THE LAST EARTH

". . . and the last will be first"

RANDOLPH KAY

ISBN: 0985458909
ISBN-13: 9780985458904
Library of Congress Control Number:: 2012941412
UpWord Media
Carlsbad, CA

Dedicated to every truth seeker who seeks the face of God,
and who trusts a loving father they cannot yet see,
knowing beyond reason that he loves us more than words
or form can express because of the promises God makes.

ᴄ Prologue ᴅ

"So the Word became human and made his home among us. He was full of unfailing love and faithfulness. And we have seen his glory, the glory of the Father's one and only Son."

—John 1:14 NLT

At first the light warmed her, before it seared her flesh.

It eased over her like a shimmering ray of sunshine. It wasn't the winter sun that flooded through the kitchen window onto her feet, though. This radiant beam penetrated the ceiling with sparkling flecks that danced within the light while bathing her with pleasant tickles. She couldn't help recalling her husband's near-death experience in heaven after his accident. The light. Joy. Love being the only language spoken in consummate relationship of one to another.

Funny how she could immerse herself with such pleasantry given the initial shock. She was oddly at ease. Strange for a person who became anxious even over the tiniest disruption—like how spoons misplaced with forks could ruin a dinner. This didn't fit with reason.

Something was different about the light—like a soothing drink of hot cocoa. She absolutely loved hot cocoa. It reminded her of Christmas Eve. Only, this drink was scalding.

Startled again by her casual acceptance, she tensed on command, face taut. Her heartbeat began to increase, and the feeling of her skin returned, causing the slightest sensation of having been out too long in the sun. Only, this wasn't from the sun.

She pressed her palms against the sink, turned the faucet to cold, and splashed her face, but to no avail. Her mind went hazy; she felt dizzy, ready to fall, but she couldn't fall, propped up by the engulfing force. Silence.

Muscles went rigid, feet stuck to the tile floor. She bent down to touch her feet, brushing at first the cool tile. Then her index finger pressed into the dimpled surface of her foot, and instantly she lunged back from the heat of the scorched dermis.

Real panic set in. She couldn't break free from the light. It entrapped her like a bug in hot ice. Nothing made sense. This wasn't a dream; her senses peaked like never before.

No pain though—just the full sentience as when stunned by a pleasant surprise. An ethereal awakening resonated as when reading the Tennyson poetry she so enjoyed and little understood—only better. No need to rationalize. She was numbed into a surreal place of enchantment . . . She let go.

A thud from the door slamming into the entranceway wall alarmed Amanda to her friend and neighbor, who Amanda presumed must have seen a light beaming overtop the house.

"Amanda—what's going on?"

Lila's booming voice pulled Amanda from her slippery state. She took offense at the intrusion, as she was beginning to drift away from life. She couldn't answer, though. Her mouth was frozen, or rather, scorched—she couldn't determine what was going on within and without. The two conditions seemingly diametrically opposed because she was oblivious to her burning body while mesmerized by some comforting sedative.

Lila lunged over to rescue her friend, but her hand was unable to pierce through the impenetrable light. Amanda turned toward her, emitted a courtesy smile, and then tried to return to her contemplative mood.

"Amanda!" Lila pulled out her phone with a trembling hand and nervously dropped it. She turned toward her stiffened friend. "Speak to me! Say something!"

Amanda could not. Her semiconsciousness was now absorbed into a world of lustrous textures and colors, soothing perfumes, and jollifying music. More than imagination, these pleasures saturated her mind as though she had been born into Shangri-la, lovely. Words could no longer explain the ecstasy with which she pranced inwardly. An unfathomable richness of being.

She was being pulled inwardly, her insides in some spasmodic tug wanting to be released into the light while her body burned.

"Amanda, my beloved." An audible voice from somewhere she knew not. This wasn't Lila's voice. It was a man's, a lovely man's. A tender tone she would wish for a father's voice, the one she'd always wanted but never had in this life.

"Yes," was all she could say.

"Will you come with me now, or stay?"

How would she know the answer? She knew in her deepest place that this was indeed her father—her heavenly Father. The one she'd always longed for.

"I want to do your will," she replied without thought. She could trust—finally. It felt right.

"I am pleased, my dear child," he said. "There will be suffering, and I will consider nothing less of you should you decide to come to me now."

"What do you want?" she asked, more mindful now.

"I want to use you," he said. "I want to show the world my love. But, most of all, I want to be with my children in a way this world cannot yet comprehend."

Her essence began to float from her body as though unzipped. She would need to decide, quickly. Peculiar how she knew this, her awareness greater than the sum of her understandings.

"Do you want me to stay?" she asked almost penitently, because she so wanted to go—so desired to stream with the light into peace and absolute love.

She knew the answer though. Otherwise, why would her Father ask her? He really wanted her to stay, to do something—an unfinished work.

And then there was Will. She didn't want to leave him alone. How could she abandon the two loves of her life—her Father and her soul mate?

"I'll stay for you, Lord," she said inwardly. "Will . . ." her final answer resonating into the environs.

In a flash the light disappeared, and with it left every idyllic comfort beyond the pale of this world. She returned to the shrill sounds and stale smells of her sparse apartment, and the cold of a winter's morning. And Lila . . .

"Oh God!" her friend cried as she hugged Amanda and sobbed frantically. "Are you all right?"

"No," Amanda replied. "I am not all right," she said, her mind still waking from pleasant slumber. "I am a foreigner in this place." She looked at Lila with the reluctance of a child regrettably awakened from a dream.

This was life now. Made strikingly barren in contrast to her glimpse of paradise. She felt the tug of her spirit, had longed to give in, and decided to stay. But, for what?

She could perhaps imagine the feeling again, but not really. Her vain attempts could only serve as a paltry excuse for the main course of heaven almost served her, having briefly tasted its delectable appetizer.

She thought of Tennyson, or Browning, some words to express her current pit, and found none. Because no poetry remained. Only the hope that one day, someday, she would release into the light.

❧ Chapter One ❧

S tiffened faces were etched by fear, living creatures baked with hardness and walking like zombies on the crowded sidewalk, not dead—at least not yet.

An aroma of burnt pork permeated the blustery air. Streetlamps illuminated the charred sidewalk, splitting the darkness. The fog was low, and there was a line of cars abandoned by their drivers that stretched up to a stoplight flashing red. Flecks of gray blew like snow in the wind; a trickle of gasoline wetting the ash-strewn road crept down steaming drainage grates.

Two young people clutched each other's hands on the walkway. A kind of doom was spread over them and the scene, and everyone appeared conscious of the doom and made somber by it. People turned to each other, mouthing words, not listening.

An officer stared at me. "Hey, you—fellow, what's your name?"

"Will," I answered, not wishing to divulge my last name.

"Better clear this area for safety," he said.

The policeman turned to his partner. His voice rose under the black smoke over the burning wreckage of the streets. "How many dead?"

"No tellin'," the cop's partner said, wiping his eyes as he directed cars dusted the color of tombstones. "I've counted at least twelve."

"Evaporated or dead?"

"Two bodies, ten or so MIA," the partner answered.

There would be more dead. I knew that. But real death, inner death—that was the horror I knew.

In the middle of the crowd, with matted hair, torn clothes, and an unwiped nose, a woman began weaving in and out until darting into the street oblivious to the officers' warnings.

"Aliens have taken over!" The woman ranted. Shapely legs showed through a torn skirt, yet I dared not dwell upon them lest giving in to the titillation of a world where anything goes—and I mean *anything*.

A familiar tune lingered from a distant saxophonist through gray sky awash in a blurred canvas of ashen life, part familiar, part distorted . . .

I wept for the loss of innocence, the darkness that had befallen men's hearts, and the evaporation through the air of my friends and loved ones less than an hour ago.

I heard sirens going off.

"Don't panic, people," the policeman said. "Try to go about your normal lives."

So this was the new normal? Normal used to be taking things for granted. Someone elbowed me.

A couple walking together halted. The woman's partner turned. "How can we do that? This ain't no regular day—with dead people lyin' around and people turnin' to dust."

"It'll be OK," the policeman said—or was it a question?

Walking home among the deadpanned faces of people moping along the sidewalk elicited forlorn pangs of longing for what it had been like before God lifted his presence, turning death inside again. Before, I could still my spirit by getting alone. Now my spirit churned down a bottomless rollercoaster.

Sure, I knew God existed. I of all people should know this after experiencing intimacy with Jesus in heaven after my accident—a near-death experience, they call it. But, now it was like awaking into a nightmare of the soul where it was perpetually three a.m. As though looking into a mirror—seeing that God was only a projection from a very bright and ordered past.

At one time I understood my faith no more than a child did, just expecting things to work out in the end. But in this desolate place I began to reason faith, and I learned to think that I couldn't instantly enter into his presence because no evidence of goodness existed, and I was left remembering how effortless faith had been.

A gust of wind slapped me in the face. I passed a three-story gray-brick building with planked windows. The structure seemed to tremble with the muffled backbeat of profanity-laced rap music, as though chilled from a fever. A wash of screams and turned-up music drifted across the sidewalk when a woman and her grade-school-age daughter, gripping each other for dear life, quickly darted away from a gust of marijuana smoke that emitted from some teen pushing open the door while puffing on his joint. The woman glanced at me, clasping her girl's hand with two hands, and walked in my direction. A cold breeze arched the mother's back as she turned her head from me, checking to see that the teen wasn't following her, and then she breathed out a cloud of smoke—as though her soul might be flaming.

"Honey, don't let go of my hand, whatever you do!" the mom said as if wanting anyone within hearing distance to know.

"I won't, Mommy. Promise I won't. You won't leave, will you?" The slouching woman let go of her tight grip and just held the fingertips of her little girl; the child's bright-pink bow atop her head lay unraveled on one side. Her tailored outfit was ripped. A dried tearstain was etched on the girl's alabaster face. Her head turned in my direction, and for a brief moment I could see into the girl's raven eyes that tunneled into an evil place. She wasn't all human.

"Where did Daddy go?" she said to her mother.

"Into the light, honey—he's in the light." And with that the mother pulled her black coat over the child as they stood still, eyes fixated on a flickering lamppost like two flies lured toward a bug zapper.

The air felt thick with the smell of burnt rubber wafting over New York City, making cheap the self-indulgences all around—people snorting cocaine on café sidewalks, pleasuring themselves in every possible physical way regardless of who watched them. Yet it all reeked of decay. Even the formerly pleasant aroma of broiled hot dogs from the street vendor smelled of spoiled meat. So much for comfort food.

"Fellow." A bug-eyed postman reached his shaky hand out toward me and pleaded in his trembling voice. "Do you . . . do you know what this is all about?"

"God's no longer here. He left," I said. Though true, how could the man possibly understand what it's like to drink from the fountain of God's soul only to find all inspiration suddenly dry up?

"Fool!" The postman flicked his shoulder in disgust with no regard for the undelivered letters dangling from his hand.

I looked up into the early morning sky and viewed the sun struggling to break through the starry sky. The galaxies above used to evoke a certain reverence, in that they were always there, though untouchable, like heaven. Once my divine companion had been a kindred part of me. I was comforted by his unfathomable nature, yet now truly God's presence was beyond reach. Burned away in a lost world, with me its orphan.

This was life now—barren and busy at the same time with nowhere to go and no direction to get you there. Everyone just going through the motions seeking after pleasure, and wanting . . .

I looked up, shaking with spasms of grief, or was it hope? I so much wanted to believe. My hands reached for the heavens. "God, you wanted me to stay, but you left me. Please . . ."

A hit of biting air awoke me from my stupor. Then, she came to mind again. She'd never left, really, but I didn't want to lament her loss any longer. Love never leaves—or so they say, though I hoped she had.

"Amanda, my bride." Where was she? *Oh, God, she's in your hands, isn't she?* Or had she, too, resisted the light, choosing to stay behind? My muscles awoke with a pulsating rush of adrenaline. Until now I had been sure she was in paradise, but maybe . . .

"No. No. God, let her be with you now!"

I called. No answer. Left a text. No response.

I took off, puffing out vapor trails, running on automatic, bumping into lumbering bodies.

She had to be gone. This was my choice, not hers.

"God, where are you? Don't let her be in this hellhole."

If I could've just said some last words: "I miss you. Love of my life." If I could've been given something to pardon my detachment from the wellspring of emotions I'd failed to share.

4

Now I was caught in a wind tunnel; the gushing current pressed against me, reduced me to slow motion—gotta . . . get . . . there—push. Even the tides of nature fought against me.

My legs carried me past abandoned boxcars, vacant lots overgrown with tall grass and empty cartons, parked storage trucks and dingy sheds under the tunnels known as convenient rape zones, and deserted dockside streets lit under humming overpasses. Several blocks of the city's grandest slums passed as I huffed with my final breaths before sighting our townhouse.

One block to go before reaching our home—still *our* home? A mass of people congregated in front of my townhouse: strangers, neighbors . . . and Lila Foster, Amanda's friend, her chocolate skin and distinctive hair weave in plain sight. Too attractive for her own good—for my good.

"What happened?" I asked. My lungs were just about to burst out of my chest.

Lila turned her head, raced to greet me with wide-open eyes and arms flailing about. "They took her! The police came to the door—they took her!" Mascara ran down her tear-drenched face as she cupped her cheeks, caving into my chest. My blood pulsated with her embrace. Finally I was able to retrieve my breath.

Lila's familiar perfume eased my senses. Or did my return to some modicum of sanity derive from the knowledge of the love of my life being on the same earth as me? Surely the latter. "Where'd they take her?"

"I don't know. They just came in with machine guns and . . ." Lila's voice broke with retching. "They said that she was part of the . . . insurgents."

"Insurgents? What else?"

She clawed at my purple sweater, her long fingernails inflicting needle-sharp pains. Gave me her puppy eyes and that pleading smile, which tensed me like a hormone-crazed schoolboy. Gotta refocus . . .

"They didn't say much, Will. I was in the kitchen with Amanda. The light came down on her—"

"What'd she say? What'd she do?" I threw politeness aside, shaking Lila as if she were a package, wanting the answers to fall out.

"It was weird. She went listless, and said . . ." Lila stilled herself. "Will. Your name. That's what she said."

Every muscle went soft as I fell out of myself. She'd turned down paradise, resisted the light. For me? I felt a tinge of guilt wanting her here. Was I being selfish at my relief, or justified that for once I felt linked to this world by more than just my own existence?

Amanda gave me purpose—to find my love. Perhaps that sounded trite, yet in this feckless world all affections spoke anew.

I glanced sideways and saw the rising sun for the first time. Its yellow glow rising quickly, producing a thin red arc that cut into the dark. More bright than yesterday. Though perhaps I'd imagined it that way knowing Amanda still graced this world. A bite of chilled air brought me back to the present crisis.

"I've got to get to the police station—they must have taken her there," I said.

"Does anybody know where the police station is?" I shouted to the assembled bystanders. The blank faces around me appeared unable to cope or think of anything but their own distressed lives.

I pulled out my cell phone to call Information. A squealing woman answered, gave me the address, and then connected me to the station.

The phone clicked. Some programmed gatekeeper answered. "We can't give out arrest details because of the terror threat associated with the recent disappearances."

I hung up. "I have no recourse but to go to the station, Lila. I'll hail a cab."

Lila still clung to my sweater. I wanted to embrace her too—for comfort, not for love. "I'm going with you. She's my friend too."

Several cabbies passed before a pockmarked taxi pulled to the curb. As we hopped in, the driver turned to ask us about our destination, speaking with a Russian accent.

"Forty-nine Chambers Street," I replied.

"You in big hurry," he said.

"My wife's just been taken by the police."

"Why?" he asked.

"I don't know. Please, can you go faster? Please!"

"I take detour. You no want to get stuck. Lots of accidents."

The radio played a news report detailing the bizarre events. Lila pressed her head into my arm after clutching my right hand. It felt good.

"They say gamma rays or high-energee particles caused people to go." The driver shrugged his wide shoulders.

"Something like spontaneous human combustion," Lila interjected. "I was listening to the TV news report."

"That's stupid," I said.

Of course, anyone tuned in to this craziness must have known about the rapture. Perhaps that's the reason I was left behind—to share the hope through this misery. Surely there was a reason, and maybe Lila was to be the first to benefit.

"Did Amanda tell you why people just got zapped up?"

Lila tried to smile politely, but her face erupted with laughter. "She said it was the rapture," and then Lila continued her raillery like some schoolyard kid too proud to admit her ignorance. "You know that I can't buy into that God thing," she said. "God knows you and Amanda tried, but it always goes back to why, if there is a God, does he permit this kind of suffering?"

I decided not to pursue the matter now. Maybe later, when Amanda could join me. She was always better at sharing contrary messages with a dose of sympathy. *Amanda's the gentle one, the likable one. I'm the one who keeps quiet and lets others do most of the talking, except when it comes to God, then I can . . . used to . . . talk a hurricane.*

No, I wouldn't share because I was unsure if my words might sound too harsh. Now I was only half a whole. My beautiful wife complemented my view of life in black and white through softer lenses that perceive varying shades of brokenness.

The cabbie looked in the mirror and chuckled. "Mister, they say lights over people came from explodin' star." He scratched his balding head. "Yeah, high energee particles . . . pulled heat from earth and . . . puff. Wind blew ashes."

Lila lifted her head to eke out a few words. "They also said it might be UFOs. But, they think it probably has to do with that giant supernova above us."

Lila sank back into my chest. The security forces probably blamed Amanda somehow. They'd claim that she was part of the conspiracy; that she contributed to the disappearances. We only held prayer meetings in Central Park . . . How I hated that she had to suffer—and for me? She

7

used to embarrass me by saying I was her "knight in shining armor." Oh God, if I could only live up to that now.

"How long before we get there?"

The driver scratched his scraggly beard and shook his freakishly oversized head. "Not long. Maybe ten minutes or so."

I checked my text messages. David Levy—in Israel. His message: "Call me," followed by his number. Seven text messages, all from David, except one—from Amanda, almost an hour ago: "Police taking me. Trust in God. I love you!"

My heart felt like a floppy fish out of water. I could picture her perfect fingers typing in the words. The most perfect hands in the entire world. Smooth, graceful, and soft skin that used to melt me at the slightest touch. My imagination followed up her arms to her tender shoulder and then the face. A face framed with wavy auburn hair and green eyes that stilled my heart.

Why did this have to happen?

Just before the life got sucked out of this world, radiant beams had hovered over believers. The light tugged at my spirit as if my insides were being comfortably eased out of me through an anesthetizing massage. My passion for heaven so intense it begged to be satisfied.

Next I heard a rich and affectionate voice. He wanted me to stay. I knew it as clearly as that childhood day when my dad and I sat together at the airport terminal waiting for me to depart from home for the first time. My father dreaded the imminent arrival of the plane as I glanced through the terminal window anxiously awaiting the big bird. And though he didn't say it, I could see he wanted me to stay, through the hidden tears in his eyes. So unlike then, I told my Father I would stay this time. Life sometimes brings us to a crossroads—one path leads to adventure, the other to the grander purpose of staying home.

After telling him I would stay, the brightness disappeared. My body had released like a two-ton corpse.

The others? Those believers who gave in to the light were consumed as logs in a ravenous fire, their souls sucked into the light, to heaven, presumably; in a New York second they disappeared. I'm not sure how many had been chosen to remain. The ones that just died, their bodies falling like someone had pulled the plug out of them? I have no idea.

I just know that my job wasn't finished here yet. At least that's how I reasoned it. But why?

The cab came to a halt in response to the obnoxiously red stoplight. A figure at the corner fixated on me with menacing owl eyes, its bloodless face opaque white. Curses poured out of it like a bloody rag wrung over me. Mouthing words. Vile words. I turned my head, though its haunting visage still lingered in my mind.

God, save me from its curses. In Jesus's name. My prayers were more programmed now. Since he left, I'd become dispirited . . . aimless . . .until Amanda. I wouldn't be alone anymore. Moreover, I didn't want her to be alone. I imagined her pleading eyes. "Oh God, let me find her!"

I glanced down at my cell phone again. Four of the messages had come from David. A terribly long pause followed my punching in the lengthy international numbers.

"Shalom."

"David, this is Will."

"Will, so good to hear your voice! You are the shining star of mercy in this place of judgment. We chose to stay behind so our Lord could come again." David spoke with a faint Hebrew accent painfully enunciated in the King's English, and his voice was a soothing concerto in contrast to my dismal surroundings.

"So good to hear from you, David. I thought that I was the only one left until I got your text. Tell me, what's going on in Israel?"

"I am in an abandoned shelter in the hills, a ray of light our only connection to the outer world. There are many here, Will. Dr. Munny Chin helped bring many converts before he left."

Ah, Munny. The vaccine had been too late for him. "You saw him die?"

"No. Witnesses say he went to God in a whirlwind, just like Elijah."

My Cambodian friend twirling like a frolicking, chubby middle-aged man in the wind while being pulled into God's embrace—just like him to defy the norm.

"Awesome! David, tell me, what's the mood like there?"

A slight pause. "It's like the time of Moses in the wilderness, brother. We Jews probably understand that better than others. Our Father relates to us now from a distance."

9

I closed my eyes—mulling David's words for a while. "He gave them every last chance—"

"Yes," David said, "three hits and you're out."

"What?"

"That's how you say it in America—is a baseball idiom, is not?"

I turned away and cupped my mouth to stifle a most welcomed laugh. "Oh, no. It's three *strikes* and you're out," I said.

"Oh, I am sorry, my friend."

My thoughts quickly returned to Amanda. "Please pray for my wife. The police took her into custody—"

"Shalom to you, dear brother. I have, as they say, a bad feeling about this."

Strange comment. Not the encouragement I'd hoped. "Did God give you a word?"

"Yes. He still speaks to us."

"I'm not so sure about that."

"It's like Old Testament times, Will—through visions, angels, signs . . . and even directly, as he did through the prophets."

A warm wind brushed my cheek, stilling me in thought. I wanted to trust the words that played in my head like some familiar song whose lyrics played over and over. It said for the most part:

"The blood of the Lamb will be spilled onto the hills of desolation, and the wind shall blow onto the lost children, causing the blind to see. Then the torrents of hell will be released, leaving the unholy as the crown of my defiled temple. With you as the last son of Adam."

"I keep hearing the same words in my head," I said.

"Ah—the prophet's ears hear that which is silent to the rest of us."

"The voice called me the last son of Adam. Like some ghost was whispering thoughts into my head. As though an angel leaned into my ear. Got the picture?"

David's throaty "ahem" jarred me. Did he think me a nutcase?

"I do not have a photograph, Reuben," he said.

"What?"

David let out a long breath. "You asked if I got a picture, and I did not."

"No, I wasn't meaning a literal picture when I said . . . never mind. I was just asking if you understood," I said.

"Ah. My friend," David thankfully continued, "have you ever thought of yourself as a modern-day Moses?"

Where did that come from? "Hardly." And if so, I guess that *would* make me a nutcase.

"Will, we must come together as a people. In Jerusalem, our homeland. You must bring us together, Will. You must bring the believers from America to the land of Canaan."

Come on. Maybe I wasn't the wacky one here. My friend's boldness proved refreshing, though—maybe even true. I decided for the moment to liberate my normally ordered way of thinking. OK, I'd play along. "Why?"

"To deliver his presence to the Promised Land again."

OK, now I began to wonder if the radiation had burned away my friend's reasoning. But then again, weird and acceptance proved strange but common bedfellows in this place.

"And where, then, is his presence? It's gone," I said, stating the obvious.

"His presence can be found in America, Reuben."

"Hard to believe." Now I tried my best not to accuse my friend of being one card short of a full house—maybe a joker, perhaps. I rolled down the taxi's window to let in some fresh air, clear my head, as in inhale drafty fumes and listen to the sounds of commotion. Honking car horns, shouts, screeching brakes. New York was returning back to life after being shocked into submission. The frenzy calmed me enough to ponder David's crazy assertions.

"Allow me to explain," David the end-times "professor" continued. "The ark of the covenant housed the very presence of God after the Jews escaped Egypt on their long journey to the Promised Land in the time of Moses. God's presence needed to be placed in the Holy Land for him to reestablish relationship with his people."

"It contained the Ten Commandments given to Moses."

"More, Will—it contained his Spirit—the very presence of Yahweh."

"Like what? God's spirit in a box—?"

"Somewhat" he said. "God inhabits the praises of his people, and in the time of Moses God's presence resided not in the flesh but in the sacred place of their worship.

"The exiled Jews felt as we feel now—abandoned and alone, nomads. Just as he needed to then, God must reestablish his presence with his people in the place of his promise—to bring forth his thousand-year reign."

If not for the fact that I had experienced heaven after my near-death experience from the car crash, and watched people recently vanish in a sunbeam . . . well, I guess just about anything was possible. "And you say that he needs to bring his lost presence back to Israel?"

"Yes. He promised as such—he will reign again, my brother, stronger than before."

"Then why do you think his spirit's in America?" I felt "One nation under God" had disappeared a long time ago.

Though his contention seemed farfetched at first, his words now resonated with that "you just know that you know" kinda confirmation—something like smelling the comforting aroma of a cooked dinner without knowing where it comes from—the life of faith I once embraced but now found incongruent with this godless place. Time, perhaps, to just trust again.

"The idea of building the New Jerusalem for the early settlers was foundational to American nationalism," David continued. "At its founding many looked upon America as the new Israel, the City on the Hill—founded upon Jesus Christ, as was no other nation in all of history.

"When God lifted his presence from the world, he left a remnant—just as he had with the exiled Jews in Egypt, and just as he has today with the exiled Christians in America. In order for him to create a new earth so his people can once again commune with him, his presence must be brought back to Jerusalem."

"A new earth?"

"The restored garden of Eden," he said.

My thoughts raged with possibilities—a new Genesis—a new beginning for this godforsaken world. "And you think I'm meant to somehow find God's presence—and bring it back?"

He answered in the affirmative. By now I was just going with the flow. A streaming video played in my head—of Jesus planting a seed in the soil of Jerusalem and watching a new earth growing out of it—crazy, exciting! Or, just plain crazy. "God told you?"

"Yes, without a doubt," David said.

This was all too much to digest in one talk. And where would I find the lost presence of God?

The taxi driver pulled in front of the police station. I said, "I need to go now, David. We've got to talk more—this is all too bizarre."

"Go now, Reuben; find your wife."

After we hung up, Lila's body slinked against me as I reached into my pocket to extract some money for the driver.

"Be careful," the driver said.

I lunged out of the cab inhaling a lungful of exhaust fumes. Lila and I started rushing toward the front door when she tugged at my sweater. "Hold on!"

I forced a hard stop.

"I need to show you this." She pulled out her cell phone and scrolled as I shivered. The wind stung, but not as much as the glaring stares of strangers drilling into us. Why, I had no idea. "Look, I took this picture just as they were taking Amanda," Lila said.

"Yeah?"

"What do you see?"

"Amanda, and a cop holding her arm."

"Look closer." One of the bystanders nudged me, almost sparking a return shove.

I strained to better view the photograph, cupping my hand over the phone to block out what few rays managed to break through the clouds. "Oh my goodness!" Lurking behind Amanda was a faint figure with fierce red eyes—expressing a feral snarl. Its barbed teeth poised to clamp down on Amanda's neck.

"It's a demon, Lila. We've got to save Amanda before it . . . let's go!"

Lila froze, her squeaky voice like a panicked two-year-old's. "But they might take you too! Let me go in alone and ask."

"No! She's my wife, Lila!" Reason had no place with me. I ran up the stairs of the ornate limestone building and opened the thick glass door, hit with the smell of Lysol as I entered the almost-empty foyer. A stern-faced desk attendant perked up in attention to my rushed entrance.

"Amanda Simon, my wife . . . she was taken from our house. Please tell me her whereabouts."

The attendant's eyes widened as she stiffened, fumbling around with some papers on her cluttered desk. "Mr. Simon?"

"Yes."

After a moment's hesitation, she glanced at the side door, then picked up the phone and punched in some numbers. "Mr. Will Simon is here; can you meet him please?"

She said *Will* Simon. *How did she know my first name without my telling her?* I nudged Lila, who stood at my side.

"Go to the coffeehouse across the street and wait for me," I told Lila through clenched teeth. "Now."

Lila backed out through the door, turned toward the street, and began walking at a brisk pace. The attendant's eyes remained fixed on me. Two policemen walked through the side door, one about six foot three, with eyes as slits and a curved nose you could slide a marble down; the other one was stocky, with his chest puffed out and a crunchy pumpkin face.

"Mr. Simon," the taller man said with a Brooklyn street tone.

"Where's my wife?"

The two men turned toward each other with that "should we tell him?" look. Or was it that "should we grab him now?" look? *God, give me wisdom.*

"She's been transferred, Mr. Simon. She's not here." The man's pasty complexion turned bloodshot as he sneered, his fists clenched.

"Where is she?" If looks could kill . . . Mr. Pumpkin Face gave an angry jack-o-lantern expression.

"Come back with us," the stocky man demanded as he threw the door wide open. "We can talk about this, but not in the lobby."

They'll isolate me so I won't cause a scene, then they'll arrest me just like they arrested Amanda.

"Just tell me where she is."

The tall man reached out his gorilla arm toward me. "We can't do that, Mr. Simon. Let's just go inside."

He was about to grab my arm when I stepped back, causing both men to lunge forward. In a nanosecond I would need to decide: run like a torched animal or play this game out. This was one of those crossroads in life. I ran.

Not daring to look back after streaming through the glass doors into the shivery city air, I hoped that the Hill Street cops remained inside. The sound of footsteps hurriedly clapping against the tell-all cement said otherwise, prompting me to pick up the pace, their shadows now within sight.

Up ahead I could see the crisscrossing New York traffic. Do I stop, or zigzag through the over-the-speed-limit cars? Either way I calculated my premature death at thirty-seven having been denied the top two items on my Bucket List—finding Amanda and now God's presence in a lost world.

"Stop!" demanded a hoarse voice.

I turned my head ninety degrees to catch a peripheral vision of the two men running, the taller guy at least three feet beyond the shorter one, and almost fifty yards behind me. One appeared to brandish his gun.

A stone's throw away the traffic-laden street lay ahead, and in the distance the rude sound of a siren grew closer. The footsteps clapped more loudly. I was losing the race with the big guy. They couldn't shoot me without endangering someone in the streets, could they?

With a rush of speed, I crossed over the sidewalk and into the crowded street. A *whoosh* and a brush of air signaled a near miss. Another car honked unceasingly, though from where I knew not, except the sound of screeching tires instinctively turned my head in the direction of an oncoming car going too fast to avoid me. As it turned toward the curb, I leapt in time to avert a collision, sending my body forward onto the unforgiving sidewalk, which sent shooting stings through my not-so-funny bone.

Lying on the pavement, I looked back to note the status of my pursuers. Mr. Crinkly Face—the short guy—was caught in the middle divider, trying to stop cars. Mr. Munster—the tall guy—appeared nowhere in sight.

By now the increasing sounds of the sirens overwhelmed the urban noises.

What happened to the tall cop?

Like a spooked horse, I just ran. Fast. Darting from the alley, a raggedy man with mop hair jumped in front of me. Pressing my right foot into the asphalt stopped me within a nose of him.

"Please," he said. "In Jesus Christ's name."

"Get out of the way."

He lightly grabbed my sweater and smiled.

"Come with me, please." He led me into the littered alley, no more than ten feet, then opened a rusty door and pushed me through as the squeaking noise momentarily drowned out the shrill bedlam outside.

The abandoned room was rank with the smell of dried urine and fresh rat feces. A lantern light eked out a few rays to divulge the peeling brown paint and graffiti that read: KILL THE INSURGENTS. An old newspaper on the floor, brittle and yellow around the edges, reflected the same sentiment with its headline: Insurgent Attempts Assassination—another fabrication. A frontal view of the man's face exposed his marbled brown eyes set deep within a bony face.

"He told me to get you," the man said with an apologetic voice.

"Who?"

"God."

His breath smelled fresh; his clothes had the soapy fragrance of having been recently cleaned. Odd for a homeless guy. Was he the real deal—a true believer—or just a delusional derelict? "God doesn't seem to speak in this world anymore," I answered.

"Yes he does. I heard his voice." He reached out his pencil-thin arm. "My name is Ian, and yours?"

"Will Simon. So he told you to rescue me or something like that?"

"Yep," he said. "You're a believer, right?"

Ian's crisp enunciation sounded like one of my professors from Northwestern. His comportment scholarly in contrast to his calloused workmanlike palms befitting a person tinged by this coarsening world.

I hugged him as a brother. "Absolutely, Ian! It's so great to be in the company of a fellow believer!" My enthusiasm swelled. "Are you a . . .?"

"A?"

"Are you living on the streets?"

"Since I lost my job at the library, yes. It's somewhat liberating. You resisted the light also?"

I answered in the affirmative before the urgency of my situation knocked at my mind again. A small window eked out some rays toward the back wall, affording me a look outside. Three flashing squad cars hugged the curb. Two officers stood next to the cars, talking to the tall cop who had chased me. Four other cops huddled on the other side of the street. Who knows how many roamed the street—in search of me, presumably.

"I've got to get out of here."

Ian placed his weighty hand upon my shoulder. "They're after you?" His compassionate tone assuaged my angst.

"Yeah."

"Why?"

I swallowed carefully. "They took my wife. We're insurgents. Have you ever heard of The Way?"

"Of course—the Christian blog. It was the foremost way to share with other believers—number one Christian site." A clearly proud Ian gave his head an approving shake, causing his red pigtail curls to bounce.

I was about to blow my cover. "I was the blogger—Reuben."

"*The* Reuben!" His eyes widened and his mouth dropped open.

"Shh . . . I'm incognito."

I darted away from the window just as I noticed, from out of the corner of my eye, a cop approach. Stooping, I motioned for Ian to be quiet and join me in the secluded nook. Just as we pressed our bodies against the stone-cold wall, a man's shadow overlaid the only ray of light emanating from the window. A beam shot through the darkness as the cop's flashlight crisscrossed the room, edging the tops of our heads.

Then the room went dark again as the shadow disappeared from the floor's crescent streak of sunlight. I crawled over to the dim space just below the window and slowly unwound my body upward toward the glass, listening for any sounds. After waiting a few seconds, I peeked from the ledge to view the plain sidewalk. No cop. I looked full on, side to side; the coast appeared clear.

"He's gone," I whispered to Ian.

"There's only one way in and one way out," he whispered in return. "They're not looking for me. How 'bout if I go outside and act as the scout. When the coast is clear, I'll knock twice slowly, followed by three times fast."

Lila came to mind.

"OK, but there's something I need you to do first. There's a woman by the name of Lila waiting at Starbucks across the street. She's wearing a white jacket, jeans, brown boots, and she's African American. Please go get her, and if she questions you, tell her that Willy sent you. That's the name she and my wife like to call me. That should allay any doubts she might have about you."

"Will do—no pun intended." With that Ian crept toward the door and opened it slowly before disappearing.

My head thumped against the wall as the rest of my body went limp. "Lord, where are you?"

For what seemed like an eternity, a dead silence stayed in the room.

"God, please speak to me."

Silence. My hope faded into the dank air.

It was hard to believe that only months ago God's spirit rained upon a thirsty world made hard by a one-world religious movement, causing thousands to find Christ, and that I had been a part of it by operating a cyber-church that shared the good news to millions across the world.

That now seemed like eons ago. How quickly this world had gone dark. I was left with the nagging question, "Why am I here?" For that matter, why were any believers still here?

☙ Chapter Two ☙

While waiting, I was afforded the luxury of dwelling on rat bones and beetle shells that littered the damp concrete floor of my humble abode. I played an imaginary card game with the scattered deck of cards stained with mold, gagged on the smokeless cigarette butts, and tasted a brewski from the broken beer bottles that lay in sooty corners. None of these things could I remember from my past life, mind you. I could only guess what a life of indulgence might be like.

A thin beam of light from the outside created the illusion of life. Enough perhaps to think about loftier things—like faith. The only way of expressing faith was to relinquish control . . . that sounded decent. Sitting alone in an abandoned warehouse and waiting for Ian might as well lead me to place of greater contemplation.

I pressed my palm against the cement floor before pulling it back after some slimy thing greased it. Back to faith—as when the external facts—sensory experiences—must be subjugated to blind confidence in God's providence, which, when fully given into, evokes a pleasant ennui.

Indeed, Jesus had taught me this during my after-death experience, not in so many words. OK, I know . . . I'm a bit wordy. I overthink.

Actually, I can never settle for answers before coming up with another question. I'd been this way since I can remember."

For me it was always about squeezing in one more minute before bedtime, one more question before I took the test, or getting one grade better in school, one higher title in work. And now I have no job; I was fired from Global Press for writing "from a biased Christian perspective," then fired as a bag boy at a grocery store for proselytizing. No status to attain. I'm a lousy bum in this world's eyes—an insurgent, which levels all expectations.

For me, victories or successes always placed the next hurdle too high. I gave up on most sports because I wasn't very good at them. I'm really a klutz; still, I felt that I needed to do better than below-average in order not to embarrass myself.

And since my sports prowess lacked considerably, academics became my game. Studying late hours sometimes gave me a headache. The first time I got a D at Northwestern, it was like someone had punched my gut—which actually made my head feel better. Failing brought relief, though I wouldn't admit it to anyone, least of all myself. Truthfully, though, the bar was lowered, and when I started getting Cs and Bs instead of all As, that wasn't all bad.

"Being the best," that's the ticket, "the very best." Funny how the words of our mentors, parents, siblings, society, prejudices, experiences and so forth turn into expectations that trigger blaring speakers in the brain anytime we have to perform. And of course insecurities always get in the way when trying to please others, as they do me, when in truth . . . I'll admit it—I'm just trying to please myself. And I'm never quite satisfied.

This all ran contrary to what Jesus said. I just needed to spend time with him, he told me. Find a quiet place, sit at his feet, chill out. Well, this certainly was a quiet place for now. *OK, I'm listening, God. Speak.*

Someone's rude pounding rocked the door with nervous urgency. Not the two taps followed by three quick ones previously agreed upon with Ian. This came from someone else, someone hurried, angry . . . someone bad—dare I ask?

"Open up!"

Who? A man. A brazen, winded man.

"Open up, Will! Open up!"

"Ian?"

"Yes. Open up!"

Maybe. The voice sounded deeper. "You didn't knock like we agreed."

"Forgot. Are you going to open? I have Lila."

A puff of exhaust fumes hit my face upon opening the heavy metal door. Lila lunged her body against mine as her hands clasped behind my back, pressing the wind from my lungs. Her desperate touch seemed amplified in contrast to the icy detachment of my surroundings. I so much wanted to feel Amanda this way.

"Here's a muffin and coffee for you," she said while holding out a bag that I fiercely grabbed, given my unbelievable hunger.

"My stomach thanks you very, very much."

"Coast is clear. The cops are at least four blocks away," said Ian.

"Where can we go that's safe?"

Ian rubbed his neck. "There's a church one block over. Let's try there."

Instinctively, we rushed out the door and onto the crosswalk, dodging the plodders around us. A blinding sunbeam glanced off the church's metal cross into my eyes, forcing me to look upward into the gray clouds wishing to shroud any remaining daylight.

A terrible stench instantly filled my space, followed by a tap on my shoulder. "Hey fellow, got any spare money?" The woman wore her skin like a full-bodied leather purse—an extremely baggy one.

"I don't have much left, I'm sorry," I answered, "but, here, take my muffin and coffee." I handed them over to the anxious woman as though I'd given over my prized Rolex watch—which, come to think of it, I'd already pawned last week.

Less than twenty feet away, an ill-omened haze rested upon the drab gray colonial church trimmed with white squared fence posts. As we approached the opened doors, two hovering auras about ten feet tall stood guard with arms folded, heads like Komodo dragons, their spiteful eyes following me as we passed through the foyer into the Gothic sanctuary.

Lila clung to my arm while Ian spanned the stained-glass windows adorning both walls, a large wooden crucifix prominently displayed to the right of the lectern; words from the Koran and from the Bible appeared side by side on a wide screen up front.

A gray-bearded man adorned in flowing black raised his arms through restless sleeves, causing his turban, for a moment, to move like Jell-O, and chanted gibberish while sprinkling water on kneeling worshippers up front. People bobbed up and down chanting indiscernible words, until the stern man at the pulpit waved his arms, quieting the crowd.

"Allah!" he said while staring blankly at his congregation.

"Allah!" the audience shouted in return. Most of the women wore traditional Islamic garb, their heads covered with hijab scarves. The men wore all kinds of clothes, even torn jeans in a formal cathedral with long interior walls lined with short candles. A stone water basin rested in the front. Shoes lined the back of the building. An old drape imprinted with a star and crescent hung in the front. An even older crucifix covered with cobwebs stood in the back corner.

"Fellow sojourners," the man continued, "we worship united, as testified by all the religions of this world. Muhammad bore witness to the prophecies of Jesus, whereas he became the final prophet who has returned as our beloved Muhammad Bakr, Chief Priest of the Universal Church, to declare righteousness once and for all.

"The terrorists have been struck down by God, vanquished. Because many tried to kill your sons and daughters. No one who is not prepared to leave their father or mother, or sister or brother, for God is fit for his kingdom. Long live our redeemer. Praise Allah, the God of Yoshua!"

"Praise Allah," returned the congregation in unison.

I stealthily walked to a pew as Ian and Lila followed, hoping to evade the transfixed worshippers. However, my conspicuousness emerged as a gentleman behind me hit his head against my back, tensing my muscles, pushing out of me a reactive and overly loud "ahh!" that could be heard by all. The perturbed minister stared squarely at me with the growl of a disturbed Doberman, pointing in my direction.

Waving his hands once again, the man's thick voice echoed through the high ceilings: "You, in the back, standing. Do you have a word?" He clutched a worn Koran in one hand while waving it in the air, and in the other hand a small new-looking Bible tucked by his side.

If I could have crawled under the pew. Instead, my mind went numb, and rubbing my eyes I witnessed a radiant figure ten feet tall with luminescent wings stretched wall to wall. I blinked, thinking it a mirage.

Though no one else appeared to even notice, he appeared to me like a Milky Way of flowing diamonds. He streamed from behind the lectern, all seven feet or so of him, filling the front section with his massive expanse. The figure's gleaming face softly smiled at me as he glided forward, his silky garb brushing against my cheek, sending out the sweet fragrance of carnations. I stood frozen, awed at the gentle majesty of his countenance.

"My name is Rhome," he whispered into my right ear. "The Lord has opened your spiritual eyes. Speak."

My palms sweating, I cleared my throat and then gave myself a pinch for good measure. I was certainly awake, though the possibility of being delusional did enter my mind. The angelic figure leaned forward and whispered to me pleasant-sounding foreign words that evoked within me an overriding peace. The first absolute peace I'd realized since God's disappearance. Then my muscles tensed, my bravado surging in a rush of confidence with an involuntary urge to speak, akin to the need to sneeze or to clear my throat. And then instinctively I declared in a full throaty voice for all to hear:

"The God of Jesus Christ has not vanquished his people. No, he has taken them home. Those not cloaked with the righteousness of Jesus Christ are now subject to their own condemnation. Hear the word of the Lord Jesus Christ! Repent, and be saved!"

My body went limp. Did I just say those words? *God, protect me!* A battle in the spirit realm immediately ensued. Angels and demons in incandescent garb intertwined in a battling tornado swirl. Serpent-like demons spewed out a flood of murky fluids in shades of grayish brown, which fell upon the audience, causing them to ooze with hatred. Was I in a dream state? My Lord, this was playing out real enough.

Churchgoers snarled, cussed, and shivered with anger. At the same time, Rhome and six other towering angels drew airy swords comprising what I instinctively knew as God's glistening expressions:

"Holy is the Lamb of God!" declared Rhome.

"Mighty is the Lord of Hosts, the great I Am!" declared another.

Rhome and two other giant angels encircled me, their eyes like fire and ice as one, spreading their luminescent robes against the angry taunts of the demons and the blistering stares from the offended churchgoers.

23

Each time a demon whispered into the ears of a congregant, inciting one of those near to reach out to me, my protective angels waved their hands and declared Christ's authority over me, causing the people's arms to stay glued against their defenseless bodies. Altogether the paralyzed congregation appeared like a maze of Egyptian statues.

"Let's get out of here!" Ian said.

Lila pulled at me as Ian rushed out of the pew.

"Go," Rhome said to me, sending adrenaline surging through my veins. "Flee this place."

The congregants remained frozen as we rushed out the door.

After running about two blocks from the church, a deafening explosion vibrated against my eardrums, followed by a gust of hot air pressing through my clothes and a consuming cloud of smoke blanketing everything in its path.

"Get down!" someone shouted.

My back slammed against the hard dirt, knocking the wind out of me. After taking my first gulp of smoke, I tried to hold my breath for an eternity in the sooty shroud until the debris settled and the fumes began to clear. My nostrils were filled with the air's tinny chemical smell as I looked back toward the steaming rubble where the church we'd just visited once stood.

Lila screamed. "What was that?"

"I don't know," I answered. Loud sirens punctured the din of screams coming out of the church rubble.

We began to dust off our clothes while moving away from the ruckus as police converged like crumb-drawn pigeons on the scene of the former Universal Church. A few coughing survivors emerged from the rubble covered in ashes, some wondering aimlessly, and one clutched a cop in heated conversation.

Endless minutes passed as I tried to make sense of it all.

"God did it," Ian said after breaking our dumbfounded silence. "Judgment."

"No, Ian," I replied. "Those people brought it on themselves by the same hatred that they levied against others." But had God done this, and if not, who or what had?

Ian's eyebrows came together. "So what are you saying, Will? They killed themselves?"

"They were victims of their own doing."

Ian pressed his lips while moving his clamped hands in my direction. "You're forgetting the God of the Old Testament. Wiping out an entire people . . ."

Ian's comment unraveled my tightly woven argument with that lingering conundrum as to how a loving father could do such a thing. Had God really killed those people? And if not, he seemingly allowed it. Having witnessed the loving eyes of Jesus, I couldn't fathom anything from him but compassion, mercy, and love. How could I respond? My head just fell.

"I have to admit I've struggled with this a little. . ." I reluctantly admitted.

Lila nudged me. "Let's go, guys. Did you forget that we're being hunted? And that your wife is out there somewhere?"

Credit Lila again for bringing me back to reality, though she always refused to see outside the limits of the obvious by denying the reality of the unknown. I think Amanda saw her as a wounded soul who could never look beyond her desires. I saw Lila as a hurt puppy in need of fixing. And then it appeared that Lila saw something on the horizon by the way she darted her eyes.

Over my shoulder I viewed an overweight policeman running up to us while trying to tuck in his shirt and puffing out a long sigh. He stopped maybe a foot from my nose and looked me up and down with razor eyes, then spoke in a breathy voice, "You OK?"

I hesitated. Did he know we had created the ruckus that preceded the explosion? Was he after us? The officer lowered his head with eyebrows knit together in a V-shape pointing to his protruding lower lip.

"We're OK," I answered. "Any idea as to what just happened?"

"Some religious zealot—an insurgent, is what I heard from one of the injured." His chin lifted in sync with his narrowing eyes, chest puffed out like a rooster ready for a fight.

I tried my best to suppress my nerves from forging a Botox makeover. "Any idea who?" Hopefully he'd buy in to my feigned cluelessness.

"Someone saw a guy running out of the church. We suspect he's the same insurgent whose wife we apprehended earlier. About six two, dark-brown hair, blue eyes—"

He looked at me with intense eyes that sent shivers down to my toes.

"I saw him!" Lila quickly interjected. *What?*

The officer continued to size me up and down with those elevator eyes. "Where?"

Lila pointed down the street to a row of brick homes—nice decoy. The officer's stoic appearance didn't say much, however, except his silence rang alarm bells in my head. *Wisdom, God give me wisdom!*

"Come on, Lila, how many guys have dark-brown hair and blue eyes? Heck, even I meet that description," I said, trying to make light of a possible thunderstorm. I also tried scratching my neck with my stubby fingernails, glancing toward the sky, anything to look nonchalant. Hopefully he didn't notice my trembling fingers.

Thankfully, Ian and Lila picked up on my gig and laughed with me. The question remained as to whether the officer would go with it.

"What's your name?" he asked me, his hand now firmly placed over an unbuttoned gun holster.

Ugh. "Reuben." A decade-long pause followed. The officer rubbed his square jaw sounding out irritating scratches. He spent at least ten hours . . . uh, seconds, doing that.

"Yeah. Well, the person didn't mention anyone with the guy." The officer's hand moved only slightly away from his holster.

"What's his name?" I quickly asked.

"Simon. Will's the first name."

Attempting to act casually, I glanced around. Old oak trees with burls like pupils stared me down. A house with yellow-curtained windows glared at me. All eyes seemed upon me—accompanied by that *tick, tick, tick* of the policeman's finger against his back hand.

"Let me know if you see anything," the officer responded with his head still half cocked. A truckload of bricks fell off my back as the officer nodded and proceeded forth. *You confound the wise, God.*

Meanwhile, Ian had been texting all this time. "I found something," he said. "One of The Way members tapped into a police conversation about Amanda."

"No way!"

"Who's The Way, guys?" asked Lila.

"It's a cyber-group of Christian believers who've been left behind. What'd you find out?"

Ian continued pecking away at his micro keyboard. *Come on.* "Just checking. There it is."

"What?" I could perfect my patience in heaven, I surmised, but not here.

"Alcatraz."

"The Rock—the San Francisco tourist attraction?"

"Same one," Ian said. "It's been renovated and now it's back to being a prison. That's where they're taking all the insurgents."

"Are you sure?"

"It's even online in the news, Will . . . uh, Reuben. See—they're rounding up all the remaining Christians and taking them to Alcatraz."

"That's it. That's got to be it." I grabbed Lila and Ian by their arms with little regard for their sensibilities. "We're going to San Francisco!" I couldn't believe it—I, Will Simon, who planned everything months, even years, in advance was ready to drop everything on a hunch and a wish. For a moment I felt that freedom of release.

I allowed myself a few seconds to view four stacks of beer that had been dropped and broken in the street. The truck driver was pulling cases out of his trailer when the boxes tumbled out and spilled several bottles, some shattering into foaming crystal pieces. All the people around had suspended their activities to run to the spot and scurry away with the unbroken bottles, including a chubby kid in shorts whose doughy legs carried him away pronto. One bruiser guzzled a bottle down on the spot. Such was the abandoned quality of people. I remembered the day when people actually helped to overcome others' misfortunes.

I wished I could go back to those days because, in retrospect, I wouldn't have bothered so much to referee actions as right or wrong. Just being still with God, as the Scriptures say. Amanda helped me deeply breathe in life and to exhale all the stresses of meeting deadlines and expectations, either real or, more typically, self-imposed. She not only stopped to smell the roses, she drew them into her heart so that she could often revisit their affect. Life for Amanda represented a reservoir of experiences from which to choose a corresponding poem or some other measured response. She catalogued her adventures, whereas I just sampled them like a box of chocolates and moved on. Soon, very soon, I hoped to share life afresh with her. I knew now where to look. However, my sunny determination soon thereafter elicited a gloomy groan from Ian, which darkened my one ray of hope.

"Reuben, you're a wanted man. Do you really think we can use your credit card, or money, to catch a flight?"

"OK, then I'll go by myself."

Amanda was everything to me now. I had to find my soul mate, while hoping to rediscover my own soul. The hum of cars speeding from the neighboring highway several hundred yards away settled in with the sound of my own breathing. Neither could drown out the raging thoughts of losing Amanda forever. Perhaps Ian was right. Maybe I couldn't do this.

Ian's voice faded everything as he brought my senses in line with reason. "I've got it," he said. "The library. I still can use my global card. Every nonbeliever has one, right?"

"Yeah . . ." I could almost hear Ian's ticker ticking. "But you were fired."

"My access code doesn't expire until my severance time expires—government know-how. I worked there for almost fifteen years."

Lila raised her hands in a hurry-up gesture. Police and probably some vigilantes looking for the church bomber scrambled about. A young bodybuilder type darting in and out of alleys. A university-aged man who looked at every male within his range of sight. I wondered if I would ever again have the pleasure of leisure dreams or thoughts absent paranoia. Somehow, I doubted it.

"Well, I can call flight reservations using the number from one of those global cards," Ian said.

"Airport check-in. Picture IDs. We can't fake our identities."

Ian pressed his lips. "OK . . . OK. Listen, I know a guy who fakes passports for illegal immigrants." Ian checked his smartphone again. "Give me about four hours and then meet me at the airport at five p.m. at JFK's Trans Air terminal. There's a seven-fifty flight to SFO."

"OK." Time to go with the flow. "Lila and I will catch a cab to someplace near the airport. Pretend like you're my wife for now, Lila, honey." Unequally yoked and all.

Across the street, a young man stared at me. The bodybuilder moved in my direction. I contemplated whether they were after me, wishing they had concerns enough of their own to keep them from spotting me. Thankfully a bus pulled between us and the approaching men, concealing us for a few seconds.

Taking advantage, Ian hurriedly raced toward the library while darting around poles, newspaper stands, and parked or abandoned cars, fading into the thickening dark. And Lila and I . . . well. We ran while trying to hail a cab, and then would wait at the airport—for only God knew what.

Such is faith.

☙ Chapter Three ❧

Before embarking on the flight to San Francisco, Amanda had been tossed onto the bus like a rented piece of luggage to the airport, but only after being repeatedly clubbed in the legs for calling the Hitler-ish official a "nincompoop," and a few other angry words she thought she'd never ever say. Her right leg throbbed with the beat of pounding drums. She dared not look twice at what appeared to be a fractured tibia bulging underneath her jeans.

The other leg bled from a cut from when the wood had splintered, landing a sharp sliver deep inside her outer thigh. It burned as though a fire exploded inside. Someone had pulled a dirty rag from the floor to wrap her wounds and another gave her some pill that managed to knock her out for most of the flight.

After disembarking the flight, another bus ride ensued from SFO to a boat dock in Sausalito, then she was moved onto a ferry to The Rock. Expansive views of the towering Golden Gate Bridge as backdrop and the tree-spotted mountain of Angel Island to the south belied their ominous destination.

Her bandage was now soaked with varied colors of dark red, white pus, and perhaps a shade of blue. Over and over she played the same mantra: *Did Jesus just turn a deaf ear as I shouted his name, as the police violently hit me over and over?*

Her futile questioning turned to random thoughts. The chewy beef jerky someone gave her, the springs bulging out of her seat, the skyline of San Francisco, the black stare of the guard, the memory of better days in the arms of her beloved Will; she wished to know the eventual reason for these things. *Show me the sublime meaning of the lofty spiritual design, as there is always a design, a loftier reason,* she thought.

Let me see every detail fitting with the ethereal wisdom that weaves into God's eternal plan . . . and then the thud of the bus rolling over something startled her, followed by the silent bay, and the stale aroma that dulled the light and drowned out God's poetry. As the world existed no longer by the rules of order in response to this messy miscarriage and stilled cry of a lost soul pining for an answer. There was no artistry, no grand architecture, only an *accident* that reached beyond the farthest ends of meaning. The alchemy of it all confounded her.

A sudden stop jarred Amanda from her mental escape. She felt relieved of the chicken-soup-smelling sweat of her fellow prisoners as she stepped from the ferry into the fresh Pacific Ocean breeze. She could taste the misty salt, albeit tainted by the faint gassy odor wafting in the air from prison exhaust pipes. Not fifty yards away the piss-colored stone face of Alcatraz made a mockery of the picturesque surrounding San Francisco Bay.

Its structural bones jagged, malignant, and craggy—every vista skewed the dearth of life in this place. The city skyline seemed oppressively bleak despite its hazy water frontage. A wrought-iron gate beckoned her inside as the prison's rock face lined with windows told her that she would never see its glassy orifices from the outside ever again.

"Step it up!" the guard shouted.

Her legs still ached, only more so. Thirty or so prisoners had accompanied her on the trip from New York. They joined fifty more in the waiting area, so that all could shed their clothes and adorn purple scrubs, the color of royalty. Together the motley bunch marched down the prison hallway—wide enough for a gurney on the right side holding a still figure draped entirely with a white sheet. Two of the insurgents propped Amanda up so she could walk while dragging her useless leg. The cool dampness pressed her legs like a vise grip.

"My legs hurt," she said as she caved to the ground.

"Get up now!" the burly guard insisted.

But she couldn't get up. Her leg muscles had turned to mush, and the dull ache in her shoulder socket served as a painful afterthought. A buzzing light overhead swelled in her mind to the sound of a chainsaw she wished would just cut her leg off. Moreover, the pain of abandonment made her retch with dry heaves, and the suffering clung to her soul like a wretched parasite, sucking all hope.

She felt cut up now on the outside just like her father used to cut her up on the inside. The memories of adolescence surfaced—her father saying, "You make me ashamed," and the ugly nights when he would strike her across the face or toss her to the floor for the littlest thing. "I wish you was never born," he'd said so many times.

The weight of abandonment had reshaped her as much as the late hours hunched at the college library desk. The only time she had really straightened was after her mountaintop experience.

She'd become, as they say, born again. Feeling as though all the questions had been answered in the person of Christ with no need to know or understand the answers. And for one who always needed an answer, that in itself was a miracle. She had been healed with an injection of love's antibiotic—she'd met God . . . and then she'd met Will.

Memories blossomed in her head, with a bubbling relief that filled her bosom. During their first date Will suggested they compete in a staring contest, and he had won. "You're appropriately named," she remembered saying back then. She admired him more for his steely determination than for his handsome ways, though the two in combination weren't all bad.

Most likely, he'd be worried sick about her. He was still in this world. She felt him. Mr. Chivalry, her knight in shining armor. When she cried, his eyes sometimes welled up too, in a much more understated way. She respected his reserved nature in contrast to her extroverted ways. But, most of all she loved that he always kept his word in a world where broken words abounded.

One day while walking through Central Park, on a misty day, he had suddenly stopped and looked at her with those beaming blues and said, "If I ever lose you, I want it to be because you found someone who will give you more joy, though I'll try—God knows I'll try—to make you happy." That one other person was God.

The two loved her unconditionally. With them she felt, for the first time, at ease. No need for appearances, which was odd for a woman who spent hours detailing the perfect makeover despite a perfect complexion and naturally full-bodied hair.

Though finally loved, she had lost both. Her damaged psyche fed off loss.

Diagnosed with borderline personality disorder in her teens, she lived most of her life just waiting to be rejected for her thorny barbs, as most people in general did—a self-fulfilling prophecy of rejections. Wired to sting like a hornet if disturbed, to flitter like a butterfly and as creatively blessed as one—only to write—and now she only wanted to write her obituary:

"She loved, was loved, and lost love each time—once as a child begging for understanding, and once as a young adult who lost the love of her life, and the one who gave her love, constant love, a real father's love." Now that father seemed only to push her away again—abandoned, just as she'd figured it would always be. There's no such thing as a father's love. Cruel fate.

A sudden thump against her ribs shocked her from the other pains, but only for a second as the hurts produced a surreal moment she wished could end in either unconsciousness or death, preferably the latter.

Rain-cloud-layered hills hovered above. A sickening feeling portended the doom she would inevitably incur. If only she had accepted the pull of the light. Except for Will she might have left this world—that and the tender voice of Jesus telling her to stay, or so she remembered. She had so much wanted to release into the warm light. Life was hard. The memory was kind. Perhaps in time she would understand why.

She breathed in the irony of them being further apart than ever, unable to exhale the misery and suffocation, with no possible way to exhale the emotional toxins inside: the doubt, hopelessness, and worst of all—God shrinking away into a concept rather than the constant companion he'd been before.

"Get up now or I'll knock your head in!" Within a few seconds she felt the knuckles against her head, and then nothing.

#

She awoke to the horror of it not being a nightmare, lying in the jail bed, the stink of disinfectant from the recently cleaned cement floor infecting her nostrils. The taste of blood rested on her tongue.

It was all real enough, and bad enough to look for something to end it all. God would accept someone who committed suicide, wouldn't he? The faint glow of a lone electric light barely broke the darkness of her cell. She glanced at the cement wall covered in graffiti. One in particular slightly amused her. Someone had written with childish penmanship, "Nietzsche says God is dead," and then beside it some other meticulous writing responded, "God says Nietzsche is dead." She knew the latter to be true. Not so sure about the former.

One slight movement brought back the excruciating pain as she peered over to her blood-soaked pants legs, not daring to look under the sticky jeans caked with body fluids lest she observed the bone protruding from her flesh. Why did she have to wake? Too many whys circled in her mind. It could have been different. She could be in paradise now. Death could save her now—perhaps only death.

Heavy footsteps clip-clopped down the hallway, growing louder. Outside her cell, the cavernous space of the two-story hallway echoed with the sound of creaky hinges. The clang of a stick thumping against prison bars played an ominous tune, until it turned silent. The footsteps stopped outside her door. A broad-shouldered, heavily weathered woman with more wrinkles than face stood at the doorway. "You've got a compound fracture from a fall," she said. "We wrapped it. You ain't in no more pain?"

"Terrible pain," Amanda replied. "Do you have some pain-killer medicine? Aspirin, anything?"

"This ain't no hotel, lady. You were told—"

"I was told that I'm an insurgent, a threat to others. Do I look like a threat?" Amanda cringed and crawled as the agony grew.

She'd never even cussed until of late. Vices amounted to sneaking in a tabloid magazine now and then—that's all. Bound by the goody girl she thought would ingratiate her with parents who never praised. A revolving door of friends she heaped gifts upon only to face their abandonment when she tested their commitment by lashing out with caustic vitriol when threatened—which always proved her theory that she did not merit love.

Countless charities and a heart for the lost—a heart now that had gone stone hard. This was the thanks? Maybe her morality was just some masochistic way of depriving her of the carnal pleasures others seemed to unashamedly enjoy. Maybe she was all wrong. People live and die, regardless. Then what? Time to die; if only she knew how to die.

The guard's clanging voice broke a few seconds of miserable reflection. "Insurgents like you have killed who knows how many people, lady! There's martial law in effect. You and your killer husband are threats to society."

"We didn't kill anybody! Haven't you heard about the rapture?" As if given a shot of Novocain, the pain turned into just numbness—an answered prayer.

"Rapture, my foot! You people released radiation into the air. I don't know how you did it, but you and your husband—"

"My husband! Where is he?" Just the remembrance of Will struck the chords of hope again.

"We'll get him too. He escaped. Blew up a church!" With that the crass guard departed, and Amanda stared into the dark corner, alone, but not really. Something was there. She felt it, sensed its threatening presence as if someone stared from behind—then the fumes of bloated bodies in decay, and that steely stare she remembered from her father. It mocked her, feeding off her misery through its salivating fangs.

"Who are you?" she asked. Her heart pounding like a ticking bomb ready to explode. Caught in a living nightmare with no hope to awaken.

No answer. Instead, the invisible entity played hide-and-seek, taunting her with its threatening cloud raining down despair. She felt boxed in with malaise, suffocating; her heart fluttered and her chest pulsated to no avail.

"Go ahead and kill me!" she declared, struggling to breathe. "Send me to . . ." To where? Where was God? Had she missed her chance?

"God save me!" The presence still loomed. "In Jesus Christ's name, save me!" Still no relief from the stifling oppression around her and now within her. Hope had been sucked out of her, and it felt like a freefall down a dark tunnel; she just wanted to crash against the hard bottom and be finished. But there was no bottom, no end. The presence just kept dangling her over a pit of hopelessness.

This was hell. Hell on earth. "God save me! Where are you! Don't desert me!" And she heaved, her chest aching with crying that was too deep to come out. She didn't deserve this.

"Will—at least save Will, God, even if you've turned your eyes from me."

The guard showed up again, this time arriving in silence as though she tiptoed to Amanda's cell. With a dismissive push, the lady's leathery arms slid a plate of brown-gray mush, bread, and meat that smelled of canned dog food through a slit in the bars. The presence fed off the putrid smell and slithered from above Amanda through the door and into the guard, penetrating the rough woman as she straightened, the now visible vapory demon snaking through the guard's lanky body and filling her rippled skin until it blew her up with bravado.

Strange how Amanda knew all this—could see into the invisible world through intuition, or a hunch, or some ethereal sensing radar— sights she'd rather not see at all. Amanda was revolted by what she saw. The guard's skin looked as though it had been ripped off of her, making visible raw maggot-covered sinew. She smiled through jagged stained teeth and then growled in a voice part woman, part beast.

"It's over, Amanda. There is no God, honey. God is a myth. You take up space and then you die, you worthless piece of meat."

Something had gone terribly awry. It shouldn't have been this way. She'd lived and felt the most pristine refreshment that love can give. And then wanton lava turned tender love to cinders. Then the pain returned, shooting from Amanda's leg with the force of a thousand volts, causing her to reach out impulsively.

"Save me!" *Anyone, just save me.*

But no one did. She was left alone with just the drip, drip, drip of a leaky faucet that would not stop.

"Hey lady," the guard sneered. "You need to wash your pretty little face."

The guard turned on the squeaky faucet to let the basin fill. She poured something into the water, soap perhaps.

Not wanting to further irritate the woman, Amanda pulled herself over to the sink, using every last ounce of strength to lift her body onto the rim. As her head lowered, she collapsed into the water, completely immersing her face. Feeling a thousand needles driving into her skin, she jerked backward trying desperately to wipe away the liquid with her scrub shirt. The digging heat pressed into her face as she screamed into the solitary space of hellfire. Rolling back and forth, she touched her scalded face.

Skin the texture of goo peeled off into her hand. Layers of it.

"God, no!"

ᵔ Chapter Four ᵓ

O n our way to the airport, Lila and I had walked so many alleys
and bypasses, had hurried across so many avenues into so many
dark backstreets, that I for one became not only lost but also
confused. Buildings appeared angled or waved forward at odd degrees.
The potholes in the pavement under our feet resembled leopard spots,
making it seem as though we straddled atop a dormant beast.

The city, ever towering, seemed to imprison us within its walls.
With the confusion came a growing anxiety that compelled us to sprint,
although no one appeared in immediate pursuit of us.

As dusk approached, we walked into a narrow side street surrounded
by mostly brick-faced shops stained with graffiti. We encountered a store
window filled with ghoulish faces and splattered blood, knives, and a red-
stained butcher knife. "Max's Costume Shop," the sign overhead stated.
For a few minutes after stepping inside we turned childlike, breathing in
the plastic aroma of several masks and laughing as Lila tried on a donkey
outfit, and me a Freddie mask from *Nightmare on Elm Street*, which actually
appeared all too real for the circumstances.

We finally settled on a mustache for me, a Jamaican wig for Lila, and I dyed my hair jet black in the restroom. Lila ran next door to buy new jackets for us, and after our transformations, I couldn't get away from feeling a little bit like a cheap gigolo. I took a quick picture of myself on my cell and sent it to Ian asking if he could fudge my new look onto a fake ID. He replied with a yes.

Exiting the store into the bustling streets again, I could not help but notice that debauchery abounded in the open gathering places and tucked-back streets alongside the city's walls. A neatly dressed group of three shooting up heroin at an outdoor table and placing their needles like cigarettes in an ash tray, a couple contorting in the alley, while a woman frantically tried to steer her son's head away from them.

"Tolerance" was the first value esteemed by the Universal Church. "A guiltless life" being another. They reasoned that by "freeing" people to indulge their natural desires, no one could judge, and thereby peace could prevail. Except, no peace inside existed.

At first it shocked me, and then I resented the arousal that snuck into me, then my disgust grew at the feeding frenzies, and then worst of all I became almost oblivious to it. Perhaps I am a prude, as Lila says; however, isn't restraint what keeps our basest parts from intruding on our loftiest duties, like sacrifice and selfless love?

The flesh feeds off this kind of thing like a hungry sweet tooth over a freshly filled bucket of Halloween candy. You could do anything and get away with it even though it eventually sickened. The imagination feeds our self-indulgences. One just hopes God isn't looking should one's mind partake. And I couldn't help but wonder if he wasn't looking anymore.

"We need to go." Lila spoke with an assumed comfort only two people in crisis can share.

We caught a cab and tested our disguise—the driver graciously paid no attention. Lila snuggled this time in the backseat assuming no need to guard against affection. Her Chanel and come-hither eyes pulled me deeper into her embrace. I allowed her to press into me, reluctantly, longingly, with mixed emotions punctuated by my devotion to Amanda. Her smooth chestnut skin raised a minefield of goose bumps as she stroked my arm.

My purpose in life used to fuel my resistance to temptation. But what did it matter, if your purpose was to spend time with a God who had removed himself from this world? Let alone the fact that I could no longer rely on his Spirit to direct me. I had only his Word, and words seemed of little comfort now.

"We need each other," Lila said.

"We need to find Amanda," I replied. As if Lila could take the hint. She did not, and began stroking my hair.

"We just have each other right now, Will. It's not bad if it feels right."

I looked down to meet her yearning eyes and Cleopatra looks. Her nose rested at the tip of mine. Her breath was fresh with spearmint, her lips full; her hands rubbed my back with tickles that resurrected my dulled emotions. *Amanda, I need you.* I imagined her in place of Lila. *God, deliver me from temptation.*

Lila pressed her lips against mine, and in that second I wished to surrender into her with every surging whim. And in that moment my eyes closed and all I could see was my need for pushing forward. I wished to honor Amanda always, and to tell God someday that I held firm in the face of my Bathsheba, or Delilah. Character, as they say, is demonstrated by what you do when no one is looking.

I pulled back and pushed my arm into Lila's shoulder. "We can't do this, Lila. You're too good for this." If only I could muster the right words.

She melted away into a ball of isolation.

"It's not you." Another lame consolation, as I couldn't think of any other.

With the timidity of a scolded pooch, she looked up at me again. "Society has changed, Will. It's open now, and you shouldn't feel guilt in following your passions. It's liberating."

"And Amanda?"

"She'd understand—love between friends, you know."

Thankfully, the airport signs and lights loomed ahead. And I figured that silence would be the best solution to our divergent perspectives. Hopefully, Ian had waited at the airport, as I noticed a swarm of police officers darting around curbside. One of the officers eyed me as half my mustache fell lamely from my upper lip, hastening my run into the airport lobby while pulling Lila by the wrist.

Looking round, Ian was nowhere, and then didn't answer his cell phone. My floppy companion in tow followed me to a secluded row of seats facing outward, where I hid my face from the scurrying masses so that I could open up my laptop to first message Ian—and then The Way distribution list. I wrote:

"Brothers and sisters in Christ, I am sending you this message not knowing if I will ever be able to do so again. Those of us who heeded God's call to remain behind as the remnant church find ourselves as the hunted, with the Universal Church being the only condoned church throughout the world.

"I believe now that we must reassemble in Jerusalem. I've been informed that God will somehow reestablish his design for perfection—a new earth, if you will. I've also been told that I must find the presence of our Lord and bring him back to the Promised Land. Perhaps he will meet me on my journey. I don't know. We have only our faith now, beloved, however weak that may be given the despair in this world. Be strong in the Lord.

"Love in Christ, Reuben."

An elephant of fear pressed against my chest after I sent the message. Somehow the authorities might track me, or the recipients. I closed my laptop and then fidgeted while waiting for Ian to contact me. After about ten minutes of twisted nerves, my phone buzzed with a message: "Reuben, meet me at the security check-in by the kiosk."

Apparently my rejection had drained the emotion out of Lila. She tagged along like a speechless toddler as we rushed to security. Ian stood there dangling a ticket.

"I've got two tickets to San Fran, bro," he said.

"How?"

"Don't ask."

"My ID—no way they'd let me through."

"Got that taken care of too, oh thee of little faith. My connection can forge anyone in a matter of minutes. Have a nice trip, Mr. Kusch."

Ian handed over one ticket while guarding the other.

"I need Lila's too."

42

"She's not going. It's you and me, buddy. No way can we jeopardize your lovely lady there." Turning toward Lila, he said, "Honey, you can get your own ticket to San Fran—they're not looking for you. It's safer this way."

After a brief protest from Lila, I realized Ian had given me a "get out of jail" card to escape from my temptress. A disheartened Lila didn't even protest, saying a mere "OK" as both Ian and I walked toward the security desk. My heart drooped a bit in thinking that I'd abandoned her. "We'll talk, maybe even meet soon," I rationalized—and then what?

Ian plopped down his ticket for the TSA agent and revealed his driver's license without incident. My turn. The twenty-something guard reached for my ticket, then impatiently insisted that I fork over my ID—my moment of truth. She shined her blue flashlight against the ticket, and then eyed my ID with the look of a wanna-be detective.

A double take signaled danger, which forced me to think of an escape route should the police suddenly pounce. An emergency exit to my left appeared the best out. She looked at me, then forced a smile.

"OK," she said, giving her golden approval.

We eventually boarded the plane, the great getaway almost complete, although each person along the way fed my paranoia—from the hawk-eyed flight attendant to the beady-eyed passenger in the aisle seat next to me. "Trust no one" seemed the prudent adage to follow.

My angst lifted with the plane into the air, and a bag of peanuts midflight assuaged me all the more, though the scowling fellow to my right refused even a response to my hello. Ian, for his part, didn't say much either.

In fact, he spoke maybe five words, if that, stretching his neck frequently, peering out the window with glazed eyes and occasional scowls in place of the happy lines he showed before our departure.

"You OK?" I finally asked.

"Yeah, fine," he said curtly. Ian squirmed in his chair, tried standing up, rubbed his face, sat back down. Looked at the man a couple of rows up.

At the risk of further perturbing him I said, "You don't seem OK."

"I'm fine."

No he wasn't. He was making me feel nervous. The Grinch on the other side of me leaned his head toward our conversation.

"Ian, have you ever been to San Francisco?" I asked, trying to make light.

"Yeah."

Another man, suit and tie and weathered face, approached the other guy sitting next to me, then looked squarely at Ian, who proceeded to rise from his seat.

"Where you going?" I asked.

"Toilet," Ian said. What was with the short answers?

Ian crawled over me and starting walking toward the rear. To my surprise, the man in the aisle then clumsily climbed over me to reach Ian's abandoned seat.

"Excuse me," is all he said.

"Excuse *me*, sir," I responded. "This is my friend's seat."

No response. He just sat down assuming I'd be OK with his intrusion.

"What's going on?" An adrenaline rush sent my ticker into double time while I hoped for some plausible explanation.

"Just sit still," the new guy responded calmly as he buried his chin into his chest.

Red flags popped up everywhere as the man on the aisle motioned to someone standing two rows ahead, prompting him and another gym-toned man to move from out of nowhere from the rear to the adjoining aisle. Now two strangers loomed over our seats.

I immediately texted Ian but to no avail.

"Tell me what's going on!" I demanded. Passengers robotically focused on typing, reading. And then I noticed that all but four of them were men—not a single child was on board.

"You need to stay calm, sir," insisted the guy by the window. "Stay calm and everything will be just fine."

My heartbeat increased tenfold. "You guys arresting me?"

"We'll discuss that when we land."

Why—was Ian part of this? "Where's my friend?"

"He's not your friend," spoke the acne-scarred man sitting to my right. The guy gave a sinister smile.

"He's a spy?" No one answered—they didn't need to.

The man by the window laser-beamed his charcoal eyes into mine. "I'm going to handcuff you now. Stay calm. This is a restricted flight, and we have several agents on board, Mr. Will Simon, aka Reuben. You're going to debrief us, and if you tell us what we want to know, you'll be free to go when we land."

Right. I'll believe that when hell turns into a resort.

"You'll take me—" I said, and then I caught myself. If they took me to Alcatraz, I'd be where they took Amanda. I could help her escape, or just see her.

"OK, I won't resist; don't worry."

"Hand over your phone and laptop," Mr. Charcoal Eyes said. They could trace every believer from The Way distribution list—I couldn't.

Lord, give me wisdom to know what to do.

A booming blast came from the left engine, followed by a sudden drop. The floor gave out. My body swung toward the ceiling. The plane rocked like a seesaw. Overhead bins opened, spilling all kinds of luggage. Creaking and groaning noises reverberated throughout the cabin. I grasped the seat in front with one hand to keep from ramming into others while grabbing onto the dangling mask and placing it over my face with the other hand.

The two standing guys in the aisle fell and rolled down the aisle as the cabin tipped forward. It fell backward, then sideways. I felt like I was in a drink mixer.

My insides churned. Organs jostled inside me, feeling as if they were tearing from my insides. My heart felt ready to burst from my chest, and I grew light-headed.

An endless swirl of motion erupted through a fade-out of grinding noises from the engines—a distinct cracking sound of metal against metal. My seat belt sucked the air out of my belly, pushing barf through my nose.

The sputtering engines ground out smoke, sounding a whistling death knell through the twilight. There was nearly continuous lightning outside. The plane took a drunken sideways lurch. I felt like I was strapped in a terrible carnival ride.

Dark. Everything went dark inside. A person screamed, setting off a chorus of screams. Something hard hit me in the head—a suitcase maybe. It was freezing in the cabin. Horribly cold.

A hard thump, and then I was pulled to the left. And then to the right as the engine sputtered to a halt. I heard gasping noises. Incessant tossing caused me to throw up, feeling as if dangling from a rope. We were caught in a windstorm just waiting for the crushing blow. I was at the mercy of everything but me.

The bottom dropped out again, and my bobble head lunged forward in response to the sudden downturn. My arms braced against the broken headrest in front. Face masks dangled amid dying screams, and the guy next to me wasn't even breathing. *We're crashing!*

ᔕ Chapter Five ᔐ

Chief Priest Muhammad Bakr slithered into his Dior leather chair filled with scarlet macaw feathers after having breathed in the crisp desert air from the new Babylon. He lounged in a hexagonal chamber where the last Middle Eastern insurgent had been martyred. The interior of the room was mostly gold, the floor crimson so as not to tell the difference between its natural color and blood. It possessed an eerie glow, this interrogation room, fitted with a large stone fireplace that burned with rare teakwood.

He could have anything. Anything, that is, except selfless love. Love in service to oneself, yes—luxury, pleasure, amusement, gusto . . . appetites indulged. But not the love that denies itself, returns good for evil, and that sort of nonsense.

That belonged to a vengeful god, the one who imposed guilt and denied one's natural inclinations. No, he would impart freedom so everyone could live life to the fullest.

Manmade treasures adorned the room. Gold trim ran along the ceiling and ancient marbled flooring. Ornate chairs with the rarest fabrics from around the world sat below heads of endangered species mounted on the walls with their fierce looks glaring down upon all who entered. Even polished moon rocks were used as door knobs. And in the center of the room lay a rug made out of mummified skin overlaid with exotic furs. Artifacts sat on pedestals that once entertained spectators from the most prestigious museums.

All of these things. And for what?

Another trophy stood beside him—the distinguished Serge Amato, trusted collaborator, chairman of the World Security Alliance, whose anticlerical views made him a perfect fit for the one-world church oligarchy. "Father Muhammad." Amato broke Bakr's contemplation. "The asteroids are falling."

"Damage?"

Because of the steeliness of Bakr's most earnest stare, Amato surely knew his question arose from malice and not concern. "At least fourteen sites identified. Three over the Sierras in the US, and one has hit the plane carrying that insurgent, Reuben."

Bakr chuckled at the irony. Reuben—his cyber nemesis who had attracted millions of Christians and seekers before the rapture falling victim to God's judgment. *You have a funny way of showing love, Yahweh.*

"Reuben's dead?" Bakr asked, flashing a smile.

"Yes," Amato answered after a moment's hesitation.

Bakr closed his eyes, assumed a Zen position, and deeply breathed in.

"One more thing." Amato winced before continuing, four even lines of wrinkles creasing his forehead. "We intercepted a message to the insurgents. From Reuben—or Will Simon, as we've discovered. He contacted the insurgents before his death."

"That would be those left in America or Israel," Bakr interrupted. "We've intercepted all of those in America—correct?"

"Those who remained after the light fell on them, yes," Amato answered.

"The rapture . . . so be it." Bakr's face warmed. "So what did this Reuben or Will character say?"

"He said that God would build a new Jerusalem and that he—Reuben—would bring the presence of God back to Jerusalem."

"Hmm, fat chance of that happening now." Bakr rolled his eyes and, in spite of himself, smirked. The aroma of fried onions and eggplant from the moussaka had escaped from the kitchen to soothe his ire at the thought of Yahweh interfering with his plan.

"Has not Yahweh already relinquished his presence in this world?"

Serge nodded with a hollowed-out stare. Though revered by the rest of the world, and of scholarly comport, in the presence of Bakr he regressed to that wet-behind-the-ears stage of a student again.

"Fools," Bakr said.

"Father?"

"*Love,*" Bakr said it as a foreign word. "I once loved him, Serge." Bakr curled his fingers to prevent their trembling, tightening the almost-black veins on top of his hands. They branched into a pentagram, he had decided—the Devil's trap. He brushed the left hand in a spherical rotation with the right, as though casting a spell.

Bakr's confidant and longtime ally gave him that quizzical look again. "You loved who?"

"Him, Yahweh, the almighty 'I Am' and all that bull." Bakr's soul felt as dark as the night outside. "No human could understand what it was like to love purely, selflessly, and then fall out of favor, abandoned to the emotions of wanting . . . just wanting." He stood and walked past a stuffed lion toward the gold cross beyond. Seven feet tall, over two-thousand year-old olive wood gathered from Golgotha lay underneath the gold plating. Emblazoned across its horizontal arm were the letters *INRI*—otherwise noted as "Jesus of Nazareth King Jews." His most prized possession.

He meticulously brushed his hand over the lettering, his back to the wall. For a minute he felt more like a teddy bear than a grizzly. Serge stepped near him and broke an awkward smile.

"You're uncharacteristically pensive tonight, Father."

Bakr rarely revealed his vulnerability, unlike Amato. Once a dapper dresser, Amato donned clothes that appeared as though thrown flippantly on a clothes rack. His drapery neck contrasted to his once-toned skin, and his gray hair combed straight back now receded on each side, thinned so much that portions of his scalp showed their age spots. This for a man not even in his sixties. The once-stately six-foot-four Serge stooped at least an inch shorter since the recent crises had begun.

Bakr, by contrast, stood taller, at only forty-six years of age. His vitality inspired by each catastrophe that breathed confusion. Chaos breeds opportunity, after all. Next to Serge's pale white skin, Bakr's was the burnished color of a bronzed Adonis. Though the heat in his face from thinking of his enemy had probably turned him a shade of red. "Such puritanical smothering. The Ten Commandments—don't do this, don't do that. Yahweh was always about the rules, and if you broke them, you were out."

"But, Father, you freed us from the shackles of that puritanical rule."

"Jesus—he did it."

"Sir?" Serge followed Bakr to the center of the oval room. Bakr pressed his hand to this temple.

"He descended from the throne—became like the humans—a human, for God's sake!"

"But, the rules—Yahweh's commandments—they condemn," said Amato.

"Not now—not since Jesus broke the contract," replied Bakr.

"The contract?"

"He rewrote the rules—you know, love God with all your heart, love your neighbor—for him it was a state of being rather than doing, just by being fueled with his spirit." Bakr's disposition matched that of the growling grizzly bear head mounted on his wall.

By now Amato appeared like a confused first-grader attempting to learn calculus.

Bakr continued: "Anyone who wouldn't bow before that human was condemned. Imagine, Serge, the loftiest beings in all the heavens bowing before a mediator in human form!"

A pop from the crackling fireplace catapulted a smoldering piece of wood onto Bakr's alligator shoes stitched with custom-made linen twine, prompting him to flick it off as he had done with so many other irritants and diverting his attention back to the strategy that would unalterably change Yahweh's plan.

"Serge, the high-frequency waves or electromagnetic pulses—which caused the recent deaths?"

Serge stood taller and lightly squeezed the bridge of his nose, lowering his voice in an attempt to sound more authoritative. "The high-frequency waves, we believe. The test detonation over the Atlantic only marginally disabled some grids over New York."

Bakr mulled his response. "I was informed that the oscillating electric waves could have fried some pacemakers."

"Perhaps, but the HCP test program proved to be more lethal."

Energy—it was always about power. "Never mind. How many watts did they put out?"

"3.7 million—74,000 times more powerful than the largest legal AM radio station in the US."

"Enough to control minds—that was their intent. But how did the first test end up killing people?"

Amato's spine straightened for the first time since entering the room. "As we discussed, Father, the low-frequency waves are at the same frequency range that the human brain works in. The best our people can determine is that the intensity of the signals triggered cerebral aneurysms in those predisposed."

"Collateral damage, I suppose," said Bakr with a shoulder shrug.

"And the ashes, Father—we couldn't reason that—and the lights." However, Bakr knew—ashes to ashes in the effulgence of Yahweh, as he pulled his slaves' spirits like insects out of their cocoons, incinerating their encasings with blazing glory. He could have them.

Bakr rested his nose upon his index finger and reached his other hand to a globe nested within an antique table once used in ancient Rome. "Our geologists tell me that if we were to inject liquid under high pressure deep in the earth, it would release stored energy in the rocks, causing more earthquakes."

Serge's face tightened. "Pardon me, Father, but why all this?"

Bakr closed his eyes while tossing his head back. "Serge . . . asteroids, earthquakes, mind control. What happens when people are thrown into chaos?"

"They'll look for someone to cling to?"

"They'll die on the inside. No anchors. No preconceived notions. They turn on the emptiness within—hopelessness. And then, we take Jerusalem, rebuild the temple, and we, not Yahweh, build the new earth." Bakr sighed. "Because the earth will implode, all flights will be grounded except ours—the perfect race protected within our underground acropolis. And when the new earth takes form, we take possession of it."

Demons brilliantly adorned in gemstone garments manifested in the room. Their auras shimmered in the light of Bakr's brilliance, basking in their master's plan. All stood gallantly in a circle around the Egyptian, Roman, and German designs carefully placed throughout the oval-shaped room.

The same plan he used to foil Yahweh in the garden of Eden, the same plan of rebellion instilled in the first humans, in Cain, and soon . . . in every godforsaken human remaining except those perfected through the first DNA sourced from . . .

"The Adam Project, how many cloned?" asked Bakr.

"Twelve," answered Amato.

"All from the first humans—no imperfections?"

"Our scientists have reimprinted the original human epigenome—yes."

"Perfect." These will never die. He had destroyed Yahweh's plan before; he would do so again. Human want would triumph over obedience—again.

"Father," Serge spoke. "Alcatraz. We could say that an asteroid destroyed it. We are looking for an opportunity—"

"Shh . . ."

Serge froze. Muhammad's angels tensed. A breeze blew through the room, blowing curtains at one end of the room and out the other like white flags, twisting them up toward the crown-shaped chandelier—and then waved over the scarlet-colored rug, making a shadow on it as dark as the night.

"We can't talk now," Bakr whispered.

"Something wrong?"

"He's here," Bakr continued to whisper. He sensed Yahweh's presence the way a child smells the scent of his parent's perfume after being caught stealing from the cookie jar.

"Go now, Serge; leave quickly."

Amato rushed through the door leading to the adjoining hallway. The demons drew vapory swords that appeared as dust clouds, emanating from whispers that elicited wanton emotions and foul utterances evoking in mere mortals the basest of their desires, leading not to death but to despair.

"Those will do no good against Yahweh," Bakr said to his outcast angels. "Leave by the same way Serge left," Bakr called to the demons. "I must talk to him alone."

The whistling breeze stopped, leaving in its place an expectant pause that gagged all of nature's subtle vibrations.

After the demons departed, Bakr brushed through the flowing silk curtains onto the pillared veranda and into the perfectly still night. One exceptionally bright star gleamed above the other surrounding diamond glitters against the black velvet sky. The oncoming wind sang through desert canyon music boxes until resting its flowing melody in Bakr's presence, causing him, in that hallowed moment, to bow.

"Creator."

The wind firmly spoke with the reach of an echo and the intensity of a roaring lion: "Why do you test me?"

Yahweh's familiar voice convicted him once more, and reminded him of their infinite separation. They had been close before. If only Bakr could weep . . . yet the river of tears had long since dried, leaving the memory of what was and is no more.

Always the wind's mighty calm overwhelmed him—although in heaven it soothed away the cares, whereas now it tensed him like a schoolboy called into the principal's office for gross misconduct.

"Yahweh, they will only deny you again. Why give your all when they give you nothing?"

"Why do you call me by that name? I am not Father to you," the wind said.

Bakr looked down and rubbed his head. "You were Adonai—lord over the entire universe and the angels. And then you made the humans—made us serve *them*," Bakr said.

"I became their Jehovah," God said.

Bakr reached as if to grasp the air. "Did we not love you more?"

"When you lost love, Ra, you lost your ability to understand the answer," Yahweh answered.

"You abandoned me!" Bakr wished to cry but could only heave with regret, and then only without remorse.

The wind rustled against the pillars, abated for an instant, and then blew with such gusts that Bakr almost fell over. "No, you denied me who

I am. For if I am not your all, after your having seen my fullness, I am as nothing to you."

"No one gives you their all! Certainly not the humans!"

"To lay down one's life is all to me, as I have laid down my life for all. So those who deny themselves receive me, and I them. For it is not what they have done that merits my grace, Ra, but what I have done for them."

Whirling thoughts raged within Bakr. Laying down one's life—nonsense. Worse, it denied reason, as if a person could simply surrender, and in so doing be made whole through blind trust.

"You denied me, Yahweh. I loved you more than them, more than you loved me!"

For the first time in such a long, long time, Bakr felt the warm glow of the wind upon his flesh as more than the singeing of his nerves, though his heart pined. The soft blush served only as a pitiless reminder of his loss.

Yahweh's voice rippled with the wind. "Your words condemn you, Ra, for you understand that to know my love you must allow my Spirit to take dominion. To you I was not El Shaddai, the one and only Almighty God. I was to you Elohim, one of many gods"

More like a stepfather, Bakr mulled. Bakr strutted toward the railing, chin up. "I deserved more, and now it is as though I never knew you."

"You never knew my full measure, for I did not sacrifice my all to you. In the children of Adam I see the reflection of my Son."

Confounding logic. "You look upon the spirit of a person," said Bakr. "I look upon their flesh and blood—give me that! Just as you gave over to me Cain and all of his descendents because they considered themselves equal to you—"

"Enough!" cried the wind. A lion's roar thundered throughout the environs causing Bakr to fall prostrate to the ground.

"It is done," Yahweh declared.

Bakr fell to the marbled floor and crawled on his knees to look upon the radiant star above, wishing for a moment to curl back into his chair. Leave the world to its demise and just be done with it. But he could not. The forces of carnality and of the spirit were pitted against each other with him as the lord of these worldly ways.

His plan would be fulfilled. He would finally have his way—flesh that would not die. Desires that would not end . . . and no more contrary believers.

Reuben came to mind like a rush of ingested rage. Bakr's neck muscles tensed and his face shivered in heat. "Yahweh, if Reuben is to die, then let me have my way with his wife."

As a couple they had done more to harm his cause than most any other—bringing the believers together through their broadcasts, inciting disparate Christians to worship with one voice, leading thousands to Yahweh before the rapture. "Relationship over religion" and all that stupid foolery.

"I can turn her soul to me, and prove to you that your love once planted in a human will invariably wither away."

The wind turned cold. "She will bear your wounds, Ra, but not your stain. Go then and do your evil deeds. Reuben and Amanda are faithful to me; they will not deny me to the end, for I am with them, and my love is sufficient."

With that the wind withdrew into a vacuum of space, stilling the dense air again and fading the lone bright star into a mere fleck among a multitude of stars in the sky. And there stood Muhammad Bakr, chief priest of the Universal Church, gallant by the standards of the world, and dark inside, waiting to be filled with all that the world could give him.

And empty inside.

No one is more dangerous than the woeful soul whose only redemption is revenge.

↶ Chapter Six ↷

"We're going to crash," shouted the pilot's voice over the intercom, followed by a thump and a groan turned silent. Electrical burning smells filled the cabin.

I felt like I was speeding down a grinding roller coaster with no ability to stop. Hills and trees below grew larger through a long vertical tunnel at lightning speed. Just waiting for the final blow.

A grassy knoll in plain sight grew as through a zoom lens. Branches broke . . . *thunk . . . wham . . . womp . . .kwoohh.*

\#

Awaking to a bleary and agonizing state of mind, smoke hovered over the crisp night air. Crackling flames showed here and there that I preferred to think as fireflies, though they were more like funeral fires. Twilight shaded plane parts and ashen red limbs strewn all over as I peered through the open metal sides of the plane. Some sat dead in their buckled seats. Others were like crushed tomatoes and smashed watermelons. The night was redolent with charred flesh and burning metal.

I was alive, I think. Though, oh, how I wished to awake from death to see the eyes of Jesus again. I was the unlucky one.

"Help." Hope against hope. Was no one else alive? I looked around to see the outlines of trees highlighted by the fire glows against the breeze, and strewn wreckage—and no one.

Detaching my seat belt, I crawled over the dead agent and leaped onto the plowed dirt looking for life. My wobbly legs caused me to fall and I scraped myself up. Two bodies on either side lay in flames. A detached engine on the ground, breathing in monstrous sucking heat as if alive, exhaled fumes and grinding noises. It wasn't until after a while that I noticed the blood on the ground had come from me. From where I cared little.

"Is anyone alive? Say something!" Only the sound of popping fire answered back, cruel, as it evoked thoughts of logs on the fireplace at home, which couldn't be farther from reality. I tried avoiding both metal and organic debris as I walked, although a few crunches under my feet here and there nauseated me; I dared not look down to see what they were.

"Hello," came a wonderfully welcoming voice. "Are you all right?"

Coming into view through the haze, a scraggly backpacker with cropped brown hair and uplifted arms came running toward me until reaching me face-to-face and touching my arm ever so gently.

"You look OK; are you hurting?"

"No." I thought how crazy that was—just shaken while others lay dead. "Is anyone alive?"

"Not a soul; I've searched all over. The only one alive is you. It's a miracle you made it." He began unraveling some gauze and doused it with an iodine-smelling liquid, then handed it over. "You've got scratches on your face and arm."

"I need to get out of here," I said while waving away his offer.

The stranger arched his head. "Why are you in a hurry? I've called for help."

"They're after me. I'm an insurgent. If they catch me, I'm as dead as those around here. Please—"

"OK, brother, let's walk toward those clumps of trees. I'm a believer too."

I'd heard that one before. No doubt undercover plants were all over trying to root out the insurgents, just like Ian. No way could I trust this guy, at least not from the get-go. Besides, I'd heard that all of the insurgents had been arrested and taken to Alcatraz.

The limber man continued to hold my arm—my bleeding arm. We briskly walked through the timbered forest away from the plane. Truck sounds came rolling from opposite our position as the flashing lights signaled oncoming emergency responders. Much to my relief, should anyone have possibly survived.

Not a hundred feet into our walk an explosion came from the wrecked plane. As we turned, almost the entire plane had been consumed by a ball of raging fire, illuminating the surrounding sky enough so that we could see over the next arching hill and lights from the valley below. Both of us stared in shock.

"Maybe some homes over there," the backpacker said.

"Where are we?"

"About forty miles north of Sacramento."

"And how far from San Francisco?"

"Not quite three hours by car."

A three-hour drive and I'd be near my beautiful wife. Oh, how I'd give anything to look into those emerald eyes and vanish into her familiar caress again. This time with all of the intensity of my renewed passion for the only one who could wear my feelings as her own. The thought made me want to hitchhike in order to get to her, if not for my near-catatonic state.

The faint rolling hills studded with oaks in the far distance stretched across to a flatland dotted with house lights even farther out—too far to reach. The dying lights of the wreckage behind me glowed now like tiny amber lights, and then some glaring light beams shot out from the crash site. They waved back and forth—searchlights.

"Do you want to go toward those lights, find a house?"

"We've got to get out of here," I said.

"But don't you want to get help?"

"No," I quickly protested. "No one can know that I survived. You're a camper, right?"

"Yeah, I was hiking the hills."

"Then let's hike far from this nightmare and camp out, please. I don't mind sleeping on the grass.

The man gently smiled in deference to my recent trauma and began looking for a site toward the north end of the hills. After a brief but far enough walk, he found a familiar spot and begin pitching his ample tent. When he finished, I just instinctively caved in, suddenly convicted that I had not even asked my rescuer's name.

"Elian, Elian Davidson," he answered to my query while reaching out his calloused hand. Elian slid his body onto the other side of the open-faced sleeping bag with his lit lantern placed between us, which illuminated his rugged face and his fresh sunburn that was making his nose peel.

"Thank you," I said. "I hate to leave the scene of an accident."

"You're welcome, first. And second—you escaped, correct?"

"Right."

"Tell me about yourself." His question sounded a little like scratching nails on a chalkboard.

"Not much to tell." I didn't want to share again with a possible turncoat like Ian.

"All right, I understand. Can I at least ask you where you were going?"

"To visit with family."

Elian seemed sincere enough, but in this world, appearances meant very little. A little test might do the trick. "Tell me, Elian, what's your favorite Scripture?"

Elian scratched his nose. "I like them all." He mulled. "Let's say I John 4:16: 'And we have known and believed the love that God has toward us. God is love; and he that dwells in love dwells in God, and God in him.' "

OK, he passed the first Scripture test. Even Satan knows Scripture. Next, "That's a good one. Tell me what Jesus means to you." Someone dishonest, who never knew Christ, would come up with some trite answer. You could always tell a true believer by how much adoration they exhibited while they spoke of Christ.

"He's my all," is all Elian could say. And even that he spoke with the enthusiasm of an undertaker. Certainly not passionate enough to allay my suspicion.

Regardless, I would have to take a chance on this guy, as he could be my ticket to Amanda.

"Is there a train to San Fran, or maybe a bus station you can drive me to?"

Elian pulled out a map from his backpack and unraveled it slowly, painfully slowly. Mysteriously slowly. "I'll go one better, bro. I'll drive you there after we hike back to my car tomorrow. How about if we get some sleep now?"

Who was I to argue? Though it did seem a little odd that Elian would go to so much trouble. Ian had also gone out of his way—just so that he could lead me to the authorities. Then again, I didn't have much choice. A ride closer to Amanda was worth the risk, and for now, I needed to surrender to my tired and beaten condition. A good night's rest would do me well. That is, if I didn't wake up to a horde of police officers.

☙ Chapter Seven ❧

Amanda awoke in the recovery room of a hospital staring at the ceiling. A slightly perturbed-looking nurse fixed her intravenous fluids. Upon noticing Amanda's alertness, the nurse gave her a courtesy pat.

"Ms. Simon, you've just had surgery." The nurse motioned for a white-gowned doctor to come over, who immediately began sizing up her monitors before turning attention to his patient.

"Amanda,'" he said, looking over her chart. "Amanda Simon. You developed some life-threatening infections in your legs. In order to keep the infection from spreading and killing you, we had to perform a gangrenous amputation of your legs."

Her life became a shadow with those blinding words. No longer represented by flesh and blood. Not even her broken spirit could walk. Thoughts of freaks in a circus show degraded her self-image to this acquaintance.

A tear dangled off the tip of Amanda's nose, and she was unable to wipe it because of the straps tied to her hands. A mirror over her bed reflected green eyes mixed with red bloodshot ones, into a muddy shade of brown. She cocked her head, the only part of her body she could move, though her hair didn't flow because even her curls were entombed in bandages.

"No!" she growled.

"Now, Ms. Simon," the emotionless doctor said, "People do quite well without their lower extremities. I assure you that there was no other choice."

Not only had the nightmare continued, but now, having been removed from a prison torture chamber thinking no worse could happen, she had awakened to a mutilated body. With clenched fist, her palm almost bled from the digging fingernails, and the other hand writhed in a vain attempt to break free. With every ton of rage she ripped that hand from one of the straps and reached for her warm forehead to feel the rough gauze against her palm.

"My face. Show me my face." She tried in vain to pull off the scratchy bandages. "What's happened to my face?"

The doctor simply paused with that sterile look of detachment almost everyone on this godforsaken planet seemed to portray. "Burns, Ms. Simon. I had the plastic surgeon look you over. The scarring—third-degree burns. If the prison permits, we can possibly do something about it."

How the . . . how had that happened? The prison guard—the demon who possessed that ugly woman! Acid—now she remembered. The water in the sink, splashing her face, the million beestings needling her skin, the penetrating fieriness that kept digging mercilessly through the peeling flesh until there was no more pain to be had.

Where was the justice! Her misery had turned into loathing bitterness. Degraded beneath the ugliest beast. The downtrodden believer had become a malignant monster. She ripped the other hand from its band and frantically yanked her intravenous lines.

"God! No. . ." and on she went.

"Nurse, grab some other restrainers before she hurts herself," the doctor ordered.

"Oh, God!" *You've truly abandoned me. I loved you—and I thought you loved me.* "Let me die!" And the floodgate of tears opened to a river of mourning over who she was and what monster she had become. So much so that she could never see Will again. He adored her beauty as much as she loathed her ugliness now, and never the twain could meet again. She would have to let him go. That would be her final act of love for him.

After being strapped to the bed, the nurse injected her with something—poison, she hoped.

Left counting stains on the faded white ceiling, she pined while imagining their enchanting wedding in Yosemite three years ago. Cradling waterfalls spilling over mountain faces as she drew back her veil to kiss him with the passion of committed love, for the first time as his wife in what seemed like a truffle of heaven with Will's sweet breath the delectable center.

She mourned the loss of her lover and husband, surrendering herself for the first time to the inevitability of true love: to sacrifice her desires for the sake of giving Will over to someone else, anyone who could give him the joy he promised and delivered to her long ago. The joy they once shared. Never had she trusted so much, and never again would she have the pleasure.

She wanted to give up on God, but she couldn't. This time she couldn't run away, and she couldn't run toward him. She was stuck. An amputee in body and soul.

She could, however, kill herself.

☙ Chapter Eight ❧

Sherlock Holmes would have been proud of my probing questions to Elian in an attempt to uncover whether he was helping me or leading me to the police, the verdict still being out. Paranoia ran rampant in a world with no trust and every reason to fear.

Our long hike to his car in daylight revealed the cause of my plane's crash. In the far distance, fleecy clouds lay laced over smoky mountaintops crusted with whipped dirt and skirted the green hillsides. A hollowed-out crater appeared as though a giant had taken a bite out of the snow-coned slope. Steam rose out of its open sore with a rocky tumor protruding from the cut mountainside.

Chemical smells of old electric cars and heavily chlorinated pools permeated the air. As soon as we got in Elian's old truck the color of dried grass, I turned on the radio. About a mile into our drive, and after details of the recent meteor shower, the announcer's attention turned to me:

"Smaller asteroids have pummeled at least two sites in the Sierra Nevada Mountains, causing the crash of that plane carrying suspected church bomber Will Simon, who authorities have also linked to the number-one insurgent site in the world. Many would recognize Mr. Simon by his broadcast name, Reuben, on the so-called 'The Way' site.

"All of the flight's passengers are presumed dead, ending a several-months' search for the notorious Reuben, who with his faceless broadcasts rallied together insurgents from around the world before the recent mysterious disappearances, now most likely attributed to high-energy particles released into the atmosphere, possibly by the supernova that has now thrust these recent meteor showers onto the earth.

"Scientists are still trying to determine any other aftereffects of the asteroid, and are particularly worried about possible earthquakes from the ground disturbances caused by the asteroid impact . . ."

"So you bombed a church?" Elian asked while I turned down the volume.

Like an avalanche, the irony that Elian now had more reason to mistrust me flowed through my mind. "No, I didn't. I was in that church before it exploded, but I had nothing to do with it."

Elian's raised eyebrows revealed that we were now on a level playing field of suspicion toward one another. My attention turned to a loosely tied bag lying to his right as he fingered what lay inside, presumably a gun. *Lord,* I prayed, *just let me get to Amanda.* I had to take the chance, despite my reasonable suspicion.

"You believe me?" I asked.

Elian's eagle eyes fixed on me. "Tell me, Will, or Reuben—why did you refuse the peace that the Universal Church offered? Muhammad united all the religions of the world, did he not?" His face remained alarmingly placid, like a cool cat ready to pounce.

"You know the Bible, Elian—tribulation—the rapture—a one-world religion—Christians being persecuted—doesn't any of this register?" Even having to mention these tell-all descriptors, as if not obvious, further signaled Elian's disingenuousness.

"I know," Elian said, "but the question still stands. Why go to all this trouble?"

"Because Jesus Christ is my Lord. What about you?"

"I can't exactly say that, Will, but you can."

That was it! A nonbeliever couldn't muster enough deception to acknowledge Jesus Christ as Lord—to do so would be heresy to them.

Not a one could do that, for a fact. *Do I dare call him on it? No, play along—he's my ticket to San Francisco.* Maybe I can ditch him at a gas station—a quarter full. I could wait.

"So, Elian, do you think this is God's judgment on the world?" I could have some fun with Elian while it lasted.

"Define judgment for me." I could detect a faint smirk on the guy's face.

The answer was easy. "His wrath. You know, Old Testament wrath. Like destroying Sodom and Gomorrah, or when he ordered Joshua to kill every man, woman, and child in Canaan. Or what about the time when he caused the flood, killing everyone but Noah and his family?" Debating an imposter would be a little fun, especially since I was feeding him red meat. Besides, I struggled with the answers myself.

"These people sacrificed their own children to their gods, Will. They were corrupt in every way." Elian straightened.

"Like today," I chimed in. "Except I haven't seen any sacrifice of children—discounting abortion. Still, he's judging this world, isn't he?"

"You still haven't defined judgment for me." A little irksome, I thought.

OK, I'd play this one out. I stared into his eyes thinking I might see through the stranger's façade. "I suppose God's ultimate judgment is rendering a penalty of death to anyone who denies him." Not exactly my best, but I was playing with Elian. "What's *your* definition?"

Elian would probably give some New Age rendering. He slid a hand behind his neck and bent uncomfortably closer to me.

"I believe God's judgment is letting those who choose the world to suffer the consequences of abandoning the protective grace of God," he said.

Wow, a truly esoteric comment—Universal Church doctrine: no sin, no need for forgiveness—everybody's perfect in their own right. Something about his stoic face, his brown hair that waved every which way, gave him an undercover cop look.

He was too controlled, too unassuming, and not the least bit willing to show his cards. I'd have to play this one like a poker player. "So you're saying that left to their own ways, people will just naturally succumb to the evils of this world?"

Elian turned his head in the direction of the strawberry fields around us, his hand still upon the gun-shaped item in his bag. "God created every living thing to live by his laws, providing a life made perfect only if those laws were kept. When humankind rebelled, the seeds leading toward destruction in the world were planted." After that glib answer he leaned back with the satisfaction of a well-satiated predator.

I wiped my moist hand on my shirt, something I wouldn't normally do except for the out-of-control circumstances. Then wetted my mouth wishing for a stick of gum, or some lip moisturizer. "OK. So what about Christians who, through no fault of their own, suffer—like now?" My voice didn't sound like my own—a little too high-pitched.

Elian licked his lips with the lusting of a hungry cougar. "Suffering is the disease of a fallen world, and that affects everyone, including Christians," he said back stiffly.

"With the final judgment being death," I said, catching my second wind.

"Do you think God sees death as the ultimate end of a person?"

Oh, Lord, would this guy ever give in? "No," I answered frugally.

"So neither suffering nor death is the final judgment. Separation from God is the final judgment." His voice spread softly through the air, articulating an answer that could preserve the notion of a loving God.

Nice debate switch, a clever chess move—queen to pawn. From the sound of it this guy had played in the classroom setting. Professionally trained posture, surgically precise enunciation. It was the somewhat disheveled appearance that threw me off.

"Are you a teacher, Elian?"

"It so happens I am a teacher. But again, do you think death is the final judgment?"

He reminded me of my first-period pedagogue, Mrs. Sharp; get to the point.

"OK, no. From God's perspective no one really dies. Their body dies, but their spirit lives on—in heaven or in hell. And suffering is temporary—a blink in the scheme of things."

"And hell is the place where God isn't—you told me that, about your near-death experience in hell," Elian said with a more sympathetic tone of voice.

"Right." Knight takes bishop.

"So death isn't the ultimate judgment. Being apart from God is. And if people choose to be apart from the God of Jesus Christ, because they don't accept him for who he says he is, then God is just letting them have their way."

Checkmate. Elian grinned and I noticed his face for the first time. I expected frown crinkles, which is to say a heavy face. But his were smile lines, the skin relaxed. I had to wonder if the sun hadn't prematurely aged his thirty-something appearance such that it fixed a kind of upturned crease around his mouth.

For the first time since we first met, my thoughts of Elian turned from a match game to a talk—possibly between two brothers. His cogent answers even allayed my own doubts about the compatibility of God's judgment with his love. God was just letting people have their way, perhaps knowing them enough to extrapolate whether their hearts were too hardened to ever change their minds.

Death was inconsequential in the larger scheme of things—sooner or later everyone would exit the world's stage through death's curtain only to reach the realm of the spirit world.

All this time I'd been thinking of death as the executioner when in fact it had only been an escort into the living space of God, or the dying space apart from him. That was the moment when I supposed that if the Almighty had to choose between taking evil out and leaving me to enjoy the creature comforts of home—which would mean the status quo—he would take the former.

The smell of old burlap from his backpack and dried sweat from my ordeal grew stronger now that Elian and I drew closer together. I let down my defenses enough to challenge Elian to divulge the content of the bag at his side. Truth be told, I couldn't stand the suspense any longer. In response, he eased his hand into the brown pouch and pulled out a banana—a rather overripe one from the smell of it.

"Do you want it?" he asked.

Perhaps I had misjudged Elian. A true friend would be nice . . .

Just then a strange murmur resounded through the truck window, followed by trembling. Both increased, at first steadily by perceptible stages, and then suddenly by swift degrees, to the full roar and energy of the climax. A few hundred yards away from a nearby river, the sound came across the water from the west-southwest, agitating the leaves of the roadside trees.

"The car's swerving!" Elian shouted. Followed by a shock and a boom.

I turned the radio volume up as the announcer's voice jiggled with the rolling pavement ahead of us. "Something . . . oh my . . ." For what seemed like minutes, the radio went dead. Elian slammed on the brake before shooting over the embankment.

"Earthquake!" the announcer continued. "Listeners, we are experiencing an earthquake. Wait . . . how big?"

Thankfully, the car behind us came to a stop before hitting us, the ground now stable and the quiet returned. A collapsed shed and a few bent fence posts served as remnants of the recent shaking, along with our agitated nerves. The radio announcer returned to state that the earthquake measured 7.8 on the Richter scale, enough to collapse some bridges and do major damage, but it wasn't the big one. The announcer stated that this was on a different fault line than the San Andreas Fault that ran 810 miles through California. That one lingered below us with the intimidation of a goblin underneath our bed.

For now, at least, we could continue driving, but to where, and to what?

☙ Chapter Nine ☙

"Get me Medvedev," Bakr roared as he exited his helicopter onto the rocky soil about a hundred miles northwest of Basra, Iraq. A pyramid trimmed with ancient Egyptian hieroglyphs spread its girth against the desert, within a stone's throw of Bakr and his entourage.

The giant structure was framed by a river. The mighty Euphrates announced its flow with rippling waters that pounded against rocks, echoing the deep roar of its cold blue gloom beneath—grave to unrepentant insurgents. It overflowed its banks as if to defy nature, serving as a barrier of protection for the chief priest's fortress.

This haven would serve as the incubator for his new world. But first, Bakr would need to establish his supremacy over the old world.

Bakr hastily grabbed the phone from his assistant.

"Prime Minister Medvedev, my pleasure . . ." Not.

"You called, Muhammad?"

His teeth pressed into a vise grip. "Yes." Bakr breathed deeply. "Well, first let me say that we all sympathize with the many deaths caused by the recent viral outbreak in Israel. You are well?"

"Fine. The purpose of your call?"

Such gall! He stood as though slapped. And then rage simmered with such building force that it took every gram of strength not to lose all restraint. Did she not know that he could call on all the leaders of the world to rain down justice on Israel?

Three deep breaths later . . . "I wish to seek your cooperation so that we might join together for the dedication of the temple, Madam Medvedev." Better to cut to the quick before the expletives spilled out.

"Why, Muhammad? What does our temple have to do with the Universal Church?"

"Madam Medvedev, with all due respect, can you not simply receive the graciousness of my offer with the generous intentions in which it is offered?" His face flushed.

"Muhammad," she said, then paused, "I would welcome you on the condition that you recognize that we, Israel, maintain full control over the temple site."

"Of course."

If she wanted to play liar's poker, he was all in. And for a brief moment he breathed in the citrusy fragrance of his voluptuous companion's perfume to arouse more pleasurable feelings.

"Well then, I suppose we could arrange for a meeting to acknowledge the support of the Universal Church."

Medvedev's bullheaded audacity—assuming that he would tacitly acknowledge their rights to the holy site—Islam's second holiest site and all. He had assuaged the mullahs' concerns with his actual plan, the eventual outcome, despite its peculiar Jewish design. What better folly than to have the Jews unwittingly build an Islamic mosque? Mecca for the Universal Church, of course.

"Splendid, Madam Medvedev. Serge Amato and his team will coordinate their arrival with your assistant," he said, and then clicked off the phone before crunching it with his fist. By the time she ferreted out the truth and rebuffed his takeover, it would be far too late.

"Get me inside before I kill someone!" And with his command the twelve-inch-thick metal doors to the building opened like an inviting Pharaoh. Massive doors backed by a huge grating that slid up and down in vertical grooves, backed by yet another massive door behind the inner one, and then another all of which opened successively with the sounds of hydraulic machines pounding metal with thuds and rattles.

When the final door opened, they walked along the ancient Persian marbled hallways. Bakr felt his heart almost flush with a father's love with the anticipation of seeing his most treasured possession, though it was more akin to the feeling one gets when preparing to feast on the most savory stew of roast lamb, pomegranates, and spices to die for.

The six men stopped, turned, and one of them pushed an elevator button. Once inside, Bakr pressed his thumb over a sensor and looked squarely into the camera, contorting his face for the fun of it, and then upon receiving a blue light, pressed number six, sending the cylindrical womb downward at a hair-raising pace. A gradual slowing commenced after the elevator rocket traveled for several minutes, penetrating thousands of feet deep into the surrendered earth.

Upon exiting, their footsteps echoed down the long arched hallway constructed floor-to-ceiling of lustrous stainless steel. With synchronized steps they marched down the lighted corridor, turning to the left before Bakr stopped reverently before a silver door. A solid sterling door accepted Bakr's handprint, opening to him with a mother's outstretched arms.

Moving to his right, Bakr's five assistants stepped carefully back three steps. Muhammad Bakr, lord of this world, master of all pleasures and liberator of the oppressed, cowered, nervously wrung his hands, and peered impishly through the glass panel behind which lay a child not yet one year old.

"Kain," he whispered. "My son." His likeness smiled slightly, impishly, but what would he know about children? To him they were germ incubators. But this one contained perfect cells, perfect everything. And it was bone of his bone, undying flesh of his dying flesh.

A sanctuary of silence filled the space between father and son. He felt the lad's eyes follow him into a pit deeper than this subterranean space. Mutual empathy if but the tiny tot could understand the depth to which his father had searched for the first human DNA that brought him into existence, reaching the exact location of the once-teeming—but now only clay remains—garden of Eden.

Energy from the birthplace of earth drew him back. He amused his scientists and geologists enough so they could roughly determine the general whereabouts of the lost Eden. Only he and Yahweh knew it, drawn to the familiarity of his childhood home, like the pull of a magnet to Bakr's metallic heart. He had rediscovered the place where it all began, and where it would soon begin again.

The dead earth called to him from below, yearning for its resurrection through the child that lay before him now. "Perfect seed gave life to modern man," Bakr said almost lovingly.

Bakr turned to the men gathered around him. "Is his DNA replicating flawlessly?"

A ball-headed fellow adorning his "Project Adam" lab coat dared to speak up. "Yes, Father. The insertional vectors are working to ensure genetic consistency, and we've defined the DNA code to eliminate any imperfections. He is perfect in every way."

"And he will always be perfect, the father of a generation made in the image of perfected man. And he will lead a generation that will never die, on a new earth more glorious than the world has ever known, free to indulge all that the flesh desires. Glorious—sing praises!"

"Allah, God, Almighty . . ." The five men shouted all the superlatives they could nervously think of, using their piercing singing voices and jerking their nerdy figures to worship the god of this world—and the next.

Bakr would rest in his underground asylum for a few days. However, in that brief moment, for the first time since heaven vomited him out, Bakr cried, because the only one to whom he could relate to—truly relate to—had been born.

Chapter Ten

"**D**on't you have someplace to go?" I asked Elian.

"Nope."

"Someone always has somewhere to go," I said.

"Only if they have a destination," Elian said.

"And you don't?"

"Well, I used to, but I lost my job." Elian threw a rock from the walkway bordering the beach leading toward the Golden Gate Bridge, which stretched itself hundreds of feet away. "That's how I ended up camping before I found you."

"So you're just a nomad?"

"Sort of."

"So what's Plan B?" I asked

"Well, I could tag with you if you don't mind. You seem to be on a great adventure, and I'm always up for an adventure."

"Sure," I answered. God knows I could use the fellowship.

Waves the color of whipped cream bowed over the pebbly beach as we walked toward the Golden Gate Bridge, the wind breathing its melancholy sounds through the bridge's two rusty orange arches with cables I imagined as harp strings. Elian told me that I like to paint with words. I suppose I do—a little overdramatically at times. Anything to escape. I so wished to be able to paint what the mind sees, in words, but alas, I could only express a small measure of the profundity often thought, more felt, but meagerly expressed.

I sat upon a bench, quite relaxed by the pulsing waves spilling over and retreating into the folds of oncoming waters, as the motions repeated in constant rhythmic symmetry. The cycles of nature speak continuity and familiarity—touching the chords of comforting words like *faith, hope,* and *love.*

Words . . . I pulled out my pocket Bible to read John 1:1: "In the beginning was the word, and the word became flesh . . ." What an odd beginning to Jesus, as if one could speak life into being. But then I faintly remembered my time in heaven—when God spoke, life indeed came into being. And when Jesus touched that life—a sparrow, or a flower— it grew into splendid vibrancy. So yes, God's words set in motion everything that thrived.

"You're deep in thought," Elian said, his feet kicking the sand with winsome joy.

"It's beautiful, enchanting," I replied. "Something about the golden arches separating the bay from the vast, deep waters of the ocean. The waters get darker, deeper, more mysterious once we leave the safe confines of our own little world."

"You have a very full soul," he said.

"Do you ever wonder what's it all about?" I asked Elian.

"That's an answer you're going to have to figure out for yourself," he said.

My notebook fell from my front pocket as I stooped to pick up a seashell; instead, I retrieved the blue book and dusted it off.

"Do you journal?" Elian asked.

"No. I used to write, but not anymore."

"Why the notebook then?"

"Just in case, I guess . . . there's nothing I want to remember about this place."

"Perhaps you could just write about what you expect God to do," he said, "about what it will be like after you find the love of your life—"

"Amanda, this world—I feel like I'm gasping for air."

"Maybe you're grasping for answers, Will—or do you prefer Reuben?"

I stopped for a moment to breathe in the fishy air, waiting for the aftertaste of the salt breeze to cleanse my mind's palate, and for the fog-laced hills to still my heart. "Reuben—I like Reuben. That's the name Jesus gave me in heaven." It meant one who has seen the Son. I relaxed and glanced up at the churning sky. For the first time in a long time, the inspiring sight of it elicited wonder in my heart. Even the whistle of a faraway boat struck the chord of awe and hallowed longing. Everything appears different against the backdrop of quietude.

Alcatraz's ruined confines jutted out of the bay to the south of me—The Rock. How sadistic it must have felt to the prisoners then and now about their circumstances when overlooking the majestic bay from prison walls. Like glimpses of heaven from this world, I suppose. The thought of Amanda being there sullied the view; she was so close and so very far away. My heart pined, wishing I could just swim toward her, but we would have to wait until the next ferry left the dock—at least a day away. *God, keep her safe until then—take this as my greatest prayer of all.*

I knelt down and dug my fingers into the sand and wiggled the tips to leave three triangular holes. Then I turned one dot into a smile. You can draw a happy face on just about anything, but the fingers of the ocean waters will wash it away. And then the beach will be smooth again. No more happy face. Which face will I wear after getting to Alcatraz? Which face will Amanda wear? And will the forces of evil wipe our smiles away for good?

Elian placed his hand upon my shoulder, causing my surprised muscles to tense. He bent down to pick up a little hermit crab from the dry sand and set it carefully in the water, then followed the crab's spastic getaway with eyes transfixed, then turned, and with that laser look began to tunnel through my hardness.

"Brother, it's hard to have faith when you can't see the destination; I know. However, you've seen him, and still you struggle. So faith isn't seeing, is it?"

"No," I answered. Then a helicopter broke our contemplation with its bombastic sound, flying over Sausalito and its marina stacked with resting boats, then over the town's hills dotted with bay-view homes, and then curved toward the makeshift hell of Alcatraz—our final destination.

Elian had the presence of thought to continue. "Faith is what you know in your heart to be right, isn't it?"

"Or wishful thinking. I can only wish that Amanda is safe." I decided to play the devil's advocate again—or perhaps in reality I was the advocate speaking my own doubts. No one ever accused me of being too trusting.

Elian paraded around the beach. He was, in my fair estimation, a far-in-excess trusting South American–looking fellow who was currently pressing his narrow feet into squishy sand that quickly filled up with ocean water, and mustering to pull up his oversized and too-short pants that had been obviously fitted for someone else.

This mystery man did manage to briefly untuck his ribbed crewneck shirt before deciding to stuff it back under his waistline, evidence of the slightest doubt as to whether he should wear the shirt as an inny or outy. I envied his carefree attitude.

Elian grinned, picking up a pebble and looking at it as though something were hidden inside. "This stone probably came from that vast ocean you see out there, and yet it only became real to you when I picked it up. Before that it just existed, but not in your reality."

"Yeah."

"So our perception doesn't legitimize faith. What makes someone or something relevant is its relationship to us. However, what makes something real is its very existence. When we practice faith, we accept the reality that in that vast unknown there exists a presence and a place for us completely beyond our perceived reality." Elian paused.

"Go on . . ."

"Trusting in the unknown says that all things are possible, including a God who would pour his Spirit from the vast ocean of heaven into flesh made of molecules, just so that the world could behold him. However, the world rejected him, still does, because he didn't fit our perception of God. What he really wanted from us was our faith that he is who he says he is, and for us to trust in his provision.

"But he could just show up and tell us what to do. He could just tell me Amanda's well. Why do you think he doesn't?"

"Perhaps," Elian answered while combing his fingers through his head, "he wants his word to be his signifier, so that his reality can be conveyed through eyes that can see the unseen."

An epiphany set off alarms the magnitude of holy cathedral bells at noontime. "Yes—yes! It's back to the word, isn't it? I was just reading about the word, how it all began with a word. We either accept that the words written about God are his, or we deny their legitimacy. We simply interpret them as man's perceptions—or as the breathed words of God's very story!"

"Even more," said Elian, "a word represents what's inside you—birthed from your heart through your head. It's an expression of you."

"Words are our creation," I said, almost giddy with God's revelation.

"A *shared* expression," he said. "The word shared with another makes a part of you a part of them. I believe God used others to express his words because he wants them shared through the objects of his love."

Yes, that was it—connection. Jesus once said "You are my friends if you do what I command." God is love. And love translates into friendship when love is shared. And friendship with Jesus begins with obedience. No wonder God created humans in his image—he wanted a friend, someone to love.

A gush of wind drew me toward the ocean again, so wonderfully complemented by the blue sky. Blue is the color of peace as reflected in the vastness of the firmament to the surface of the sea. Why did God reflect blue in the light of day, and black in the dead of night? Maybe God's love, his light, must be absorbed through us to the depths and the heights of his unfathomable kingdom to evoke within us a peace that surpasses our limited understanding.

"We just need to be reflections of his love," I said. "I think the way of love is to see ourselves for who we are, and to see God for who he says he is." Elian patiently endured my reflections. I think the fatigue triggered a pensive mood; my thoughts probably resonated more profoundly to myself than to anyone else.

"I believe he's leading us in the way we should go, whether we know it or not," Elian replied.

"I trust he's leading us to Amanda, and that she'll be OK."

"God loves her infinitely more than you do," Elian said.

Elian gave me a knuckle bump with his fist. God had left me with no options but to trust him. I supposed that's where he wanted me to be.

"There's something wonderful that happens when what we want to express is filtered through the soul of another so that we understand each other," Elian said.

"And how do you think God's word became flesh—Jesus Christ?" I asked.

Elian threw back his head and closed his eyes and shouted toward the sky: "Jesus is the expression of God, to be shared so we can relate to love!"

My now whimsically giddy friend ran toward the frigid water and splashed his feet in it, lifting his legs up as though kicking a soccer ball clear to the old Mason (Civil War) Fort at the base of the bridge.

"Hey, Reuben," he said, motioning me to join him, "do you think the words about your experience in heaven and hell will be accepted ages from now?"

Sadly no, I didn't. They were mine, only my experiences. "I can only hope that others would accept them."

After resigning himself to the fact that I wasn't going to join him in the water, my soaked friend sprinted to join me at my side. In typical fashion his eyes beamed into me as though nothing else mattered. I admired him for that ability to screen out the world in unbroken connection to others, unalterably fixed on the object of his attention, and stilled in the moment.

Grasping my hand with no intention of letting go, he whispered, "Hey, Reuben, I believe your words."

This meant he believed in me.

"Which means that I have faith in you," he said. "Even though I have no idea where this journey of ours is leading."

"It always leads into the arms of God," I said, remembering my first love.

Impulsively I broke Elian's hold and began running along the sandy beach. "Race you," I yelled to Elian while in full stride.

"To the old Civil War post at the base of the Golden Gate," Elian shouted back.

It felt good to be carefree—if only for a brief time.

☙ Chapter Eleven ❧

Just the snapshot scenes brought relief to Amanda—of life, as the ambulance passed through San Francisco. Painted Victorians cramped against each other. She witnessed people straining to walk up the hills. Chatty Chinese men bickering over checker games as they munched on fried rice and sweet-and-sour pork, the fragrances of which seeped through the driver's partially opened window. A cable car—and the pleasant electric smell when its brakes pressed against the metal cable beneath the road surface. These smells, no matter how pungent, seemed like perfume because anything beyond herself spoke life, and she had . . .

Nothing. These teeming vignettes of city life would soon end on her way back to Alcatraz after being prematurely discharged from the hospital. It taunted her with the reality of what could never be hers again.

Scars lined her once smooth face. She had been ruined, she thought, her throat tightening at the memory of how Will once ran his palm gently against her face. Sobs shook her, and she gave herself in to them for the first time since leaving her home—heaving, shuddering spasms of anguish that convulsed her entire body.

When she thought through her previously catalogued imperfections before being abducted, however trivial they now seemed, she could not believe that she was the same being whose thoughts were once filled with hope and the belief in goodness. The mangled beauty had become a tormented phantom. Even the enemies of God had company in this fallen place, but she was alone.

The ambulance pulled into a street bordering windowed houses overlooking Alcatraz and the bay framed by undulating hills with gracefully branching trees. She felt the enlivening crispness of winter and followed the dancing leaves and the flitting of birds, and though these should have caused her to weep even more, they served as surprising consolations.

Then she realized why these things spoke to her—they awakened her to the continuity of nature, and as she turned to look north to the sea , toward the open field with children running carefree, kites in tow, butting against the walkway trimming the bay waters, life spoke again.

She saw a man. More than a man. Her man. She knew the backside of his walk as well as she knew the back of her own hand. His long gait awoke her from the slumber of a bad dream into the hope of that frolicking little girl who ran through an open field of daises knowing no end to the freedom of living . . . just living . . just being in the presence of what you love.

He brought her back to the freedom of breathing in the melody of life and the carefree abandonment of needing nothing else. He was the only man who dared to allow her to be her unabashed self. Yes, this was definitely him.

"Will!" she shouted, then let her cry fade away. No, she couldn't let him see her this way.

As the ambulance grew closer, his angelic face came into view. His familiar jaw, his lovely strands of hair, his hands gesturing characteristically as he spoke to a man with winsome eyes who walked by his side.

"Why now, God?" She didn't know that she could scream so loudly. The love of her life, her husband, walked no more than twenty feet from her. Yet she was thousands of miles from being able to share in life with him. Wrenched by utter isolation

"Shut up!" the ambulance driver shouted.

Then she noticed his head turn in her direction, his eyes open like a switch, and in that instant it was as if they felt each other. She knew he felt her too. Not a shout back but rather as when distance plays no part, and two spirits wrap themselves in the knowledge of being together—despite the chasm of their separation.

His pace increased, his eyes fixed in her direction, perhaps propelled by her spirit that reached out to him with the pull of a thousand love letters imbued within their souls. Their feelings looped together to express love's heart again.

"My forever friend! My lost love!"

But in the cruelest turn of fate, her glimpse of what had been faded into what was now. His slender frame that first stood out like a giant Welcome Home sign began to fade into a long good-bye as the ambulance passed him. Until, despite her silent cries and his futile pull, only a speck of his figure remained, and then eventually he faded back into her memory again, out of sight. Love lost again.

Around the bend up over the Golden Gate, through the tunnel with brilliant vistas of the artsy bay that only accentuated her isolation, the final stretch left her wanting Will all the more and knowing it was now too late. Past the golden hills onto the desolate roadway to her waiting tomb—Alcatraz.

Grinding engines and slapping waves were all she could comprehend after closing her eyes to guard against viewing the scenic bay en route to The Rock. When the ferry docked, she tried desperately to keep her mind closed as her eyes opened to a contemptuous officer who grinned with a full mouth of partially gold plated teeth. As he wheeled her to the entrance, she sucked in one last breath of the salty air before entering the musty hallway as her chair squeaked like the rats here and there, and into her three-walled hellhole where she would rot with the rest of her deserted brothers and sisters—insurgents brought in from around the United States.

Thankfully, she fell quickly to sleep and into a dream that would last forever.

He came to her. Bathed in crystalline winds that made his flowing hair shine over piercing eyes that infused her with power and with grace. Her legs grew out, and her spirit burst with the vibrancy she had often felt in the bosom of her soul mate: tender embrace, warm showers, and the feeling of shouting from the mountaintop. She was full of life and bolder than she had ever been—on top of Half Dome, Yosemite, overlooking the brook near where she married Will.

"My beloved, I am with you," he said in soothing whispers.

Amanda's eyes sprang open. Somehow the light had translated into sound. Her mind was soothed back to reality as she registered the misty apparition at her side atop the warmed cement, spreading its comfort through her. "So good to hear from you again."

"Fear not, my beloved; your suffering will not last much longer."

Amanda closed her eyes again for a brief moment to savor the respite. "How long must I suffer?"

"My beloved, you shall be in paradise with no memory of your suffering, and so your suffering will be as never having been." In the background, angels sang soft reassuring praises with the single voice of a thousand tenors. The sound stroked at the ears of her mind, causing her to feel pleasantly lightheaded.

She hauled in a breath. "So why do I suffer?" Her questions, though challenging, elicited no fears of retribution from the majestic figure.

"Dearest Amanda, your suffering will be restoration to all who have lost hope in this desolate world that has denied me."

Amanda floated in the billowy silk of the majestic's outstretched garment that swirled within a vaporous cloud. "And why, then, are we here?"

"So that my light might remain in this world, beloved." A wisp of smoke blew in the wind and churned into a spiral. It spun with at first the slightest glow until building to almost blinding effulgence. The heat raged but did not burn.

She rested in its calming embrace for what seemed beyond the reach of time. Then the radiance dulled to a flicker and finally to nothing. She awoke to the stark reminder of her misery in that cold, damp cell. But not alone. Someone reassuring stood over her—at least ten feet tall—his brilliance highlighted by a blinding beacon reflected over the strapping titan, and yet she beheld his reassuring face as fiercely ready to avenge anyone who came against her—and none did.

He was dressed in linen, with a glittering belt of gold around his waist, with a body like amber, his face aglow, flaming eyes, arms and legs as if a bronzed statue, and his voice the magnitude of hundreds. A lightning countenance and his vesture snowy white.

"Be comforted by the promises of God," he said.

The demon that had once taunted her in that place, struck her with doubt and fear and every baneful thing, dared not come against this one lest it be crumpled underfoot and returned to hell.

And then the presence spoke again in a resounding voice seemingly audible to anyone who could hear: "Fear not, Amanda, for the Lord your God will deliver you and reveal to you a love deeper than what you had before in this world. A love that cuts to the very core of God, stripped bare of the deceptive love that is of this world."

Though these words first puzzled her, she felt altogether relaxed. It would be so good to be loved again, only this time . . . well, this time the love would be perfect and would never end.

☙ Chapter Twelve ☙

"**H**ow many insurgents not incarcerated?" Bakr asked of Eid Sammi, a heavily scarred ruffian who served as his chief security consult for the Universal Church.

"None, as far as we can tell," he answered. "We've not identified any insurgents outside of the US thus far—strange they would only be in the US. We've transported them to Alcatraz as planned."

Muhammad Bakr paced inside his Roman-styled office waiting for the president of the United States. He was late—a slight rebuff from someone demoted now to head of a second-class nation. Perhaps he and his congressional delegation had found it difficult to maneuver the intricate maze of his underground palace.

Sammi continued, "And, Father," he whispered, "if we can eliminate those at Alcatraz in one fell swoop, that will leave only the insurgents in Israel."

Bakr responded with a more than generous smile.

"Sir," the shapely assistant said as she opened the door, "the president and his party are here to see you."

Good. Now was the time to make sure that the US was on board with his plans. On the surface, the president had acquiesced to Bakr. But his avoidance was strange, speaking volumes about his uncharacteristic silence. And there seemed something not quite right about him, not the least of which was the president's speeches about the need for diversity. No, Bakr thought, only one race was imperative in a world homogenized by selective genetic engineering.

Bakr reached the door and let the entourage through. Four others joined the downcast president as Bakr motioned to them to sit around an authentic Roman table. A statue of the Greek monster Medusa stood in the corner, marbled snakes on her head, whose very looks, legend said, had the power of killing or turning its victims to stone. Sammi's eyes glassed over while looking at Medusa.

If only, Bakr contemplated, they understood the one behind the great empires throughout all history. Then they might feel more gratitude for the freedom he granted to all who would embrace the gods of the Greeks, Hindus—even the god of themselves.

"Father Muhammad, so generous of you to welcome us to this amazing structure," said the president.

"I call it Masada, a name for Herod's royal citadel," Bakr said.

"Quite impressive." The president bowed.

"Masada in history was also where Jews committed mass suicide instead of submitting to Roman capture." Bakr stretched his neck.

"I've never witnessed any shelter like it—it's beyond description," the president said while wiping his brow.

Bakr sneered. "Our generators will allow us to survive underground with no access to the earth above for hundreds of years, Mr. President, and with the asteroids heading our way, well, there's plenty of room, as I said, for you and your supporters to join us."

"Thank you, Father," the president responded. "You are very kind."

One senator's irksome habit of scratching his nose caught the chief priest's attention. The man's very presence somehow brought out the lion's revenge Bakr felt when sensing his pride threatened. Why he felt this way, he couldn't tell. Perhaps it was the smell of the senator's blood— his spiritual blood.

"Excuse me," Bakr said while looking at the senator, "have we met before?"

"Senator Brown, from California, sir, and no, we have never met." The man's cream-colored suit contrasted against his black skin, which only served to heighten the discord Bakr sensed, his attention now solely fixed on the placidly irritating fellow.

"Tell me, Senator, are you in agreement with our imprisoning the insurgents in Alcatraz?"

"Can't say I am," he said in a matter-of-fact way.

"Why?"

"I don't believe that evangelical Christians pose a threat to the US— or any other entity, for that matter."

The hairs on Bakr's neck almost catapulted from his skin at the man's very Christian-like response.

"Please indulge me for a moment. I am most curious as to your persuasion. Do you have a problem with the exclusivity part of Christianity that you have to accept Christ's lordship and receive his forgiveness before entering heaven?"

"I do not, sir," he said, which confirmed the man's position.

Bakr felt like a cat now dangling its mouse before the kill. He would toy with this contrary senator for a little while; he was amused at his temerity, if not disgusted by his stupidity.

"Then tell me, Senator Brown, why would a so-called loving God send to hell those who do not accept his way as the only way? Is this not contrary to how love should be—accepting all and refusing none?"

The senator fixed a stare upon the Medusa statue, then folded his arms, somewhat grabbing his heart, and closed his eyes for just a spell before speaking.

"Think of it this way, please," said the senator. "Say someone offended your values, your rules for living, even denied your lordship over your own home as though you were no more than a nuisance, and then later came to your home's doorstep and asked you if they could live with you. Would you invite him into your home to live there?"

Bakr refused to answer; he simply nodded. "Go on . . ."

Senator Brown turned his attention to the president, prompting Bakr to straighten up and scowl. "Mr. President, would you in that situation refuse that person entry into your house knowing he threatened the very foundation upon which you've established your home and your family?"

The President answered yes while quickly darting his eyes toward the wall.

"Then, Chief Priest Muhammad Bakr, so does the God of Jesus Christ. It's *his* home."

With that the senator sealed his fate. How could an insurgent enter his protected abode? How had one of them infiltrated his secured stronghold? And why wasn't this senator imprisoned with the rest of his kind?

With all the hatred he could muster through his heart, Bakr looked upon the man with that Medusa look—causing the man to grope his chest and fight for breath. He huffed like a pig about to be slaughtered.

"Ted"—the president nervously reached out to the senator—"are you—"

"I can't breathe." His face paled.

Bakr motioned for one of the security agents to come to the senator's aid. A large Ethiopian quickly ushered the senator into the hallway and began closing the door, but Bakr darted through it to join the two men outside. With equal swiftness Bakr closed the door behind them so that no one else could hear.

He proceeded to whisper into the gasping man's left ear: "We had identified what we thought were all of the Christians after the rapture, Senator. How could we have missed you?"

Crunching to the floor, Brown lifted his blue-blushed face enough to look Bakr in the eyes. "The . . . Way," he mumbled. Like a fish out of water he sucked in another breath. "Reu . . . ben. He . . . Je . . . sus . . . loves me."

Bakr snarled and then motioned for the agent to usher him away. "Send him to his God," he said.

Reuben again. Thank God he was dead.

Returning to the room, Bakr fluffed his collar and wiped his brow before sitting in his macaw-feathered chair. "Gentlemen, we've sent Senator Brown to our top-notch infirmary. He's in very capable hands, and the best thing we can do now is to finish our business. Eid." He motioned for his emotionless assistant to speak while the others strained in their seats.

"Thank you, Father," Eid said. "Mr. President and distinguished dignitaries, Alcatraz poses our greatest security risk in America. There have been two attempted breakouts there already—thankfully, they were put down. However, the prison remains an insurgent time bomb, ready to explode, and unless we eliminate this threat—"

"What are you saying?" said one of the congressmen while retracting into the sofa immediately after speaking.

"Sir," Eid answered, "we confirmed with the president the insurgents' assassination attempt on his life. Insurgents have incited violence, warfare—and lest we forget—the recent disappearances. All were insurgents. And then their leader bombs a church—a church! How much more do we need to endure before acting, gentlemen! Once that threat is gone, we're left with Israel as the only roadblock to peace once and for all!"

"Mr. Sammi," said the president, "what do you want me to do?"

"Your stealth bomber," Eid said. "There will be an attempted breakout; our guards will be evacuated. It will put down the final insurgent attack." The room fell morbidly silent. "When your nation bombed Hiroshima to bring the Japanese to their knees, did your then-president Truman not save tens of thousands of lives of men who would otherwise have been killed?"

The president slowly nodded, his face drawn. "But they pose no threat if incarcerated."

Bakr's face burned at the president's impotence. He fixed a stare at him. Bakr's eyes were more than the product of a world's evolutionary limitation. He had the ability see into one's soul and beyond the here and now to the trajectory of a being's path, especially those headed to hell. The president was no more than a politician, always wishing to strengthen his position, even at the expense of others.

"Mr. President," a now calmed Bakr said, "the insurgents pray for our destruction, and sooner or later they will find a way to kill more innocents if not stopped–not to mention that the very site of Alcatraz threatens the world with their presence."

"And you're saying that they would be collateral damage in our war against the insurgents, to further isolate Israel, and to prevent any undue sympathy for their cause," the president said.

"Yes, Mr. President," Eid said. "This will also make it easier for Israel to acquiesce since it will signal our resolve and unity. Plus, Alcatraz is an easy, isolated target."

"And," chimed Bakr, "you and your family will be secure here until the asteroid crisis is over."

"We need to at least inform Prime Minister Medvedev," said a notably Jewish congressman. "There are Israeli citizens in that prison."

How much longer Bakr would tolerate such insolence depended solely on how permissive Medvedev would remain by letting him dedicate the temple—his temple. On second thought, alerting her to the preemptive attack might also strike some fear into her, someone who had, or so he'd heard, accepted the foolish ways of the insurgents. A Christian Jew—a paradox right up there with an omnipotent God who would allow his people to suffer and die.

The conundrum finally settled itself when Bakr deduced that Christ's God was neither perfect nor all-knowing. Heavily flawed humans after all, having been made in his "perfect" image?—laughable. They denied the pleasures of the flesh for a god they could not see. A god unwilling to accept any other way than his way. Bakr had once tried to reconcile it all until it proved too futile to even consider further. He had a better way.

"Father," the president said to Bakr, "are you all right?"

Rudely awoken from his muse, Bakr agreed that the president or congressman or whatever lackey wished to contact Medvedev could do so. Eid then shared the details for the attack on Alcatraz, the fated end to America's experiment with Christianity.

"Gentlemen," interrupted Bakr. "Do you not find it ironic that narrow-minded, bigoted Christians once remained so divided on this earth, and now, because this now-dead Reuben had blasted their names over the Internet, we were able to round them up like a pack of sheep?" He no longer cared what the Americans thought. Besides, Christ's God did this to them. *A loving God, my foot!*

Bakr sat down and looked at the wilting plants potted around the room. Some leafless twigs reached out like bony hands from the grave of confusion. Up above this subterranean hole, the ancient hills were hidden in the darkness, their dying olive and fig trees, and surrounding deserted homes specters of a way that once tried to preserve life. This new age welcomed the night. Embraced death as a means to make the soil fertile with a new race. Yahweh couldn't save this decaying world this time. The seeds of confusion had been planted.

Besides, Bakr had died a long time ago, and God didn't save him then.

༒ Chapter Thirteen ༒

The manly old house peeled from too much sun, its roof bald from decades of neglect. Its once-military charge relegated to standing watch over lines of white crosses marking settled bones. An abode that had once entertained generals. And now, the body of an old wood-paneled dwelling fitted as a youth hostel contained, for now, two enemies of the state. How ironic.

"I heard this Presidio used to be teaming with soldiers," I said. Elian ignored my idle comment while intently peering at washed-out seascape pictures on the wall. His whimsical nature in the face of travesty never ceased to amaze me, the way he looked upon the slightest details with childish wonderment.

At first I thought he was seeking an escape hole through which to climb into another realm, and then I came to believe that he chose to see the hand of creation, whether a painter's insight upon a brushed canvas or a child building their masterpiece sand castle.

He was, I assumed, an empathic spectator wishing to profoundly understand those who sought to create expressions greater than themselves, intently focused on the worker behind the work.

And in some strange way, I envied him the innocence of seeing new life afresh through the ruins. As if he saw no ruins at all. Only the broken handiwork of God through the eyes of an artisan.

Some would call this optimism; only, I don't believe God sees it that way. I was beginning to view God's persona in three parts: as a maker, a restorer, and in his consummate position—as an artist. In the beginning God the *maker* created the earth and everything in it. Then each of us at one time or another decided to live apart from God's authority, so he allowed people like me to screw up—that's when the *restorer* facet of God came into play.

God as *artist*, according to my interpretation, happened when someone just gave up entirely, after having been immersed in proverbial hot water, leaving that person like putty in his hands. Then, and only then, I surmised that inspiring beauty could arise from the fallen ashes—at least that was my theory. That "putty" state which permits God's artistry is where Elian seemed to reside.

If I could only just *be*, as is Elian's state. Alas, my earthly dad tended to pontificate like me. He used to tell me that everything eventually came to an end, but more and more I hoped to realize that every end came to a new beginning—that was optimism, in my estimation, and that's how I wanted to be.

"Meditating again?" Elian asked.

"Ah, yes," I responded. "We all have our means of escape, I suppose."

"You fixated on that ambulance the other day—why?" Elian asked.

"Something, I can't explain. I was on autopilot." More, that person in the ambulance haunted me for some reason, tugged at my heart with the desperation they must have felt. Hurt, just like I was hurt, and my legs had moved to catch up with my heart. Silly.

Elian shook his head. "It's been days," he said.

"I know, I know. I'm just waiting for God to give me a word."

"Like what?" said a half-joking Elian. "Like a certified letter?"

"Look, Elian, I can't just go up to Alcatraz and save Amanda like Prince Charming. We have to get permission to enter, and then there's the visitors' boat that leaves only on certain days. I did call the prison the other day and they listed Amanda as an inmate. And then there's this thing about finding God's lost presence."

Elian showed that perky grin and pitched eyebrows of a man who wouldn't settle for settling. I'd have to explain that last comment.

"David told me that I'm like a modern-day Moses, and that I'm to find the lost presence of God in America." *There, I said it.* I thumped myself into a chair in front of Elian's laptop, waiting for one of his sarcasms.

"You're a modern-day Moses—looking for God's lost presence?"

I turned hesitantly away from the laptop to look into the eager eyes of my companion, expecting a laugh at any moment. He said nothing. He barely moved.

"That's right. I know you think it's strange, but it's one of those things you just know that you know."

"Trust," Elian quickly said.

"Not my strong suit," I replied.

"Do you trust me?" he asked as he leaned forward.

"Not entirely, but that's just me." I was itching to share more. "Say, let me get your take on something since I shared with you the Moses thing already. Someone once called me the last of Adam's bloodline—strange, huh?"

"Hmm . . . and what do you think that person meant?" He sat back and tilted his head toward the gray ceiling.

"Well, maybe I'm the last generation of humankind." I let out a short chuckle. "Whatever. God doesn't seem to be hearing me these days."

Elian stood up and looked over the cemetery with the proper pose of a general—stiff back, chin up, ready for the fight, "ol' chap."

"Reuben, you can't always wait for God. Sometimes you have to go out and find him."

Funny thing to say. "He's omnipotent. He can always find me," I said.

Elian resigned himself to a worn chair that blew up a cloud of dust as he pressed into its wilted cushion—innards of the old manly house.

"Physically, yes, I suppose," Elian said. "But the spirit is different, isn't it? A person's spirit can drift away from God."

Here we went again on one of our spiritual walks. "The Spirit of Christ is within us, right? Certainly that's a kind of homing device for God to find us anywhere," I said.

"You're a wise man," Elian said.

"Let's go for a bike ride," I suggested.

Elian pressed another dust batch from the armchair as he lifted himself and trekked over to the two weathered, rusted bikes chained outside. It took moments before we saddled our two wheels and pedaled toward the ocean, along at least fifty rows of white crosses, past more stately houses in disrepair, over a bridge topping cars whizzing toward the Golden Gate, and up a hill scattered with Eucalyptus trees, until skirting the cliffs on our dirt bike path overlooking the ocean. Draping bluffs framed the inlet on either side. A lonely barge crawled along the water's surface with rusted building blocks atop its back. It slowly and silently crept along the ocean waters toward the bay with the urgency of a snail through fog-laced spiderwebs.

We stopped for a time to breathe in the pristine air.

"So, Elian. You agree that God can find us—he knows all, has authority over everything?"

As was typical, Elian reached with his head out toward the grandest picture before us as I followed his stare. This time his gaze took me to washed hills and onto a finger-shaped cliff pointing toward crashing waves that purportedly raked over old sunken ships denied by Lady Golden Gate. The ships lay entombed beneath its waters. Reminders of my sunken mission. *God, help me find it again.*

Elian continued, "I think God traded free choice for love. Relationship isn't bound with love unless the one loved is set free."

I was beginning to wear my esoteric conversations with Elian like a warm yet sometimes itchy woolly blanket.

"OK. So what about God being able to find us—me? It's not like he doesn't know." Indeed, I wanted God to break through this mess to speak as plainly as before. Or, perhaps I was the one too encumbered to hear him speaking.

"Ah," Elian replied, "You need to return to him, my friend."

I felt the knot in my stomach constrict as Elian eyed me.

The porn sites I sourced on Elian's laptop—he didn't see them, did he?

It had been a temporary lapse, but one I'd never have made before God removed his spirit. My eyelids began to twitch. I'd lost the clarity of vision I once enjoyed. I used to operate one of the largest Christian sites in the world. Now what? I was debased into looking at women being dehumanized? *God, forgive me.*

Elian cleared his throat as though expecting me to say something. My mouth felt like cotton balls had been stuffed into it. "What?" I said to Elian.

"Nothing," he answered.

"The world robs you of what you thought you knew," I continued.

"So what did you think you knew?" Elian asked.

"I thought I was supposed to make a difference." I answered.

Elian failed to respond, much to my consternation. We hopped on our wobbling bikes and continued to ride while locked within ourselves. We spoke not a word for several minutes, just listened to the sacred sounds of the ocean while eyeing the silently adoring hills.

These scenes allowed me to pray more effectively, though I must concede that my prayers were more palatable without people around. Even within the circle of Christians before the rapture, we had become a society that spouted out answers to problems too routinely for my liking, though I'd like to think that every problem had an answer that the mind could fathom. Despite my open-minded self image, what I really wanted was to be told the answers so that I could close my wandering brain. When the going got tough, I wanted the instruction manual.

I dropped back to ride side by side with Elian.

"You know, I never did come to terms with why God just doesn't end the suffering," I said.

"He would if he could," Elian replied.

"That's a joke. God can do anything."

"No, he cannot. God can't lie; he can't break the law—"

"And he can't prevent suffering," I said.

"Some suffering he can't prevent or it would destroy his plan toward redemption," he said. I was suddenly aware that I was wearing a short-sleeve shirt—almost always a bad idea during any season in San Francisco; I wasn't sure if the goose bumps on my bare arms were caused by the chilly air or not.

If only I could blithely accept the imperceptible answers about suffering in defense of God as Elian did. To do so would be like defending that perfect person who could not have possibly committed the crime even though his fingerprints were all over the evidence.

Elian continued after waiting for me to say something. "Corruption led to suffering, so God had to create a different pathway—"

"A way to right a wrong," I said. "Even if someone has to go through pain to get there. Even if they'd rather die than suffer?"

Elian rubbed his chin, awkwardly balancing his wobbly bike with one hand as he spoke. "Say I need to get to the hospital for a critical blood transfusion and failure is not an option—because I would eventually die if I didn't get there. The problem is I don't want to go to the hospital. I'd rather die. So while walking away, I stumble and suffer a severe bone fracture, and the only option to relieve the pain is to go to the hospital and have the fracture mended."

"Hence the suffering," I said. "And your fracture gets you to the hospital so that you can also receive your life-saving transfusion."

"Precisely," Elian said. "Suffering on the way to complete healing is always worth it, don't you think?"

"So God chooses not to relieve some sufferings if they will eventually result in complete healing." I was finally drinking the Kool-Aid Elian had to offer. Seriously, his analogy helped reason suffering as best as possible, I supposed. "God cuts a new path through the storms of life." I liked that. More important was that he would never leave us in the midst of it.

"I'm heading back; you go on," Elian said while pulling away.

Biking alone proved therapeutic—and dangerous. Thoughts of Lila came to mind. The porn—a looping video that taunted me to enter, and I darn well couldn't enter—didn't want to enter. But, Lila—I hated leaving her like I had at the airport.

I needed to know about Lila—she was so vulnerable. And so I stopped and dismounted my bicycle enough to breathe in the intoxicating air before dialing.

"Lila, this is . . . Will."

She screamed for an unsettlingly long time. "Willy! No, Willy—they said you were dead! You're not some sickie, are you? Willy, is this you?"

"It's me, Lila. I survived. I'll even prove it to you—Remember when you showed me the picture on your cell phone of Amanda being attacked by a wolf, the demon, before she was arrested? And us buying wigs in the costume shop?" Darn, I could only hope that Lila wouldn't snitch on me.

"Willy, this is so incredible. I've missed you so much! Where are you?"

"In San Francisco." Now I was really into trusting Lila. No turning back now.

"So am I Willy—just north—I'm in Mill Valley—my aunt lives here. I took the next flight out after you left New York—then I heard. It was terrible."

Conviction overruled my senses as pictures of Amanda's sacrifice—staying behind—her puppy eyes. "I've got to find Amanda, Lila—she's out there."

Lila didn't respond for the longest time. "Did you hear me? I need to find Amanda."

"I'm so sorry to have to tell you this, Willy." Her voice quavered.

"What?"

"She died."

"No, she's at Alcatraz."

"I tried to contact her at the prison. She died yesterday. The person I talked to told me—" Lila spoke with a toxic voice that swallowed my mind into oblivion.

"No!" Madness snapped inside me with the jaws of a pit bull. This couldn't be. Not now. Not ever.

"Will—she's in a better place now." Lila's trite attempt to calm me only proved more irritating.

"No. How?" My emotions raged in a stew of anger, disbelief, and remorse at not having been able to save my one and only. This just couldn't be—

"I know it's hard,.."

Her condolence served only to fuel my regrets. "I've got to go, Lila."

"Wait—let's get together. I have to see you, Willy."

"Later. I can't talk now. I'll call you after I clear my head—are you sure?"

"Yes," answered Lila.

I pressed the red button like it was a detonator, wanting to blow up the whole world and be done with it. Then I hopped on my bicycle and pushed the pedals with all the angst I could muster.

This was all wrong—hope deferred turned to hope denied, with God at the core of it all.

I saw demons like they were insects crawling out of the dark places—but God? Nowhere to be found! He had taken Amanda, my love potion, and left me with the foul stench of fear-induced sweat.

And then the reason behind all this baffled me the most. Why did I have to stay? Did God have something to teach me, or did he want me to help save souls? I felt like a hamster spinning its wheel with no destination and no way to get off. "I want answers, God!"

I pedaled out along the pathway edging the cliffside that fell down to the bay waters north of the Golden Gate, then wrapped around a corner onto pavement wanting to just check out. A long columned French pavilion jutted out in the distance, and to my left a lone fountain sat surrounded by a circular pond the color of emerald jewels.

Before me stood the familiar edifice with a gallant archway leading to a U-shaped museum. I couldn't remember the name . . . Palace . . . Legion . . . the Legion of Honor. I remembered its regal stature. It was like a mini Louvre with "The Thinker" statue poised upon its pedestal in the center of the slate courtyard. A wide walkway led to the bowed entrance and a façade with swags and all kinds of sculptural enrichments.

Before Amanda and I got married in Yosemite, we toured the city, and this place stuck out like a royal oasis amid the natural wonders. I stopped near a bench where she once sat, then tired from our journey through the art museum.

I had taken a mental picture of her then, as I do when hoping to capture a point in time that will pass too soon. There she sat again. I was afresh with the memory and a doleful wish of wanting that moment back.

She appeared pensive that day, perhaps from fatigue—more contemplative really, unusually vulnerable. Her normally amorous bravado turned to gentile belle, head bowed, tendrils of hair blowing wistfully in the wind against a face drained of all pretenses.

I loved her so much in that second, wanting the moment to never end—but knowing it would wilt as do all of life's most poignant blooms.

Her flowered dress pressed and released from her svelte body at the mercy of gentle breezes. The dark hair falling down her back curled in the air with almost a life of its own. And then she looked at me with the impulse of a child who'd found a four-leaf clover, wanting to share it with me—luck, or love—yes, guileless love. No words. Just the eyes of devotion—that's what I saw. And they were for me . . .

Why can't we stay in the moment? Why can't love last until we soak in its soft touch deep into our soul? Too many whys.

"Hello."

I turned and saw a homeless man wearing splotchy clothes standing behind me, his hair matted, face smudged, and his putrid scent of baked sweat hit me in the face. "Spare some change?"

His eyes were dark, and instead of round pupils they appeared as slits—more like a lizard's than a man's. He sneered with jagged brown and black teeth.

"Who are you?" I asked.

He made a gurgling sound. "Jesus."

"No," I quickly replied. I knew Jesus—would recognize him anywhere. "What's your real name?"

"Not Jesus?" He rubbed his whiskers, making sounds of irritating sandpaper scratches. "I'm you, Will."

Chills ran through me. "How'd you know my name?"

"Really," the man said with a chuckle, "I know you, and you know me."

A demon, or a possessed man. I could almost smell the decay in his blood. "What do you want?"

"Oh, Willy." His countenance grew stern, and he spoke in another more feminine craggily voice. "You don't really believe. No one really believes. It's all a dream, sonny boy." He began humming an Irish folk song.

I picked up my bicycle and began to mount it.

"Willy." The man stretched his neck from side to side. "Dead is better than this."

He reached out his hand with long dirty fingernails. Before I could move away, he thumped it on my shoulder, and as he did, it felt as if something contagious instantly crawled inside me. I wanted to jump in the shower. To scrub out my insides and kill the parasites that infected me with his touch.

"Willy, sonny boy, it's dark inside you now. You lost him and you lost her. There's no point in it anymore. No point at all," he said with an Irish accent. "You can't win, laddie boy, can't win 'em, so why try? It's hell out dere." His crooked mouth formed a creepy jack-o'-lantern smile.

He let out a sickening raucous laugh upon releasing his hand from me, and then bored into my eyes while snarling with his razor teeth. He laughed uncontrollably again while bending wildly back and forth and howling to the sky like a wolf.

I hopped back on my bicycle and peddled like there was no tomorrow as the demon man's laughter began fading away. I was determined to see Amanda again, and to get out of this mess. It would have to be in heaven, through death's doorway. I could have just gone with the light's pull—I would've been in heaven. Now I had to force it. God would understand my running over the cliff, pulled by the current into the sea. He could accept that, right?

I pedaled up and over the hills darting between meddlesome bushes and intrusive trees, catching patches of dirt and thumping over jagged surfaces. Faster, faster—I could leap over the edge like a two-wheeled parachute feeling Amanda grow closer and closer with each second of freefall into my icy grave, and wake up in the warm pool of her sea-green eyes.

Faster, faster I pressed toward the ground waiting for my airy release over the unforgiving precipice. The dense forest obstructed me from what at any moment might be my final flight over the edge, and then it came into sight: the vast ocean topped by staggered white layers of breaking waters against a backdrop of ruddy cliffs. Pounding sounds of rushing water glazed by rippling tides. And deep within those currents teemed sea creatures that pulled their human victims out . . . Out—that's where I wanted to be—out.

Faster, faster—seconds from launching over the cliff as the wind pushed my back as though it were an accomplice. Faster, faster—now— now . . . *let me fly, Lord*. Only a few feet to go before leaping over the edge and through the biting wind into the deep.

The next second, my bike flew into the air. Something butted against my tire throwing me sideways as my body plowed into the dirt. My brain rattled inside my thumping head with legs and arms wobbling at the mercy of uncontrollable forces. The gravelly ground stabbed my flesh with needle-sharp pains.

Everything faded away as I lay prostrate in my surrendered state, staring into the sky, lost to weariness, yet feeling at once wholly vulnerable and anxious. It had the effect of a trance, taking me out of the ordinary relationship with my environment, and inclosing me in a sphere by myself.

A hard wind pressed down against me. It rolled me like a piece of dough, sending shock waves from nerve to nerve until my entire frame felt plugged into an electrical socket. Spasms consumed my body as an overwhelming heat seeped into me to the point where I wished the skin would just peel away to release the fieriness.

Blinding light in shades of yellow-orange encased me. I saw nothing but the swarming sea of hot colors, paralyzed now by an awestruck sense of someone or something hovering about me, reaching into me with its revealing fire, sucking the air out and breathing into me absolute reverence for the sacred place about me, and now within me.

Nothing felt hidden anymore. My stripped self felt undone in the presence of something. The fire took on a personality—fearsome, threatening to kill me if I did not acquiesce to its strength and just release myself to it. The burning slid through my veins like a snake, straining to take control.

I could literally smell burnt leaves and charred wood as all my cares and concerns melted away in the steeped fear of raging fire within and without. The me of me was burning away. Not my flesh—my all. Emotionally and spiritually naked, I felt stifling wind swallow me into a vacuum—conscious of nothing and susceptible to everything.

And yet through it all a presence shielded me from the consuming heat—hugging me and pressing his cheek to mine. Reflecting yellow and orange rays back to the blinding white light in the distance.

"I will never leave you or forsake you." A voice as powerful as the supremacy that now fully possessed me.

"Is that you, God?" My blood pounded in every inch of my body—especially over my heart.

"Trust in me always, and I will make your paths straight." The voice rose from a gust into a blustery gale. A full-throated command I'd imagine from a trusted friend. "Yes, Lord."

A pure after-rainfall air stilled me in the moment. The sound of God's voice, the sense of it, breathed a reverent calm across the full spectrum of everything within hearing distance. Even the ground beneath me turned soft.

And then suddenly a deep surge of heat pierced the skin on my chest. I tore my shirt to relieve the fever. Red scars covered my chest. I ran my fingers over the raised lumps. They were uniformly shaped—letters. Reading down the point of my chin, they spelled something like Braille: *I am always with you."*

"Lord, speak to me again," I implored.

Not a sound returned. Instead a chill ran over the back of my neck, followed by a warmth in my chest as if my heart opened to accept a rush of God's well-being. For a few moments I floated adrift of every care and every want. Awash with comfort.

And with that the fire encircling me faded as my body numbed.

My spirit began drinking in refreshing waters. I literally felt as though quenched with chilled water on a blistering day, and these invisible streams turned the red and orange colors of my environs to lighter shades of yellow, then milder shades of green, which became comforting shades of blue until the colors faded and I saw my surroundings again, relaxed, and returned to my familiar physical awareness.

Chirping birds flittered from limb to limb against the washed skies with the stilled air bringing all the reaches of nature into view. The ocean sang instead of haunted. The cliffs spoke of God's mightiness instead of death. I was finally at peace.

Remains of my experience revealed themselves in the physical also— the ground appeared charred; even my bicycle felt hot to the touch, though my body remained unscathed, or so I thought. I bicycled leisurely down the hill this time, calling David on my cell, still winded from my traumatic encounter.

"David, Reuben here; how are you?"

"Excellent to hear from you, Reuben. Have you found the presence of God yet—can you bring him back?"

Imagine how silly any answer I gave would be—I had found God's presence, but alas could not package him in an ark or any other vessel to bring his presence to Jerusalem. Instead, I answered as best I could.

My words were clearly understated, having been wrung out like a soppy rag. I simply repeated to David God's freshly spoken words just as I had heard them. Yet I could not express the pureness of my refreshment. What we call peace in this world is just the residue of something lost. Something I'd forgotten from heaven, something one could only truthfully know in the moment of its existence, and something words only coarsened.

"Amazing!" David shouted in his boyishly innocent, however caustic, voice. "Absolutely amazing! And I have my own wonderful news to tell you!"

"Yes?"

"Prime Minister Medvedev—she has come out of the closet!"

"What?"

"Yes, yes—I believe that's how you Americans say it. She has publically declared her faith in Christ!"

After chuckling a bit, I began to share in my friend's joyful news. "How did you find out?"

"A friend in our group knew her from the Knesset and has shared your plight with Medvedev as well—wonderful news all around, isn't it?"

David's hearty speech always sounded upbeat, though especially celebratory now, and a little clunky after hearing the graceful voice of God.

We spoke a few minutes more. I knew that I would need to go to Alcatraz, to set God's people free—somehow. Though not spoken outright by the Lord, I now trusted his barometer in my spirit that called for action. As for Amanda, she too lay in the arms of our loving Father, wherever that may be. So I bid farewell to my friend, telling him of my plans to go there tomorrow.

"You must bring the redeemed to Israel, Reuben—bring them home," David insisted. "God will provide a way."

We bid adieu. God would absolutely provide a way—this I now knew. It was branded on my chest.

ᖃ Chapter Fourteen ᖄ

"**T**asa icha desaya!" Bakr's desperate cries bounced off the crystal-laden chamber of the underground cathedral. His resonance agitated haunting chimes that sounded of sorrowful echoes through vaulted ceilings. Beyond the altar, heavy shrouds lined the stone walls. The room was richly appointed in drab colors barely visible through the darkness—from the gold-embossed pentagram against the far wall to the floor-length silk curtains and marbled floor. It was stuffy with the smoke of torches, with the smell of burnt flesh and the remains of preservatives from the adjacent embalming room.

The smell of death was acrid in his nostrils, satisfying, almost inspiring. Bakr felt intoxicated by his recently ingested blood. He took out a handkerchief, crimson-stained, thinking it a grave cloth. Shadows crept from behind the draped podium, edging outward with the flicker of light reflected off a coffin by the wall. Death was everywhere.

And yet death appeared not the enemy anymore. Honestly, Bakr had been dying for a long time. Ghastly appearances titillated his fancies. He enjoyed the black floor tile, the faint glow from the candles surrounded by pitch darkness, and the sense that his protective tomb beneath the natural light was beyond life's reach.

He could not rid himself of his hideous fallen state, nor did he want to. It haunted him as a friend. The specter of his own soul comforted him as he affectionately breathed in the mildewed sofa upon which he lounged. He figured that joyful play would never be his lot, confined to his own depravity, which was all penitently satisfying.

He was the most despised creation of all time—Satan incarnate. Devoid of emotion, too fallen to remember the euphoria of love, or so they said. In fact, the inability to love does not steal the memory of it; indeed, mindful playbacks of affections tormented one all the more. This pleasured him, since loathsomeness fed his ravaged soul, serving up a delicious dish that fed off of death, making Bakr content within his being. Bakr's mission now served as nourishment: to create life in his image in a world ruled solely by him.

Yahweh created the first flesh and blood, true. However, their offspring turned away from Yahweh, thanks to Ra and the selfishness of humankind. So Bakr's nemesis, the Christ, birthed life anew through his spirit, a way to make up for human failings, if you will. Then the Christ implanted his church on earth by instilling his spirit into his believers so that the church might work on Yahweh's behalf.

So of course Ra's first objective was to destroy Christ's church, his so-called body, by leading a one-world religion that countered the salvation plan of Christ. He succeeded except for the insurgents, and all but a few remained. He would destroy these. And then Bakr and his spirit of Ra would birth the first humans designed after his kind, after the earth imploded upon itself.

Heady with pride, he wished to boast of himself to Yahweh.

"Come to me now, Yahweh! Let me hear you—I want to speak with you!"

His shout faded into a rounded alcove draped in black curtains and a granite altar lined with metal gutter drains faintly lit by candles around its perimeter. And to his side, a foul angel stood, sticky with the sweat of indulgence.

"Azael, he came to me in my desert temple. Why does he not speak to me in the bowels of this earth?"

112

The angel, who had tasted of women throughout the ages, remained momentarily silent before answering. "When I whisper to the humans words of temptation, Lord, their aroused flesh deadens the soul. Yahweh does not know death—never did."

Just the thought of Yahweh haunted Bakr, but he needed to transcend death with or without Yahweh's help.

It was the gradual erosion of the flesh that Bakr needed to overcome. The irony being that he had contributed to its demise. Some might say he had even formed decay with the mother dough of hopelessness mixed with flecks of doubt and other faithless emotions from the discharges of human will. Anything that titillated with forbidden thoughts fed the body, which invariably wasted until dying, being transformed in the afterlife from ashes to flesh again—rotting flesh in the place of Gehenna. Hell, as some less enlightened chose to call it.

"Abiogenesis."

"Lord?" asked Azael.

"Oh, I was just thinking out loud. Abiogenesis—life arising out of inorganic matter. Ashes to flesh."

"Or to a spirit body," said Azael.

"The thriving spirit body—hmm." Bakr playfully wiggled his body. "Well then, that requires a kindred spirit to Yahweh, doesn't it? We don't have that, do we? We just have the flesh, and we need to undermine the soul in order to feed the flesh. The spirit's like a living zombie to us." With that last truth Bakr's body slumped like a deflated dirigible.

"Lord," Azael continued, "if we could somehow speak to Yahweh's spirit. That's the way in which he communes with his kind."

Bakr ran his hand over the chilled altar looking, or rather feeling, for blood. The blood—it was always about the blood. Only Christ's blood fed the spirit, and of course the angels he cast out had none of that.

Not physical blood—corpuscles, leukocytes, and all that kind— though the two types did overlap in some regard; as blood is to body, ancestry is to spirit. Rather, Christ's lineage—adoption linked through his inheritance, a transfusion of Christ into the "spiritual family of God"—the term he used to describe his slaves.

"Ha, grafted onto the family tree. Christ thinks of himself as some kind of spiritual horticulturist," Bakr said, and laughed boisterously.

With a theatrical gesture, Bakr used his finger and thumb to mimic the use of a French watering can in the hands of a gardener, waving it in the air over Azael, who gave him that resigned look of man sitting in the first row of a bad comedy act.

Bakr could have all things physical, of course. The spirit of the Christ—well, in as much as no one could see the spirit less even believe it—Yahweh could keep his spirit, even if it meant not receiving the Christ's pedigree.

"Let's get the sacrifice done," Bakr said.

"Soon, Lord; they're on their way."

"It wasn't supposed to be this way!" Bakr shouted while pounding the altar. "I stand alone, Azael!"

Something watered his eyes. Perhaps an irritant flew into it, although not even a gnat could find its way into this metal enclave. If not for his charred soul, he might attribute it to the burden that befell him. No, feelings were better left to the bleeding fools, and he was certainly no fool. "Sir," a bulky guard shouted upon entering through the back door of the cathedral, "we are ready with the insurgent, Father."

Two others hurried to the altar, one wheeling monitors with IV bags hanging from their poles, and the other lackey pushing a cart filled with syringes and other medical devices.

The burly man and another squirrely character pulled their chained prisoner down the long walkway to the altar, where Bakr stood solemnly along with Azael. In his earlier playboy stage the senator knew Azael as his demonic mentor. Now this slave to Christ would soon be sacrificed as an offering to Yahweh—maybe then this appeasement would cause him to appear.

"Hello again, Senator Brown," said Bakr. "Say, hand me the knife there, would you?" Bakr motioned to one of his aids.

The half-beaten man strained to straighten his head only to meet the barren eyes of the chief priest.

"Why are you holding that knife?" the senator asked.

"Oh, because it feels good holding it," answered Bakr.

"That's crazy," the senator said.

"Ooh, I *am* crazy, don't you think?" Bakr said while childishly jiggling his head.

"Stop this now," the senator said.

"Too late."

"Why me?" the senator asked.

"Dear Christian, because you're toxic to this world. I can smell the blood of Christ in you, having accepted the ancestry of Christ, and now it is time to shed that blood so we may offer it to your jealous God."

In truth, Bakr needed the blood for his redemption—innocent blood, to stop the dying inside. A fact of life. Even plants needed compost now and then to thrive. Something had to die for life to begin anew.

A cool rush of air rustled the black curtains around the room. Misty apparitions glided about like wispy clouds, illuminated by the candlelight. They spewed Gothic words in guttural tones. Making a scene only ghosts could see.

Evil set in the thick air, in the dim space of nothingness. It left the pained feeling of a hard scratch against the skin, leaving beads of blood that sweated from the mortals in the room.

"You're evil!" the senator said before drooping his head again.

Bakr smirked. "Evil compared to your puritanical smut! But to my own, I am the liberator. I deny nothing to no one. Only the blood of Christ can infect one with the disease of righteousness—which only serves to cause senseless guilt."

"You're going to kill me," the senator said. It was not a question but a resignation as the room's coolness turned to burning heat.

"Do you know why the Jews sacrificed animals, Senator?"

The emotionally distraught man could not answer.

"Because," Bakr continued deliberately, "the shed blood of the innocent cleanses impurities. Physical blood is a disinfectant—did you know that?"

No one answered. The smell of fresh blood now permeated the air, settling on Bakr's tongue, leaving for him a pleasant aftertaste. He fancied himself as a kind of blood connoisseur, with an extensive collection that dated back from, say, 33 AD—a very fine year, the year of the Christ's crucifixion.

The stale flavor of burning flesh spewed from the mouths of the floating demons all about. Remnants of the deep dark and all things dead.

The senator strained again. "Jesus was the sacrifice once and for all."

"Such nonsense," Bakr said. "You think he cleaned you out like some kidney dialysis machine? Cured you of the disease of sin so you wouldn't infect heaven with your impurities? Ha. No, you don't understand—nobody does. It's all about relationship, dimwit. He adopted you, gave you his bloodline. Congratulations, loser. I could have given you the world. Now you die."

Then Bakr waved his hand, emitting a red glow that lit up the room like some cheap dance club, sending a sticky, gooey film that settled upon the skin of everyone in the room. Although they tried, no one could wipe it off as it seeped into them, ushering the mortals into their deepest chamber of despair.

And so the two men hoisted the senator onto the marble slab while the others pricked his vein to insert the needle, which was connected to a catheter attached to an empty IV bag.

"Give me a sample of his blood," insisted Bakr. One of the technicians quickly used a side port from the catheter to siphon off some of the senator's blood into a small beaker, then reverently handed it over to Bakr, who then hoisted it over his head with outstretched arms.

"Behold, the blood of the Lamb, who was slain so that this little peon could inhabit a slave colony!"

The burly technician's lips quivered. Perhaps because of the desolation that oozed increasing cold throughout the temple crypt, soon-to-be morgue. Perhaps he quaked because he was audacious enough to ask his master a question.

"You have something to say, Mr. . . . ?"

"Jed—the name's J-J-Jed, Father. I-I was wondering . . ."

"Speak up, man; we have a sacrifice to make."

"Sir . . . Father, there . . . I . . . was curious as to what happens when we die."

Bakr forced a smile and moved toward Jed, placing his hand upon the man's forehead in some feigned attempt at compassion. "Your soul, my child, is mine. Think of something forbidden, something lusty. Close your eyes."

Spasms pulsated down Jed's body, throwing his convulsing figure to the floor. A slow stream of bubbles trickled out the corner of the man's crooked mouth. His glaring eyeballs morphed into shark's eyes.

Azael chuckled until his amusement surged into a roaring laugh. The other technician looked in shock. Bakr leaned over the man's chest. "Be still."

Groggily, Jed came to, slowly sitting up while expressing his dazed look through clouded eyes.

"Tell us what happened, Jed," Bakr insisted.

Jed paused before composing an answer through his lethargic stupor. "It was the biggest rush I've had, and then . . ."

"Then what, Jed?" Bakr asked.

"Then . . . I felt . . . like . . ."

"Like you dove into a pool and you couldn't reach the surface, and you began to suffocate," Bakr answered. "You're suffocating inside now, aren't you?"

"Yeah."

"That's your dead soul, Jed. And that's why I'm creating life eternal. You want that, right?"

Jed nodded.

"And the only way you can get that, the only way anyone can get that, is to let me, or one of my brothers"—he looked to Azael—"to let us possess your soul."

The smell of charred meat lingered in the air as the afterglow of death's signature. Bakr liked his cooked rare, alive actually. Someone was about to die.

Bakr turned toward Azael. "My Incubator Project, brother Azael. This is what I was telling you about. We'll inhabit hosts that will never die—flesh eternal."

"You are indeed the greatest, Master," Azael said.

"Yes. Well, I had to find a way around my adversary's way, didn't I? It couldn't be through the spirit. I can't revive their spirits—he took that part. Yahweh found a way to redeem the spirit.

However, Bakr's own spirit had found a way to resurrect the body. He used simple ingredients to concoct his scheme: Take a body, any body. Blend into that body some greed, a dose of hatred (for self or others), and spice it up with despair enough to doubt a loving god. Then bake that body by turning up the heat of loss—any loss would do—of a loved one, job, well-being, you name it, until the person denied God once and for all. Finish off the body by icing it off with disease.

Then, savor the victim's dying body while a demon waited to fill its corpse, so that on the last day of earth, the dead would rise from their graves as worshipers of Ra.

If he could force the senator to deny the Christ, Azael could inhabit his dead body, and what a treat that would be.

Azael kissed Bakr on the forehead and stroked his face. "We're all dying, Master. For how many millenniums have we sought the means for living apart from the spirit, our souls dying like fallen fruit from the tree, consumed by decay? You gave us promise—that one day we would taste what humans taste, and live forever."

Bakr raised the cup of the senator's blood once more. "To self-worship and life eternal! Who needs to sacrifice oneself when one can sacrifice another!" He poured the blood over the heart of his soon-to-be victim.

"Save me, Lord Jesus Christ," the senator cried while attempting to lift his head.

Bakr fumed while pounding the senator's hand with his fist. "Shut up! We can't inhabit your kind because you're infected with Christ's bloodline—you worthless meat!"

The other men in the room nervously nodded.

"Bakr," said the senator, "my spirit will live forever with Christ."

"Start draining him of his blood!" Bakr demanded. A humming noise from the machine ensued, after which the senator's blood flowed quickly from his wrist through another line emptying onto the table gutters, and next into a large plastic container by the altar.

"This will take a few minutes, Father," the one technician said.

"Fine—I'll give you one last chance to deny your Christ and receive a transfusion from me, Senator Brown. Be a part of my bloodline and have anything you want—anything, including life forever. What say you?"

"No," he responded.

"What is that smell?" Bakr lifted his head to catch an enchanting perfume, strangely reminiscent of his time with Yahweh. "What is that glorious fragrance?" His nose twitched in a bunny-like frenzy trying to catch up with the source. It was finer than lavender, richer than gardenias, more accurately defined by the peaceful rest that it imbued throughout the frigid room. "I can't quite place it."

"Heaven," the weakened senator said. "You smell heaven."

118

Indeed, that's what heaven smelled like so long ago. Bakr's shoulders drooped. He never wanted to be reminded of it again, never thought he would be. Until now. If not for this man . . . Memories only served to pain him. If only he could taste affections the way heaven's scent rained down joy—yet neither could be had.

Then the redeemed senator's face relaxed as he drifted into a coma.

"Fool," Bakr said. "Light some incense." He stormed out of the cathedral and into the steely, sterile-smelling hallway outside, and immediately dashed into a side conference room before calling his surrogate.

"Serge, Father here. Arrange for me to meet with Medvedev within the next three days."

"Yes, Father," replied Serge Amato. "I will arrange it. May I ask the purpose of this meeting?"

"I'm going to give her one last chance to join us, and if she doesn't, we start the invasion after the temple dedication. Clear?"

"Yes, Father, of course I'll inform her, saying only that you wish to speak at the dedication of the temple in honor of its grand completion."

"Fine." Bakr hung up and immediately called Eid Sammi.

"Eid, when is the bomber going to hit Alcatraz? It's time to eliminate those infecting ticks once and for all before they suck the blood out of all of us."

"The pilot is to depart soon from the Miramar base near San Diego."

"Fine, put me through—call me on the phone in the Mayan conference room."

Minutes lapsed irritatingly while Eid Sammi worked to satisfy Bakr's command. The phone rang. Bakr pressed the speaker button, and began listening to the conversation between the flight tower and pilot.

"Tower, give me a rough time check!"

"It's Friday, Sir. Fuel check?"

"Full, sir."

"Take off runway 26, destination Alcatraz prison, landing runway 14, alternate 12. Alitalia 192—taxi to runway 26. AZ192, cleared for takeoff . . ."

Bakr clicked off to speak into the thin air, hoping beyond hope that Yahweh could finally hear him.

"Now, Yahweh, if you're listening to me now, like you do with all of your spirit kin, let me say this—your New Jerusalem in America is about to go the way of your Old Jerusalem. Not a soul there will acknowledge you as their Lord after we eliminate the remnant.

"Your little experiment failed again. Humans always reject you in the end. When will you ever give up on these fickle humans?"

Bakr slumped into a chair.

"Never " spoke a voice from some indefinable place.

Bakr had finally heard from Yahweh.

ᶜ Chapter Fifteen ᶜ

I t was early morning, within a man-crushing San Francisco windstorm, the air so full of cold it made me wish for a layer of blubber around my body. I walked back into the late eighteenth-century living room of the scraggly hostel to wait for Elian. A final good-bye to the plush but tattered place in need of renovation. It had briefly served for me as a silent retreat from the brashness out there. The day of reckoning—time to go. I paced back and forth along its threadbare rug waiting for my nonchalant friend.

"Hurry!" I yelled at Elian.

"Is the cab here?"

"Yep. Come on." I looked once more into the mirror at my stubbled face as a reminder of how changed I'd become from my BR (Before Rapture) days when an unkempt look used to make me feel squeamish. I had told Elian about my indescribable encounter with God. I didn't know a jaw could drop that low.

"See," a recovered Elian commented, "you *are* a modern-day Moses!"

"Well, hopefully this doesn't mean I'm going to spend forty years in the wilderness."

"Forty days with me is enough wilderness training," Elian said as we exited the old manly house. Lines of perfectly placed white crosses stood atop the grounds in front us, surrounded by an expanse of evenly cut grass and trees that seemed to bow to the fallen warriors. Hopefully we wouldn't join the ranks of the underground, but then again . . .

"We're off to Alcatraz—and what's your plan again?" asked Elian.

"I don't know after we get off the ferry. I've got our passes, though; I just know that God wants us to go there."

"My oh my," Elian replied, "you've turned into a man of faith."

I wasn't entirely unprepared. It turned out that a group associated with the prison system called "Outsiders Looking In" could visit the prison and conduct weekly Universal Church meetings there. All I had to do was provide the fake ID my traitor "friend" Ian gave me, and Elian's driver's license, and we could go there—in thirty minutes the ferry would depart.

My hands trembled at the thought of entering the prison that either housed Amanda or had served as her final place of torment. Was she alive? Cool blood ran through Elian's ruddy face while mine burned with angst. OK, I knew God would take care of everything. I guess I felt a little trepidation as to what I might find. I just know that my life had always been complete with Amanda. She was, or is, better than me.

"Ready?" Elian asked. One last breath of free air before we hopped into the taxi and traveled down the rippled stretch of road onto Route 101 and across the bridge. Blankets of stretched cotton disguised as fog rolled over the hills, adding a surreal feeling to it all. We rounded the hills pocked with homes overlooking the bay, and its watery enclave speckled with anchored boats.

To our right along a dirt pathway we spotted a brawl. Three men taunted a tensed-up fellow.

"Pull over," Elian demanded.

The taxi driver obliged.

"What are you doing?" I blurted out. "We've got a boat to catch."

"That man's in trouble," Elian responded.

I implored Elian to remain in the taxi after it pulled to the curb so I could run several yards to the now-assembled group of five. They all stood on a dirt bike trail in the middle of crumbly serpentine, steep gullies, and sandy hills. Plenty of secluded places to hide a body. Surly biker dudes hovered around the gangly youth like black-leathered vultures. A young twenty-something's eyes darted around at his surrounding mockers, the youth's arms tightly folded over a leather-bound book clearly titled *The Bible.*

"Give me the book," shouted one of the men.

"No," replied the frightened youth.

"Hey, guys," I yelled. "What's going on?" The eyes of those in the mob suddenly lasered into me.

"He was proselytizing one of my buds," a bearded guy said.

Only the Universal Church priesthood and other church officials could share religious doctrines with others. Police arrest awaited anyone who shared publically, especially if they engaged strangers using an outlawed doctrine like the nonamended Bible.

"Come on, guys, he's a kid," That was the best thing I could think of to say.

Another fellow in his black leather Hell's Angels regalia turned to size me up with his sinister look.

"Whatcha have to doo wit dis?" he asked in his *Sopranos* imitation.

"Just a passerby who's tryin' to keep the peace. Let's say I take the guy—I'm meeting some officials at Alcatraz, and I'm sure they'll take care of him for us there," I said.

The band of vigilantes looked at each other, apparently waiting for some spokesperson to answer. The Hell's Angels guy finally spoke up.

"You betta be goin' to Alcatraz, bud—an' do what you say, or else. We don't need nuttin' on our records either, so take this dork and go before I deck him."

Without looking back I grabbed the rigid youth and tossed him into our waiting cab as if he were a suitcase.

"Thanks," he said as the taxi driver heeded our command to "make it snappy."

Elian, in his usual collected manner, seemed almost amused by the activities.

"Nice job, Moses. Set my people free!" he said.

"How'd you become a Christian—uh . . .?"

"Hudson, the name's Hudson." He reached his wet palm out for me to shake. "My parents—they disappeared. I started to read some of their stuff, think about what they said to me—then it became personal. Are you taking me to Alcatraz to arrest me?"

"No, brother. We're going there to set the Christian prisoners free." I whispered so the driver couldn't hear.

I supposed Hudson hadn't quite recovered from his traumatic encounter as he only met my statement with a tacit nod. Elian gave him a chocolate bar he had stuffed in his jacket and applauded Hudson's courage. The Spanish-looking boy, perhaps not even seventeen, rabidly chomped on his bubble gum without making any eye contact, bouncing on the balls of his feet probably without realizing it.

Our little rescue had delayed us to the point of danger. By now the earth appeared prematurely darkened from the masking clouds. Less than ten minutes until the boat launched. Were we too late? During the ride I couldn't get the book of Revelation out of my mind: "Then I saw a new heaven and a new earth, for the first heaven and the first earth had passed away."

So was this the next-to-last earth? What would happen to it? And the new earth—what would that look like? I supposed that I'd soon find out. Thank God, because *this* earth lay in a trash bin, just waiting to be dumped into a landfill so it could be covered up for good.

"We're getting close," the taxi driver said.

Elian looked at his watch. "Right on time!" He often said that. That flippant yet good-natured declaration always made me laugh. I hadn't forgotten that Elian had helped me escape the crash and avoid being discovered alive. "Are you ready to meet your wife?" Elian asked.

That question stung me like a rabid hornet, resurrecting thoughts of her suffering, throwing a heavy ice block against my heart. Was Lila right—?

"I think she's dead." There, I said it. "I called Lila, who told me she'd died—she called the prison."

"So did *you* call the prison?" Elian asked.

"Yeah, but before Lila did."

Ever the eternal optimist, Elian's perkiness irked me. Especially in the face of peril. Would Amanda be better off in paradise, or with me in this pit? I so wanted to see her lovely face and hold her comely body again.

Hudson waved his small hands. "For real, guys, what are you doing with me?"

"Don't be afraid," Elian responded. "We're brothers in Christ, and we're attending a group study at the prison. You can go with us if you like, or, if we can't get you in, then you can walk around, no worries."

No worries! We were going to enter the lion's den, and Elian once again displayed the attitude of a child going to some amusement park, or rather, a haunted Halloween house. How did he do it?

I played over and over in my mind God's words branded on my chest. *I am with you always*, until the peace that surpassed understanding soothed over my anxieties. The buzz of the tires pressing asphalt on the highway a hundred yards from the long entranceway merged with the sound of waves crashing against cement blocks and sandy hills bordering the dock.

"Look." Elian pointed toward the ferry as they began to pull some chains across the boarding ramp.

"Fifty-six bucks," the driver said while coming to an abrupt halt.

Elian paid out of his mysteriously well-stocked wallet as I yanked Hudson out of the cab and began running toward the ferry.

"Wait, we've got three more to board," I yelled.

I ran beneath the contemptuous stares of the boat's crew. Their faces scowled down at me, scarred by their servitude to the masters of Alcatraz.

"You're too late," one of them said through yellow teeth.

"Sorry," Elian said while huffing. "Traffic and such. Wouldn't Allah let us on board?"

The man crinkled his nose. "Tickets," he said with an outreached hand.

I gave him the pass from the Universal Church prison fellowship group. *God, blind his eyes to the fact it states on-boarding for only two persons.* I could hear the profanity as the man huddled with his fellow crew members. I drew a deep breath and wondered again what I was doing with extra baggage.

The man returned scowling even more. Now they'd deny passage for all of us, thinking we'd deceived them. He stood there shaking his head. I felt like a minnow in a shark pool as the crew sized me up and down. Next, he grabbed the entrance chains and jingled them in his hands.

"Come on, get on the ferry, pronto!"

I tried my best not to exhale as deeply as my relieved impulse drove me to do. We scurried onto the deck with the speed of three foxes being chased by a terrier.

As we sat silently on the bottom level, not a peep for the entire ride, the window to Alcatraz framed a puzzle. How could we possibly find Amanda, not to mention the others? None of the pieces fit together. Before the federal penitentiary had been closed in 1963, it could hold around three hundred or so. Who knew how many fit within its restored cells now? This place used to be a tourist destination, for crying out loud—Amanda and I had even visited it once. And now . . . the massive cell house atop Alcatraz Island appeared as though someone had switched off the view of reality to a bygone period replete with the ghosts of Al Capone, the Bird Man of Alcatraz, and other sordid characters. It was all too surreal.

The feudal-looking prison jutted from the craggy island—an austere testimony of man's ability to build the most deadening structures. Our approach toward the mausoleum-looking structure reminded me that we were about to visit the near dead. Everything about the place was lifeless—Gothic lettering over the entranceway and Frankenstein bolts over the decaying windows. Giant rusted double doors dominated its façade. The paint was chipped and peeling on heavy concrete walls.

After docking, we ascended the decaying concrete ramp up to the overwhelming gloom that hit while passing under a shedding plaster-lined tunnel. We continued toward the visitors' entrance before stopping to take one last breath. We must have looked like the three unarmed musketeers heading toward the narrow visitors' doorway marked with a weathered sign above. Our threesome proceeded down a long dimly lit hallway that smelled of damp cement until reaching the security checkpoint.

A rather robust lady hidden behind two glass panels motioned for us to show identification.

"Reason here?" she asked.

"We're with Outsiders Looking In," I answered. "We brought a friend who isn't preregistered. Can he join us anyway?"

"ID," she said after looking at Hudson. I felt as though I were entering into a nightmare. At any moment the boogeyman would clamp his cold paws onto my shoulders and drag me away.

"OK," the woman answered with surprising ease, and so we proceeded to the security post after receiving our temporary badges.

After passing through the doors just beyond the metal detector, we entered into the cafeteria lined with vending machines that showcased their foods in an assortment of stale options. The place bustled with the sounds of families or friends and prisoners, with few smiles, trying to catch up with each other across round tables.

"Over there." A guard motioned toward some outside tables.

We took a seat with others while a plaid-shirted elder with a gray-speckled beard held the Universal Church Book in his hand at the front.

"Welcome to our study," he said in an artificially sedated way. Prisoners sat in purple uniforms, outsiders in varied clothing, against a gray-walled backdrop. I kept wondering how God would show up.

I spoke up. "Sir, can we check on any prisoners here?"

The instructor rolled his shoulders and pumped his arms with the amusing gesture of a welterweight fighter. "Nah." He shook his head. "If they're not here with us, we can't call them."

"Amanda Simon," Elian blurted out. "Can we please just find out if she's here—she might enjoy this."

Another unsettling pause followed while I adjusted to Elian's audacity.

"There's no way I can check. Now, let's get on with our study—let's pray. Father of us all," he continued, "we come together in unity. Thank you for the freedom—"

A sonic boom sounded over us as our bench seats vibrated.

"Hit the ground—on your stomachs now!" someone shouted.

All of us circus-seal types dropped belly-first on the hard flooring. Guards swung their propeller clubs. I could feel the brush of air from one of their sticks.

A loud siren. Red beams bounced off the walls like strobe lights.

"Attention!" yelled a guard from inside the cafeteria. "Prisoners, line up immediately by the east doorway. Visitors, we need you to line up for departure through the doorway from which you entered. This is *not* a drill."

Instantly all of the purple suits stood up and began moving toward a side doorway, while the rest of us visitors emerged from our shock enough to begin exiting. Visitors frantically threw their food away; prisoners tightfisted theirs.

"What's up?" I asked one of the guards.

"Just comply, sir," he responded.

Elian, Hudson, and I walked to join the visitors' line when another reverberating shockwave hit.

"A jet, or jets," said Hudson. "Military."

"This may be it," Elian said.

"What?"

"Did you notice a bunch of boats lined up outside?" Elian asked.

My ticker pulsed in high gear. Something was up, but I couldn't place whether this was God's or the enemy's doing.

Both lines moved quickly as we finally passed into the hallway and then through the narrow exit doorway, turning our heads as soon as we entered the misty air to look for jets above. A long-beaked jet took a U-turn over San Francisco and zoomed in like an eagle ready for the kill.

"You need to board the ferries," a woman demanded as she pointed to some vessels docked about twenty feet before us.

"Move!" a guard insisted through a bullhorn. "Once you get to the shore, buses will be waiting to take you to your respective parking areas. Find your destination site as noted behind the bus's windshield."

Like good soldiers, the numbed visitors filed onto the boats.

"What do we do?" Hudson said while turning to me.

"Don't board the ferry right now," I instinctually replied, hoping wisdom served as my guide. Instantly a surge of adrenaline filled me with the boldness of having consumed a dozen energy drinks. I turned toward the face of the prison and shouted at the top of my lungs, "Lord God Almighty, in the name of Jesus Christ, set your people free!"

Hudson looked as if a brick had suddenly hit his head, Elian shouted a "Hallelujah," and the bystanders just continued to file robotically onto the ferryboats without notice.

Within a span of about two minutes, the ground underneath threw us down. Waves of asphalt rolled toward the prison, forcing the massive building to rock like a wooden sand castle pressed by the sea. Boats rolled over and two automobiles in a near driveway flipped like toy cars as if someone had pulled the rug out from under them.

The once-intimidating Alcatraz's surface began peeling off layers of stonework in rhythmic surrender to the overwhelming vibration underneath, jiggling like hard pudding.

"Will." Elian pointed toward the prison windows as streams of vaporous apparitions swooped through shattered windows. I could barely make out their forms until a cluster of them dashed overhead, with spindly grasshopper legs, fluttering winged arms, and contorted faces crunched up in skins folds. One looked directly at me with its black buttony eyes and spewing some cursed words I couldn't understand.

"Demons," Elian said. "They're swarming out of here like flies from a dung pile. Pray hard, guys!"

They scattered through the air leaving trails of mournful cries lingering in the wind.

"Quickly, pilots, close the gates and let's take off!" The woman in command shouted through her bullhorn as the yet-to-board people scraped their bodies off the ground before hurriedly jamming themselves into the remaining boats still afloat. The boat captains began pulling away. Two vacant ferries remained—their captains looking around for stragglers.

"It's about to crash down! Come with me!" I shouted.

I ran toward the visitor exit door. A seven-foot-tall figure stood upright at the door, resplendent with a gold-plated robe reflecting what little sunshine remained.

"An angel," Elian remarked. "I think only we can see them—I see at least five."

To my delight, purple-attired prisoners, insurgents—brothers and sisters—were streaming out the door. Many had already grouped outside.

Commanding everyone's attention, four guys with muscles bursting out of their split arm sleeves, each at least six foot five, thumped against the pavement with their tree trunks, their faces about as brutish as the angry side of the Hulk. They wore brown clothing unlike the others, more similar to the guards' uniforms. The tallest guy grimaced with a big scar across his cheek, and tattoos covered almost every inch of exposed skin below his face. His frame stretched high enough to merit nosebleeds.

"Hey, guys," I squeaked, "are you guards?"

The biggest fellow looked down and grinned. "Christians," he said with about as much emotion as the upright stone slabs through which they passed.

"OK, you guys aren't wearing purple."

"They didn't have purple uniforms that fit us," another dude said. I could believe it.

"You guys could be professional wrestlers," I said, my voice returned.

"Football. Raiders—we were praying together in the locker room when the lights hit," said the strapping runt of the three, who looked to be about two inches or so above the top of my six-foot-one-inch head. No wonder the Raiders had been in first place before the rapture. I'd imagine anyone facing these guys might opt to fake an injury before lining up against them.

"Let me ask you a favor—will you board each of the two remaining boats and convince—maybe even threaten—the captains to take your fellow brothers and sisters to the Sausalito ferry station?"

They looked at each other and nodded impishly. "Of course," each said all together, and they began to walk away, the ground quaking under their feet—I wasn't sure if it was because of them or the earth.

"Wait," I said before they could step two feet. "There are also some buses waiting at the boat dock, and we need to . . . force them to take us. Can each of you take a different bus and do the same?"

"To where?" Scarface asked.

"I'll let you know when we get to the dock."

"Cool," he said.

They nodded again and then gave me a high-five as confirmation before walking toward the two remaining ferries. I couldn't help but be amused by the lily-livered expressions of the captains once our Raiders impressed their wills upon them. *Thank you for nice monsters, God.*

"Come!" I instinctively shouted at the top of my lungs. "Continue boarding the remaining vacant boats. Once full we'll take off, and then some buses will hopefully be waiting at the other end to take us to freedom. I am your brother in Christ, and our Lord is setting you free!"

"My husband." A crazed woman with hair hanging over her face dropped to her knees. "He's in there—I can't leave him to die!"

Elian picked her up and began consoling the lady while ushering her toward a boat.

"His name?" I asked.

"George Kendrick," she said.

"Former President George Kendrick?" I asked in amazement. She answered in the affirmative, to which I said we would certainly look for him, which seemed to suffice.

"He's dead. They killed him—shot him on the spot. I was with him," said one of the inmates. As the woman crumbled with hysteria, Elian picked her up again and carried her to the waiting ferry. They didn't want one of our greatest presidents to threaten the current scoundrel's power, I deduced.

My phone rang. "Reuben, David here. Tell me what's going on."

"We're boarding Christian prisoners onto boats to escape from Alcatraz—"

"Sounds like a movie," he said.

"I've got to go now, David. I'll call—"

"No—listen to me. I told you that we contacted Prime Minister Medvedev. She was informed of your plans and said that there is another plan to bomb the prison in order to execute the remaining Christians in America. She is sending a jet to meet you at the San Francisco airport."

"When?"

"Sometime today—we sent the message that you were liberating the Christians at this time, just as you said."

Oh my goodness. "David, if that's true, then we've got to get to SFO. Is that all?"

"Yes. Now hurry! Make waste!"

"Haste," I said, and with that we clicked off.

A sickening explosion came from a short distance, followed by a giant plume of smoke rising upward. I looked for the jet fighter that now streamed northward sounding like thunder through ripped clouds. Nothing in sight at ground level except for the steaming rubble that once was Alcatraz.

Screams poured out from the amassed prisoners as they jostled to board the remaining ferryboats. I strained to look for others through the melee. A few men and women on crutches and in wheelchairs looked at me with the somber eyes of the doomed and nodded blankly.

"You!" I pointed to some able-bodied men standing about. "You help these people!"

These men obliged as a few coughing and limping people continued to walk toward the docks. The feeblest were last—about four of them . . .

A cowering woman in a wheelchair bended just so. She rubbed her hands together. Anyone else would never have noticed, but the bend on her pinky finger resembled the break caused by our backyard game of catch long ago. Moving forward, I noticed a familiar blemish on her right arm shaped like a freckled starfish. Her muffled hair the color of maple pancakes we cooked each Saturday. She had to be . . . could she be?

"Amanda?"

She cupped her hands over her face, though I think I caught a faint glimpse of those green marbled eyes as her fingers slipped from her forehead

"Amanda! Look at me!" I ran to her side, touching her auburn hair ever so lightly. I began stroking her unkempt locks, knowing in my heart of hearts this was she. But why didn't she answer? "Say something."

"No, I'm not Amanda," replied that voice of a thousand together times. This *was* she, yet those muffled words knocked the wind out of my rising hope. I wanted to shout my rejoicing to the outermost galaxies, paint the sky with her favorite lavender color, but . . .

"Amanda, I know it's you—look at me!" ,The blanket over her lap fell revealing Amanda's bottom limbs dangling over the wheelchair rim, and in that instant I grasped the horror of her amputation.

"How, Amanda?" I tried to conceal my shock through hidden tears.

She increasingly tightened her hands against her face with each futile attempt by me to pull them away.

"I love you so much," I cried.

"Go away; leave me here!" She jerked the chair with her body.

I closed my eyes, remembering for a brief moment how she was, how I'd hoped she would be in my arms again.

"Stop," I pleaded. "I'm your husband." My emotions ran the gamut of confusion mixed with a sadness. What terrible things had happened to make her so? Limbs or not, I still loved her.

132

A trickle of tears dripped through her fingers as she heaved, spastically bending up and down.

"Oh, God," she said, "What a fool's introduction this is!"

Her words befuddled me. This should have been our grandest reunion. But no, despite our being together, she only wanted to be apart. What a twisted turn of fate. Had the world taken not just her limbs but her love? *God, I don't know what to do. Make me like you. Give me the right words.*

"Amanda, please!" I looked up again as the sound of the jet engines echoed in the distance again. The fighter jet was making a U-turn. We had to go.

"Wheel her onto that boat," I said to her escort while pointing to the only ferry not yet fully boarded. I followed my wife as her face remained hidden from me. Why?

"What happened?" I asked again. No answer. I was talking to the wind. Elian wrapped his arm around my shoulder while walking beside me, Hudson to my left.

"She doesn't want to see me," I said to Elian as we walked up to the pier.

"She's afraid you won't love her the way she is," Elian responded.

"God knows I love her."

The moment was too raw to ponder. Besides, the fighter jet was heading our way, so all of us hopped onto the ferries. I gave orders for the Raider-compliant captain to start moving while I looked toward the horizon—instructing the other boat to follow us as we passed it.

Several seats back my wife still sobbed as my heart ached and rejoiced at the same time. Through sickness and in health . . . she had to know I loved her despite her lost limbs. I was just in shock.

The other boat fell in line behind ours.

"Let's get this thing over to the Sausalito pier," I said to the captain, "that's where the others were headed." With the Raider's encouragement, the pilot drove like a speedboat racer with the others trying to keep up. The second boat pulled away from The Rock, and not a minute too soon. An encroaching swell of smoke signaled the final fall of Alcatraz. I hoped that all had gotten out, but if not, paradise awaited. I stepped six rows back to sit next to my shivering wife, covering her with my jacket to protect her from the stinging winds that sucked the air out of our lungs.

"Honey, I will always love you, despite anything—you know that. Now, let me see those sparkling eyes again."

With that Amanda dropped her hands and lifted her head so that her teary eyes stared through me as though she could see everything hardened and imperfect inside me.

"This is me now," she said. A gust pulled her hair back and blew wide her cheeks to reveal Amanda's clenched teeth and gums . . . and that skin . . .

My face tensed as I beheld the grotesque scars that hid her once-smooth complexion. Her waxen skin drooped like some melted candle over a once-spotless countenance. Varying shades of flesh colors were drawn over a sticky mask as though reflected in a distortion mirror. And her once-ravishing eyes protruded from receding eyelids, making her appear phantomlike. I tried my hardest not to cringe. Oh God, was this her?

"Amanda, what . . . how?" I was on auto-control.

"They tortured me," she said while covering her face back up and throwing her head against the seat in front.

If I could but pull off the mask to stop this cruel hoax. A whirlwind of memories jumbled into a ruined mess. *God, help me love* this *woman.* My joy had turned to a repulsive nausea— my beauty turned into a monster. *God, I didn't just think that! Make it right. Do something, please!* I turned my head so as to not heave over Amanda.

"See, Will. I should have died," she said after turning her face away from me.

I couldn't answer her. *God give me the words, the eyes to see through the scars. Make it go away.* What a failure I was—I couldn't say a word! What a weak, despicable, shallow man I was. What could I say? I didn't know. I needed to be strong for Amanda. *God, make me strong!*

"I . . . it's the inside that counts." What a banal thing to say!

Amanda's piercing eyes cut into me. She stroked my face with those familiar hands.

"So lovely," she said. "Just as I remembered—"

"I'm so sorry."

I closed my eyes dreaming of our "remember whens." Of better days. *Oh, God—this should have been a better day!*

134

"I . . . missed you," I said, unable to muster the strength to even say "I love you."

"You're still missing me; this isn't who I am," she replied as she reached her other hand to cover my eyes. "Remember me as I was, please. And forget this beast."

Elian had moved to the front—he wouldn't dare try to assuage my angst now. I needed him now, though—someone to talk to. So I rushed to the front and plopped next to him.

"Now what do you say, Elian?" I whispered. "Man with the answers. My lovely lady looks like the bride of Frankenstein, and she's even dead inside. So this is the new pathway God has created—is it?"

Elian's eyes drooped. He reached over and engulfed me with the tightest hug I'd ever experienced, and spoke not a word.

"Will, get over here!" Hudson shouted as the pilot began to slowly pull the boat close to the pier while others threw ropes over the dock posts. "There are some buses over there. I saw some of the guards getting onto some of them and driving off."

"Good, let's get to those four empty buses."

"Board those buses," I yelled to our passengers and those docking behind us. "We're going to the San Francisco airport, where a plane should be waiting to take us to the new Promised Land of Israel so we can again enjoy the presence of God. Wait after you board your bus, and wait until I step onto the last bus and pull ahead, then the other buses must follow my bus."

The four Raiders pushed to the front.

"What do you want us to do, Boss?" one of the guys asked me.

"Thanks for asking. I'll give you the thumbs-up, and then you need to follow the bus that I'm on. Each of you needs to take a separate bus, and if needed, you can take the driver out and replace him with someone more trusting—who probably will be anyone other than the driver. You OK with that?"

"Got it, Boss," said Mr. Scarface as the four Raiders ran to board the buses first. Purple-gowned bodies filed out in orderly fashion onto the pier and walked briskly toward the empty buses. I asked Hudson to help with the boarding and to wait for Amanda, Elian, and me, so that we could all get on the final bus not yet filled.

Amanda patiently waited along with Elian. She cowered while he politely rubbed her back. And when I was finished making sure all of the Christians had disembarked their boats, I picked up Amanda and gently placed my bride into her wheelchair as we began heading for the bus least packed with people.

Once on the bus, Mr. Scarface sat behind the driver, who appeared like a scared rabbit ready to take off.

"Hudson, I want you to drive our lead bus," I said. Hudson started to disagree before I strongly insisted he take the wheel, after which he passively obeyed. Mr. Scarface pulled the driver to a seat near him in order to allow Hudson to take the driver's chair. I was amused at how the recently licensed Hudson lightened, as he rubbed his hands around the steering wheel with an impish grin. When everyone was settled, I gave Hudson the thumbs-up to move. Sounds of the other bus engines igniting played like rallying music.

"Sirens," Hudson said, "we're being followed!"

As instructed, Hudson pulled ahead of the other buses and they followed in hot pursuit—along with a cop car now in sight behind us. Our engine popped and whined as Hudson revved it to maximum output up the hill, while the others struggled to keep up.

"Who—how many squad cars?" I asked without time to think.

"Not sure. At least two cop cars—maybe some others I can't see."

"Can you go faster?"

"Remember, we have buses behind us. By now one squad car's running alongside the rear bus."

"Just get to the bridge, Hudson—just get us as far as you can." If only I could command Amanda's face out of my mind. I blinked a few times with some childish expectation that her disfigurement might vanish.

Hudson reached down and turned on the radio. ". . . reports along the San Andreas Fault of unprecedented destruction. If you are trapped or injured, try to remain calm, as responders are moving as quickly as possible . . ."

We topped the hill and entered onto the stretch of highway leading to the bridge. Looking through two crisscrossing clouds in the distance, I observed a leaning tangerine-colored post that stuck out from an ocean pimpled with debris.

The Golden Gate Bridge was gone.

Rounding the bend gave us a clearer picture. Two huge ladder-like structures jutted out of the ocean waters—its former towers. Both peaks curved inward and in between them existed a giant gap where the road once joined to them. Jagged pieces of rust-colored metal peeked through the waves. On either side of the towers, abandoned cars sat as masses scrambled to reach land. Several crisscrossing chunks of asphalt implied the wreckage of the former connecting road.

"What do I do now?" Hudson asked.

"Take that side road over there—it leads down to the water's edge."

"But we'll be trapped between the police and the water."

"Just do as he says," insisted Elian from behind.

The sudden jerk to our left jarred everyone, causing some to fall out of their seats. Thankfully, the other buses remained upright, though one appeared to almost tip over while rocking from side to side.

"Are you all right, honey?" I shouted to Amanda. She didn't answer as I glanced to see her new face glistening from tears, and oh, how I wanted to dry those tears.

As the bus headed down the slope, we vibrated over the uneven road toward the water's rocky edge. Skies were milky gray, giving off a corpse-like pale. Foreboding tides rose high and crashed against the littered beach. Restless waters seemed to wave us into the bay's watery grave.

The bridge ruins now appeared surreal because of their close proximity. Surrendered metal and broken cement peeked through oscillating waves. Pounding sounds of crashing waterfalls drowned out alarms from the burning city of San Francisco across the bay. Sirens whistled with increasing volume as they drew closer from behind.

I crawled two seats back after Hudson was forced to a stop because of the waterline. Two squad cars were now parked on either side of us with more on the way. My broken wife sat to my right as Elian rushed to my side. I looked back and forth to both for answers, but found none.

"We're in a pickle," I said. "We're stuck."

Elian puckered his lips and gave me that childish grin again. "You're Moses; ask God to part the waters."

Normally, I would laugh at Elian's perceived sarcasm; only, he said it matter-of-factly, and this certainly wasn't the moment for any levity.

"You're not kidding, are you?"

The absurdity of Elian's suggestion mixed with God's words, "Trust me," distilled within my mind, and the words *I am with you always* branded on my chest.

"Accept God's promise over your own understanding," Elian said.

Boldness. *I can do all things through Christ*, Philippians 4:13—like Moses parting the waters. But then doubts popped up again. After all, Moses possessed an instrument to elicit God's miracles. I had nothing.

"Moses had a staff—I don't have a rod." An excuse, I know, but come on—parting the waters?

Only after saying this did the silliness of it really sink in. A staff, for crying out loud—as if that mattered.

Two officers from afar with drawn guns increased my sense of urgency.

"OK," said Elian, looking up. "Let's try to figure this out. The rod of Moses represented God's authority over all the earth. The rod also propped Moses up—made him stronger. Think, Will. What do you have that represents God's authority, something that makes you stronger?"

I let my mind wander. Something came quickly to mind, and the irony of it struck me, as my marriage was presently crushed with disappointment.

"My wedding ring."

The deepest of compassion surged within me as I looked at Amanda for the first time without revulsion. "Remember, honey, when I placed that ring on your finger? It represented to us the circle of love. God had joined us to him. And the diamond—he's our rock, and our salvation."

Amanda folded her hands—in prayer, I hoped.

"Hold it up," Elian declared. "Hold the ring toward heaven and declare God's authority over those waters!" This was crazy—crazy right!

Amanda cupped her mouth.

By now, creeping waves reached just beyond the front tires of our bus. We could hear the waves as clearly as the wind pressing against the glass. Both converged like brushing sounds through the thick ocean air. The bay water encroached slowly over the beach so that in a matter of minutes it would be over the tires and splashing against the sides. We sat glued to our seats, peering at the line of buses parked bumper to bumper behind us. Hoping. Praying.

My faith turned to expectancy—God *would* do it, my spirit declared in bold colors! I'd seen numerous miracles already—all things were indeed possible through Christ. Our new path would bring us to God in a circle of strength, through the eye of the storm. I removed my ring and it framed the sky and ocean waters through my eye, the gold trim isolating me from everything but my peephole into the vast glory of God's heavens. "In Jesus's name, part those waters."

A knock came against the bus door. A policeman clumsily pulling up his left pant leg while tiptoeing through the water pointed his gun at Hudson. No waters parted, nothing at all, and I would have felt like a fool if not for the present danger.

"Open this door now!" shouted the policeman.

Hudson reached for the door's lever just as a thunderous sound of converging waterfalls burst out before us. Both of the ruined Golden Gate's leaning towers slammed against the ocean surface, sending a surge of water upward.

What happened next could only be described as a grand miracle. A curtain of waters draped over a developing ridge formed from the caving earth. On both ends emerged an ocean floor. A bridge of land!

Floods pounded on either side of the elevated crest that stretched across the bay, forming an earthen pathway in place of the Golden Gate. Waves pushed outward toward the endless ocean. And on the other side of the bay a newly formed dirt roadway lay directly in front of us!

Our jaws could have dropped to our chests if not hinged. No superlative could explain our amazement. "Praise you, Lord!"

"Wow," Hudson said in the most understated manner possible. He wore a goofy-looking inverted baseball cap—a "rally cap," as he explained it. Oh, the playful ignorance of youth. If donned a cap, I would turn it inside out as well!

"Drive!" I insisted to Hudson.

He slammed his foot against the gas pedal, sending our bus and those trailing it into a mad dash. The exposed ocean floor still dripped water from the receding sea. Our passengers cheered with praises to God. I imagined how the Jews must have felt upon crossing the Red Sea.

Behind us a stunned group of police officers stood mesmerized before scurrying toward their cars. But by now the final bus in our succession had wormed its way onto the ridge as we sped to avoid sinking into the drenched sand.

As I looked back, the long string of police cars sped a few hundred yards behind in heated chase. And then the pressing ocean waters ripped into the makeshift bridge behind us, causing it to buckle under the waves' pressure. About thirty feet or so behind our last bus the waters finally collapsed onto the pathway. Cakes of the makeshift road crumbled into the sea. The two leading squad cars attempted to make a screeching stop before tumbling into the rushing waters and disappearing into turbulent foam from the churning waters.

A domino effect of crashed police cars appeared behind us. They formed a slinking black-and-white caterpillar row of disabled vehicles.

We continued on our path making a final push through the dirt and onto a paved path at the foot of the Old Fort Mason. And up the road and onto Route 101 toward the San Francisco airport we went!

"Hallelujah!" shouted Elian. "Was that a trip or what?!"

"Check for that fighter jet," I said. No time for celebration yet.

"Not a trace of it," someone shouted from behind, while another confirmed.

And no more police cars for now, though that would probably change very soon.

Hudson arched his back to see me out of the corner of his eye. "Now what? We get to the airport and just wait?"

This had been a journey of faith. Why stop now? The smells of burning rubber still lingered from our stop-and-start speed chase. However, a renewed confidence in God's providence overfilled my spirit, sending glorious refreshment.

"I have no idea," I said. "I only know that we're to get to the airport and trust God to make a way out of here."

"Where to?" asked Hudson.

"Israel," I answered. "Supposedly the prime minister has sent a jet to take us there."

Lila came to mind. I had abandoned her once, and felt terribly guilty about possibly doing so again, especially after our abrupt ending. This time I had to make it right, so I pulled out Elian's cell phone and clicked on her name.

"Lila, Will here. I've got Amanda—she's OK."

"Willy—"

"Listen, can you right this instant get to the airport?"

"What . . . why . . .?"

"Look, there's no time to explain. If we don't get out of here now, it's never."

"But all flights are grounded, Willy. The airport's closed."

"Don't worry about that. Can you just get there now—and I mean this second?" Lila reluctantly answered in the affirmative saying that she would use her aunt's car, and so we agreed to speak again after she arrived.

I was surprised that no other police chased our very conspicuous line of buses as we drove through lines of stucco row houses. Chipped housing facades and leaning trees evidenced major damage from the merciless force of the quake. Rooftops had collapsed on several structures leaving heaps of debris and weeping people eyeing in shock their former homes.

Perhaps the police had too many other emergencies. Or, they were waiting for us at our destination. A helicopter above signaled such a possibility.

Sitting down with Amanda again refocused me. I managed to look at her for only brief seconds at a time, choosing rather to view the vestiges of her old self: her wavy hair, her smooth hands, her eyes. If only I could see them in exception to her face. I held her hands, imagining better days. Disgusted by my shallowness. Wanting better of myself.

Our hurt emotions iced over the embers of our untainted love I so desperately wanted to rekindle. If only I could love her in the same way— or a better way. If only she could trust me. Could I see the beauty through the scars? Could I get beyond my own flesh to see beyond hers? Could I be the person she perhaps thought I was—and give her joy?

The irony of our situation struck me profoundly. We beheld such miracles that should have caused us to rejoice regardless of any trials, and yet the cares of this world continually yanked us back into the muck. It was true, that seeing the eyes of God doesn't always pull us away from the filth that we see through our own eyes. At least, that's the way I figured it.

I held Amanda's hand. "As long as I have you, that's all I care about." Sounded good. I wanted to believe that. Maybe I did. *God, make me the person she needs.*

I knew deep down that the essence of my beautiful bride—the spirit of her—remained. I kept trying to remind myself of that. Her outer deformity was revealing my inner ugliness. Maybe we could discover blind love between us, deep down.

"Say something, Amanda."

She turned her new face upward, and for the first time smiled.

"I love you, Will." She swallowed deeply. "Let me go." She shushed me by pressing her finger to my lips. "It's OK. I had to let you go."

"No."

Amanda returned my grip and turned an apologetic gaze toward me. "Will," she said, her eyes burning through everything dishonest in me, "you need to let me go, just like God let us go."

"No, he never lets us go." But he had. Not in the sense of denying us. More like when Mom let me board the school bus for my first day at school. I'd never been away from home like that before. I was by myself—really—for the first time. *God, I feel like a child again.*

Elian placed his hand upon my shoulder while leaning toward me. "I think Amanda needs to know that you'll return to her with a more genuine love than before. One that truly goes beyond appearances."

"And how do I know when that happens?" I asked.

"When you don't have to try anymore," he answered.

"Is that true?" I asked Amanda. "You want me to just let go of what we had—"

"It's different now." Her voice broke with emotion. "I learned to love you in my suffering more than ever before." She paused to rub her eyes. "And yet, I couldn't have peace until I gave you up."

I turned to see the lake of tears in Elian's eyes. He reached over the aisle to give me a big bear hug and a soft smile. "It's OK, my friend," he said. "Letting go doesn't mean giving up. It sometimes means giving love the freedom to be stronger."

This all didn't play out well with me. "I pledged to be with you, Amanda, till death do us part, and I intend to keep that pledge."

"It's not about abandoning Amanda," Elian said. "It's about letting go of all the surface desires that were between you both, so that you can attain a deeper love."

"Is that right?" I asked Amanda. She nodded.

"So be it, then," I said, a little tired from too much thinking and a whole lot of shock and awe. "I won't give up on you, Amanda." Her muscles relaxed for the first time.

I got up to speak with Hudson. Leaned over his shoulder. "How soon to the airport?"

"About a mile or so," he answered. "And then what?"

That was a question only God could answer.

Hudson grossly underestimated the miles, as it took forever and a day to finally see SFO. Runways were ruptured open like sliced arms. Several cars lay flipped over in the parking lot. Others sat stranded at the terminal. The airport looked like a ghost town with empty buildings and just a handful of people moping about like lost children.

"I want you to take the exit route toward long-term parking, Hudson," I said. "There's a gate there that leads to the runway. Hurry!"

We reached the chained fence separating the runway from a parking lot. It looked like a bumper car arena, support vehicles jammed against one another. We stopped. Our relieved bus riders began disembarking. I felt like the Pied Piper walking with at least three hundred others in tow toward the open gate.

We filed through onto the tarmac strewn with newspapers and food containers. The outside mist anointed the marooned planes as the fog reached its lumbering arm over the sky and fingered the ground. Abandoned planes crisscrossed runways, some leaning on their sides with broken wings, their emergency rafts hanging out like yellow tongues. Other planes waited patiently at their gates.

My phone rang. "Will, Lila here. I see your buses. I'm parked at the terminal and headed your way."

"OK, Lila. I'm with Amanda. Be careful—can you see where we're at?"

"Yeah, I'm walking your way—see me?"

Lila's svelte body ran like a gazelle toward us. I looked around in a panic for Amanda, unaware that Elian had wheeled her to my side.

"And now what, my friend?" asked Elian.

"Wait for God," I answered.

Lila slammed into my body with an air-sucking hug. I reintroduced her to Amanda. Lila's face sank upon noticing my wife's disfigurement and lost limbs.

Our introductions were cut short by the sounds of sirens drawing closer. I had known that sooner or later the cops would come after us—military too.

Bending down, I tentatively cupped Amanda's cheeks with my hands. "Pray."

"You pray," she said while turning away.

Now I could see the procession of squad cars and flashing SUVs heading south toward the airport.

"Faith." That speechless voice spoke to me again within the inner chambers of my soul. It had always been about faith, and obedience—trust. That's all we had, as our soon-to-be captors snaked around the airport ramp heading our way. Two buzzing helicopters converged above to heighten the drama.

Father God, protect your people from the snares of the enemy. Provide a way for us to escape to your restored church in Israel.

The screeching sounds of tires against pavement introduced us to at least ten cars as they spun to a stop. Immediately doors opened with men and women in flak jackets leaping out, guns drawn.

"Fall down on your stomachs now," someone shouted from a megaphone.

"Down, everyone," I shouted. Instantly all three hundred or so Christians belly flopped to the ground, except for the disabled. Amanda outspread her arms and tilted her head backward as if to say "shoot me." It broke my heart again. I eased my reluctant Amanda out of the wheelchair so that we could lie side by side, Elian to my right.

"Pray for wisdom, guys," I said to my friends.

"Already am," responded Elian. "And whatever happens, know that God is on the other side of it."

An alarming silence remained for several minutes. Then the megaphone guy spoke again. "We're going to approach you now. Any movement and we will shoot."

A long horizontal line of officers moved slowly toward us. Guns pointed down at innocent heads on the ground.

"Will," Hudson whispered. "Look!"

A muffled sound like thunder grew more pronounced through the clouds. It built to a resounding jet engine noise until the clouds parted in submission to a 747 plane emerging overhead. Within seconds a Star of David symbol appeared clearly on its tail.

"El Al," I said. "The Israeli airline."

All the approaching officers stopped to look up. A few from our side pushed themselves up to view the massive airliner descend upon an open runway within plain sight. Though I could barely see the jet through the corner of my eye, the resounding engines announced its presence as royalty through bent clouds and a plumed trail of exhaust fumes.

As the tires screamed down upon the runway surface, police officers scrambled back to their cars. More than half sped off as the two leading SUVs crashed through the fence leading a parade of squad cars and military Humvees toward the Israeli airline. Sirens ablaze with the leftover odor of burning rubber wafted in the air.

The plane turned toward the circling vehicles and came to a stop less than three hundred feet from us. By now our group sat up watching the drama, oblivious to the waiting cop cars behind us.

Two side doors from the 747 opened, and two giant rafts flew out as if to stick their tongues out at their waiting adversaries.

"This is an unauthorized landing," spoke a voice through some intercom speaker. "Come down the raft with your hands clasped behind your head. Anyone who does not comply will be shot."

No one responded. Several minutes passed.

"Will." Amanda tugged on my arm. "What's happening?"

"Freedom. They're here to take us to Israel. Hey—"

A megaphone appeared from out of the corner of one of the plane's open doors. "Let the Christians peacefully board this plane. We do not intend any hostilities. We come in peace, with our only mission to rescue these persecuted people.

"We will lower a ladder and some of us will depart to aid in the rescue. Please acknowledge that you will allow us to peaceably board the Christians."

Silence. A huddled group of men knelt behind one of the SUV's open doors until one stoutly fellow in a ruffled tweed jacket raised a bullhorn. "You can disembark up to four unarmed persons to negotiate a settlement."

My gut tensed knowing there was no way they'd allow us to peaceably board that aircraft. However, true to their word, four men slid down the rafts, two from each door, followed by rope ladders thrown out from the two doorways in anticipation of our escape.

The four men wore Green Beret–like outfits and stern faces as they walked deliberately toward our group, seemingly oblivious to the cadre of vehicles circling the airliner. The stout fellow emerged from behind his SUV to confront the four would-be rescuers. For a few minutes he and a rather short Israeli man spoke calmly to one another.

Then the four Israeli soldiers continued through the barricade, proceeding through the broken fence toward our amassed group.

"Mr. Will Simon—are you here?" shouted the Israeli leader.

"Over here," I said while waving my arm.

The four men walked up to me. The leader stopped no more than a foot in front of my face, his strong cologne striking me as odd for a soldier. I met his outreached hand for a firm handshake.

"Very pleased to meet you, Mr. Simon," he said in perfect English. "Prime Minister Medvedev sends her greetings and blessings to you, brother."

"Thank you," I responded. "God bless you!"

"We're in a very tight predicament, as you can imagine," he continued. "The police and soldiers will not allow us to peaceably board you, so listen carefully. I need you and your group to calmly reboard the buses. I will join you."

"But will they let us?" I asked.

"They think that they're going to escort the buses to a holding area. But once I board with you, they'll know something is up. So, after we board, I want your drivers to immediately and quickly drive through that gap between the two squad cars closest to the airplane door. Then I want the buses to form a barricade by lining up around the open side of the jet so that our troops can descend and meet fire with fire."

"But they'll shoot us like caged animals in those buses." While in my mind I knew nothing was impossible through Christ, reason always struggles with faith. The plan seemed fatally flawed.

"We've got some massive firepower on board that plane, Mr. Simon. There is no other way."

So I sent a chain of command through the group, telling them to whisper our plan to each other as people began to peaceably board the buses again. They crouched down on the floors of the buses upon entering, as instructed.

Thankfully, the police didn't budge. Until, that is, I boarded our lead bus with the four Israelis. Hudson slowly turned on the ignition. The police drew their guns as we revved the bus engines and proceeded toward the plane.

"Stop now!" shouted the officer. We continued moving as our buses crossed through the circle and formed a line along the plane. Eeriness permeated the silent environs with the calm of a cat sneaking upon its prey. And then it started—bullets snapped against our underside as the bus tilted and then sank from the deflated tires.

Deafening blasts opened from the circle, shattering the bus windows. Screams poured out, along with the sting of broken glass. Metal fragments blew like confetti. From the plane's doors Israeli soldiers returned fire, spraying rounds of bullets, and the heat of explosives pressed into every space while Israeli combatants temporarily diverted the assault from us to the plane.

Soldiers with shields slid quickly down from the other side of the plane. Both sides continued peppering their opponents in an ear-splitting assault. *Ting, boom, kaboom . . .*

Fire raged from Israeli guns and blanketed the encircled vehicles as others raced to join their ranks. And then thunder snaps of bombs crackled unnervingly all around us in an indiscernible pandemonium for a forever period of time. Until at last, the shots began subsiding to a trickle, and then to silence.

I peeked up through the shattered window to notice the retreat of our opponents—what was left of them. Most of the vehicles lay in flames and as charred remains.

Then I panicked expecting to see bloodied bodies strewn across our bus. No way could our people have escaped the onslaught. To my amazement, neither I nor any of those around me appeared injured. No blood anywhere.

Then I noticed the most spectacular sight: angels—giant vaporous figures illuminated with sparkling gold colors lay on top of all the people, engulfing them in a jellyfish-like umbrella. Their gelatin-like shields completely covered us without notice, until now.

"Go now," whispered a voice into my ear. I turned around to see Rhome, my guardian angel—his gargantuan figure bowed so as not to touch the bus ceiling.

"Thank you," I said.

"Thank our Father," he returned.

"Let's go!" I shouted.

People began awaking from their shock and filed out with me onto the pockmarked pavement. I shouted to the other buses to disembark. Israelis began ushering us to the rope ladders. I stayed behind with Amanda and Elian.

The sight of America's remnant believers climbing aboard the El Al 747 elicited for me profound emotions. Our final departure from my beloved country was about to begin. Our destination—the restored Jerusalem. My heart ached for the country that had once welcomed God with open arms.

I began singing our National Anthem.

"Oh, say can you see by the dawn's early light,
What so proudly we hailed at the twilight's last gleaming;
Whose broad stripes and bright stars, through the perilous fight . . ."

And then, slowly, others joined in until a chorus of voices, Americans and Israelis together, proudly sang the song of a blessed nation for one final time. The most prosperous nation in all of history. "Land that I love."

We silently wept together. "Good-bye, America."

Finally, it was time to board the sick and disabled, as our retreated adversaries appeared nowhere in sight. Uniformed rescuers from the plane tied the disabled to flatbeds and then pulled them on board. When it came Amanda's turn, I kissed her chapped lips and told her, "I love you." She remained silent, showing those puppy eyes that saddened me with their barrenness.

Finally it was my turn—the last of the Americans. I climbed the rope ladder taking one final look back to breathe in the smoky air of my country for the last time. Farewell "Shining City on the Hill." Soon, a new earth would shine brightly again—and I longed to breathe in its perfect air.

And then I boarded. Amanda sat next to me by the window, Elian to my right. We taxied uneventfully before speeding for liftoff.

As we rounded over the Pacific Ocean, instead of ocean blue we saw copper-colored waters.

"Look!" I said to my flight partners. "The ocean—"

"It looks like the Dead Sea," Elian said. "The earthquake, the asteroids—the earth and its waters and every living thing is dying, my friend. Without the breath of God, everything dies. But don't look down, Reuben. When all is failing, that is exactly the time to look up."

And look up I did, to the blue sky. And I also looked for the jet fighters again. They wouldn't give up. The troops that attacked us had probably retreated in anticipation of sending the jet fighters to finish us off. I felt an uneasy knowing that they lurked within the clouds.

God, take us home. One way or another.

☙ Chapter Sixteen ☙

When I look down upon the sea
Waves of copper look back at me
Once viewed the mind did soften
Yet now the ocean seems as dead
With buried creatures bleeding red
Making the sea their coffin

— Amanda Simon

Somber words flowed from Amanda as she sat back pretending to sleep. They consoled her with the comfort of funeral melodies. Words expressed what the mind yearned to come out, and she liked that. God's words—well, they used to comfort, but like the once-calming sea, now seemed dead, and their bloodied meaning entombed a myriad of hopes and dreams.

The seeds of despair had been planted back when she lost the baby just fourteen months after their marriage, born silent into the world with the gentle countenance of innocence resting over its restful face.

She didn't realize how hard it would be to say good-bye to someone she didn't even know.

When the future of what could have been her daughter's life started streaming into Amanda's thoughts, a match was struck that burned inside for a long time. The twilight haunts had often manifested through mascara smears from her tears. Tears she tried to hide from Will, because his pain burned deep and she wished to assuage his torments.

She used to enjoy using her beauty to pleasure Will. Ever the gentleman, he never took advantage. The first time they lay together was in the tenderly awkward night of their honeymoon. His boyish cheek-boned face and a contemplative personality complemented by his supple wit charmed her more than she let on. He excused her brooding waves and mistakes, because as he said, "love is stronger than rightness."

Truth be told, she had always struggled with depression, hoping her outward appearance could mask her often inward darkness, and when she lost that, she lost her protective shield and decided just to give in to the despair. And now she could not crawl out of it, having fallen down a sloping chute greased by low expectations, and then futility trying to crawl up again.

Despite the miracles, despite seeing her beloved husband, these things only served as reminders that *her* miracle had not arrived. Perhaps because she was unworthy, or maybe God forgot her. She longed to be free to taste the wonders that happened despite having lost the sense of wonder. To bask in the awe of what God had done . . . or not done. She turned down the vent above her; it was so cold. Had she become so chilled, so hardened, as to lose the sublime?

But she was the sensing type (to use the Myers-Briggs language of personality styles), her take on life ultimately determined by the physical reality of trusting experience first and trusting words and symbols less. Will was the one governed by intuition—trusting impressions and metaphors first, and facts second, or third.

The cabin air was so cool and her mind so numbed that everything seemed stripped bare of superfluous subsistence, reduced to the purity of impression. She tucked her blanket under her truncated legs, accepting the brisk ventilation. Amanda thought she could actually see better in the crystal-clear air, that it offset her nearsightedness. Her glasses had been taken after she was abducted, which forced her to be more content with seeing distant objects.

The vastness of the sky as she looked outside the cabin window appeared beyond comprehension. The surface of the clouds in abstract clusters, wind-brushed to obscurity and imagined shapes, fluffed against the white-blue breadth of heaven, and with perspective limited, the entirety of it looked like a sanctuary spreading forever, the bended clouds becoming wedding arches under which to marry the ideal image of her bridegroom.

The endlessness of it brought her littleness more in line with the grandeur of God, the great I Am, and here she was, and is—I am, she thought—deformity and all. Her condition drained her of all superfluous subsistence. The longer she tried to make sense of it, the more the whole idea of this jumbled world just got away from her.

She used to find solace in just opening the Bible and reading the answers. They were clear, concise, and nicely packaged. The irony was that she knew the Bible backward and forward, had memorized countless Scriptures. And yet, the words only teased her now as empty promises. She witnessed now a judging God. A God that would allow her and the world to suffer. And for what?

None of it made sense, least of all her picture of herself. She wasn't a bride. She wasn't anything like a bride. Her sanctuary only led to further isolation. No union, no more fellowship. She had become strange even to herself. She felt like she wore some other person's skin. God threw it over her as though he no longer cared. She was sitting in someone else's nightmare while others looked casually in the mirror with no thought for who looked back.

Something had died—call it her world, call it her view of herself and everything around herself. And why . . . why had God rescued someone who wanted to die? That was the cruelest reality of all.

Amanda tried blanking her mind in order to sleep. She wished to never wake up. But if she awoke in heaven, with a new body, then all the best. If she had to remain on this plane as a broken doll sitting next to her Prince Charming . . . well, she'd continue to push Will away, hoping he'd be happy again.

Maybe Lila could make him happy. She was beautiful, after all, and she always seemed to have a crush on her husband before they married, which she excused because, after all, wouldn't anyone be attracted to Will's allure?

That was it. Her final sacrifice. She would leave Will one way or another. And then she would be left with only her words:

Adrift in loneliness I did fly,
Hoping someday to master the sky,
And trying not to look down,
Lest I play again the clown.

Amanda's thoughts drifted into the strongbox tucked within her memory bank. No one but she could enter into them again but her.

If you are there, God, let me leave this place with no more memory of it.

↜ Chapter Seventeen ↝

As the plane taxied to a stop, Bakr expected a swarm of waiting Israeli dignitaries to greet him outside his window. He saw but a smattering of peons, a few military, some other nondescript persons, and then a black limousine pulled up with a small Israeli flag flapping against its antenna, followed by a long parade of cars.

Two black-tied men immediately jumped out and opened the side door closest to the Universal Church's jumbo jet with *The Peace Plane* imprinted across its nose. Out walked the very stiff and stern-looking Prime Minister Abra Medvedev. She waited for Bakr near the steps, hands firmly clutching a red purse. No red carpet for the most esteemed man on the planet. How many insults would he endure?

Soon, Medvedev and the entire world would be forced to acknowledge his divinity. The show of shows was about to begin. Glory unleashed. But first, he would need to take the temple.

Bakr began walking gallantly down the stairs with an air befitting royalty. Serge Amato followed behind with a forced elevated posture. Medvedev stood below. The year following her appointment as prime minister had been unkind to her, hardening her features and adding shadows under her eyes augmented by fleshy bags beneath.

As Bakr reached the final step, Medvedev stretched out her arm. The two clasped each other's hands with competing grips.

"Welcome to Israel, Muhammad," she said without regard for the offensive informality with which she greeted the high priest.

"It is a pleasure to finally meet you on your soil, Madame Prime Minister," he graciously replied, albeit feeling his pulse spike. It wasn't his cordiality that flooded his face but the strain in maintaining it.

The two proceeded to the waiting limousine while Amato was ushered into a car behind them. The prime minister met Bakr's invitation to enter first, with a heavy sigh, followed by a sturdy huff of irritation from Bakr; as heaven is to hell, never the two will meet, although these two could do so only on an earth situated somewhere in between.

During their ride toward the temple square they spoke nary a word for at least three miles—Bakr's only consolation being the ample supply of champagne between them to toast the completion of the restored temple, the place to which they traveled. The question remained as to who would raise the first glass, whereas Bakr felt obliged to not waste the bottle.

Seeing that Medvedev would not defer, Bakr took the liberty of reaching for the filled glass, taking a large gulp, and then slamming the empty glass squarely in front of her. An uncharacteristic belch from Bakr signaled his respect.

"Good champagne, Abra," he said. "I look forward to our toasting the dedication of the temple."

"And to whom do you think we are dedicating the temple, Muhammad?" she replied matter-of-factly.

"Why, to the people of the world. Do you not agree?"

"This is the restored temple of Solomon, Muhammad—I thought we had agreed." Medvedev stared at him with the eyes of a bull seeing red.

"Abra." He leaned over, feeling as though the taut vein on his neck might pop out at any moment. "Neither of us wants a holy war. The peoples of Islam have been assured by the Universal Church that the temple will be a shared site—simply called the Holy Temple. If the Universal Church is seen as the face of the temple, we can assuage all concerns."

Medvedev grabbed her glass of champagne and held it up while painfully squinting at the bubbly. "Muhammad, when we speak at the podium, we need to speak with one voice. You'll be speaking to a group largely comprising Israeli citizens—"

"Yes, but the televised audience will be made up mostly of Universal Church members—the largest group being Islamic."

"Granted," she continued, "but I need to inform you of some recent changes."

Bakr's face tightened. "Yes?"

"We intend to welcome the presence of God within the temple."

Normally Bakr would feel flattered, assuming he would rightfully inhabit the temple playing the part of god's presence. But of course Abra did not think of him as a god as did most others. His miracles of healing the sick, raising mortals from the dead, forging peace throughout the world through a one-world religion—these weren't enough for her. Even rising from a fatal ingestion of poison hadn't convinced her.

She had become, by all accounts, a Christian, which, coupled with being a troublesome Jew, made her nothing more than a pariah on the world's stage. He, in contrast, had the ears of all the world leaders, being their priest and chief spiritual consult—all, that is, except hers.

Ever since her declaration of faith in Jesus Christ on an American news station, she'd been like a giant boulder inside the Universal Church life raft, weighting down all ecumenical efforts to unify religions and immovable on voting against condemning insurgent activities. She would not budge, but she had buoyed every attempt (like her countless trips to Washington) to defend Judeo-Christian believers, by making Israel a sanctuary nation.

Still, he needed the temple—the very place that Yahweh's presence resided—until his favored son paid the ransom for those shackled by the self-indulgences he freely embraced in exchange for their souls. Bakr enjoyed defiling sanctimonious people and places. And not from the sidelines, either. In Tehran, all it had taken was one meeting of the mullahs to convince Islamic factions to unite in favor of coercing the divided Christian religious leaders to accept a nuanced means toward salvation. It was either that or face political pressures ranging from the loss of tax exemptions (in North America) to stiff penalties for discrimination (in Europe, Central America, and South America) to economic sanctions (in Asia). Bakr was far and away the most successful change agent toward eliminating the greatest cause of war throughout history—religious conflict, by bringing all religions under the Universal Church's tent.

Noncompliant fanatics who practiced religious doctrines that established a deity in exception to the universal god of all faiths were in violation of antidiscriminatory decrees, subject to the rules of international humanitarian laws. If Medvedev was foolish enough to receive the Spirit of Christ to serve as her makeshift temple, she could have her savior. As for him, though, he would reclaim the holy temple in order to assume his rightful place.

But then, what was Medvedev referring to as God's presence?

"Abra, I would welcome the opportunity to present myself within the temple, but I suspect you have something or someone else in mind?"

Medvedev arched her back. "We're expecting God to show up," she said. "The real God."

At first he wanted to rip her throat open and spit out her voice box, and then reason took hold. Instead, he would indeed show up in all his glory. A manifestation that could not be denied. The world would finally witness the glory of god.

For the remaining ride, Medvedev's tapping fingers could be heard through the tense silence. Through kibbutzim, industrial plants, and collective farms the two rode apart like magnets of opposite poles. They passed a small farm. Bakr rolled his window down to a crack. The air had a rotten smell. Soon the thaw of spring would force wild mushrooms to bulge from Israel's sludge before dying after their brief emergence, before their life sank into compost in wait for another spring so that others might devour them.

Another few miles and a mass of thousands appeared. Heads straining like baby birds wishing to feed from Medvedev's wormy promises of a born-anew Israel. The caravan wound its way through a side street, sirens intermittently blaring.

Then the temple emerged: its front a lattice of white stone walls from which rose six turret towers eyeing visitors at each corner. Several marbled steps surrounded the face like a jeweled necklace around its base. A patio trimmed in gold faced the forecourt.

The two dignitaries exited their car without Bakr acknowledging any others; he was too transfixed to think of anything except the sanctuary set before him. He ascended the steps with regal care taking no notice of Medvedev, who closely followed.

Stepping through the porch between two massive bronze pillars, a three-story columned tower jutted out from the main compound in striking contrast. The Holy of Holies inner room would be in this building. God's place. His place.

Around the temple appeared a walled-in compound faced with ivory columns and rooftops trimmed in gold like some ornate citadel. It still breathed forth the fresh smell of sanded stone and cedarwood that lined the walls and made up the golden marble flooring. Wall carvings of palm trees, cherubs, and blooming flowers in buttercream brass served to inflate Bakr with the air of supremacy. A fitting monument.

Bakr moved unapologetically toward the main building, the outer room comprising an incense altar, table, and ten lamp stands made of gold, and in the front, a swirling sea within an immense bronze water basin supported by twelve bronze cattle. A bronze altar stood to the side—for the sacrifice. He stepped forward toward a gold-trimmed doorway.

"Muhammad, please, you cannot—"

Medvedev's warning not to enter the Holy of Holies was summarily dismissed by Bakr. He walked through two enclosures until finally reaching the inner room—where the presence of god—his presence—would rest.

He lay back upon the floor taking in the magnitude of his position. Once, the ark housing the tablets containing the Ten Commandments resided in a similar place, long ago. The presence of Yahweh indwelt the ark, and then his presence was deposited within the inner sanctum once Solomon's workers finished its construction.

Of course the curtain separating the priest from the commoners no longer remained. Jesus took care of that. The Christ preferred instead that his spirit reside within his foolish believers.

"I will emerge from here after you announce me," Bakr said to Medvedev as he stepped outside.

Medvedev's fists clenched as she pursed her lips. Certainly she would acquiesce if only not to make a scene before the cameras, he thought. She growled before turning to walk toward the temporary shelter behind the podium erected alongside the temple.

Bakr stepped back inside the holy chamber taking in a deep breath. Grating noises eked through his sanctum. Masses began to chant all around, at first indiscernible, then clearer in unison: "*Yisrael Adonai Eloheinu Adonai echad*," which in English meant "O Israel, the Lord our God is one Lord."

Bakr contemplated whether the chanting crowds had indeed adopted the Universal Church mantra: "One church, one god in many forms," and so forth. If true, his claim would be as the unifier of all the gods into the one true godhead—priest of all—and chief of all gods. Or, they spewed Jewish lies. Either way, he would have his way.

A lanky man outside the inner room, earphone attached, shouted to the other suited men around him: "The Lord our God is one Lord. Jesus and the Father are one!"

"Heresy," Bakr shouted back. "How can you as a Jew say such a thing?"

Such visceral rants peeved the two-headed serpent that struck with vengeance against his insides. One of those heads being power, satiating him with its entree. Not even the temple could contain his worldly stature. He felt altogether comfortable in the Holiest of Holies, though. The other head of the snake, the meaty fuel of hatred, ate through his insides with an acidic burn. Indeed, it propelled him to destroy his enemy, but it also sometimes turned on him.

A forty-something assistant to Bakr dared to enter the inner room despite protests from the outside, and sat upon the floor with Bakr. "We're ready, Father. The jumbo screen is loaded, the music cued, and the lighting perfect. All the media is anticipating your speech."

"I won't need the lighting," Bakr replied with a wink. "I have something special planned." He smiled at the thought of Medvedev fretting that her nemesis was usurping *her* spotlight in *her* country. Little did she know.

"Now leave me alone." After shooing the man away, Bakr shut the door to conjure the spirits of this age. "*Shala imbuk imom da kasak.*"

Auras of every shape and size began to fill the room with their melancholy and seductive voices. "I can smell the blood," said Bakr.

Spirits swooped in a whirlwind of writhing forms imparting trails of red. The night creatures filled the space with groaning sounds of perpetual longings, as the room became awash with odorous decay. Bakr danced in one grand, decadent celebration with his kindred vapory figures.

Bakr felt his spirit push against his muscles, itching to come out. He who possessed Bakr wanted to escape its fleshly confines—Ra. The grand spirit of the unholies issued forth a refulgent ray of light almost blinding to the natural eye.

Bakr dispersed a glowing mass of shooting rays. His luminescent body spun like a human strobe light, while the other spirits in the room frolicked in anticipation of their master's forthcoming revelation. They reveled for almost an hour.

"It is time," shouted someone from outside.

Bakr's spirit regressed into its dormant state as if turning off a light switch. Ready for an encore.

The rousing music outside obliged as Bakr straightened and knocked gently from inside, signaling the guards to open the temple doors so he could step majestically into the open air. Camera lights blasted from waiting reporters. They doggedly followed him toward the podium outside as the blaring music built to a crescendo. Timed perfectly for the greatest peacemaker of all time.

While Bakr walked with the confidence of a king to his coronation, his escort Amato shuffled with the air of a drunken man.

"Too much champagne?" Bakr asked.

"No," hissed Amato. For a moment Bakr seemed perplexed, until it dawned on him. Amato was possessed by Asmoday—the prince of demons who had spoken to Eve in the garden.

"Asmoday—you own him now?" Bakr smiled.

"Yes, as I did with Eve. And Cain. To allow Amato to perform miracles." They laughed. Bakr took his regal seat beside the stage, just beyond sight of the audience with a serpent's eye toward Amato.

Though Amato walked upright, his contorting body slithered its way toward the podium.

Medvedev spoke from the podium. "And now, fellow Israelis and people of the world, we will hear from the president of the Universal Church, Dr. Serge Amato."

Fireworks shot into the cool afternoon air in tempo to a kingly melody as Amato walked onstage to a polite yet alarmingly subdued clap of hands. Yet it all played out differently to the broadcast audience on preprogrammed speakers, sounding more like twenty stadiums filled with ravenous college fans cheering their football team's offense with just two yards to go for the victory.

Asmoday returned reason to Amato as he spoke: "Fellow sojourners for peace, we come today at the most momentous of all times, a time when—"

A mob of seven angry men interrupted Amato by charging the podium, knives and guns in hand. The raging men stunned everyone to a dead silence as they defied the attempt by guards to impede their progress. Amato eased his head in their direction with the coolness of a serpent ready to zap the offenders with its tongue, and turn them into food.

Amato shouted as his words faded into a hissing proclamation: "Withhh . . . the authority sss . . . of him who isss . . . all-powerful, I call upon the legionsss . . . of this world to engulf these insurgents with the firesss . . . of hell!"

At that moment a ball of fire arose, consuming the men, and reducing them to ashes.

Amato turned back to the audience and declared, "People of the world, you have just witnessed the judgment of our Lord upon the wicked. Fear not, for as he has protected me, so shall he protect you!"

Amato hissed one more time before puffing his chest to the crowd. He acknowledged Medvedev by nodding to her as she sat like a perturbed grizzly next to Bakr in the wings.

"Now," said Amato, "it is my highest honor to give you the guardian of peace and the protector of his people—the holy and hallowed chief priest of this world, Father Muhammad!"

And then a deep-voiced announcer spoke through the speakers, sight unseen. His voice echoed down the podium and through the masses:

"Friends, all the peoples of the world, welcome the author of peace, the brother of Jesus, the bishop of Rome as elected by the College of Cardinals, and the most esteemed of all, the Mahdi for whom we have all been waiting—bless us now, Father!"

Another programmed sound bite of riotous celebration blared forth as Bakr approached the podium wearing a royal robe of blue and white, and an outer cloak of fine purple linen that he nonchalantly spread out with his hands in a show of resplendent colors. The jumbo screen reflected his marbled onyx-colored eyes shining fearfully through the mascara that encircled them.

"Fellow brothers and sisters of the world union," Bakr said while awaiting the taped cheering to subside, "I come to you with love and a grateful heart for those who have chosen peace over division, enlightenment over tradition, and freedom over dogmatism. Today, we stand united as a people who honor the best of humanity's values: tolerance, openness, and respect for the peoples and institutions that treasure our commonalities. That which unifies us makes us stronger.

"Your Universal Church is honored to dedicate this place of worship for all the religions of the world, as a place to praise Allah, God, the prophets Mohammad and Jesus, and to honor the principles set forth in Buddhism, Hinduism, and the many other religions that honor the sanctity and sacred rights of the individual."

Programmed applause blared through the loudspeakers as church representatives ensured that cameras remained focused on Bakr and the few who cheered. The Universal Church security agents especially warned the cameramen to avoid Prime Minister Medvedev, whose scowl wrinkles rivaled that of a tensed shar-pei.

Bakr continued to wow the global audience with all the right chords, convincing most that a world devoid of bigotry translated into harmony. Whereas fundamental Christianity, which insisted on a mediator, only served to isolate people from a direct relationship with Allah—God, or so he tried to convince the audience.

"Islam," he spoke, "promises hope and assurance, and coupled with the philosophies of Eastern religion, these religions serve up a plate of prosperity for a world hungry for gratification." Even a healthy dose of agnosticism could balance out the potpourri of faiths, he thought.

As he began to close, a prurient music eased its way into a lusty resonance over the intercom, inciting a rush of adrenaline across the wider audience, filling spectators with splendor and swank.

However, as the music blared, no one but Bakr could understand the true dimension of excitement in the air. His spirit released its pent-up dynamism into a surrounding field of demons charged with metaphysical energy the world had yet to discover. And when their currents met, a beam of light engulfed Bakr so as to blind every watchful eye.

He became in that instant like the sun. Grand and too magnificent to behold. Flowing in rays of sparkling stars like threads of priceless jewels washing over a people too awed to comprehend anything beyond their mesmerized state.

Never before had the world been exposed to the glorious light that once belonged only to heaven but was now perverted into a sideshow to highlight the master of this world. And no one could help but reverence the one who introduced brilliance to a world grown dull. Bakr basked in his glory.

After a few seconds of this unparalleled demonstration, he raised his arms to still the flow of his spirit's glory, sucking its energy back into his flesh, returning him to mere mortal. Then he quickly exited before the audience could quite awaken from its stupor.

Before departing into his awaiting car, Bakr stopped to acknowledge the prime minister, whose stiffened posture and aloofness about twenty feet from him signaled all he needed to know. Surprisingly Medvedev moved toward him, and leaned over to whisper into his ear. "Amazing, Muhammad—I don't know how you did that. But remember, that the temple is the holy site of Israel."

Bakr reached deep into the pit of his titanium will to avoid a murder of first degree. After releasing his clenched fists, he robustly shook Medvedev's hand for all to see, then whispered into her ear, "Remember, Abra, that if you deny Islamics their rightful place of worship, there will be hell to pay."

With that Bakr quickly headed for his limousine with Serge Amato while scrubbing his hands with a disinfecting wipe. After climbing into the car, he quickly phoned Eid Sammi.

"Eid, Medvedev has no intention of letting anyone but the Jews use that temple. I'm sure you know what that means?"

"Yes, as we expected, Father. I will contact the members of the World Security Alliance, as I am sure they will opt to execute project Al Malhama."

"Yes, I'm flying toward my compound now—keep me informed, Eid."

As Bakr hung up he turned to Serge, fists clenched. "That idiot! I'd like to—"

"I know," interrupted Amato. "But we knew she was a traitor to our cause. Besides, we have other concerns."

"The war to end all wars—been there, done that."

"Perhaps bigger than that, Father. The asteroids that hit earlier were small in comparison to the one headed toward our atmosphere. This one is perhaps as much as a mile wide."

"When?"

"No telling—days, months, perhaps never."

"Enough to destroy the earth?"

"Plenty enough."

Bakr closed his eyes and sighed. "One way or another the earth will end."

"I've been following our scientists regarding this for a while," said Amato. "They say there's a huge hole in the earth's magnetic shield, so that some destructive particles are coming through its crack at an alarming rate. And the way the sun's polarity is flipping, the earth will be susceptible to the sun as never before."

"Serge, it's always been about energy. With the change in polarities, we can master the grids, thereby mastering the world, and Yahweh can't do anything about it—just like he couldn't do anything to prevent the fall of Eden the previous time. We'll have a new earth—our new earth."

⌐ Chapter Eighteen ⌐

S treams of clouds passed underneath as I peered over the pilot's shoulder, and the sky—well, the sky was perfect. For a moment I just enjoyed the ride, until the pilot reminded me of our precarious position.

"Two Russian F-22 Raptors have been following us for a while now," he said.

"And what do you think they'll do?" Stupid question, I know.

"All of our jets, including this one, have antimissile systems installed—canisters that produce heat to divert the missiles. We just need to stay alert."

"No radio contact with that enemy fighter?"

"Nope, they prefer it that way—they know who we are, and they've got the advantage. My job as directed by the prime minister is to get you to our homeland safely, and I'll do my best."

With that bit of ominous news I scurried back to my seat. Hudson and Lila sat together in familiar conversation. Too familiar for my liking. Amanda still slept while Elian peered intently out the window.

I sat clearly awake. My spirit uplifted with anticipation as we neared the new Promised Land. My feelings were consistent with the nostalgic son who nears home after a long absence. Remarkable how our destination felt kindred to my soul, as though I knew her as an old friend—not so much because of the land to which we traveled; rather, the Promised Land indeed reflected the very promise of God—his word—his intended home for us in more ways than just a place to stay. The site of Israel was where God would plant his presence again, thereby establishing a fresh relationship with his children. The "New Genesis," as David called it.

In contrast to my rising hope for our new home, I felt terribly unsettled by my soul mate's rejection of me. My old life with Amanda still burned within me, but more and more of it had been reduced to the ashes of memory in hopes that it might be resurrected into something stronger. After much prayer, the sense grew that I, not her, needed to change. I couldn't help but think of the story of the old tree whose leaves prevented the sun from reaching its young saplings. What in my life needed to die in order to allow the light of Christ to shine into that part of me struggling to break through?

"She won't let me love her," I said to Elian while sitting down.

Elian didn't respond at first, just matched my glare with his blues until I spoke again. "I don't know how to make her love me back."

"Don't need to," he finally responded. "Love just loves."

This time I punched Elian in the arm out of frustration. I wanted some plausible advice—not that esoteric stuff.

Elian rubbed his arm and took another glance out the wild blue yonder before turning my way again.

"I take it that wasn't a love pat," he said while grasping my arm, presumably to prevent another blow.

"I'm sorry. I just lost my head." I felt terribly guilty. All my life, I've been about fixing things—people too. And now Amanda seemed beyond repair. My success in life, I suppose, calculated like a decent batting average, a little less than .300, which meant I knew failure all too well, which also meant that I need to rely on the Almighty to make up the difference. Obviously God could do anything, but he needed a person's will to do it. After witnessing so many miracles, I was not about to doubt

God, but I did doubt my wife's will to persevere, and my ability to help her. I doubted me.

"My friend, I think you're trying to validate your love with Amanda's love. She's trying to love; I'm convinced of that. And so are you."

Was I just *trying* to love? Amanda's disfigurement altered the equation, the passion, perhaps.

"Eros love—marital love," I said. "That can change. But agape love stays forever."

"True, Elian replied. "The love of the spirit is agape, and God is the only one completely true to agape love."

"I thought that I loved Amanda with agape." *Thought* being the operative word.

"I believe that most who care for another person practice more of a nuanced form of agape love," Elian replied.

"You mean not really pure love?" I was hoping Amanda remained sleeping.

"Yep. Pure love comes from being sold out to God, and who can say that—truly?" said Elian.

I agreed that we need to be emptied out so that God could pour his love into us. But, it was the emptying part that caused us problems. "No one can completely purge themselves enough to allow God's Spirit to fully govern their desires."

"Really?" said Elian.

"No way. For example, love doesn't simply manifest for a stranger— you have to get to know someone before you can love them," I said.

"Love doesn't just happen?" Elian said.

"Right."

"You're getting to the point, I think, Reuben. To love a stranger requires more than ourselves."

"It requires God," I answered with the obvious.

"God knows and loves that stranger, even if we don't," Elian replied.

"Because," I said feeling a bit like a child in Sunday school, "no one is a stranger to God." I was looking forward to how this tied in to my love, or lack thereof, for Amanda—and perhaps Elian had some welcome insight as to the love she felt for me.

"You made my point," he said. "Only a supernatural infilling of God's Spirit can instill unaffected love in us for another, even love for a stranger."

"Kinda like cupid—God shoots us with love for another."

Elian cupped his mouth so as not to wake Amanda with his chuckle. "God as cupid," he said. "I'll remember that one. I believe, though, that God's love is innate to some extent."

"Give me an example," I said.

"OK, like a mother's love for her unborn or newborn child. Most have it, though the child is like a stranger to her mother."

"Of course," I said. "Because it's instinctual—the baby lives within her."

"Precisely." Elian smiled. "Once God's love is inwardly birthed in a person, through Jesus Christ, it thrives regardless of knowing. You can't learn to love. Agape happens through an inward transformation of one's spirit. Eros happens through an outward response of the flesh.

"And loving a stranger is the most profound evidence of knowing God. And then, loving an enemy—well, that truly requires the power of God's love."

"That's it!" I proclaimed. A sudden surge of adrenaline signaled a revelation the likes I'd not felt since before the rapture. "I've got it! God's grace is that he lives in us, so that he can perfect his will through us!" How does God package profundity in such simple wrappings? Maybe profound only to me—God speaks the language of each individual, which can sometimes be foreign or obvious to others. "Amen." And then Elian gently patted me on the arm, no doubt a reminder that I'd punched his arm earlier.

Amanda indeed seemed like a stranger to me. Walled off and hardened. Hard to love. But not hard for God to love.

Though I wished to rekindle the relationship we had enjoyed before her trauma, that might never be. I would simply have to ask God to take over, replacing my failed eros love for Amanda with his spirit's life-giving agape love. My part would be to simply give everything over to God, including my desires—hard for someone who wanted to fix things.

A gentle rub against my right shoulder at first startled me until I looked over to see a very prim Lila.

"Are you OK?" she asked.

"Fine, thank you—and you?"

"Some amazing stuff took place back there—hard to believe." Lila rubbed my back as I nervously leaned forward.

"I've never witnessed anything like it," I responded. "Those were some Old Testament–type miracles—parting the water . . . say, you can't still doubt the reality of God?"

Lila glanced down at a satin-covered box stuck tight in the clasp of her hand. "I can," she said. "For every good thing this God of yours may have done, if he's really all-powerful, he's also allowed many more bad things to happen."

I wished to further engage Lila with a rebuttal, however the gold-laced box she clenched intrigued me. "What's in the box?" I asked.

"My mother's wedding ring."

"Why'd you pull it out?"

"When you held your wedding ring, the waters parted. I tried asking for my miracle through this ring—it didn't work."

"What's your miracle?" I asked.

Lila rubbed her fist into her wistful eyes and stared into a space of nothingness. "Once when I was a little girl," she explained, "my father bought me a Slinky that I loved. Upstairs, I would release the Slinky from my palms, or throw it up to see it wiggle in the air. Elongated, it resembled to me a sanctuary, because its wires spread over twisting circles that I pictured as a tunnel through which I could travel to anywhere I liked."

"And now, where do you want to go?" I asked Lila.

"I want to go back to the way things were," she answered.

"That's never possible," I said. "You can never go back and it is the same. But we are going to a safe place, Lila. Say, are you open to hearing about Jesus Christ?" I must admit, the recent parting of the waters fueled my evangelical push a bit.

"Come on, Willy, we've been through this before." I glanced over at Elian, who stared unabashedly at me.

"God's really the only one we can lean on." I was feeling like Billy Graham on hormones—well, maybe *hormones* wasn't the right word . . . "Surely what we've been through must have changed you."

"Willy—stop. All I want is some love right now."

"I can't—"

"Then make a miracle for me," she said with a seductive voice.

"Lila?" interrupted Elian with a smile. "Miracles are matters of heart," he said. "Some who knew of Jesus's walking on the water might have accused him of not being able to swim. If miracles were all it takes to believe, why was Jesus rejected by most who knew of his miracles? So if you want a real miracle, ask Jesus Christ to change your heart."

Lila barely looked Elian in the eyes, choosing instead to end Elian's comments with a period by looking squarely at me. "Willy, will you ever care for me?"

"Not like Amanda," I said. "She's my forever love."

Lila just stood there, head down, looking like a homecoming queen who'd just been informed of a recount. While Elian and I talked about how God saved us in more ways than one, she had been affecting an amorous denial by studying the speckled blue carpeting, but now she looked up, and it was her turn to feel embarrassed. She looked at me up and down, with an expression that was both dismissive and insulted, then straightened and moved toward the lavatory without another word.

"You look deflated," said Elian to me.

"After all that she has seen, I thought she would finally be open," I said.

"I only have one question," Elian said.

"And what's that?"

"Do you think it's your job to save her?"

"Of course not," I said, but after saying this I realized that I had been trying to be the fixer again. I used to be a columnist, a renowned minister, and a devoted husband, and currently I was flying in an Israeli jumbo jet unemployed, an exile, and with my wife, who didn't want me to be her husband anymore. I guess the fixer had now become the one in need of repair. "The bigger God gets, the smaller I get," I said.

"The smaller we get, the more God can use us," Elian responded.

My heavenly values seemed to me a paltry sum in comparison to where I wanted to be.

"Why me?"

"Why not you?" Elian responded.

"Some modern-day Moses I am."

"Most of the real heroes I know," Elian said, "have been gone for a long time."

"I was supposed to bring the Lord's presence back to the Promised Land. I failed."

"So were you supposed to bring him back, or did he really want to bring you back to him?" Elian asked.

Touché.

"Try finding the word *success* in the Bible—you can't." Elian continued, "You can only find *obedience* and *faith*."

That God doesn't care about our success was an epiphany. So I supposed the reason I was here had less to do with my success in bringing the exiled Americans to Canaan, or in reinstating God's presence in the temple of Jerusalem, and more to do with being an obedient child. I couldn't fix Amanda, so I wasn't successful there. God simply wanted me to heed his voice, to be at his beck and call. To follow him one step at a time, trusting in *his* final destination.

What a paradigm shift. I couldn't even love Amanda without being filled by the spirit of God, who is by definition love. I was completely helpless without God. I felt like a child in his cradle just waiting for Daddy to pick me up and feed me. That's what I was in the company of an all-knowing Father—a child, and very young child. "Give me a bottle, Daddy. Feed me, Daddy. Take me to where you want to go, Daddy. I'm in your hands, and I'll do whatever you want, go wherever you want me to go. Just tell me what to do. That's all I need."

No longer need I fear what to do, or where to go, if Daddy leads me. No worries. Satan? Daddy will take care of him. Amanda? Daddy will take care of her too. All these people needing help? Daddy can do it. *I need you, Daddy.* Daddy will take care of me, comfort me, take me home . . .

Never again will I forget whose child I am, or that I *am* a child. Never will I try to crawl out of my crib to get to a place that can hurt me. Never will I try to fix someone when only Daddy can do that. Never will I feel like taking the keys so that I can drive the car when only Daddy can take me where I need to go. Never will I forget that without Daddy, I'll starve, or I'll get lost, or I'll . . . Never will I forget that Daddy loves me more than anyone else does.

Never will I forget my time in heaven, when Jesus supplanted his purpose in me, to have me simply dwell in his presence and allow him to assume control. Never will I forget how he birthed me into this world to serve him, to spend time with him. Never will I forget who is God, who is Daddy, for as long as I live in this world . . . until he takes me home. Never.

Awakening from my childhood romp, I noticed Amanda rumbling from her fetal position. She sat up and rubbed the sleep out of her eyes.

"Do you mind if I talk with Amanda?" Elian asked.

To which I replied, "Not at all." I trusted my friend to do the right thing. As for me, I closed my eyes to pray, knowing that the next few minutes would answer the question as to whether we would be shot down by those jet fighters. But then again, everything would be OK, because Daddy was now in charge.

ᖾ Chapter Nineteen ᖿ

Amanda watched as Elian moved four seats over to join her. She blinked the slumber from her eyes and nervously adjusted the blanket to cover her phantom legs.

"May I chat with you awhile?" Elian asked.

"No—I mean yes, of course."

He took out a small pocket Bible, opened it to Romans 8:28, and read, "And we know that in all things God works for the good of those who love him, who have been called according to his purpose." He then took Amanda's hand and gently placed it upon the open page.

"That's a promise to you, Amanda."

She wished not to cry again—the wellspring of tears could not possibly be deep enough to cover her broken dam of emotions. So she said nothing.

"You think he's forgotten you," Elian said. "Of course you have every right to question, every right to feel abandoned. However, you must also know that God intends to wipe away every sadness from your life."

"How?" She turned her drained face to look at him for the first time.

"By loving you into eternity. By taking every bad memory and erasing it in heaven."

"And where is he now?" she asked, trying not to sound too apathetic.

Elian's moistened eyes sank into a tender gaze. "He'll never leave you, never forsake you . . ."

Those often-spoken words that once gave encouragement only rubbed against her callused heart, making it all the more hardened. Once, Amanda had preferred to think in poetic language, condensing life through a viewpoint that elicited emotion via sounds and imagery. Rhythm and metaphor enveloped her words, creating an obscure view of life that dulled its harsh reality. Beauty threw thorns. Escapism for the soul through carefully measured lines of poetry based on the beats of the words.

Not anymore. She reasoned now with the tepid discipline of a detached schoolteacher:

Christians were imbued with the notion that belief systems proceed from faith, because that was what initiated relationship with God and others. The relationship of God and humankind could work the other way around, however: people could create belief systems first and then devise faith that would satisfy their need to feel that their life was worthwhile.

Amanda had already prayed to receive Christ because she believed in a system of blessings and promises to those who placed their trust in God, and when the system failed, though her faith lessened, she had already become born again, and so she couldn't just deny God and all that Christian stuff altogether. Which left her still a Christian, with not much else.

Elian didn't quite look the part of a Christian. Not at all pious. He came off too much like someone who would take you up on a dare to skydive without a parachute. Well, maybe not that trusting. Then again, maybe so. He seemed to not care about dying.

Perhaps he cared little about anything—or rather, God didn't care. She felt the blood drain from her head, followed by tensed muscles and a surge of anger. Without thought she grabbed Elian's arms so tight she could feel his bones.

"Since God's a God of miracles, why didn't he save me?" No pat answers would suffice now.

"I can't answer that," Elian replied.

"What do you mean, you can't answer that? God's omnipotent, all-powerful—"

"Who can reason the mind of God?" Elian said quickly.

That was so disgustingly true, she thought. Who can reason God? She realized her grip now, withdrawing it a little embarrassed, more composed, and no less disappointed.

"So, I'm to blindly trust his allowing this . . ." Amanda fell back into her seat. That was it, she thought, that was always it.

Elian refused to take his eyes from her. "Can a blind person help others to see their way?" he continued. "Did Job's suffering not comfort countless people through his account . . . did not Christ's pained separation from his Father on the cross allow believers to know togetherness with God through his Holy Spirit?"

Amanda politely listened. She sighed, rubbed her eyes, and then closed them. When she opened her eyes again, she saw Elian staring at her.

This time Elian grabbed her arms, only lightly. "Can I talk in confidence with you?" he asked with a softer voice. He was breathing deeply.

Amanda responded with another sigh. "Sure."

Elian looked side to side, then spoke quietly. "Someday, Amanda, your loss of limbs will lead others to walk with Jesus Christ. Your scars will heal the open wounds of a lost generation."

She closed her eyes wishing it were so. *Hope is all we have.*

"May I pray for you?" Elian asked.

"Yes," she answered. Though it mattered little.

"Father," Elian whispered, "instill hope within Amanda, that she might again trust your promises over what this temporal world has stolen. Comfort her with your words, and make them hers again."

Elian straightened up and held her hands.

"May I tell you a story?"

She nodded. At least she wouldn't have to talk.

"OK. There was this young lady who lived with her father in the country. One night as the father was tending to chores in the field, a thief broke into the house. The young lady screamed upon seeing the robber, who then came after her. He tore her dress and hit her across the face. She struggled free and ran shoeless out the door, never looking back until stopping about two miles down the road.

"With her bare feet bleeding and being out of breath, she crumbled to the ground weeping. Then she heard the faint clomping of footsteps in the distance behind her. She assumed the thief must be running after her to finish his dastardly job. So she got up, and despite the pain tried running again. But the person behind her ran faster, and soon she could hear his footsteps as clear as though he walked beside her. She resigned her fate to being beaten again, hoping this time she would die.

"The young lady finally stopped and turned, succumbing to the terrible suffering she believed was inevitable. But instead of seeing the thief, she beheld her father. Panting from the long run, he walked over to her, held her hand, and said, 'Dear daughter, I heard you scream, and ran as fast as I could. But you had run so furiously and so far. And though I called out your name time and again, you did not hear me through your panic.'

"The daughter's cares melted in the familiar embrace of her father. And the two wept with the joy of finding each other."

Two tears ran like soothing ointment down Amanda's cheeks, refreshing her insides with warmth. The love she once knew and wanted so desperately to know again—could she find it? Could it—he—find her?

"Amanda, please stop running. Let your Father catch up to you," Elian whispered.

What did she have to lose? She was twenty-eight and had no legs and an ugly face. She wore smelly purple scrubs that were torn from where she ripped out her IV line, and now the only one who could find her was someone blind to all of it.

She'd been running so long. Too long. It would be good, perhaps, to stop and let her heavenly Father come to the rescue. And in some strange way, she'd known that all along.

↶ Chapter Twenty ↷

C louds swirled about like lacy curtains blown by the wind. The sky darkened to a faint lavender, bathed in a wash of prayers. I awoke from my prayerful escape to the suffocating stale air of our cabin, thick with anticipation. We were almost in Israel, minutes to our descent.

I also became heavy with the haunt of deepening gloom. Something was up. I could hear it in my spirit like the clapping of thunderclouds through the sky. Worried lines etched at the corners of Amanda's eyes too.

I reached over in an attempt to console her. Under my sweaty hand I could feel the tremor of Amanda's controlled anxiety over her left forearm. The good news is she didn't pull back. My heart beat double speed. A delicate azure cloud drifted away to reveal the faint sight of a jet fighter hovering over us with its steely stare, breathing out its dishwater-colored smoke. The sky turned blood red, and then infinite shades of gray.

In an instant a jagged spear of fire launched from the jet toward us with demonic accuracy.

"They've launched a missile!" I yelled at the top of my lungs. Before I could finish, a brushstroke of fire rocketed from our plane, cutting through the soggy clouds. A plume of black smoke rose outwardly into a grease-hued sky.

The pilot said nothing, so I got up and raced to the front, then pounded on the door like a madman.

"They're attacking us!"

The silver cockpit door opened slowly. "They've been doing that off and on for about thirty minutes now," answered one of the too-cool pilots.

"And we're OK?" I asked not too politely.

"One of ours is on its way now, Mr. Simon. Then they can duke it out. Ooh—yeah—there she comes now."

A silver knife cut through the butter clouds directly toward the attacking jet. A lightning flash emerged from the Israeli, jet just missing the Russian fighter. Apparently the Russian took the hint, because in the next seconds the fighter jet streamed into the distance with the urgency of a wolf being suddenly charged by a mountain lion.

Finally at ease, I returned to my seat. "It's OK, brothers and sisters!" I yelled. "Some Israeli fighter jets have come to the rescue, and there's no more threat." I could tell Lila wanted to jump out of her seat and squeeze me, but by now Amanda's softer shade of emerald eyes telegraphed a hint of encouragement in my direction.

"Love, are you OK?" I asked her.

"Better," she said. I began moving in her direction until Elian motioned me with a "Hey."

"Yeah?" I responded.

"So what did he say?" he asked.

"What?"

"God—you prayed. What did he say?"

"Oh, as a matter of fact he said something very profound."

"And?"

"I feel that God has something for me to say to all our brothers and sisters on this flight."

Elian lifted his shoulders and opened his eyes wide. "OK, then say it."

There was something I felt compelled to do first—and I hoped my friend would oblige. I pulled out of my bag a small bottle of oil I had used for my dry skin.

"I want you to anoint me."

"Anoint you? Anoint you with what?" He responded like a child thrilled for the chance to do something really bizarre. I gave him the bottle of oil, and he quickly twisted off the cap and demanded I sit down.

"This is serious," I said.

"Then get serious," he responded. Elian reached his dripping finger over my head and pronounced, "Father, in the name of the Son, I anoint my brother Reuben Simon as your deliverer. Fill him with your Spirit now."

My body and mind went numb as I fell back desperately trying to brace my fall against unforgiving chairs on either side. Once grounded, I settled into a comfortable crouch on the floor while recovering from my daze.

Shaking my head and jiggling my cheeks to further my return, I stood up and approached the pilots' door again.

"Sir, Will Simon here again. I hope you don't find me too presumptuous, but to be honest with you, I think I have a word from God for everyone on the plane."

A pause followed. I had overstepped the boundaries, I know. Finally, the pilot spoke.

"OK, you're the man, Mr. Simon—by order of the prime minister. Here's the intercom."

I squeezed the microphone with perhaps the same command as— dare I say—Moses held his staff. *Lord, still my spirit and make me a sounding board.* I remembered how God used to speak to me, after my praying that he would possess my thoughts, and then through sheer childlike confidence declaring whatever came to mind hoping or believing the words came from him and not me.

A friend of mine once asked me if I checked my godly "hunches" against Scripture, to which I said "yes," usually, and I also measured their accuracy by the outcomes of what I presumably heard from God. The way I looked at it, a renewed mind of Christ tended to reflect the words of God almost instinctively.

A cough and a deep swallow later, I was ready.

"Brothers and sisters, this is Reuben. For many months I had been speaking to you over webcasts as part of The Way, God's end-time cyber church.

"Through our Lord's miraculous outpouring of his Spirit, we realized the grace of God as never before, until this world pushed God out.

"Now, my beloved friends, we are the remnant of believers from a nation founded on the principles of Jesus Christ. We were chosen to remain after the rapture, to carry the light of Christ, and to welcome his return.

"God has also called us to lead the battle against Satan and his minions. We are like Gideon's army—small yet endowed with God's strength, destined to face the mightiest army ever to be assembled throughout the world.

"We are Americans by birth, Jews by adoption, and heirs to the throne of grace through Jesus Christ! I fully expect the word of God to be birthed again in the Promised Land, and with it the presence of our Lord will reign again over a new earth.

"Now, brothers and sisters, take up the armor of God. For the greatest warrior in Christ is not one who stands with gun in hand, ready to kill his enemy and claim his territory, but rather the servant of the Lord who wins the battle in the spirit realm is one who kneels with the word of God in his heart, ready to love his enemy and claim God's authority over all."

Somehow I think the angels must have joined in the cheering and clapping, as our small band of three hundred sounded like a thousand colliding hands within a blithesomely rowdy echo of cheers and hoots.

"We're landing now!" shouted the pilot. "Please take your seats!"

Indeed, the eagle was landing!

⸂ Chapter Twenty-One ⸃

"This is insane." Bakr hurried a sip of vodka. "Will Simon alive!" He rolled down the limo's foggy window to throw out his empty glass.

Serge Amato slinked back into his seat. "We thought—"

"You thought!" Bakr's right hand cupped his fist. "You've failed to get rid of that scoundrel."

"In due time we'll—"

"If you don't do it," Bakr snapped, "I will."

"The plane's arriving within the minute, Father," a crouching Amato said.

Of course Bakr knew that. He had delayed his departure to greet this enigma.

The Christian church had become divided, inbred, and self-serving before Reuben and his minions changed all that. Its pastors and priests disenfranchised their flocks by taking control, assuming center stage while making their flocks useless spectators. Millions of Christians went to church to assuage their guilt, appeasing themselves by giving Yahweh their token commitment while countless outside their church walls suffered and died. The demise of Christ's body, his church, all worked out perfectly until Yahweh used this Reuben or Simon character to bring his church together through the web—ingenious, perhaps, though ultimately futile.

Then Reuben escaped certain death. And, with the luck of a cat on its ninth life, he was leading the insurgents to freedom. But Simon's lives stopped at nine—his final breath would soon be exhaled on earth.

"This Reuben character being alive doesn't change our plans, does it?" asked the sheepish Amato.

Bakr practically had to pull his gritted teeth apart. "Christians fit neatly into my plan before his movement," Bakr said. "Their private parochial schools only wanted perfect little boys and girls with good grades; they rejected kids who had behavioral problems. Abused youth and families too poor to afford their prestigious schools didn't fit their convenient standards and therefore were rejected from Christian institutions of higher learning and success. All I needed to do was remove any mention of God from the public schools to capture these impressionable rejects who had been dumped into an overwhelmed system.

"And then there were the derelicts, drug addicts, the emotionally disabled, and mentally ill—outcasts and rejects—they were undesirable, stinky, devalued lowlifes disgusting enough to ward off the mass of Christians who preferred their tidy little men's and women's gatherings to getting their hands dirty. I fed off of those rejects just as the Christian churchgoers fed on doughnuts and crumb cakes. A soul is just a soul to me regardless of their position. All I needed to do was destroy their bodies so that I could take their souls. I accepted them when the Christian church rejected them, Serge. I became their god in drugs, depravity, and despair."

"But there were always Christians groups that fed the poor, took care of the sick, and that sort of thing," Amato said.

"Less than ten percent of those Christians did so," replied Bakr, "while millions suffered. The vast majority of mainstream Christians gave even less of their time to their God in prayer, service, and study. They played right into my hands until Reuben and his mentor buddy Munny Chin challenged them to come together and seek the face of their God. It was because this body of believers came together that Yahweh poured out his spirit and changed the hearts of a people desperate to know him."

Bakr felt his fingernails piercing into his palm. He burned with the fires of hell struggling to calm the heat through soothing thoughts of finally, *finally*, beholding the dead face of Reuben. The question now: How did Yahweh plan to use Reuben? Bakr would need to increase his efforts. That's why his fondest demon stood by his side with its sixty-six legions. The mightiest of all, Baal, with his chiseled chest, spanned five feet wide, his arms rippled, and his legs were like that of a tyrannosaurus rex.

Baal's entire form exuded blistering heat, though most intimidating was his face—lava-colored eyes and rows of razor teeth lining his gaping mouth. Bony spikes covered his body in place of skin. All his features were veiled within a spiritual cloak invisible to humans.

The rain-scrubbed air on the tarmac could not mask the smoky underworld that seeped through the physical with a stench of burning sulfur.

They waited, and plotted. Baal had won battles against Yahweh. Human choice could not be denied, even by Yahweh. And humankind, left to its own desires, always chose self.

"There it is," one of the guards called out. Like a hot silver dome breaking through the snowy clouds, the plane dipped—an eagle in hunt. Anticipation waited on both fronts, yet only Bakr knew of the real outcome. So-called biblical scholars knew only half the story.

Reuben's flight touched down hard, and then rolled itself toward the streaming band of police cars and fire engines. Israeli military had been ordered to protect its entry. So, too, Bakr's line of vehicles headed its way.

They would finally meet.

#

"Reuben is in the plane," joked Hudson. "Showtime."

All but a few now stood on the tarmac inundated with press corps. Those of us remaining at the plane's doorway deeply breathed in the smell of freedom.

"You go first, Hudson, and then Lila, then Elian, and I'll carry Amanda," I said.

Carrying a willing Amanda felt wholly wonderful. I could have sworn her scars had faded somewhat, though she insisted otherwise, and of course that would be impossible. It was more likely they didn't matter as much to me now. My heart gave way to the tenderness of a blind kiss, a flower's drifting smell, and all things beautiful beyond the pale of sight.

Amanda for her part went limp, and given that she no longer fought my touch, I considered that a victory worth celebrating. I felt like Clark Kent trying to win Lois Lane's affections. I was a little unraveled, but still looking after her, hoping she'd find her Superman.

Noises of screeching vehicles, swarming people, and clicking cameras filled the space at the foot of our stairs as we finally touched Israeli soil.

"Reuben, Reuben!"

I strained to see whom the hoarse voice belonged to in the distance.

A heftily built man whose red-bearded face darted in and out of the crowd hurried toward me with arms gleefully open. He unabashedly kissed both Amanda and me. "My friends, this is the moment for which I prayed," he shouted while compressing the air out of my lungs with a bear hug.

It finally came to me through his raspy voice. "David?"

"Yes. Yes!" He reluctantly let go. My only Israeli friend—he was taller than I expected, with a slightly protruding belly and forearms through rolled-up sleeves that reminded me of Popeye's. "I'm pleased to punch you—"

"As pleased as punch." I corrected him again—wondering if David was really so clueless about these colloquialisms or just being funny.

"So good to see you, my friend!" I continued, hoping he wouldn't bruise a rib with another hug.

"Here," David motioned me to put Amanda in a waiting wheelchair.

"You know what this is about, my brother and sister?" David asked, his square face and large frame reminiscent of some professional wrestlers you'd see on TV.

"Well, I'm not sure what you're getting at," I replied. "I did come as a messenger, I believe."

"Yes, yes, and . . .?" Bundles of energy raced from my friend's brain to his shaking hands, yet I'm not so sure he was completely aware of how to control his brain's synapses to stop the wild gestures. He always seemed a man of impulse, which is perhaps why he could so fluidly interpret God's messages. Contrast that to his precise enunciation—maybe because he wanted to ensure those words always came out right.

So what was I to say? David continued wringing his hands waiting for a response.

"His presence, Reuben," he finally answered. "He has to return to complete the cycle," David said.

"What cycle?" I replied.

"The cycle of redemption. To right that which was wronged," David said with an awkward touchdown dance.

"To start anew," I surmised.

"Tell me, brother," David insisted. "Why must God start anew?"

Not knowing his strength, David shook me like one of those old magic eight balls, as if wanting the right answer to come through my mouth.

He couldn't wait for my response. "He has to start over! The cycle of redemption means everything must be made new, including this world."

Starting over—was that what this was all about? But how? "By destroying the earth?"

"Yes," answered a velvety smooth voice from behind me, followed by a sudden cold that chilled my bones, and the most intriguing scent of burning brush.

I turned to see a striking Adonis man adorned in an Armani suit with a blazing red tie and Windsor knot pressed against his thick neck. He had chiseled features and jet-black hair, skin the perfect blend of topaz, and the darkest eyes I'd ever seen.

The corners of his eyes were creased with disgust. "The God of Moses wanted to kill all his people," he said. "All the people whom he freed from Egypt—he wanted to simply wipe them out, start over, because they didn't do what he wanted them to do. Is that your God, Will Simon? A God that kills his people just because they aren't perfect?"

"Don't talk with him, Reuben!" David shouted. "He's not human." David began to lunge at the man until I reached out to restrain him.

The man's entourage dressed in business black stood stoically in wait, though I sensed more around the man. Something within the sensory depths of my spirit sent out flashing red signals. Discernment. An evil presence reeked of the familiar decay of hell that surfaced as the odor of mold upon the earth. As if rage permeated the aerial unknown, ready to pounce.

"Are you—?"

"Chief Priest Muhammad Bakr of the Universal Church," he answered as I received his cold hand grasp. "It's indeed an honor to meet today's Moses, or so I've heard. As the story goes, Moses had a meeting with God, or shall I say with a talking burning bush? Pray tell, did you have an encounter with the big guy?"

Was I looking Satan in the eyes? I had expected to instantly hate him—to revile the agony and destruction he spewed upon the earth. Instead, I saw in this man the same emptiness I once witnessed in the schoolyard bully who taunted me as a child—a person who fed off people's fear. I would *not* fear him. I would instead pity his lost soul, making him revile me all the more.

"I know you. You're the Antichrist."

Bakr cupped his mouth in muffled laughter. "I'm the father of this world—don't you know, Will Simon, or shall I say Reuben?"

"I know Jesus Christ, and therefore I know love," I said.

"Love!" he retorted. "Love as in abandoning you and every godforsaken believer in this world? Love as in taking your wife's limbs? That's love?"

Bakr walked over to a trembling Amanda, riveting his stare onto her glazed eyes like a cat in hunt, then whispered loud enough for me to hear, "Amanda, I feel your pain. Come with me, my dear, and I will heal your scars. Your limbs . . ." He tenderly stroked her stumps. "These can be as new. You can be whole again. Come with me, dear—"

"Enough," I said. "She's not going with you."

Bakr remained fixated on Amanda. "My dear daughter," he said smoothly, "I can give you the father's love that has been cruelly denied you. The love you so desperately want. I have the finest doctors and scientists from around the world. I've proven that I can perform miracles. We can now grow out new limbs from tissue cells; our best plastic surgeons can make you more beautiful than before—"

Her torso bobbed up and down in some palsied convulsion, and she shook her head in a frenzy. I thought she might fall to the ground in a grand mal seizure.

"Stop!" I insisted.

"Let her decide," Bakr shot back. "She's not a prisoner. She can choose. Her faith has been pointless, the suffering—the rejection . . ."

"Leave her." My anger spilled over.

Amanda lifted her hand in a halting gesture toward me. "No, Will." She tensed.

"I have nothing," she said, her face drained. She looked away for an endless span of time without the slightest hint of emotion.

"And so I have nothing else to lose," she said, her body deflated.

She then looked straight at Bakr with that steely determination I'd not seen for so long and said, "Yet I have everything to gain. I choose Christ."

I knelt down and reached my arms around her, and what's more—much more—she wrapped her arms around me.

"Fools!" Bakr stood and faced me again. "If that's the level of your stupidity, you can have your godless life—you've been left with nothing."

"You left the world with nothing!" My spittle landed on Bakr's pressed shirt as I yelled nose to nose with the chief priest. "Your false religion denied Jesus Christ his authority, lifting his protective grace from over this world."

"Bull," Bakr seethed through clenched teeth. "You insurgents always believe what you want. It was your God's judgment that caused millions to die."

"Death is your legacy, not God's." Was it my surge of adrenaline or a supernatural infilling that gave me such courage? Maybe both.

Standing face-to-face with Bakr, the hot air from his nostrils snorted out like a wounded bear and at once inflated my courage. I felt like a bull, hooves to the ground, ready to charge.

Not more than ten seconds thereafter it felt as if I'd stepped into a freezer, my heart squeezed as though someone had placed a twenty-pound bag of ice over my chest.

"Your God's presence is gone—and he intends to destroy this world, but my people intend to save it," Bakr continued.

He turned to the reporters who had been kept at a distance and raised his pitch in a statesman's voice for all to hear.

"Mr. Simon, aka Reuben, is here to help the so-called God of Abraham destroy the world, just as he destroyed a church in New York City murdering hundreds. Noble warrior indeed—this man is no more than another crazed murderer who feels that he's on a mission from God to execute judgment on a fallen world."

He wiped his sweaty upper lip and then threw his handkerchief to the ground. I began to reach for him, wanting to punch the living daylights out of him, just as Elian grabbed my arm.

"Don't engage him, brother," Elian said. "Let God prove his faithfulness through this as he promised."

"There's a presence here, Elian," I said while striving to breathe.

Elian place his hand over my chest. "I bind the spirit of hell from Reuben."

Bakr turned his black-holed stare on me, then whispered in my ear, "I have legions at my command, kid. You and your prison escapees might feel safe now, but in short order all of you will be burnt offerings—to me."

With photographers frenetically clicking shots and newspeople pleading for some words, Bakr leapt in through the open limousine door and slammed it. His line of vehicles sped like scurrying ants toward an awaiting jet.

As they departed, the oppressive unseen storm that had pressed its piercing cold against my chest began to dissipate. I could take full breaths again. The stifling sense of futility left with it.

Elian walked up to a group of huddled believers in prayer over Amanda.

"You embraced the Father," he said to Amanda.

"I stopped running," she said.

Elian smiled and rested his hand upon her shoulder. "You overcame Bakr's temptation. I'm so proud of you. You have no idea how much that means."

Elian then turned toward me, digging his eyes into my soul. "You didn't back down," he said to me.

"He's my all."

"As he gave you his all," Elian said, his tone more subdued. "One can't receive the free life God offers without first forsaking the false security of this world."

The warmth of my Lord's encouragement melted into my heart like hot butter on a warm muffin. Elian spoke the truth.

As I stood there pondering on the lost, conflicted world, I thought of God's glory when I first bathed in the clear streams of Jesus's living waters in heaven. I'd traveled a long way to get to that pure oasis, and my dreams of heaven had appeared so distant that when I stood upon its soft field of gold I could hardly grasp it. I did not know then that heaven had been placed in my heart, somewhere back in that grandiose obscurity beyond the imagination, where the darkness of this world faded under the light of Christ.

I believed in the pure light, the bright future that recedes in a barren world. Once hope eluded me, but now, no matter what, I would stand taller, stretch out my arms to God farther . . . and once again touch the face of Jesus.

༺ Chapter Twenty-Two ༻

Ticktock, ticktock . . . the countdown to the end had begun. It had been several weeks since my direct encounter with Bakr, after which his allies launched their missiles against Israel. Their warriors invaded shortly thereafter.

Smoke-laden skies drizzled with sulfuric wisps of deadly chemicals. Now the world dragged on minus the sights and sounds of birds and animals. Marauding scavengers hunted for valuables on human remains stacked like firewood. People gnawing on organic waste flashed their russet-stained teeth through snarls. No one smiled.

Armageddon, the consummate battle between good and evil, would take place sometime in the future, the very near future.

Our drive toward Megiddo took us past rusted tanks and other stranded military vehicles imbedded in the dense forest roads like giant antique ornaments on Christmas trees, left as monuments of the 1967 Six-Day War in which Egyptian forces invaded Israel.

Modern-day Russian tanks had come through Egypt only three weeks ago, tried the same, and they too lay disabled along the roadsides. Left as play toys, making a mockery of man and combat.

At least 200,000 lifeless bodies now made up the death toll, mostly Israeli forces. World Security Alliance (WSA) forces casualties were surprisingly low. Jets and helicopters swarmed like engined hornets overhead, and I heard an occasional boom that elicited images of giants pounding their fists into the ground. I wished to think of it that way, and not reflect on the hundreds of bodies scattered as debris from nuclear fallout. Ragged children with patches of gray or peeling skin lumbered in the streets. Was there anything not infected with the disease of war?

Words circled in my head to relieve the sounds and smells of war. *Hate. Love. Fate. Choice.* I tried to fit them like a crossword puzzle into some mindful escape. None of the spiraling chaos around me made sense.

After leaving the war-torn Jerusalem, we traveled for hours to the final battle stage as explained in the Bible, praying God would manifest his power there. Which words now fit this field of blood called Tel Megiddo upon which we camped? *Ancient. Epic. The end.* Or was this the beginning? Sometimes it's hard to tell the difference.

Blooming flowers everywhere emitted their lovely fragrances mixed with the intermittent acrid smell of smoke-laden skies. Seven ancient cities lay entombed underneath the soil of Megiddo, fertilized with human compost comprised of fallen soldiers—ancient Egyptians, Canaanites, Judeans, and those from the Ottoman Empire. Gideon famously trampled over the defeated Midianites in this very place.

Nobody survived here anymore. Not the former soldiers who wrote letters to their wives, not their brave commanders with false notions of victory, not the scribes who recorded history that most forgot. Everybody but our three hundred lone survivors from the United States of America was long dead. Megiddo was a vision of portending doom, a junkyard of hubris mixed with flesh, a killing field that fell deceptively silent except for the pesky fleas that danced mercilessly around our ears.

I tried recording our last day's experiences in my journal, but found no taste for it. Words alone were dead. Coupled together they evoked the stories that gave them life. Stories left behind by those who died—if anyone cared. What truly remained were the imprints those lives made in the grand scheme of God's plan. His word, God's words, mattered most, and the most welcoming of these were: "Well done, my good and faithful servant."

We sat chilled by the morning air overlooking the ashen-colored ruins of Mount Megiddo. Vast plains below served as home to countless prior battles. The scene before us now appeared more like an Illinois farm field, with us living atop a raised circular ashtray of ancient rubble.

Would our flame be extinguished? Would we join the layered ashes of fallen Egyptians, Romans, and Assyrians that fought here before? Armageddon—the final battle. And we were just waiting for it to happen. And who would record our battle? Why, I suppose, God would record it in his book.

My cell phone rang. "Reuben, David. The commander here in Jerusalem said their intelligence knows of WSA troops heading your way. They'll arrive in about two hours."

"Do they know we're here?" I asked.

"Yes. They know that you and your three hundred so-called insurgents are camped out at Megiddo, and they're coming after you."

"We've got enough rations from the Israelis to sustain us for awhile, David, but no arsenal," I replied.

"You should have accepted the general's offer to provide you with military cover," David said with an unusually gruff pitch. "Tell me again why you did not?"

"I prayed about it, David," I replied. "I felt God wanted us here by ourselves." I prayed now that my sense of God's voice was correct, with not a little tinge of doubt, mind you. Elian had agreed with me. I prayed we were both correct.

"They've got air cover," David continued, "and they just overran the Israeli forces as if they were schoolchildren playing like soldiers. You've got to get out of there now!"

Elian remained perched on a countryside hill to my right, Amanda to my immediate left. I wished to share my angst with Elian—but of course, he just placidly sat there. As for Amanda, I wished to not further alarm her, yet she balled up like a pill bug after hearing David's warning through the phone.

"OK, thanks, David. I'm not sure where we could go. Let me talk this over with Elian and Amanda."

"Don't tarry, my friend," David warned. "These guys broke through the Israeli barrier north of here, and without any arms your group would be, as they say, sitting quacks."

"Ducks."

"What?"

"Never mind," I said. "So why haven't they just bombed us if they know our position?" I asked.

"No telling why," David said. "They may have already tried—only God knows."

"Shalom," I said before hanging up.

"You OK?" I asked Amanda.

"Yeah," she said. "I don't really fear death anymore."

I moved closer to Elian. "There's a WSA battalion moving in our direction. We've got to get out of here now."

"To where?" Elian said.

"We'll take a roundabout way toward Jerusalem and hope to connect with a friendly Israeli army."

Elian lowered his head, briefly closing his eyes. "Don't you think they're tracking us right now? With that helicopter that flew overhead."

"So what are you saying?"

"They can find us anywhere we flee to. We're like Gideon's army, right?" Elian waited for my response.

"You're thinking we stand firm?" I asked in disbelief.

Elian placed his hand against my back and tensed his jaw. "Where's the real battle?"

"Here, Armageddon—the last battle's going to take place right here according to Bible prophecy."

I checked in with Amanda to see her peering misty-eyed over the camouflaged pitched tents of the group we now affectionately termed the United Soldiers of America—the USA—prayer warriors. They congregated as pilgrims under clearing skies unaware of the menacing cloud approaching them.

My heart went out to these nomads. I needed to protect them, somehow. Right now they were sitting ducks, or "quacks," as David would say.

"What if the battle isn't in the physical, Reuben?" Elian asked.

"What do you mean? Troops with guns are coming after us—"

"And we don't have guns. We have faith, and we have God," Elian replied.

Chapter Twenty-Two

"I know what you're getting at. This is foremost a spiritual battle?"

"Right," he said.

Amanda rubbed my calf after Elian and I stood. "This is about judgment day—it's the final battle where Jesus shows up in his glory, right?" I said.

"It's about relationship," Elian responded. "It's always been about God restoring relationship with his people."

"Why, then, do you think we're going through this living hell?"

Elian sighed. "God's presence held together all that is good—you know that." He picked a dandelion and blew its seeds to the wind. "The flower's dead, right?"

"Yeah?"

"Not really. The stem continues to live through its seed, and eventually through its progeny that take root," Elian said.

Allegory time again. "Get to your point, please."

"Think of God as the creator, the foundation of that dandelion. That dandelion represents his church—his children with whom he relates. When God removed his church, he left behind some seeds—you and your team, and the Jews who believe in Jesus Christ.

"He then planted these remnant believers in this fertile land, the Promised Land. So together all of these human implants could take root, sprouting forth a fresh relationship with God."

"I've not felt close to God in a long time," Amanda interjected.

"Precisely," Elian said. "You could say that it hasn't been since the garden of Eden that there's been an intimate relationship between God and humankind on earth. Now you see him dimly—"

"Then face-to-face," I said. "That Scripture is about seeing God in heaven."

"Maybe not. Perhaps we'll see him face-to-face on earth," Elian said. Amanda peered over my shoulder to the empty fields behind us.

"So what does this newly formed relationship look like?" asked Amanda.

"We'll see soon enough," I replied. "But for now, let's pray."

Elian and I knelt down as the three of us banded together, seeking God's wisdom and strength.

Before we could finish our meditation with the Lord, an epiphany rang through my head as clearly as if someone had placed a speaker system inside my brain. By an epiphany I mean a sudden spiritual portal through God's perspective—if I may be so bold—to transcend all reason in submission to my absolute confidence in what I was hearing. Without any doubt whatsoever I knew that we needed to take a stand.

Gideon's name kept playing over and over in my head. Then I began to remember his story, how he started with thousands of soldiers until God whittled the numbers down to only the most dedicated of them—three hundred of the finest soldiers, the same number as our remnant from America. What separated them from the rest, I deduced, was their willingness to do even absurd things in obedience to God's voice. In fact, instead of using weapons, Gideon's army made loud noises to defeat their enemy, or something like that. It dawned on me that we could hide within the remains of Mount Megiddo's pinnacle, and then, crazy as it might sound, shout at the top of our lungs for God to engage us in the spirit battle against the WSA army.

A rush of adrenaline drove my new-felt rush of faith that surged up to the raised goose bumps across my arms. I picked up my bullhorn and with a General Patton pose declared to the USA, "Brothers and sisters, we have the high ground. Some WSA forces are on their way, presumably to take us.

"They have worldly weapons, but our weapons are of God, and they are mighty for the pulling down of strongholds. I want you to conceal yourselves as best you can behind the stones when you see the WSA soldiers marching. And then when I speak through this bullhorn again, it will be a call for you to shout praises to our Lord. And, dear ones, I expect God to show up!"

I wheeled Amanda around the camp as the three of us spread the word. Our brothers and sisters scurried about to gather their wares and fold up their tents. Hudson, beacon of mercy that he was, was assigned the task of helping the less able-bodied. Though, his new companion, Lila, followed him like a lost puppy. *God protect Hudson from her seduction.*

Within an hour or so, every person had hid behind the mask of fallen relics that served as nameless tombstones for the ancients that had fallen before us. The question remained as to whether this place would serve as our burial ground—or as our victory mount.

The tiny insect-like stampede of troops down the dusted road in the distance was the final thing I saw before closing my eyes. I wasn't just praying; I was *expecting* a word that would lead to a story for the ages.

ᴄ Chapter Twenty-Three ᴅ

"**L**ord, open my spiritual eyes to see what's going on," I said while sitting atop a pebbly knoll. I tried finding a smoother patch of dirt on which to lie down, close my eyes, and drift into the surreal realm of God's kingdom. After finding one, I lay down. At first, the uneven ground poked me like a bad shiatsu massage, yet after praising God for a few minutes I rested on the most billowy cotton imaginable, completely oblivious to my surroundings.

Then my eyes beheld sights beyond words—things for which no words existed, as though watching a dreamlike film in 4D viewing, with an empathic understanding of everything around me. My otherworldly sensing became a pulsating organ as effective at identifying life and reality as the eyes, ears, and nose—as feeling as the skin. It suppressed my physical nature so that the supernatural could have absolute dominion for just a time as this.

Celestial figures raced through the spirit world in a supernal place unmarked by human fingerprints, leaving behind an after-gust felt only faintly in the physical. They resonated as impressions to humans—of well-being from the angels, and of oppression from the demons.

Unlike other days, today would determine the eternal fate of humankind, of heaven or of hell. Life or death. With or without God. This I knew as surely as I knew that Jesus would return.

These speeding spirit bodies that inhabited the ethereal space clearly spoke a language all their own. They battled in a space where love or hate existed as tangibly as a kiss or a slap might be in the world of matter. Unlike the physical world, where appearance largely identified someone, these beings' distinctiveness came from their character—truthful or dishonest, genuine or manipulative, caring or thoughtless, courageous or cowardly, and so forth. In the physical, it would be similar to a person giving off good or bad vibes.

The angelic spirits traveled toward Megiddo through Christ's life-giving words that fueled their journey. Conversely, hatred and all expressions thereof charged the demons as they fed off each others' vitriol, thereby strengthening their resolve. Each opposing group raced to the battlefield in opposition to the other.

Those humans below who heeded Christ's expressions obtained comfort, similar to the same way that an aroma of freshly baked bread speaks of home and peace.

Lingering trails of confusion issued from the demons eliciting baffled expressions on the faces of angels, much like the angst one senses after waking from a deep sleep in the bottomless, unscalable pit of despair. The angels writhed with each expression from their adversaries just as a physical human would squirm after being called a do-nothing, stupid, ugly—you get the point—just as anyone would suffer through abuse.

Soft perfumes of flowers in bloom lingered after the angels' flights. Demons could not shake off the repugnant smell of rotting debris. They emitted lingering aromas in what I might experience if laying within a field comprised of fragrant blooms and crushed onions. A mix, part flower field and garbage dump.

Two diametrically opposed forces, and only one would gain the power to change everything.

Though he walked in human form, Jesus Christ could still sense all of it, communicating with his army of angels while encamped in the flesh. I could not see his face but he was most certainly Jesus. He never really left the invisible arena of the spirit. He remained ever present with those he called his children, yet he communed with his angels through a spiritual effusion that flowed as mist into the spirit world. And that mist blushed with colors was inhaled by the angels, making them glow and expand likes sparks fanned into flames

I faintly saw above me the first two levels of heaven as lush firmaments joined by a cascading waterfall, and then from the first level a waterfall poured down upon the earth as crystalline angels traveled through the waterfall. Hell appeared as a black hole, through which the demons struggled to move upward through a kind of sludge. Jesus viewed the gathering of opposing forces that timelessly traveled through either the first level of heaven or the abysm of hell toward the consummate battleground of the spirits.

"Gabriel, my beloved, stay far from the fallen ones," Jesus said in a thundering voice to his beloved angel. Only the glorified angels could hear Jesus, through the deepest realm of the holies. The demons seemed deaf to his words.

"Yes, Master," Gabriel answered as he pierced the vacuum of space all around him. "We're trying our best to avoid their curses. They speak the law against us. They lie, saying that your love cannot change the course of humankind's desire for self-control."

"They are condemned by their own words," said Jesus. "My servant Reuben leads a mighty army. If they hold firm, we will prevail."

"And if not?" asked Gabriel.

"Then my enemy will rule for a thousand years," Jesus replied. "We must get there first. Faithfulness is all."

Faithfulness is all. What a curious thing for Jesus to say, I thought. In these environs appeared a triangular struggle—a ménage a trois—between the angels, demons, and their masters in a place constructed not as heaven. I knew this because I had once glimpsed heaven.

No, this place of spiritual battle was not heaven, or hell. It resembled a pattern of crossing worlds that I had imagined from computer animations—an ethereal contrast of brightness against darkness. The few colored beams that illuminated the spiritual beings along their journeys intersected degrees of latitude and longitude along varying shades of lighted paths, like dust particles moving through a beacon being pushed by the wind.

And then it hit me. I witnessed a bridge between heaven and earth, or between hell and earth for the demons. I would call it the spiritual grid because it was made of waves of light that broke into different colors through their points of intersection. And then this high-tech-looking field of battle quaked with an indiscernible roar.

The angel Raphael (I knew him by name, for they all declared their names) butted up against a demon spewing words of anger.

"Hearken unto the word of the Lord," Raphael said to the demon. "You have no authority over the chosen!" The angel's words ushered from his mouth as particles like molecules that clustered together into an indescribable form that grew with every utterance, and then these declarations served to glue the demon's mouth shut. The muted beast writhed in fury because of its now-paralyzed tongue. "Well done, Raphael," Jesus said. "The fallen angels strive to forget my truth."

"Lord," Raphael said, "I delight each time your truth binds the fallen ones and frees the deceived to hear your word again."

Jesus sent a fresh breeze to cool the heated air between the demon and Raphael. Michael dove to join his brother Raphael in the fight; however, Jesus called him off.

"Continue forward, Michael—to Megiddo. Raphael has turned the demon's anger against himself."

"Yes, Master," said Michael.

"Now, the first to reach Megiddo will be the first to stake their territory."

"And if we fail to reach Megiddo first?" Michael asked.

"Then, beloved, the accusations and lies of our enemies will cause the hearts of some in Reuben's army to turn away, and the forces of my adversary will be emboldened to kill them."

"You shall declare your righteousness on earth for the first time since you declared it on the cross?" asked Michael.

"Yes," Jesus answered, "only, this time I will speak it over those accursed by evil."

"Judgment," Michael said.

"Conviction of sin leads to death; my forgiveness gives life," Jesus replied. "Judgment declared at the dawn of time will be meted out to all who deny me once I remove my protective covering."

Michael expanded his eagle-like wings and puffed out his chest while shouting praises to the Lamb of God. With bent head he spoke to Jesus through the ethereal world, "Your righteousness, Master; we hear only your righteousness."

Indeed the angels could hear only Jesus's words, and of course me. I couldn't see his face in the physical, though. A thick haze cloaked everything around him except a faint impression of his figure. He waved his hand as though pulling a curtain back to reveal the spiritual grid apart from the world, exposing two dimensions of existence as separate as water is to air. Words ushered from his mouth into the spiritual grid.

Jesus spoke words of comfort, of the free-flowing rivers of refreshing peace, which always brought forth his presence regardless of whether he stood in the flesh or freely in the spirit. Truly Jesus's words formed living waters that the angels drank to refresh themselves, and whereas the angels' words took all kinds of forms, only the river of life exuded from Jesus. All of God's words spoke life and renewal, causing everything in their path to thrive as expressed by those brilliant colors of his light.

"Bring my grace to the world that I might have *koinonia* fellowship with my children again. As it was in the very beginning," Jesus proclaimed to his angelic warriors, "so it shall be in the end!"

"No separation," Michael said.

"Face-to-face," Jesus affirmed.

The forces of good and evil converged within a span of only minutes before reaching the humans. I could see WSA soldiers marching within range of firing their missiles at the USA army. Multitudes galloped on horses. Tanks preceded at least five thousand soldiers carrying M360 laser-directed machine guns and backpacks loaded with mega-grenades. Grinding truck engines strained to pull the latest "smart" launch missiles, able to visualize their targets through robotic sensors.

"Kill!" the war-painted soldiers shouted in perfect cadence. Lock, step, lock, step . . . A smattering of demons encouraged them with words of hatred. And, unlike the angels who breathed warmth and assurances, the demons' foul words turned into crawly figures I could best describe as a swarm of murky maggots that devoured anyone who came in contact with them . . . unless . . . unless the angels spoke the words of God, and then the living waters engulfed the maggots until they disappeared.

Soon the legions of demons speedily journeying toward the WSA combatants would meet them, forming an almost invincible killing force. At this rate the legions with the so-called Baal would get there first, empowering the WSA with the determination they would need to win.

As I learned from the various words spoken, unless the angels could slow the demons somehow, the victory would go to the enemy. God's full presence would again be denied. As happened in the garden of Eden— generations lost to sin. "Would human will again choose self?" asked one angel.

"Lord, let us pass the demons. Blind them to their destination," implored Michael. "We must deafen the elect to the demons' lies by shielding them with your truth!"

Stillness filled the void between the now-separating teams of angels and demons. They split from each other like a flock of birds. One side headed toward the WSA, led by Baal; the angels hurried to the USA army, headed by Michael.

The angels lifted their heads for a word from Jesus, as they appeared to always do before going into battle. This struggle would determine the fate of humankind—the demons shouted as such. And the angels were losing the race to Armageddon.

"Lord." Michael's voice rose with the warming sun that now blended the worlds of spirit and of matter. "Do not tarry. Speak your truth, Master, so that all might bow."

A mighty wind pushed down upon the demons from heaven, unraveling their V-formation and making them scatter like frenzied birds.

"I declare the righteousness of God unto the world," said Jesus in thunderous tones. "Now hear, you mighty army of Reuben: My grace shall be your all, for my all is love. Now, declare that which is rightfully mine!"

The demons flew in confused circles.

The USA army must have heard the rumbling in their spirits because they cheered for no reason but for the pure celebration of God's power.

Crackling thunder roared from the heavenly realm. It struck momentary terror throughout the demonic ranks.

The angels sped faster with each word spoken by Jesus until they finally passed their foes.

The demons continued their crazed dance of the scattering beasts until Baal regained his composure enough to speak. "Yahweh has forsaken you. He has forsaken the world." On and on he went, filling his ranks once again with bravado. Now composed behind their leader, the demons raced ahead with blurring speed.

"Manifest," Baal shouted as ashes swirled like metal shavings to the demons' magnetic aero-forms. And so the demons began forming flesh to spirit. They morphed into sinewy frames and skins of varying pigments, from weathered bronze to flesh colors. They developed burly figures at least ten feet tall. Their eyes burned with rage and they gnashed their teeth, and horned protrusions as sharp as knives dotted their bodies.

"We are ready, Lord," said Michael.

Now it was the angels' turn.

"Let us make the angels in the image of man," declared Jesus. With these words the angels spread forth their essence to take in the radiant light that shone gloriously from heaven.

A blazing beacon poured intensely over the angels as they formed flesh from spirit, their bodies shades of precious stones and metals—bronze, silver-gold, pearl, blue azure—and donned breastplates of iron. Their eyes glistened like diamonds; with beaming faces they shouted sounds of joy and resolute purpose.

They drew vapory swords that reflected the spoken words of God through some visceral transfer that manifested as a mirrored expression of Jesus's own sentiments. As though the sound of Jesus's own thoughts formed into words that morphed into the images of these words.

The best I could describe it would be like imagining something—say, the most wonderful spring setting with flowing fields of flowers against the backdrop of a baby-blue sky, and then taking a photograph of it and then watching the photograph come to life. Through my enhanced awareness I could sense each facet of the Lord's expressions. *Oh God, how mighty are your ways!*

Suddenly clouds retreated into balls of fading smoke. The sun, a yellow orb, gave way to a partial covering of darkness.

"The hand of God," said Michael.

God breathed the wind toward earth, pushing every spirit closer toward the battleground. Their backs bent in response to the pushing force like falling parachutists. Faster and faster they fell. The angels first, heavy from God's abundant words—words of judgment and of righteous anger.

The demons followed their opposing angels, impeded because they could not travel through the space of God's impartation. Their descent continued only after the expressions of God dulled into a fading echo.

The demons' calls of destruction were emboldened by the shouts of the WSA soldiers who shouted, "Kill, kill!" The men continued to rant with words of hatred, further enlivening the demons.

"Save us, Lord," came the cries of the USA army—which strengthened the angels' flight. "Glory be the Lord of Lords, the great I Am, Lord Jesus Christ," came varying forms of silent prayer from the believers, which, when ushered into the spiritual grid, caused the angels' frames to expand with renewed energy.

With each word of praise from the USA army, responsive shouts from heaven came as declarations of God's providence, and God answered with impartations of his assurance to the USA believers. I could picture the prayers of the saints rising toward heaven, and God's outstretched hands holding a cup into which the prayers flowed. Once deposited in the cup, these prayers turned into God's living water. And when the cup became full, he poured the water of life over the praying souls, who were then filled with wonderful peace and comfort.

"This water is my presence," Jesus whispered in my ear —how he did so I have no idea because he was nowhere in sight.

Then a bombastic boom burst throughout the environs, shocking those above and below. The skies literally shook, and a clear glassy opening between the spirit world and the earth became visible.

Through this translucent porthole, the spirits descended unto Megiddo for the final battle of spiritual dominion.

☙ Chapter Twenty-Four ❧

I awoke from my incredible vision in a fright, unaware as to whether I dreamt it all or truly viewed the spirit world—though I really knew the answer because it appeared as real as my former near-death experience in heaven. It mattered not as I looked upward in response to crackling thunder.

"Amanda—look!" I shouted. In the distance—through the sky—hordes of gargantuan beings swarmed downward. "Oh, God Almighty!"

Amanda spread her arms, tilted her head back as far as her neck could go, and grinned as wide as her cheeks would allow. She flopped backward, oblivious to the pebbly dirt, and began laughing hysterically.

"Isn't it wonderful!" she exclaimed with a thousand-mile stare into the sky. I looked over to Elian for his response only to find him kneeling, his hands covering his face as tears leaked through the cracks of his fingers.

"What's going on?" No answer.

Marvelously sculpted hulks continued rocketing through the sky, some adorning glistening armor. Others had sagging leathery skins and bloated faces that spewed out masses of small crawly creatures toward the angel-like figures. The parasitic insects engulfed their victims, eventually devouring them into nothingness.

I much preferred the sight of the brilliantly adorned creatures breathing out varying shades of colored light that pressed against the guts of the beasts, causing some of those decadent creatures to cringe in agony before dissolving into a swarm of the pests they had formerly breathed. The ravenous fleas or flies devoured their flesh until their once-threatening frames blew away as ashes in the wind.

Opposing sides chided each other in a swirling flight of warriors. Marvelous and frightening.

"Angels and demons," Amanda surmised.

"They fight with the expressions of their spirit, Reuben—words of truth," came a familiar voice. A massive shadow towered many feet beyond me.

"Rhome!" My guardian angel.

Rhome spread his wings over Elian, Amanda, and me to guard us from the pressing heat of the tormenting demons.

"That which you see is what the world calls a war of words—the spoken language of a person's core, or heart," Rhome said. "The very essence of good and evil is imparted from the spirit to the flesh."

The war raged about us as I dwelled on Rhome's statement.

"How can mere words do that?" I asked. "As kids we'd say that sticks and stones can break my bones, but words can never hurt me."

"Words spoken from the depth of one's spirit can take root in another," explained Rhome, "and when they do, those words from the shared core of that person transform their character, their soul. That which comes out of a person reflects that which resides within their heart. Truth, from the angels—the shades of light you see—convicts the demons of their fallen state, turning their depravity upon themselves."

"And they die?" I asked, while warriors slithered through the thick air like forms in a lava lamp.

"They cannot remain in the world once their depravity is revealed to them," continued Rhome.

"Which kills them?"

"Not a death as you know it," Rhome further explained. "Believing the lie sickens the soul. The demons' spirits are already dead to God, meaning they have no relationship with him. A sickened soul leads to anguish, which degrades the body."

"And the angels," I asked. "Why do they vanish?"

"They accept the lies of the enemy as truth, and once accepted these lies take root, defiling them until they can remain no longer in the fight," Rhome said.

"Vanquished?"

"No, they are rendered useless in the world, and so they return to God so they might be restored." Rhome watched his fellow angels hold their shields against the fire-spewing demons.

All kinds of colors swirled with the entangled masses as the warrior titans attacked the hearts of their adversaries—not unlike, I guessed, the war of lies and truths that waged against the human spirit, spreading spring colors to those uplifted through encouragement, or the bland colors of melancholy that weighed on the hearts of those who doubted themselves.

This battle for the heart and soul reminded me of the day my mother wept in the street one winter morning in front of our prefab house in Chicago. In her hand she held a glove, one glove, from the hand of her dead daughter, my sister, who died when a child after being hit by a car while bicycling. "I should have been there," she said, which translated into "I'm not a good mother," which she occasionally said out loud. Those words played in her head over and over, showing through her sad eyes each time a little girl bicycled along the street. The virus of discouragement and worry preyed upon her soul until her body gave in to the cancer that eventually riddled her body.

Perhaps it was my imagination, perhaps not; however, I now pictured those moments of grief that spread over my mother's face to include a scowling demon shouting lies to her, telling her she was a terrible mother. Lies infecting her soul and breeding inside her, repeating themselves endlessly, with the only anecdote being God's truth.

I understood that these demons served to remind others of their loss and failings. Angels, however, offered hope and encouragement. Each spirit whispered silent words into the spiritual grid that existed beyond the curtain of this life, speaking to each other and to the humans whose lives they influenced. The battle in the spirit realm was over whose words would be heard and manifested in the souls of humankind, words either of truth from God or lies from the demons. And these words constituted each person's beliefs.

I noticed a flickering light caught in the eyes of an angel who stopped in front of me. He took off his armor and came slowly toward me. The ground quaked under his feet. With his dulled array of rainbow colors he stood under a dark cloud where the iris flowers leaned so palely. Along the barren pathway behind him struggled a few wild sprouts that managed to break through the dirt. For a moment the sounds of war were drowned out.

The angel looked at me with bended head. With drawn eyes lifted to look straight into mine, he pressed his cold hand against my chest and left it there. Lastly he smiled at me and drew his face close to mine, his breath stale, eyelids heavy across azure-colored eyes.

"Recite for me some of God's words," he pleaded.

I could only recall Psalm 23 in that moment, verses I recited at my father's funeral. "Even when I walk through the darkest valley, I will not be afraid, for you are close beside me. Your rod and your staff protect and comfort me."

The angel's countenance thereafter glowed with the brilliance of sunshine, the sun piercing the dark cloud around him, the irises svelte flower petals at his feet perked up to boast of their violet blush. With fresh breath and eyes wide open, he whispered to me, "Thank you. And let the peace of Christ rule in your heart."

As the angel flew boldly back into the battleground, I knew afresh the power of words. The life-giving power of words. The Lord's words begin with the sound of a presence whispering in silence. Then an intelligible voice emerges in the realm of the unknown. And then joy surfaces when the spirit of Christ begins to illuminate the words, sending intimacy and comfort as clearly as the assurances of a close friend. Then the light of life allows us to see Jesus and to find peace within his embrace. His presence—Jesus had told me in my vision that the prayers of the saints are deposited into God's hands, so that he can pour out Christ's presence over them—refreshing waters from the river of life.

I thought now that everything of meaning arose from the mist of words, good or bad. The medium of words expressed the thoughts that were birthed through actions. They took root as a person's inner speech, which actuated the creation of something—say, beauty from the inspired soul of an artist, or destruction from the ugliness of a defeated soul.

For me, God's voice would be ever-present, stirring everything that led to peace through the silence of his presence. When God speaks, it is done. My only requirement would be to listen to God and invite him to breathe into my life the potentiality he desired.

A sudden explosion jarred me back to the surface reality of this world. By now the air emitted an odorous blend of gunfire against a backdrop blushed with flesh colors. Angels' declarations of God's righteousness continually caused the demons to cower, whereas the demons' curses over the angels caused the angels' luster to dim to a sickening pale upon the epic fields of Armageddon, as thousands of these atmospheric beings tumbled with each other. I could not help but wonder how the war would be won or lost

I turned to Rhome. "What are they fighting for?" I asked him.

"Never before since the dawn of the earth has there been such a fight, when all the powers and principalities first battled to influence God's lordship over humankind," Rhome said.

"You mean this happened when God formed the earth?" I said.

"It happened only after he created the reason for this earth," Rhome answered.

"And what was his reason?" I asked, both chilled and not a little elated by the magnificence of everything.

"You," Rhome answered. "Humankind. He did it for you."

Rhome continued while wiping his brow, the very spot where I myself felt a slight headache from all of this magnitude. "After the creation of Adam and Eve," he said, "a battle similar to the one taking place now happened to determine who would reign over the earth."

"And our team won," I presumed.

"No, the powers of darkness prevailed," Rhome said.

I was taken aback by the gravity of his answer. "How?"

"Because the first humans chose to trust themselves over God by partaking of the one thing he forbade," Rhome said.

"The fruit?"

"Not quite," Rhome responded. "Disobedience to God makes a person his own god—and there can be only one God." There was a long pause while I pondered all this.

Then I dared challenge the seeming unfairness of it all. "And why did that ruin it for the rest of us? Adam and Eve and their descendents were banished from paradise, which affected all of us."

"You are the son of Adam," Rhome said while cupping my head. "The seed of disobedience has been passed on to generations since. Has not each person disobeyed?"

"Can we break that curse?" I nervously asked.

"If God's words become your words," Rhome declared, "then yes."

I sensed that Rhome had his say and was waiting for me to respond. "How can I overcome all of my doubts?" I asked. It seemed that our remnant of believers held the key to paradise just as Adam and Eve had before their disobedience, a burden no man should bear.

"Fear not," Rhome said. "Trust is a state of being. Do you not always trust that water will quench your thirst, or that food will satisfy your hunger?" Rhome's words challenged me. How could I refute the obvious?

"What does he want from me?" I asked.

"Our Father wants you to trust him as much as you trust water to quench your thirst," Rhome answered in a calm manner reminiscent of my favorite grade-school teacher. "To trust your loving Father should be everlasting. Our Father's words, his promises, are always sufficient for the thirsty soul, and always true for those who seek the way in which they should go, are they not?"

"Yes, absolutely. God's presence is like water for thirsty souls." I liked that. "He is, as Jesus once said, the Way—the path toward righteousness."

I wondered, how would this play out? How could we win the victory this time around by establishing our absolute trust in God?

In the midst of my contemplation, Rhome whispered in my ear, "Pay attention; the battle's end is nearing."

It dawned on me to rally our troops. Hopefully, not too late! I picked up my bullhorn and shouted, "USA—shout praises to our Lord!"

If I didn't know better, I would have thought a hundred thousand voices were shouting praises to God rather than the parched three hundred in our group. Their praises sang like twenty choruses, which caused me to wonder, then to understand, that somehow God had opened the heavens so that the angels could also shout their praises with us.

"Stand firm, Reuben; the Lord is with you," Rhome whispered to me.

Hundreds of resplendent angels reflected the glory of the Lord—encircling our encampment as they declared, "Righteous is the Lamb! Holy is the God of Abraham!" And with these words came assurances that I had once felt in heaven.

"Praise you, Lord!" I shouted.

Down below a pattering of bullets echoed. Then four blasts with accompanying flares, and soon thereafter the *swoosh* of a missile before it landed several hundred feet behind our stations.

"They're at the foot of the hill," Hudson shouted. "They're coming up after us!" Explosives burst all around, pushing hot air against our backs.

A stream of brown-and-tan-jacketed soldiers filed up the mountain's stone-lined pathway with precision. Another boom—and then the sick airstream of several objects flew overhead and vanished like shooting stars.

"The Lord is your God!" proclaimed an angel shimmering in gold hues. "Hi, Reuben," he said, "pleased to meet you. My name is Michael, an angel of our Lord." He stood by my side, at least ten feet tall, looking very much like the statue of David—only, with clothes on.

"*The* Michael?" I asked.

"Well, yes—just like you're *the* Reuben. I've placed seven of our mightiest angels to guard you and your immediate circle of friends. Fear not. The Lord is with you."

"I know," I said.

The sounds of guns firing and missiles blasting through the air spoke otherwise. However, not a single shot had struck any of our USA members—as far as I could tell. At least not yet. I continued to encourage the USA to shout more praises—"as loudly and as joyously as you can!"

With each praise the angels gleamed brighter, spreading forth their arms in declaring God's authority in Jesus Christ's name, followed immediately by the retreat of all the demons surrounding them. The angels floated gracefully in contrast to the jerky motions of their adversaries.

Below and up the mountain I could better see the giant prehistoric-looking demons above their allied soldiers. They hovered over the ascending WSA troops shouting wolflike rallying cries. Some emitted croaky groans when pained by an attacking angel who declared over them words like "Today is the day of God's judgment upon you," after which their faces drooped and they emitted sickly grunts.

Amanda lay supine upon the ground with not the slightest twitch. Her chest expanded and contracted in perfect synchronization, and her eyes were closed, her calm face disrupted only by the faint smile upon it. Bright yellow dandelions framed her lacy gown. The wind gently brushed up a few tendrils of her soft hair almost rhythmically.

"My beloved," I spoke softly, not knowing if she could hear me. "I am so drawn by your beauty."

A familiar hand rested on my shoulder. "My friend," Elian said. "The WSA soldiers are almost here—no more than a few minutes away—see." The platoon walked in full view, stepping up the winding walkway below.

My tense muscles awoke me to their magnitude. Thousands marched in lockstep. We would be slaughtered, or else . . . the "else" part being a miracle.

Let my last memory, I prayed, *be the compelling tenderness I feel toward my wife—and the touch of softness expressed through her peaceful countenance as she dreams of you . . .*

"Reuben, God doesn't want you to give up," said Elian.

"Even if I give it up to him?" I answered.

"Do you know the story of Elijah on Mount Carmel? The 850 prophets of Baal who faced off against God's lone prophet, Elijah."

Crackling gunfire sounds and stones flying everywhere in submission to exploding bombs punctuated Elian's words.

"Yeah, I know the story," I said. "They dared Elijah's God to bring rain, I think—it was a standoff between the false prophets' god and our Father." Stifling smoke brought the increasingly pungent stink of rotten eggs.

"And?" Elian prompted.

"And God's fire poured down," I answered.

Chapter Twenty-Four

Smoldering fires from the explosions now pressed their heat through my clothes.

"Elijah stood at the altar—just like that one over there," Elian continued. He pointed toward a structure made of stones. "The twelve stones of that altar represented the 144,000 sons and daughters of Israel. The very believers that reside in this land today."

"What are you saying, Elian?"

"Elijah shouted these words after clearing his throat: " 'The Lord, He is God; the Lord, He is God,' and then the fire rained down."

"You're suggesting I do that? Didn't the fire also consume the soldiers?"

"It did," Elian answered.

"I won't be the cause for killing anyone," I said.

"It was their rightful time to cross the divide, brother. Everyone lives under the mercy of God until their appointed time for judgment—their rightful time," Elian said.

"I never signed up for this battle," I said. Sounds of the soldiers' footsteps now rang like annoying taps against my head.

"It's almost time to release the bride—his church—to its groom." Elian pulled me toward him. "You've been fighting your battle up till now, Reuben; now it's time to fight God's battle."

Chants of "kill, kill" could be heard from our savage neighbors—who were turning up the volume until the words shouted in my ear. Then an eerie silence settled as guns and missiles stopped firing. The dewy smoke blinded me for a moment.

"Draw weapons," shouted a commander within earshot. "Prepare to fire on my command."

Demons buzzed over the soldiers, flapping their arms and salivating with mischievous grins. I looked overhead for our angels; at least as many hovered over us almost motionless, expressionless. But why weren't our angels doing anything?

I supposed the battle between spirits had already been fought, and now the humans on either side were filled with their masters' words — ours being the truth of Jesus Christ, making us ready for the fight—the spiritual fight.

"I'm going to meet them," I told Elian, boots falling loudly against the gravel.

"No!" Amanda demanded as she sat up. "That's crazy!" Rattling metal sounds were closer now, the click of cocked shotguns. The ground vibrated. Grinding machines only yards away.

"Sorry, love, I've got to." And so I walked to the edge of the walkway no more than twenty feet now from the first line of four soldiers, whose guns were pointed straight at my face.

"On your knees!" shouted a commander, whose nose filled most of his face in contrast to his squinty eyes and lipless mouth that flapped out a stream of cuss words.

I dropped in response. "I have no weapon; none of us do. Surely you wouldn't shoot unarmed people—we're no threat to you."

"What's your name?" demanded the commander.

My stomach was growling from hunger, or fear, or whatever rose up inside me. I didn't plan this foray into the battle zone. I looked upward to see two clouds that crossed into the shape of a crucifix. An ill omen or a sign from God? "Reuben . . . Simon."

"Of course." The commander rolled his eyes. "The prophet." Three slithering dragon-faced demons encircled the commander. "I don't suppose your God is going to save you this time."

Rhome stepped up to my side along with Michael. They cast their long shadows over the commander. For the life of me, I didn't know why the angels remained silent.

"Will you protect us from their attack?" I whispered to Rhome, not a little perturbed.

"The Lord is keeping us silent, Reuben. This is your stand of faith," Rhome answered.

"What do you intend to do with us?" I asked the commander.

The commander grinned along with the hissing demons. Everyone suddenly looked up into the sky. Lightning mixed with thunder in the light of the day. Smokestack clouds stormily rolled downward like an inverted tornado.

A viscous angry growl caused all of us to cower as a behemoth figure swooped down while riding the clouds as skateboards. The ground quaked with the impact of its lizard-like legs as he landed into the exploding dirt.

"Reuben—one who has seen the Son," the demon said with a sneer. Its pupils swelled as a lone ray of sunlight exposed the beast's deep-set eyes surrounded by scales. His oblong toothy face drew into a wide-open scowl.

"Who—?" I began to ask.

"I am Baal."

"The same Baal who was worshipped by the Israelites? The same whose priests were confronted by Elijah?"

"The same."

He struck me as awesome. Everything about him screamed power and intimidation, though he grimaced awkwardly more in the fashion of a half-unsure bully after I reminded him of Elijah's victory against his minions. I watched him sway side to side, his loose flesh clapping against broken skin. This creature was a nightmare revealed in the light of day, a beast I'd have more feared if not for the confidence I felt in his chief adversary. I was a bit frightened . . . well, more than a bit. He paced the ground impatiently. His long spiky horns along his neck clapped as he moved. He appeared to me as a caged wounded animal, stalking for some prey upon which he could avenge himself.

The other reptilian beasts stood stoically, eyes fixed on their master. I grimaced at the thought of what might happen; the angels were so silent and still, like a band of soldiers ordered to a halt, their exceptional bright armor seemingly useless.

I was certain that without another miracle, like that given to Elijah when confronted by Baal, I would be a smoldering piece of flesh after being scorched with the flaming nostrils of my enemy. At first I wished to run, but Baal's hint of nervousness made me see him as someone who knew the strength of God and wished to forget it. However, he was the most fearsome creature I'd ever seen, and I could not help but feel the rapid beat of my heart as some ominous sign. Yet something strengthened me. The feeling that Jesus was near, reminding me of how I had felt with him in heaven.

"Surely you must fear the Lord Jesus Christ," I said.

The thorns on his neck shot upward as he stiffened. "Where is your God now?" He made a sissing sound through the grill of his curved saber teeth.

"He is here, always," I replied, praying nervously for God's wisdom on what to do next.

"Then call him—now!" Baal's eyes blazed red.

I prayed silently with every ounce of faith I could muster. Nothing.

Baal pounded the ground with five steps in my direction and leaned forward while cocking his head playfully. I could feel the heat from his mouth.

"You lost your way more than a few times," he whispered mockingly, "such as the time you looked upon Lila with not a little arousal, the sites you viewed on the computer—you even doubted your little God, didn't you, to the point of almost abandoning him?"

His words deflated my confidence, yes. But, I knew by now to recite God's words to counter those of my enemy. "If we confess our sins, he is faithful and just to forgive our sins and purify us from all unrighteousness," I said out loud.

"He can't save you now!" Baal shouted.

"God gave all beings to Christ that he might save them—"

"That doesn't apply to you now," Baal retorted. "Save your people by joining our ranks," seethed Baal. "I'm not asking you to deny your god. You can do as you please, and your spiritual eyes will be opened forever, knowing all there is to know about the powers and principalities of this world."

I wanted so much to just be done with it. For a second I considered that I wouldn't be denying Christ to surrender. If he and his demons would only go away. *God, give me wisdom.*

I closed my eyes hoping for an answer. Elian's words kept replaying in my mind: *Elijah . . . the altar . . . fire. Oh God, just let me live in peace.* Not a false peace, or a temporary respite. I wanted the real deal that could only occur after being obedient to God.

Amanda came to mind. She was strong. She had refused Bakr. She had broken through the fears and the pain to embrace her heavenly Father. If anyone deserved to let go, she did.

"Let me go to the altar," I said. Baal nodded in amusement while snarling his nose and clenching his elongated fingers into a tight fist—playing along with me for the moment, at least.

I stood tall and proceeded to the amassed rubble that formed a semblance of an altar. Then closed my eyes. *Lord, increase my faith.* Hoping beyond hope.

I shouted at the top of my lungs: "The Lord, He is God; the Lord, He is God." My profession echoed throughout the valley below—followed by silence. Not a word was spoken for what seemed like several hours. I waited. *God, show up. God, do something!*

"Don't be a fool." Baal roared with laughter. "Hear ye, hear ye, all you spirits of this world and of Yahweh. We are gods—and the God of Abraham is impudent! Stop this foolishness!" Baal continued to laugh until his voice rolled into a putrescent gurgling sound.

"Lord God," I shouted in abandonment to any thought, "in Jesus Christ's name I pray. Not my will, but yours be done. You are my everything, and everything I give to you."

In that instant an undeniable conviction consumed me. In total surrender, God's Spirit possessed me to the point where I could not discern his words from mine. I was caught in a maze of mirrors reflecting God's holiness. Consumed in the moment. Not me . . .

"I AM," came the sweet whisper in the wind to my ear.

"I love you, Father!" I shouted with the full force of my lungs.

With that, my flesh went numb as I burned with anticipation and seemed to float without consciousness of my physical body or surroundings. Everything went blank. No thought, no pretense, only complete surrender. I had jumped into the sky thousands of miles above myself with no parachute.

Shouts of praise and ear-piercing screams broke through my detached space, though I could sense little beyond my immersion within God's holy presence, as though caught in a wind tunnel with just those faint sounds outside my echo chamber while immersed in a mystical playground of the mind.

Gradually the world's presence broke through my hypnotic state as the muffled noises eked through until resounding to the full measure of their expressions. My eyes opened to the world again, and the brutality of agonizing rants rang in my ears.

Demons shrieked like caged animals being prodded with electric rods, shouting profanities and curses that would embarrass the most salty of characters. WSA soldiers burned with fire; their bodies convulsed while trying to fight off flames that devoured their flesh. They scurried about in morbid dances until caving to the ground in submission to their fate.

Baal stretched out his reptilian limbs as if wanting to break them from his body. His vein-laced wings frantically flapped with black beetles parading up and down his wasting frame in a feeding frenzy.

Angels shouted, "Glory to the King of Kings and Lord of Lords! Holy is the Lamb of God!" They joined hands and stretched their vaporous wings upward toward heaven, singing in perfect unison.

Michael towered over me. "All authority will be given to our Lord Jesus Christ once he is returned to the temple, Reuben," he said. "You must go to Jerusalem. Bring his presence there so that he may ascend to his throne and take his rightful place of judgment. Do not tarry."

I jerkily shook my head trying to awake to the fullness of what was transpiring before my eyes—devastation on one side and adoration on the other.

"Must we go now?" I asked Michael.

"Go now, before it is too late. For just as your enemy is being destroyed by God here, the enemy is destroying your brothers and sisters in Jerusalem. If the Savior does not inhabit his temple, darkness shall reign again for a millennium. Already Satan has declared victory. Now go!"

The battlefield was dripping. WSA soldiers crawled down the hillside, dirt and stones were wet with blood, and the sun broke through a clear sky—no more spirits inhabited its space. Our preparations were made and our way clear. There remained only one more thing to do before we could realize the second coming of our Lord.

I lingered for a moment on the edge of a boulder, watching the enemy vanish into the shadows under moving clouds. I had some questions; the end had been prearranged with the only plans being those for here and now. God never lets you get too ahead of him. And while those plans clearly led to the Lord's next move, letting one's questions go seemed the nature of a believer's life. Some questions were better left unanswered.

Such was the meaning of Armageddon and the eventual outcome in Jerusalem. The final battle would be over whose voice would be heard, and over who would answer the call. As for us, God would speak, and we would follow.

❧ Chapter Twenty-Five ❧

My life was fraught with pain
My heart pained to be free
And then I found the answer
On the other side of me

—Amanda Chapman Simon

Amanda cared no longer about the rhythm or meter of her poetry as she tossed her notebook, and then on second thought reached down to stuff it in her pants pocket. She only wanted now to speak her soul, no matter how it sounded. This was pleasantly odd to her.

The entire USA army drove on the roads of Israel near Shechem, framed on either side by jagged mountains en route to Jerusalem, having received word of Prime Minister Medvedev's hideout, where they would rendezvous. Amanda rolled down the vehicle's back window as Will rubbed her back, and as Elian napped while Hudson drove with Lila at his side.

Amanda drank in the light's rays as they streamed over her bare shoulder. The road cut through towering rock faces. Man-cut cliffs

225

through whaleback peaks reflected shades of amber against the brilliant sun. The sun's tentacles embraced everything within sight, anointing them with glistening kisses. Nature's behemoths mellowed against a slight haze in the air, making them more surreal. Gentle giants come to life through their burnt sienna unmasked by the sun. Gale-formed buttes, swarthy rocks, and striking sandstone formed mazes through which the wind sang her song.

She cared not that the wind toyed with her hair, or that scorching heat had burned her nose, or that others stared at her clothes torn from too much wear.

All her life had been about following the rules, wearing the right mix of colors—earth tones with greens—and using the correct sentence structure—never ending a sentence with a preposition. Everything ordered down to the perfect God, who demanded perfection. Only, he didn't. She knew that now. Nature spoke it.

Craggy mountain faces framed the USA's traveling caravan on the way to Jerusalem, enchantingly uneven in their design. Enormous red monoliths and sketchy desert hills randomly shed their rocks on either side, ruggedly beautiful in their asymmetry. Randomly shaped into a profound inspirational design. God's impressionistic handiwork made foolery of evenly lined ancient temples jutting out from jagged cliffs. Manmade trinkets that stuck out like pimples on bloodshot stones.

Amanda turned down the car's radio music and listened to the perfectly choreographed notes drift through echo canyons. From perfect pitch to an enrapturing melody dispersed by the wind that blew where she wished without thought or care.

How marvelously flawed the Father's artistry appeared. Perhaps not flawed at all. Perhaps he purposed life in free flow, with each part joining to another. Constructs freed of finite calculations or limited understanding made great by their creator, whose signature lived within each crevice, canyon, hilltop, and valley. How futile man's attempt to make its tailored constructs as striking as God's inspired art.

No, God did not demand perfection. Nature proved it. And neither would she demand perfection of him—strange as that sounded. Not that he wasn't perfect—only that her definition of perfect wasn't. And so Amanda Simon relinquished her role as judge.

He could judge her—that was true. After all, he *was* perfect. God didn't need corrective lenses to see truth; he had 20/20 vision. Truth's distortion through the human mind's finite understanding produced a blurred reality that misinterpreted all kinds of things, including love. Leaving faith as the clarifier of truth.

Faith. A word. No more than a concept before she'd witnessed the love in Will for her. Real love. The kind that shares in suffering despite one's sincerest attempt to hide it. The kind that wills itself to God so that he can craft his handiwork through a pliable mind over bended knees. The kind that gives in and gives up to God, who knows the final masterpiece because he first sketched it perfectly in heaven.

Will looked through her with lucent eyes, into her, and loved her not for who she was but because of what love was. A gift. A presence. Will looked at her through the mind of Jesus Christ that gave no thought to human-conceived beauty—with personified love that flowed freely over wind-sculpted canyons through Jesus's rivers of living water.

How refreshing this freedom was to her. Love needed no reason to write its script upon the heart, she thought; it needed only the author to do so. Love came as naturally as breathing to those created by love. She stopped trying, and exhaled peaceful relief into the obscure unknown.

Slowly and deliberately, Amanda pulled the notebook from her front pants pocket, set it lightly upon her lap, and gently lifted a pen from her shirt pocket to write. The words fell out of her with no care or thought:

I knew my God within my heart
As love did tear myself apart
And left me on the other side
Of me

༺ Chapter Twenty-Six ༻

"**F**aster. Can't you get this stupid car to go faster?" Bakr barked maddeningly at his driver. "We've got to get to Masada."

"We radioed ahead," Amato said. "Your guards will open the gates as soon as we approach the entrance."

"And why wasn't the helicopter waiting at the airport?"

"I don't know," responded Serge Amato.

Bakr's entourage, not twenty miles from his underground fortress, found themselves followed by a string of military vehicles adorned with launchers and automatics guns.

"How far back are they?" shouted Bakr.

"Maybe a mile, maybe less," answered Serge.

"Israelis? Who? Get me the answer! I need to know who's chasing us!"

"Our drone detected someone speaking the Dinka language," said Amato.

"Sudanese," said Bakr. "Imbeciles! They're part of the World Security Alliance! Why?" A rhetorical question.

Now barely visible through the desert haze, Bakr's pursuers wound around the flat bend snaking their way through masking dust. Their faint outline grew visibly larger by the millisecond.

Bakr arched his head while simultaneously pounding his fist against the back window. "Why can't our jets take them out? Where's our frickin' air cover!"

"Two of our jets are down," said Eid Sammi. "Russian jet fighters—can you believe it!"

"Spineless idiots! Get me Egorov—now!"

"We tried reaching him—no answer," replied Amato as he wiped sweat from his brow with an already soaked handkerchief.

Bakr squeezed the air out of his armrest while furiously shaking. This couldn't be happening. All his life he'd been hounded by traitors. They'd been guaranteed powers, splurged at opulent resorts, partaken in orgies to die for—been offered riches that would make the wealthiest salivate with envy.

He went limp in the backseat. "Makes no sense," Bakr said.

Amato, for all his authority over the netherworld as the second-in-command, could do nothing now in this world. Fickle humans—it was in their DNA, and Bakr had used their self-serving ways against Yahweh before—but never had one of his own turned against him. Until now, only those with Christ's spiritual DNA could defy Bakr.

"Sir." Amato pointed while holding his phone away from his ear. In the distance the Euphrates River's pounding waters overflowed its embankments. Bakr rolled down his window. The rushing currents took on the sounds of slapping water fountains as a jet fighter above blasted missiles into the river, dispersing the waters and covering them with the debris of scattered boulders, which had been piled up on either side. Two helicopters dropped a four-story-high concrete highway divider that spanned the width of the river, wetting Bakr's face with its catapulted splashes.

"What are they doing?" Bakr then lifted his head knowingly. "They're stopping its flow."

"They're creating a makeshift bridge," Amato replied.

"And they've taken out our helicopter. They're making a way for those renegade troops to hit our compound. Faster!" Bakr shouted to the driver. "So why haven't they hit us yet from above?"

"Perhaps," Amato replied, "they don't want to kill us. They want to capture us."

"Take us hostage," Bakr said. "Inhabit our underground safe haven. They know we can't die—at least not I," he said matter-of-factly.

The vehicles behind them closed the gap to merely a few yards. Supercharged engines with recoilless nuclear guns were pointed at them. It would be seconds before they engulfed Bakr and his people.

"Faster!" Bakr insisted. "We need to cross that bridge. Father Ra, lord over this world, I call upon your power to destroy my enemy!"

Nothing happened. Why were his prayers fruitless?

Yahweh was in this somehow. Bakr had diverted most of his demons to Megiddo and Jerusalem, assuming he wouldn't need them here.

Bakr closed his eyes and raised his arm. "Belial."

"Yes, Master," Belial whispered from the invisible environs.

"Breathe your fire against that jet above." Bakr for once relaxed his face.

"Ours is a battle that cannot be won, Master." Belial's winded voice sounded too weak to breathe fire.

"You listened to Yahweh's angels, didn't you?"

"Yes, they've already declared victory," Belial said. "And the word—it has all been written and cannot be changed—"

"Nonsense!" cried Bakr. "You know that's not true."

"But we lost on the field of Megiddo. The humans stood on faith . . . Yahweh scripted out this time—"

Bakr snarled like a wolf. "Yahweh's words do not speak the final outcome any more than they did when he spoke perfection over the earth in Eden, or when he destined Moses to enter the land of Canaan," said Bakr. "None of these things happened according to his word."

Belial's radiance began to return. "So you can turn the prophecy of Yahweh around—it can be changed? You can defeat the Christ?"

"Of course," Bakr answered. "Did I not change the course of Yahweh's design after he created the humans?" He could feel the looming shift of control like a tempest pounding its way from the desert.

Belial's voice now spoke at full strength. "And so we can gain the victory once more."

"Yes—it is already done," Bakr said dismissively.

"But Reuben's army—they were not discouraged. They still live . . ." Belial's voice trailed again.

"Not for long. Death is assured, and when I kill the most precious one in Reuben's sight, doubt will enter into their ranks again."

"Christ's presence—will it be prevented from entering Jerusalem so that we can gain the victory?" Belial asked.

"Of course!" Bakr looked again to see the army close behind. "God's presence will never again inhabit the temple—we've blown it up!" The grinding of an engine reached him over his shoulder. A camouflaged figure astride a motorcycle came alongside Bakr's car. For several moments, the two looked at each other until one of Bakr's guards shot the motorcyclist in the head, sending him into a spin.

"One down," Bakr boasted. "Now finish off those above, Belial."

Full of renewed confidence, Belial darted up quickly into the air and blew a hard current of heat against the Russian jet, causing it to flip mercilessly like a kite broken from its string. The jet's dance of death continued into a downward spiral until touching the ground, sending out a glowing plume of rippling orange and dark-brown colors.

"Quickly, speed over the river," shouted Bakr. His car pushed through trickling waters over the top of the lumpy debris. The procession of cars bumped each other in pursuit of the entranceway to Bakr's aboveground pyramid leading to his underground palace, Masada. Massive metal doors gradually opened from the domed structure as the revving turbines of Bakr's pursuers signaled an imminent takeover. Bakr looked back to see two Sudanese armored cars within a stone's throw of his vehicle. The enemy would soon enter his compound if something was not done within a nanosecond.

Soldiers from two of Bakr's SUVs opened fire against the two opposing vehicles. Fire was returned with equal might. Rounds of ammunition clicked off in opposing directions until nothing but a steady stream of pinging bolts against metal could be heard. Bakr's car sped through the thick doors.

"Close the doors now!" Bakr shouted after fully entering the enclave.

The thick doors slowly retreated inward not a moment too soon, as Bakr's six vehicles spun around to form a wall in front of the screeching armored vehicles in pursuit. One of the Sudanese cars slammed into a black SUV before it could stop. Bakr and Amato ducked as five bullets clinked against their vehicle, one piercing the window and narrowly missing Amato's head.

Two of the guarding SUVs blew up in a fiery ball that shattered the back window of Bakr's car, cutting Amato's face with glass as Bakr blanketed himself with his jacket. An opposing Humvee smashed through Bakr's burning SUV in pursuit, settling only a few feet from the edge of the fortress's closing doors.

A soldier from within the compound launched a short-range missile into the on-charging Humvee, filling the cab with fire and causing the vehicle to drift into the steel-walled foyer of the half-circled entrance. It exploded against the thick back wall spewing bits and pieces everywhere.

Bakr let out a sigh. He braced himself as his vehicle made a hard right to avoid fragments of burning metal.

By now at least fifteen of the compound soldiers were firing machine guns while holding bulletproof shields in front of them. An explosion rocked the sterile inner chamber just as the fortress door closed within a few inches of sealing the entrance.

The blast lifted the left side of Bakr's car, sliding him against Amato, rocking it until it finally rested against the cement floor.

"How far is our nearest Skyhawk helicopter?" Amato said to one of the commanding officers within the now-sealed compound.

"We've got three that are over the scene outside now," the officer responded.

Four rapid pops could be heard in advance of muffled explosions outside. Bakr and Amato exited their car as five bodyguards swarmed and guided them to an elevator door. Once inside, one of the guards inserted his key and pressed his hand against the green sensor as the elevator descended to the fourth subfloor.

After exiting into a an empty circular room, Bakr, Amato, and three of the bodyguards crossed over into a waiting secured elevator that transported the five men into the final deep chamber miles beneath the earth's surface. The stale air breathed through the underground vault like a dying invalid, with a groan of settling bones as they stepped onto the stone floors. All was killed by the silence but the ticking of a clock. But Bakr appreciated the lifelessness. He felt it against his chest like a prophecy. Like a séance of the dead speaking of the future from the past. The specters said that the fall of man this time would reach the depths of hell.

Bakr and Amato both inhaled deeply upon exiting into a foyer leading to a long steely hallway. They entered a boardroom containing black high-backed chairs and a table that stretched endlessly toward a mounted projector screen detailing the destruction of the Jerusalem temple.

Bakr grabbed the closest chair and slumped into it. The two men breathed rapidly and then slowed as they reconnected their gaze one to another.

"They could have killed us," said a winded Amato.

"Isn't that an oxymoron, Serge?" Bakr said.

"Sir?"

"Killing us—as though we're not already dead," Bakr said, deadpan.

"But," Amato said, shaking his head, "this is about eternal life. Never dying—"

"Of course, of course." Bakr flipped his hand back and forth. "Don't worry. I won't let you die."

"And that part about having bombed the temple—how does that prevent Yahweh—"

Bakr leaned back, his confidence godlike again as he swallowed some air, kicked back, and closed his eyes. "Yahweh's presence must be established upon the earth in order for the Christ to return—correct?"

Amato rolled his shoulders without saying a word.

Bakr continued. "Yahweh's presence inhabited the temple of old until the Christ hung on the cross. After that he decided to deposit his spirit into the bodies of Christians. Plain and simple."

Amato lapped up Bakr's words. "Why did he decide to use humans to instill his spirit?"

Bakr chuckled. "Because, dear Serge, the Christ is kindred to humans." Bakr contemplated how to dumb this down even further. "Yahweh, on the other hand, is not kindred to humans—he is separate—and can only abide in a space that is undefiled and pure, as in heaven."

"So the temple was made pure—he could inhabit that and nothing else on earth?" Amato dropped his chin.

"Well," answered Bakr. "Not quite. You see, Yahweh lifted his spirit from this earth. He's needed a place to put it in order to reestablish fellowship with his little children again."

His nose twitched with the nervousness of a dog in the hunt. "He's here, on this earth, Serge. I can smell his blood."

"Who?"

"The Christ."

The space between the two men ran cold. Amato was beginning to understand. "He's here," Amato repeated, stunned.

"In the flesh," Bakr replied. "However, he cannot remain in the flesh and inhabit his place as judge over this earth until he is transformed into his glory. And the only way he can do that is to enter into Yahweh's midst—into the sacred place of their communion."

"The temple," Amato said.

"Yes, my friend. You must be listening to your inner voice—or should I say your inner angel." Bakr chortled. "But, ultimately, they must meet in heaven to consummate their union."

"And so we've bombed the temple, preventing this initial union of sorts."

"Well done," Bakr said. "The student has grown in knowledge. However, you are missing one key point. I defiled the temple when I was there. It is no longer pure—I left the residue of sin, if you will."

"I don't understand, Father," said a perplexed-looking Amato. "Why does God need a pure vessel in which to place his spirit?"

"Serge, he needs one that's been purified, as with the blood of Jesus Christ—his spiritual blood. Remember the senator? I offered his Christ-infected blood to Yahweh as a sacrifice.

"You said that Yahweh was repulsed with your sacrifice," Amato said.

"I was caught in the emotion, dear Serge. What he really responds to is to see the Christ in another."

"And how does the Christ do that?" asked Amato.

"He does that, my dear brother, by the act of substitution." Bakr tilted his ear, waiting for Amato to reason the rest.

"Aagh, never mind," Bakr said. "I'll spell it out. Yahweh couldn't relate to humans unless his spirit was in them. And the only way to implant his spirit into humans was to substitute the human spirit with the spirit of Christ—and all that mumbo jumbo."

"So this Christ in the flesh, the one here, on this earth now—he intends to sacrifice himself again, to impart his spirit once again into this world so that Yahweh can again relate to his own?"

Bakr stood and began pacing back and forth. "The Christ needs to enter the temple and give up his spirit to Yahweh, his so-called Father, who will instill Christ's spirit into a glorified body. Except . . ." Bakr waited.

"Except?" Amato obliged.

"Except I will ruin the purity of Jesus so that he cannot relate to his Father!" Bakr raised his arms until his sockets hurt.

"I—" Amato struggled.

"Oh, come now, Serge. If he tries to enter that bombed-out temple— those charred remains—he will go to the place where the inner chamber stood, and he will call upon his Father. Then, just after he releases his spirit, I will cause him to deny the will of Yahweh."

"But how? You couldn't do it at the cross—"

Bakr snarled. "You dimwit! Didn't I ruin Yahweh's perfect plan before? I knew in the garden that one man—one stupid little Adam— could deny Yahweh's plan for the perfect world, spoiling his communion with the humans. I separated God from man then, and I will do so again—only this time I will deny the Christ his position as savior!"

Amato dared not speak. Silence remained until Bakr composed himself again and swooshed back into his chair. The room's glaring lights paled Bakr's brilliance, and the large table was hard with his steeled fortitude. He took no note of Amato or any mere mortal, even as he carefully noted the picture hanging on the wall.

"Serge," he said. "I will take the Christ's place upon the throne. I am the rightful son of God."

Bakr fixated on the painting of the ancient temple of Solomon on the wall. With his mind adrift, he hadn't before noticed the scene of Jews raising their arms in worship within the temple square. He thought that he saw just a touch of vapor rising from the tips of the worshippers' heads into the air. There was still a light shining over the temple site, the so-called Shekinah Glory of God, but now he realized that the light effused from the mouths of the faithful who raised their hands to Yahweh.

Then it dawned on him. They were offering sacrifices of worship. It wasn't the destruction of flesh and blood that caused Yahweh to listen. It was their praises. He inhabits the praises of his people. And all this time it appeared that the blood of the innocent elicited his presence. Such bunk. Bakr stood and rolled his head. He could not, would not, acknowledge the lordship of an equal.

"Now, take me to my son. He will reign on earth as I will soon reign in heaven," Bakr suddenly blurted.

"To the Genesis chamber," said Amato.

The two walked down the hall with four oversized men toward a towering door at the end of the sterile hallway. Bakr pressed his hand over the door's sensor. The door slid back, opening to another steel-walled room with cameras angled over each corner, a mirrored ceiling above reflecting their tensed faces.

Bakr and the others walked through a metal detector. A bright light flashed down upon them, and then the floor began descending several feet below until stopping at a crimson-colored metal wall. Bakr looked into a mounted eyepiece on the wall, after which the wall vanished into the floor.

Before the men appeared a vast hangar the size of two football fields, with tubes dangling from the brightly lit ceiling, dripping fluids into adolescent-sized bodies on floating beds suspended by cables and attached intravenous lines.

Beeps from the monitors placed at each dangling bedside sounded like random piano chords that echoed through the massive chamber. The mass of dormant bodies swayed on their padded hammocks with the rhythmic tones while feeding from plastic umbilical cords. At least three thousand catatonic younglings awaited their awakening to a grand new world.

"Behold, gentlemen," said Bakr, "the perfect generation sourced from the first humans—the very DNA of the famed garden of Eden."

"A new earth," said Amato, gasping.

Bakr beamed. "The end of this world will mean the beginning of mine."

"Father," Amato said, cowering, "what shall we do now?"

"I need to go now," Bakr replied, "and relinquish my final gift to the world—my spirit, Ra—the god of the underworld and soon god of the world yet to come."

Amato shook his head in pained confusion.

"Serge." Bakr tapped his shoulder. "You can't possibly understand. Suffice it to say that the spirit of this age will reign over a world made perfect in my image."

ᴄ Chapter Twenty-Seven ᴅ

My kiss blushed Amanda's cheeks a rosy color. On this very day we'd reached beyond our hedge of thorns, to what was our joy to find within each other soft rose petals beyond sight, beyond the senses, within a place steeped as one in the presence of love. I found myself inside of Amanda. My rose of Amanda. The scarring had made us stronger, harder to tear apart, and more tender to each other's touch, as one in Christ.

"A rose bush lies dormant in the winter," Amanda explained to me, "until its buds push through the defrosted stem until they reach the weak light of late spring." Now was the time of our summer bloom.

I smiled outwardly thinking of her inward beauty. She danced on the inside upon seeing my smile. I would give anything to see her twirl a minuet. And she, I know, would give her all toward fulfilling my dreams. We laughed, for the first time in a long time, together at last.

Perhaps we were in love for the first time, truly.

We rode side by side in a musty-smelling four-by-four utility vehicle along with other armored trucks and cars abandoned by the WSA soldiers whose ashes now lay upon Mount Megiddo among the ancients.

Amanda, Elian, and I nestled together in the backseat. Hudson drove, his tagalong and ever-flirtatious companion, Lila, snuggled against his thigh while he intensely gripped the steering wheel.

"Do you ever wonder why we got left behind?" I asked my bride.

"Every day," Amanda responded.

"And?" I looked forward to knowing if she, like I, had found some answer.

She closed her eyes while minutes passed in silence. The sight of her so pleasantly contemplative brought a smile. She once said that I never smiled without reason—not anymore.

Amanda stroked my arm, and then rested her head against my chest. Spirited, caring, and beautiful, she sang a lovely song:

"I stumbled a way never trod
and caved from the weight of my cares
shunning the world's most ugly stares
that kept me blinded to my God.
So I reach with blind faith, and mope
wishing for answers to it all
yet I need only heed the call
and weakly trust the God of hope."

"Tennyson?" I asked.

"Nope—me, though I'm sure Tennyson's words are lingering with some similar fashion in my mind."

What beauty lies within my wife. "You always thought in poetry, my love. So lovely, like you. And so true, we need only trust our loving God. Daddy knows best." I wished to wax more poetic like my wife, but being with her, anything I might say would be dulled in comparison to her sweet lyrics. She was so beautiful.

"I think," I said, "that finding a deeper love with you was in itself worth it, and in so doing I discovered how our Lord loves us."

"Or was it the other way around?" said my very insightful wife.

Amanda leaned her forehead against mine and kissed me, her eyes glassing over. I felt the muscles in my face relaxing. "And we discovered a more genuine love for God, which was essential to finding ourselves, and each other," she replied. "This world has been stripped to its barest need for God, which left us vulnerable to each other."

"I love you," I said with the deepest of meaning.

Amanda looked intensely into me. "I adore you, my knight in shining armor," and then she closed her eyes and dropped her head against the headrest as if to sleep.

She's too beautiful for this place, I thought.

She was right about this land being bare, I thought, while viewing our surroundings. Battles had made most of the territory along our journey a forbidding mass of dirt, chopped-up clumps created by exploded bombs that left scattered metal debris. A dreary and war-swept place of grievous memory, adorned with patches of brush and ripped trees, and an occasional burned-out vehicle still hot from fire.

And the most dreadful of all could be sighted in scattered bunches within smoldering places—bodies with pale and blue faces frozen in agony, some reaching out with their twigged arms in a mournful last gesture, their shredded uniforms burned into the blackened figures.

The land flowing with milk and honey—as the promised land of Canaan was described upon its earliest discovery by the Jews—now flowed with the blood of fallen men and women.

We headed toward Jerusalem, now thirty or so minutes ahead—if no armed conflict awaited us—a big "if."

"Reuben!" Hudson shouted. "In the distance!"

He pointed to the vehicles speeding our way, which were followed by a dust trail.

"Can you tell if they're friendly or foe?" I asked.

"Can't tell," he answered. "But, they're sure hurrying toward us."

"And they've got some men brandishing machine guns," Elian added while looking through a pair of binoculars.

"Doesn't sound friendly at all," Amanda added.

"Gun it," I said to Hudson.

Hudson pressed hard on the accelerator, perhaps to no avail. The oncoming line of suspect vehicles approached us from our front at a forty-five-degree angle, which meant they could catch up to us traveling at the same speed.

"Pray!" I said.

"Lord, in Jesus's name," said Amanda, "let us reach Jerusalem."

Many of us had gathered weapons from the vanquished WSA, but few, if any, really knew how to use them. Our pursuers charged full speed at us with guns aimed high.

My phone rang with classical music—it was David.

"We're being pursued—can't talk long," I answered.

"Is that you?" he said.

"What?"

"Is that you just around the angle?" David's voice sounded a pitch above his normal baritone.

"What? You mean, are we just around *the bend*?"

"Yes. Yes. I'm with the Israeli Golani Brigade sent by Prime Minister Medvedev," he responded, "to escort you to her. And I'm hoping the line of vehicles we are chasing is you."

My heart quickened a beat or six. "You mean that's you approaching us? Can you see our white flag with the cross on our antenna?"

"Yes, yes," David said, "that's why we thought it was you. Now slow down so that we can meet."

As a Type A, I had never been so relieved to slow down in my life, so I commanded Hudson to ease up until coming to a halt. I quickly jumped out and waved my arms, then shouted through my bullhorn that the oncoming soldiers were friendly.

Within minutes our pursuers came to a screeching stop. My familiar friend leaped out like a two-hundred-pound cheetah and raced toward us with arms wide open.

"My friends!" David shouted before hurriedly kissing us. "You cannot imagine my joy at seeing Reuben's mighty army. Did you have collywobbles before you knew that your pursuers were us?"

"What?"

David waved his tattered dictionary in the air. "It means intense anxieties," he said while reading, "also butterflies in the stomach, which sounds a bit disgusting to me, though descriptive—"

"Yes," I answered. Leave it to David for some much needed comic relief. "We had collywobbles. Now tell me, how's it going in Jerusalem?"

David's expression turned sour. "Not well, I'm afraid. The WSA has bombed much of our holy city, even the temple—it lies in ruins even though our brothers and sisters are desperately trying to repair the inner sanctum in time for the dwelling of our God."

"The dwelling?" I asked

"Yes. Yes. You are bringing our Lord's spirit to Jerusalem, dear Reuben! His presence is with you—I know it as surely as I have ever heard from God."

By now several hundred Israeli soldiers stood alongside a zigzag cluster of military rigs, their uniforms dusted, wrinkled, and some torn. Bloodied rags were wrapped around their appendages. They presented sagging postures in contrast to David's bullish disposition.

Several riddled vehicles appeared like cheese graters pocked with holes in testimony of their riders' bravery—though the soldiers' appearances spoke not of heroes but of sickly looking survivors.

David informed us that a third of the Israeli population had died, based on Israeli news reports. The lingering scent of burned flesh laced through all of Israel—reminders of crematoriums, an all-too-familiar smell to the elder Jews.

Two Jewish groups remained on the battlefield of Israel: the unbelievers who fought only for survival and the believers in Christ who prayed and hoped for the glorious coming of Jesus Christ.

Was God's presence among us, as David insisted?

I prayed with all my might for God to reveal his presence should it be in our midst. Then it came to me—that moment on the cliff in San Francisco when he engulfed me with his presence, emblazoning the words of his grace upon my chest.

"I've got to show you something," I said while unbuttoning my shirt. David's and Amanda's eyes opened wide, and I could just imagine what the others thought—I'd gone mad, become an exhibitionist.

I lifted my undershirt to reveal the red scars that spelled out God's words. Elian laughed. Amanda reached her hand to feel the raised letters. David cupped his mouth. Hudson let out a "Wow," and Lila's eyebrows knitted together.

"Amazing," said David as he read the words out loud: "I am with you always."

"His promise written over your heart," Elian said with a chuckle.

"Do you think this is it?" I asked David.

"Yes!" he responded with eyebrows raised. "The presence of God is within you, my friend. These words—how did God . . . what did God say about them?"

"He said to trust in him, and he would make our paths straight."

"Pretty simple, just trust God," said Elian."

"So simple yet so complicated by the human will that wants to control everything," I responded.

"Hence the promise that he will never leave us," interjected David's hearty voice.

"Yes," Elian continued. "God's end goal is intimacy with his children, and the only way his children can acquire that intimacy is to believe God's promises and to not lean on one's limited understanding."

"That, and to be still and meditate on the Lord," I added. "I think that's what he wants most—he just wants us to spend time with him and to do what he tells us to do. So simple it sounds like something out of a third-grader's Sunday school class."

"Hallelujah!" Elian lifted his arms and wiggled his torso back and forth.

"Very cold," commented David.

"You mean, very cool."

"We need to get you to Jerusalem, Brother Reuben," David said, "to release God's presence into the world again. He's in you."

That was it! God's spirit resided within me. How could I be so dull as to not realize that? All this time and I'd been looking outside, when I needed only look within myself.

Amanda's head remained bowed as she gracefully clasped her hands while placidly sitting in her wheelchair some distance away. I didn't think she'd mind if I intruded to share my joy at the revelation of God's presence.

"Love of my life," I said as I gently rubbed my hand down her bent back.

She raised her head and looked up with dewy eyes fixed solely upon the deepest of me. "Hello, love," she said. "I was speaking to our Lord."

"And what did he say?" I replied.

"He said, I love you." Plain and simple, and so profound because he said it without speaking a word.

Chapter Twenty-Seven

"And?" I wanted more.

She smiled pensively. "Will, there's no promise of tomorrow . . . we have only now."

"What are you talking about? Amanda, we've found God's presence!" I paused to take in her words again, feeling bad about jumping in with my enthusiasm. "Love, you look sad. Tell me you're not sad."

"Not sad," she answered. "Just know that God's grace is for the present. Not for the next moment, or the one before. He's the God of I am, not the God of I was, or I will be—"

"Is that what he was telling you?"

"In a way."

"I know." This was sounding all too melancholy, and I dared not speak the joy of my revelation in this somber moment. "And right now," I continued, "right now I love you with all my heart." I dropped to my knees as we embraced.

"Yes, we *have* now," I said, "and I love you now more than ever."

"Me too," Amanda replied as our tears met cheek to cheek. "We'll never really be apart." Her voice cracked.

"I know."

"Remember when?" A game we used to play—projecting the future into the present—only now our "remember whens" were truly memories.

"Yes."

"Remember when we met in heaven, and we rejoiced together with our Lord?"

"OK." I would play along, hoping my raw feelings would not spill out into a flood of cries. "I remember our reunion—in our spirit bodies."

"We were stronger, more genuinely in love," she said. "Because God had united us in spirit as one—just as you said it was in heaven with all the spirits, right?"

Amanda's eyes glistened with starry emotion.

"Right, in heaven we're all one," I replied.

"So that's our next 'remember when,' Will." And then the floodgates opened. We were saying our good-byes to this world—soon. First, I had left America, and now I was about to leave this world . . . but not Amanda. I never wanted to leave my wife. We would be together, one way or another for all of eternity.

245

"Our next 'remember when' might be in heaven—"

"I love you, Will Reuben Simon. I love you . . ." Amanda reached out to wipe the tears from my eyes with her fingers. Like an artist, she softly brushed lines across my face as I bent to press my lips to hers.

We kissed. Deeply.

A faint musty odor entered my nostrils, startling me from my sublime moment. The colossal sound of automatic fire at close range penetrated the air, stiffening my back. And then the roar of a helicopter erupted directly overhead, followed by bright flashes from under the door like red lasers from barreled guns.

Strangely, the sporadic snap of return fire from the Israelis seemed almost lazy in response. The thud of bullets hitting dirt and the tinkle of metal shattering all around turned everything into a blur.

The firing intensified as the helicopter circled and then angled its head. Everyone scrambled into vehicles. A faint ruddy glow surrounded armored jeeps that had been ablaze from recent attacks. Desperate shouts of "Get down!" came from random voices on the ground. Now the sky was studded with four helicopters, raining sheets of fire from above, matched in part by the dirt-covered tracers from the guns of the Israelis.

Israeli soldiers too busted up to fight lay on the ground, emotionless. Other bodies lay frozen in contortions, or mercilessly facedown in pools of blood. Some corpses had already been placed in neat military rows. Coughing and cries interchangeably broke through the blur of raging ballistics.

"Here, take this machine gun and just keep pulling the trigger toward those open helicopter doors," Hudson said while pushing the weapon into my chest. "I'll take Amanda and place her safely into one of those armored cars over there." He pointed to the closest one.

Without thought, I lifted the gun and obediently pressed the trigger. I fell back once, got up, and endured the butt of the machine gun piercing into my shoulder. The sound deafened me to anything else, and the sight of red popping from the barrel over and over dulled me to everything but the menacing metal hornets spouting out their stings from above.

Then, one of the helicopters burst into fire from an Israeli missile, crashing to the distant ground in a ball of flames, followed by two resounding explosions until settling into burning rubble. Another followed, and then another. And then the final remaining one retreated into the graying sky as the sounds of battle faded with it.

A chilled evening settled in, with a slight wind filling the air with the stink of fresh battle. Elian grasped my arm and wrapped his other arm around my shoulder before pulling me to himself.

"You OK?" he asked.

"I guess," I replied without thinking.

I looked at Elian—tears washed flesh-colored lines down his dirt-covered face. He removed his arms and pressed his hands against my face as though I were a little kid. He then rested his forehead against mine, standing straight while firmly holding my arms and dropping his shoulders. I had never seen him drained of all joy before.

"My friend, Amanda's gone," Elian said.

Nothing registered. I didn't want to even think of it. I turned my head away as if to live somewhere else—anywhere else. No questions—didn't want to ask any—didn't want any answers. Skies were dark. The air felt muddy. Nothing's here or there, or any—

"Reuben, Amanda is dead," Elian said. "She's with God now."

The air felt thick. Smells . . . what was that smell? Nothing good. The stars were covered by ugly clouds. Four-leaf clovers turning into compost rambled in my head. I pictured sunshine on a rainy day, butterfly kisses and rainbow hugs . . . anything to escape. But eventually I could think of nothing but bad. As greasy as the slime that infected my dreams and the broken ground of Israel, as grimly enchanting as the lark birds that flew confused through the smoke, as grotesque and familiar as the bloodied casualties, this place of war rotted like trash that someone should have thrown out weeks ago.

Elian locked his arms around me, pressed the air out of me, and whispered, "I'm here, my friend, always will be. She's in paradise, Reuben."

"Where?" I said. "Take me to her."

Elian lifted my limp body as I stared at nothing, wanting to just blank out. *Just move one foot, then another . . .*

Lila stood staring at Amanda's corpse. They both appeared drained against the clearing sky. There was a black jeep, a line of military cars; the black truck's door swung loosely against the wind with its charred driver inside. Lila swung in the same rhythm as a raggedy doll. I couldn't move to console either. Lila moved slightly to her left, away from me, and began to walk toward a lone white flowering shrub. She picked a flower and then shuffled toward an open patch of field, toward nothing.

I visualized long strawberry fields. Green stalks of corn, heads bluntly removed. I was in another world, Iowa perhaps, or central California. Amanda was with me, we walked hand in hand. She was about eighteen, as when we first met.

In my vision, the day is flaming hot, air sucked out of it. We are on a path that seems pristine, though I have not been in this place before. I keep glancing at Amanda; she walks farther and farther from me. It's now hard to see her pale dress against the dried stalks. I hurry trying to catch up, she looks back, blows me a kiss that feels like a cool breeze, falls on her knees to pray. She stands and walks toward a blinding light; her silhouette floats gracefully until she disappears into the light, and then I woke from my dream.

Now Lila appeared in the distance, turned around, and began walking back toward me. There was a hard, bitter taste in the air, a rankness; the feeling was that something had died here. I motioned for Lila to go away. She stopped, caved to the ground, and shouted expletives to the sky, using the Lord's name in vain over and over and over.

The sun was hidden behind Lila, always has been.

I didn't want to look down. A butterfly pulled my eyes down toward Amanda as it landed on her forehead. It flew away just as I meet her half-opened eyes.

There on the dried-out leaves, my lovely bride lay on her back, a peaceful Sleeping Beauty. The magenta blood covering her scars masked all but her long eyelashes and those slightly parted lips that mouthed speechless words into the still air. The sun tried desperately to show its face after a sudden downpour, and now only partially illuminated the small patch of unscarred flesh over her left cheek. Filtered through thin clouds, the light sprayed over arching branches, raining down scattered columns of sparkling dust that danced across her body.

"You finally released into the light, my love."

"This is terrible, I know." David's harsh voice came from some unknown place close by. "Can I do anything for you?"

248

"My God!" I yelled while falling on Amanda. "No!" *God, let me wake up. Make it a nightmare.* She still smelled alive. The perfume—we had searched high and low for it . . . no, it wasn't that perfume. It was something else. Sweet, pure . . . innocent, like my love, my bride.

"She's alive," I half declared. No one smells this lovely in death.

All I could sense was that enchanting fragrance. She had to be alive. Had to . . .

Elian leaned forward. "Brother," he whispered "she is alive, but not here."

"No! God, bring her back! Please bring her back! Make her live!" I held up my ring—the one used to part the San Francisco Bay waters—held it up to the sky as far as I could reach. "Make her live!" I declared, bobbing up and down, heaving in desperation for a miracle. "God of miracles—make one for me!"

None happened. My desperate cries raged through the dank air to a deaf God in the timeless span of hopelessness. She was dead! At the moment of our most precious love. It was not fair—not fair at *all*. We were just learning to love again. "God, it was your love. How sadistic is your love?"

I pounded my fist against my chest and ratcheted my head, wanting to launch it from my neck. I yanked my hair, wanting to pull it out. This was how it worked all the time—for every minute of bliss there were hours of trials. "God, destroy this world that has destroyed love!" I declared in futility.

Elian tried stilling my arms by draping his form around me, bobbing as I bobbed, not letting go, speaking some kind of gibberish. No words would suffice now. Nothing could take away the pain of this cruel fate—love lost, found, then lost again—how cruel. How devilishly cruel.

"I am sorry, gentlemen," David said from behind. "But we need to leave quickly. They'll be back, and our only hope for survival is to reach Jerusalem." I turned my head to find David wringing his hands in a feebly crouched position.

"We'll take care of her," Elian said while lifting me.

Crackling thunder from above jarred me to look up. A jet fighter streamed by, muddying the sky with its vapor trails.

"Hurry!" David yelled. "We must be on our way." Another jet fighter flew by.

"Is that us or them?" Elian asked.

"One is ours, the other is theirs," David replied. "There is no telling which one will prevail. We have only thirty minutes or so to drive before we reach the prime minister's holdout."

My eyes said good-bye to Amanda as Hudson lifted her, the red silk dangling from her body and dancing in the wind. My look back revealed only that red glow, and then she disappeared into the dingy back end of a truck—her only vestige being that stupid red spot that bled over a vibrant-colored life.

How tacky for my lovely bride—being placed in a truck bin. Lovely trash. This world was trash.

"Come," Elian said while guiding me onto the seat still warm from when we last sat side by side, talking as lovers do. I so wanted to feel her—wanted to smell that lovely fragrance again.

Farewell, my love. This life is but a mist. Love of my life. Precious flower in a dry land. *God, give me strength to dry the tears . . . until we meet again.*

"Remember when . . ."

⟋ Chapter Twenty-Eight ⟍

Belial soared through the environs, with renewed purpose after receiving Bakr's orders. A swarm of aero-form warriors poured through hell's portal to fly beside him. He carried between his clawed hands an intricately laced case covered in gold, and on the lid were two golden dragons with their wings facing each other to form an enclosed area. It was the size of a jewelry box. Only, this contained no jewels, through it did carry a priceless treasure, the spirit Ra who had possessed Bakr. Just as the Ark of the Covenant once carried with it Yahweh's presence, the essence of Ra who ruled every creature beholden to the world lay in a box, awaiting his release for the final battle with the Christ.

Belial looked over the ant mounds of ruins over Megiddo. Because Baal could not tempt the son of Adam, there would be no dominion over this world any longer. Now the conflict would occur between Ra and the Christ for rights to the throne of judgment, and over who would take dominion of the new world.

Belial expanded his form, but he was not yet ready to fight. He was a servant brooding over his fate while keenly attuned to Ra through a transmittance that happened between the two through Belial's sticky grasp of Ra's shoebox-sized abode. Ra was a parasitic spirit who had possessed rulers past; once Ruling Prince of the Celestial Order, he descended to rule over the humans' fallen world until recently, after the battle in Megiddo, which caused him to leave Bakr's flesh.

Belial lifted his face to the heavens and let out a guttural, unearthly cry. Flaring his wings and arching his back, he moved swiftly, pumping his head up and down and spiraling through vacuums where no angels crossed. Belial's and Ra's minions floated bat-like in a thick brown mass of winged bodies like a massive dried bloodstain moving over the ethereal space between hell and earth, and over a doomed continent below.

Belial declared: "With Ra we have the power over light!" Indeed, Ra's strength had been cooked for eons over the searing coals of hell. He was god over everything Yahweh could not possess. A spirit steeled by hatred for the one who banished him there. The spirit over everything that Yahweh was not—lies, death, deception—caring for no one and nothing but unabashed desires. "Long live Ra!" Belial yelled again

Belial heard the spirit Ra telepathically. "Ra," Belial said, "upon your release not only the world will bow before you but the heavens as well."

"In due time," Ra replied. The angels had followed Ra because he promised them the next world—the world soon to come. The world Ra would usher forth when his presence was loosed to destroy Yahweh's enslavement over creation—by killing Reuben.

"Soon you will take your place upon the throne," Belial said to Ra.

"Yes," came the silent spirit voice of Ra. Once proclaimed within the world, as in hell, Ra would reign over both heaven and earth.

"Yahweh prophesied the Christ's second coming. Fools," Belial said. Coppery-scented steam wafted from the ornate box he gripped, but he ignored it, descending instead into a deep possessed focus.

"Yes," Ra said to Belial's cavernous heart, "Yahweh's spirit expects to rise from his chosen vessel, this impudent human, Reuben, and ascend to heaven as judge over all. But Yahweh will never create his perfect earth. I have never let him create *his* perfect earth and he never will."

"For a thousand years he says that he will reign, Ra, for a thousand years . . ."

Purulent smoke oozed out of the box held by Belial, inciting in each beast that breathed in its tendrils the unbridled rage of Ra. Wailing choruses of demons screamed with passions to disembowel every human, annihilate any creature in their path. Ra was consummate hatred, and every thought, every feeling, every fiber of one's being consecrated to Ra cried out vitriol for everything not its own.

The demons snarled, spittle misting through clenched teeth, clawed hands reaching out for anyone they might tear; they writhed with unfulfilled desires to brutalize any living thing into a struggling pulp alive enough to feel its pain. Belial and his tormented demons turned lusting eyes toward each other, struggling not to satiate their fury by feasting upon each other.

Still, they had the presence of mind to reason, if only to carry out the deed.

"Yahweh failed in Eden; he will fail again," said Ra.

"Did he not tell us that he would create a new earth then, and that it would be paradise?" asked Belial. "And that both angels and humans would live in harmony with all of Yahweh's creations?"

"Lies," replied Ra. "He's full of himself."

"How did you destroy Eden?" asked Belial.

"By taking away the humans' free will," responded the still, small voice of Ra, "Yahweh will never take their free will. I did that in Eden, when the lusts of their flesh consumed their will."

Indeed, Belial reasoned it as such: When Ra controlled the minds of humans, they became prisoners—addicts who became slaves to their next fix, lovers of money consumed by greed, people stressed by their worldly cares.

Ra's way destroyed human will. Yahweh's way made human will the same as his. Foolish, as self was all one had.

"Ingenious," Belial thought out loud. "You turned the will of humans over to their fears, to their desires, to the confines of their finite thinking. Rats lured into a trap because of their consuming appetites.

"You, Ra, controlled the world by breaking the will of humans. And all that time they thought that Yahweh was trying to control them. He gave them freedom to deny him, and they blamed him for the suffrage caused by their indulgences.

253

"You enslaved them by denying them nothing, because they could never be satisfied. They were consumed by wanting more. And you did this so that you could restore our rightful place above the humans."

The spirits swerved along tunneled pathways to a viscous environ mucked by eons of wasted dreams. They could hardly break through the layers of otherworldly rot that felt like a black hole of despair in the physical. Such being the space of loss that constituted the netherworld and all things between it and the world of the humans. This ghostly vortex bled over from the earth like smoke from a smokestack. Eternal death manifested. Hope vanquished through endless fermentation that was toxic to the soul.

There was only one way to redeem this wasteland: to defeat Yahweh's plan of aligning human will with his—that they might be joined to him. Ra of course never desired fellowship—not once. He simply wanted to create life in *his* image in a place where sinister pleasures reigned. And the only way to accomplish that was to destroy the will of man so that humankind could no longer reign over it. Indeed, humans were victims of their own doings—of technology that impersonalized human intimacy, pleasures that fed self at the expense of others, misguided valor that led to war, and decimation from ages of greed.

Reflections from a bluish-gray marbled earth pierced the dark as Ra's spirit eyes met the physical. Upon closer inspection, he saw green hills speckled with rectangular housing structures thousands of feet below on earth. Toylike cars crisscrossed in mechanical futility. Light broke through thinning clouds, illuminating specks of human figures scurrying below like pests.

"Praise Ra!" Belial bellowed through the vacuum in which he and his fellow warriors traveled.

Their bubbly window to Jerusalem lay before them. Below were comical human figures viewed by Ra and his minions through distortion mirrors that made the fleshly mortals appear as caricatures with no form and having no worth.

They traveled through the space of nothingness, of hopes deferred and dreams never dreamed. Soon they would enter through that window to the world, then open the box containing Ra over the Mount of Olives so that he could eventually reign in the heavens.

He would embolden an unwitting soul to mercilessly kill Reuben, thereby squelching the spirit of Yahweh within Reuben's dead body. A butterfly entombed within its cocoon, squished before it could spread its wings to fly.

Ra would be loosed—to ascend to heaven to proclaim his authority to the angels who had once defied him, to announce to them the coming of a new Eden, with humans ruled by angels—the way it should have been.

Belial's bellicose voice echoed through the horde of unseemly demons all about. They fixated on him like trained wolves.

"Angels of Ra," declared Belial, "prepare to enter the humans' world again—for the final battle. As it was in the beginning of humankind, we will triumph!"

Indeed, since they had killed Amanda, Reuben must have lost all hope. *Pity those who love, and whose love was lost.* Belial laughed. Humans always denied Yahweh when they'd lost what was dearest to them. Selfishness always won out, and that was good.

Belial grabbed the box and shook it wildly overhead, breaking the seal and releasing the maniacal incarnation of all those malicious intentions, leaving some demented humans affected by Ra with only half a soul and half a mind.

That corrosive malignity that had been simmering in hell from the beginning of humankind's fall was released to dominate even Christians who ascribed to only half the truth, those worshipping false idols like security, wealth, status, and appearance. Ra never fell down and worshiped any, but deliciously imparted his ideas to these sickened souls. He pitted himself, inflated with pureness of self, against the one who sacrificed himself on the cross.

All that torments and disorients, all that stirs up animosity, all lies veiled as truth, all that cracks the veneer of faith and stimulates the flesh, all the subtle demonization of life and thought—he poured all of it over humankind. He shook over Jerusalem the lump sum of all the rage seeped into porous humans from Adam down, and now, as if his chest had been a thinly walled bubble, Belial felt his cold heart burst with the descending of Ra's spirit over the final place of conflict.

Chapter Twenty-Nine

"**R**euben, when you meet the prime minister, do not be surprised if she greets you in a cold manner," David said. "She's the Iron Lady, hardened to survive this beastly world. Satan took her only child, her daughter, after she became a Christian. He always goes after the children—"

"Not now," Elian said as he placed his hand on David's shoulder. "Our friend is still mourning, can't you see?"

Leave it to Elian to place the soul's condition above life's circumstances. Of course I mourned. Satan—or God—had punched me in the gut. It was difficult to deduce who earned the blame. The one caused it; the other allowed it. Then again, what did it matter? My lungs stilled until my brain reminded me to breathe again.

We approached Medvedev's secret hideout in Jerusalem thankful that our sputtering Humvee had not died. Try as I might, I couldn't catch my breath. I was heaving inside. Wanting really to get beyond my soulful suffocation and pass on—to see Amanda again. To be with her in heaven once and for all. *Lord, free my spirit. At least do that.*

"There it is," David pointed. A simple hut made of corrugated tin with patched-up holes and slits with protruding gun barrels appeared before us – Medvedev's headquarters.

"Stop the car," David said to Hudson.

Hudson slammed on the brake as a rush of dusted cars broke through camouflaged cardboard covers while racing head-on toward us. Thank God David had radioed ahead. Then again, death appeared not the enemy anymore. Hudson blinked his lights which signaled all in our caravan to stop as the Israeli vehicles before us formed a blockade around Medvedev's hideout.

Before stepping outside to greet our presumed allies, I turned to my friend for one final exchange. "What's this all about?" I asked Elian, emotionally drained and barely able to think.

"You'll learn soon enough," Elian said as he rubbed my shoulder. "In due time we all have to come to the answer by ourselves."

"You've been such a good friend," I said to Elian.

I'd found Amanda only after losing her. Perhaps that's the way of life—you can only find the core of something after the shell's been broken. To live in the moment is to accept the gift of life, and love, and everything resident in that one moment. I wanted all of my "remember whens" to happen in the present. *Be still and know that I am God. Be still—* those words would resonate with me forever.

"I'm here for you, Reuben, as is God," Elian said. "He may seem distant, but the reality is that he's always with us, even now."

"My head knows that. It's my broken heart that sometimes says otherwise."

"Actually," Elian said, "it's your head that doubts. Your broken heart wants him all the more."

I was raw. Perhaps that's how God wanted me to be, needed me to be. Amanda had taught me the lesson of true humility: no pretense, real humility as in "nothing mattered apart from what concerned the one who loved you most." Humility, as in "it's up to God, no matter what."

I stepped outside of our vehicle as David, Elian and Hudson followed to meet the stern faced soldiers who lined up before us. "Shalom!" David shouted to an officer decked with medals filling the front of his jacket. The man's neatly pressed clothes and slicked-back hair contrasted to those of most of the disheveled soldiers we'd met along the way, as did his stiff neck.

"Shalom, Brother David," replied the officer. He turned in my direction as I exited the car with Lila clutching Hudson's biceps.

"And this must be Reuben Simon," the officer said while reaching out his hand in a perfectly straight line. "I am Military Chief of Staff Ram Zahavy."

"Yes," was all I could say.

"The prime minister is waiting." He straightened his back while waving us to the makeshift compound, proud soldier in a humbled nation.

"What's the status of the war?" David asked as we approached the heavily guarded entrance.

"We are very close to maintaining air superiority over the Middle East," Zahavy confidently replied.

"What a wonderful turnaround," David said.

"We are still fighting off combatants," Zahavy said, "but praise God, we are rapidly gaining." "Praise God" as in "Thank you, sir," or "praise God" as in "My heart swells at the thought of your awesomeness"? I think God is more honored by the latter; certainly he's more deserving of it.

We entered through two rusted metal doors that almost came off their hinges. Another doorway appeared at the end of several stairs deep into the dark underground. As we descended, the heavy doors flung open with a gust of stale air. Two stoic soldiers adorned with machine guns more than half their size eyed us up and down.

"Sir," one of them said to General Zahavey. They ushered us through the doors into an austerely lit entryway composed of a dirt floor and plaster walls.

"Prime Minister Medvedev is awaiting you down these stairs," Zahavey said as he opened another side door that led to a small foyer and about twelve stairs leading down to a brightly lit cavern.

"This is our ad hoc command shelter we established to protect Madam Medvedev during our fight to reclaim Jerusalem," the general said.

Sounds of busy people rumbling about and clicking office machines grew louder as we entered into an expansive room contrastingly finished with wood trim, giant screens all around, cubicles, and a glass-enclosed conference room in the center. The door from the conference room sprang open as a woman with perfect posture quickly headed my way, then paused just a moment before turning toward me and cupping her mouth.

She was tall and muscularly shaped, but not one of those overcompensating women who seem intended to one-up the boys. On the contrary, she was so distinguishingly relaxed that she seemed apologetic for her upright manner. Nor did her soft expression fit the press's description of the prime minister as having a titanium spine. The whites of her eyes were a little reddened, yet she blinked without needing to hide her unwiped tears. Her forehead was high, her eyebrows lowered, and her head bowed sympathetically in my direction.

"Mr. Simon," she said as she reached out her hand, "I am so sorry for the loss of your heroic wife."

That she would even mention my loss impressed me, though her genuine emotion moved me—she was not so iron-looking now. Even her handshake felt soft.

"This is my great honor to meet with you, Prime Minister Medvedev. Our mutual friend, Dr. Munny Chin, could not speak more highly about you, and said that you would reference my wife as a hero . . . well, you being a hero . . ."

To my amazement the prime minister moved forward and tightly embraced me before retreating back to her regal stance and clasping my hand between both of hers. "Our Lord is with you—may I call you Reuben?" she asked.

"Of course."

"Reuben, I know loss all too well, and I feel in part how Amanda's loss must be affecting you now. Words can be empty in times of loss, but *the* Word, our Lord Jesus Christ, is within you?" She tilted her head.

"So I've been told."

"Inside you." She nodded.

"I suppose," I answered while glancing down.

"His words imprinted on your chest?" Medvedev glanced at my buttoned shirt half meekly. I dared not offer to open it.

"Yes," I quickly answered. "I believe our Lord would have me share these words with your people, should you approve."

"Of course—I was about to insist that you do. In fact, I've arranged to travel with you and your fellow Americans to the temple site. There you'll find an eager audience—and there you will declare the word of our Lord."

The prime minister vulnerably smiled, then sucked in her gut and arched her back. I supposed all great leaders maintained their outward bravery through deep-seated compassions.

"One more thing," she said. "When we get to the temple site, you'll see two prophets there—you'll know both of them."

"Dare I ask who?"

"I'd rather you be surprised," she answered with a smile. "They also declare God's words."

☙ Chapter Thirty ☙

he bright light high over Jerusalem's temple pulled us east. "A
burning star," David explained.

Rabbi Horowitz sat next to Madam Medvedev in the SUV,
windows rolled down, David and Elian on either side of me. The jagged
Jerusalem skyline sketched before us with the strokes of war. The fading
sun pierced through smoke from smoldering remnants, breaking the blue
sky into muffled colors, fading the light to bronze.

The sun gradually fell down toward dusk behind fume clouds swollen
with humidity. Hills stretched for miles. In front of us tall pines dotted
a familiar landscape along with flowers that spilled over walls and ruins,
burned fragments of structures, the shadows of Israeli box buildings over
rubble streets. The wind carried the bark of a dog, the pungent smell
of chemical fires in the distance, of a flaming luxury hotel with people
watching it burn from the balcony of their apartments.

The startling vision of the pristine temple ahead conjured up biblical
stories. It was like a primeval history, constructed afresh from the
beginning of time, of the origin of God's promise to the Jews who had
escaped Egypt. We couldn't wait to get to the rebuilt temple of Solomon.

Its gold headdress came into view, beaming over its neighboring structures. Jerusalem greeted us with the familiar aura of a long-lost relative eager to get reacquainted.

Bright stadium lights exposed heavily clothed masses, thousands poised against the shadows of temple turrets facing a large podium. The cool wind introduced a faint perfume, so familiar—the same floral mix I sensed over Amanda's sleeping figure. I remembered her hair swept up like the clouds captured in heavenly ribbons.

It was an expectant time. We all knew Jesus Christ would emerge again—this time not in a manger but, rather, birthed in his glory. Would we see him from heaven or from earth? Somehow I knew that we held the key to unlock the doorway to his presence.

Madam Medvedev stood with her head bowed, eyes gently closed.

Elian's strong profile drew my notice. His slight chin jutted out in the confidence of a general ready for the fight—the same pose he'd struck before I met God on the cliff. Perhaps ready for one final showdown. His pensive gaze stretched over miles of thought.

"You've pulled me through the tough times," I said to him.

He turned with a smile. "And you, dear Reuben, have been a true friend . . . and I will always remember your faithfulness in taking in this stranger," he said while pointing at his chest. Elian's sedated tone sounded a bit unsettling.

"Have you ever wondered why God left us behind?" I asked him.

"What do you think?" he answered.

"The best I can determine is that we were just willing, that's all."

"Those who trusted him enough to postpone paradise by staying on this earth were certainly useful to God, but I'm not sure that's why," Elian said. "What's the reason God uses people?"

"To fulfill his plans, I suppose." I was almost drained of all reason. But then my answer didn't resonate with that light-bulb-going-off-in-the-head feeling.

"Does he use people to fulfill his plans, or does he use his plans to fulfill people?"

This sounded like the-chicken-or-the-egg argument over which came first. Only in this case it was clear that his children's needs came first in the eyes of God, not his need to change the world or anything in it. It wasn't about just using us—God can use anyone or anything to complete his works. It was, I believe, that "God has a work to accomplish within us," I said. "And we just need to will ourselves over to the potter's hands so that he could finish the work."

All this time I thought it was about doing God's will, when it was really about allowing God to perfect his will in us.

"Are you ready?" interjected the prime minister as her eyes loomed over dark-rimmed glasses.

"For what, Madam Prime Minister?" I answered with more than a little trepidation.

"To speak—to declare God's words to a people hungering for them. We sent out an announcement—I will introduce you, then you speak."

No pressure. Only about, what—ten thousand or so people around the podium? And TV—how many millions in addition? *God, possess my mind and tongue to speak with your voice. And give me the energy to get through this.* I clutched my handkerchief, ready to wipe my brow.

Sounds of tangled conversations, clapping, and rock-concert shouts pierced through our windows as we turned to view mobs of people waving blurred white-and-blue flags of Israel. Signs giving glory to God extended over lifted arms. Boisterous praises shouted out to Medvedev. One little boy jumped with all his might in a futile attempt to compete to see against his taller rivals, until he was finally lifted up onto the shoulders of a lanky man—after which the biggest grin filled his face.

"They seem to be celebrating victory—did I miss something?" I asked.

Medvedev giggled uncharacteristically. "Since your battle at Armageddon, brother . . ."

"You saw that?"

"Our air force flew over—we had some people stationed there in anticipation—taping it. It was beyond words. I've never before witnessed the spirit realm in all its glory. Amazing."

"Could everyone see the battle?" Elian asked.

"Some saw nothing."

Discernment, I supposed.

Elian perked up. "What happened since that battle?"

"Our forces began pushing back the enemy as never before," she answered, "so much so that we now intend to take the land promised by Abraham—that bordering the Mediterranean and the Euphrates."

"And this occurred after the spiritual battle on Mount Megiddo?" I asked.

"Precisely," answered Medvedev.

"What happens in the spirit realm is mirrored in the physical world," said Elian. "Now the final battle is about to begin."

With that ominous proclamation, our car pulled up to the stairs leading almost six feet up to the stage. Medvedev emerged from the vehicle and motioned for Elian and me to follow suit.

"And now, ladies and gentlemen," a Hebrew-accented gentleman said at the podium, "it is my pleasure to introduce to you our noble leader, Prime Minister Abra Medvedev!"

Arms lifted high, creating an ocean of waving hands over blaring shouts of euphoria. The prime minister spritely stepped up to the podium and pressed her hands downward to quell the cheers.

She spoke deliberately. "Citizens of freedom. Fellow countrymen. Brothers and sisters. For millennia the Jewish people have struggled to fight against the forces of evil, those marked by bigotry and fueled by gratuitous hatred. Innocent Jews, children, and women, slaughtered throughout history simply because of their heritage.

"Why such hatred for a people who simply wished to live in peace? Because, my friends, fomenting this hatred was the Devil and his demons, and the pawns they used to wreak destruction on a people devoted to the God of Abraham.

"And for thousands of years many of us prayed for our redeemer. The one prophesied in Isaiah as the son of God. And, as you know, I profess to know this Messiah as Jesus Christ." Shouts and praises for Jesus reverberated through most of the amassed crowd as Medvedev continued. "Our journey began as a people at the formation of this earth, and it was birthed anew when Moses freed our people from Egypt, and when God wrote his truth upon the stone tablets we know as the Ten Commandments. Moses declared these truths to our people.

"Today, my fellow believers, God has used another man to declare his words of truth, but instead of writing these words on stone, he has carved them into the chest of this great prophet of our age. And today, there stands among us this prophet, a man who, with the angels of God, defeated on the battleground of Armageddon one of the WSA's mightiest armies and the demons who empowered them. And it is with a tender heart that he comes to us, having lost his heroic wife, Amanda, whom we honor for her bravery in the face of terrible suffering.

"Please welcome my friend and brother, Reuben Simon!"

I dried my sweaty palms against the towel I quickly discarded before moving forward to shake the prime minister's hand with an ensuing genteel hug. The raucous sounds echoed through muffled noises in the distance as my mind filtered all but my solitary prayers to the God of Abraham.

In the stillness of this reverent moment, God spoke. Not in an audible voice but rather in an undeniable assurance of his presence and his faithfulness—and nothing else mattered. I spoke for an audience of one.

"The air over Israel is pregnant with anticipation for our Lord's coming," I said while pausing for an interpreter to restate my words. "Do you not sense it?" Like a roaring pride of lions, the masses responded in the affirmative. I spoke almost in abandonment of thought.

"Before I left America, I thought God had deserted me, and in my misery I began to bicycle at full speed, heading for the cliffs of San Francisco hoping to lunge over them and perish in the icy waters of the Pacific Ocean. However, God intervened, saved my life, and then spoke audibly to me, burning into my chest words that express his grace, and that which we must trust to enjoy a relationship with God."

At the risk of appearing risqué, I unbuttoned my shirt, pulling it back to reveal the raised letters of my Lord's words: *I am always with you.* The crowd remained silent while viewing the jumbo screens on either side.

"God's message is simple—trust him. He wants us to know that, however abandoned we may feel, he is always with us and he will never forsake us. And above all, he wants intimacy with us no matter the cost to him, or to us. The removal of his presence from this earth has forced many of us to our knees, a position I've found to be the best vantage point from which to seek God and to eventually see into the eyes of his love.

"Beloved, we all seek a better place, a more joyful state of being. However, lasting joy can only be manifested in the arms of our loving Father. Everything else is fleeting. And during my journey I've learned that although our path may be strewn with hardship, our Lord is faithful to carry us through the storms, and sometimes he clears another path through this foreign world—a fresh way that inevitably leads to home.

"I must admit, I once thought that I was to lead our band of American believers back to the Promised Land. I thought that I could somehow bring God's presence back with us, and all would be well. However, God had a different plan. He simply wanted me to follow him, and to let him take care of the details. I had to let go.

"Some of you need to also let go, and to simply believe God's promises. I've learned that God's words are the only words upon which we can rely. Not the world's, not even our own. But to know them we must ride the storms, listen to the confident voice of wisdom, still ourselves in the present within God's presence, and expect that everything will eventually be worked for good if only we believe in Jesus Christ. In so doing we adopt the mind of Christ, which is essential to living in the fullness of our Lord. And if we do, he will make our paths straight. Our actions, even our thoughts, will be aligned with his will. He will right the wrongs. He will give us everything we need, and even more so. If only we believe . . ."

For a moment my heart sank with the fullness of God's grace. My heart stilled deep as emotions of gratitude rose.

"This has been a hard lesson for me, my friends. I am not so much a man of faith; rather, I am a broken vessel forged in the hands of my maker. I now stand before you as a person being made whole by our loving Father, yet still broken, as one who is keenly aware of my scars, and my faults, and one who has been made stronger for them. I failed but . . ." *God, please keep me from breaking down with cries,* I prayed. I paused to realize the confidence that he gave me.

"I have failed but, God, you never failed me." One could not imagine the reverence with which I spoke those words to my Father—my audience of one. He awoke me to the masses listening silently, and so I continued:

"Though my failures often define me in this world more than my successes, I strive to remember who defines me as I am. We believers in

Christ are his chosen children, citizens of heaven, and foreigners to this world. So let us try to be content and grateful for the grace that our Lord has bestowed upon us. I hope . . . I truly hope you know as I do that Jesus stands with you, always, even when he can't be seen, or heard, or felt." I begged that God would still my tears. *Just for a little while, Lord.*

"My brothers and sisters, we are heirs to his throne, adopted into God's family, connected to the bloodline of Abraham, David, and our Messiah, Jesus Christ. It is, after all, most important to God that he establish *koinonia* fellowship with us, if only we will obey his word and let him have his way in our lives. God desires to be our all, and that through him, steeped in his presence, we might also love one another as he first loved us.

"This, my brothers and sisters, is God's word for this age, summed up in his very person—his love is sufficient."

With these words I concluded my speech and left the podium to the stillness of the crowd. Not a peep could be heard. Elian nodded and smiled at me before giving me a hug as I began to descend the stairs with the solemnity of a rejected messenger. So much for my public speaking ability.

From a far distance some chanted indiscernible words, slowly followed by a greater number of faint voices shouting in unison. Gradually the volume increased as more and more people began declaring the same mantra, still unrecognizable to me as the chorus rolled forward with increasing intensity. As the verbal momentum reached the stage area, the words rang clearly as an expression of thousands: "Amanda! Amanda!" Over and over the multitudes shouted the name of my beloved wife.

"Well done," said Madam Medvedev. "Amanda spoke to us through her suffering. She was the modern-day Job. The account of her suffering was relayed to me during your flight to Jerusalem, and I used her story through a broadcast to encourage our people. Amanda's strength and courage became a rallying cry throughout our ranks. When she rejected Bakr's offer to restore her at the airport, the news went viral. She reminded us that no matter the cost, or the temptation, we must remain true to our God. Thousands came to know Christ through her witness. And now you have encouraged us in God's strength."

How wonderful to learn that my Amanda's suffering had been turned to good, just as God promises.

"Bravo!" declared David. "You stoned."

"You rocked," corrected Hudson.

I turned and began walking toward Elian, who stood next to the TV cameraman. "You've been the inspiration for my confidence," I said to him.

"Praise God," he responded.

"I mean it, with all my heart," I continued. "I've lost almost everything and gained more in return, only I didn't know it before."

"So what's the lesson, brother?" Elian asked.

"That God never leaves us or forsakes us, even though we—I—forsook him."

Elian touched my cheek with his hand. "God wants so much to be close to you—"

"But he appeared to leave this godforsaken place—at least for this time—"

"Not really," said Elian. "The world left him."

"And I of all people, having heard from him, shouldn't have doubted."

"You're in good company, brother," Elian said.

"Huh?"

"All twelve disciples did the same. Even though Jesus walked with them, performed miracles in front of them, they *still* denied him in the end."

"True," I answered with a tingle of revelation, "the world convicted God and sentenced him. He abided, but he never left those of us who still believed. I had falsely interpreted his presence through the jaded lenses of this world. I let the world be my arbiter of truth." *Forgive me, Lord.*

I wished that Jesus was with me now so I could ask him the reason for this convoluted turn of events. Just knowing might provide some added consolation. But, on second thought, no. How could I understand the answer if it was not born through my own acceptance in Christ? A teacher's instruction is not accepted until it is received by faith, and even then the understanding comes only through the interpretation of one's mind, and in the case of Christ, through the assimilation into one's soul.

"I'll just have to trust that Father knows best," I surmised. "Wasn't there a TV show by that title?"

Elian's face glowed with the surreal expression of a delighted child.

"Come, let us go to the temple," Medvedev said while waving us toward the restored worship site about a hundred yards behind us. The crowds began to migrate toward the temple as Israeli soldiers cleared our path.

A crackle echoed . . .

"Oh God—no!"

ᕦ Chapter Thirty-One ᕤ

Belial and the demons lifted the gold box over the Mount of Olives and slowly opened its ornate lid. Peppery vapor wafted downward. The shadowy presence spread like an expanding rain cloud pushed by the strong winds until settling upon unwitting people below.

Some of Ra's victims breathed in the gray mist, which caused them to inhale with ragged gasps. Others suddenly slumped over and aimlessly rambled to some random place. Several touched by the vapor's fingers lunged forward in a feral prowl after being consumed with carnal concerns. And still others instantly seethed with the appearance of cornered wild beasts.

Such was one man who wheezed after sucking in Ra's presence through an open window. The man closed the window and lethargically walked to the middle of a room dusted with mites. His beard was long, and his tunneled eyes were barely visible to anyone who might see him because of his muted snarls, though only Ra could see him now. Before Ra took him, other demons had inhabited the man, morphing him from the inside to expose tree branch veins, bulbous eyes, a twisted face, and a yellowish body polished with bloodstains.

He sat alone, in an austere room with barren walls and week-old dishes scattered randomly throughout the adjoining kitchen. The aftertaste of decay overlaid a medicinal odor from moldy growths. Odors of liquor and vomit, boiled cauliflower, and rat droppings intermingled with the stench of meat aged like wine.

Fear fermented in dim corners in which demons feasted on their willing host, more dead than alive. He watched the peeling wallpaper, which appeared like his scaly skin.

He functioned well in the dark, the shades drawn, robotically loading his sniper rifle. He was fueled with Ra's spectral fumes. He raged a thousand times harder than ever before, fierier than when he pounded his fist through walls, and when he beat women foolish enough to want his bad-boy ways.

A cockroach scurried across the floor. He stomped it and pressed the floor with all his might, grinning at the innards that gushed from the sides of his boots and listening to its squishy crunch.

The lights dimmed without him touching a switch; the smell of blood from a recent kill wafted from the kitchen sink. Death could not have been a more welcomed visitor.

After loading his weapon, the man stood upright and expressionless. He rigidly walked toward the front door, opened it slowly, and looked from side to side while coddling his gun. He stroked it with his hands and rubbed his cheek softly over the barrel before wrapping the 81 assault rifle with his full body in a passionate embrace. He strutted over to a car riddled with dents, easing open the door before falling into the seat.

He hesitated a few seconds before starting the car, head dropped onto the steering wheel while taking in a full breath and holding it. He let out a rolling groan that built into a full-bodied growl unlike any a human should make.

Without further delay he drove feverishly toward the temple, lowering the passenger window to suck in the funeral ashes that rested within Ra's breeze. The air was thick with oppression, similar to burnt chemicals that left a bitter aftertaste.

He was stoked with a mission now—roiling in hatred for the so-called prophet whose voice spoke of God from the nearby temple.

The man sped faster with each thought of Reuben, aka "the Moses of our age." Little did he know of the prophet, only galled by the respect shown him. No one ever said a nice word about this man. And yet that weasel of a prophet was being revered with the same distinction as Israel's greatest leader. Indeed, Reuben's stature only served to mirror the man's own worthlessness. And the only way to squelch the fury would be to break the prophet's reflection.

Something oozed within. Something stale and fowl. Scorched brown coagulated blood. He had to get rid of it. Only fresh blood would do. Warm red blood. Innocent blood.

Ra now fixed his attention solely on this lone warrior. His thoughts merged with that man's thoughts. He manipulated him like a ghoulish puppet on a string. A demented clown. The kind children fear.

The man could see the temple looming larger now, its richly appointed golden dome contrasting his own destitution. He wished to bomb the whole place; but alas, killing the temple of the Christ would do.

He pulled onto a gravelly side road as his car strained to climb the hill overlooking the temple square. He parked at its peak. The valley was lit by bright lights that rudely cut into the dark. Squirming bodies below and around the temple looked whiter because of its illumination. Disgustingly so.

A lone tear-stained olive tree appeared in plain sight atop the Mount of Olives. Strange how he knew of the dried tears. Sick in their sweetness. The Christ's tears.

He popped the trunk and stepped out to retrieve the rifle loaded with only one bullet.

He walked deliberately to the edge, binoculars in hand. Reuben could be easily spotted in the center of huddled masses swarming him like maggots to crap.

He dropped the binoculars and retrieved his night vision goggles from a sack. He took one final deep breath of the intoxicating air before aiming his rifle directly at the man who carried the spirit of Yahweh.

In the heart. The bullet needed to go into the heart.

The night turned shadowy. Vapory ghouls danced in the wind with cheerful expectation. Minuets by ancients drawn to the smell of wasted flesh. Twirling vortexes of smoke amid the moonlit ashes.

Ra stilled the man for one moment to savor the end of Yahweh's perfect plan. To kill the host would be to kill the spirit wishing to emerge from its dormant state. How fitting that the worm's growth would be halted before sprouting its wings.

How delicious.

Boom. The rifle pressed painfully into his shoulder. *Crackle* . . . and the echo of a job well done.

"It is finished," declared the man—or was it Ra who spoke the final proclamation?

⟬ Chapter Thirty-Two ⟭

Elian's chest bled profusely as he gasped, striving to fill his lungs with air. Blood oozing out of his wound soaked through his left pocket spreading through his shirt's threads at an alarming rate. He groaned as though somebody had literally ripped his flesh apart.

Some gentleman stooped over Elian and began pressing his chest with a white cloth. Elian kept crying out, "Father . . . Father, do not abandon me." I couldn't bear to lose my best friend. *God, save him!*

"He saved you," someone said in the crowd. I turned and noticed a woman draped in sackcloth.

"He jumped in front of you—that bullet was meant for you," she said as my heart sank into the abyss.

"Elian, don't die," I eked out.

"Pray for me," returned his familiar voice.

"God, in the name of Jesus Christ, heal my brother Elian," I implored.

I touched his crimson chest. His eyes closed as he faded into a peaceful slumber.

#

A fiery splendor reflected off gold plates, framed on top by spikes with sharp points that would seem to impale anyone who landed upon them. Stones, some as large as boulders, shone against the bright lights in contrast to the exceedingly white walls around them. An altar appeared in plain sight, with corners like horns, and an indiscernible figure placed atop it—the sacrifice.

Was this heaven or hell? I couldn't tell. My consciousness returned only dimly, and then only through blurred lenses. Every sound was obscured by my mind's filter, I wanted to tune out the random voices and vignettes of the past as though a spectator in my own biographical film.

Where was the light that preceded heaven? The river of life? I so wanted to dip my hands in it again. Are you here, Amanda?

"Reuben, can you hear me?"

"Who?"

A fog obscured the speaker, so I reached out my hand frantically attempting to clear the air and see him. At first Elian's surreal features appeared as though from an out-of-focus camera. I must have fainted, or dreamed—something. Slowly my surroundings crystallized from a blurred reality while I braced my head with my hands in order to keep it from jiggling like Jell-O.

"It's me—Elian. I've been healed."

A heavy hand rested on my shoulder. I wasn't ready for any tactile intrusions—as I was just trying to regain some semblance of reasoning— let alone the brutish touch of my shoulda-been-a-wrestler friend David. "Reuben, this is David. The most amazing thing happened!" *Thanks for the blunt wake-up call, David.*

"What?" I asked, trying quickly to climb out of my shock.

"Elian—you prayed for his healing, and his wound just closed up— amazing!" David's face appeared in plain sight. The sounds and views of huddled people now became as clear as a digital video.

"You're not dead?" I asked Elian, not even believing the audacity of my question.

"I'm afraid not," replied Elian. "You do trust God, after all."

"How . . . it . . ."

"Don't try to reason it out, Reuben. Your faith saved me."

"No, *you* saved *me*," I replied. "You jumped in front of *me*."

I barely had time to rejoice when that decadent moldy smell permeated the misty air again. Ashes floated like snowflakes all around, illuminated by the bright stadium lights shining down upon the temple.

"Who was that I saw being sacrificed on the altar?" My vision played out just as vividly in remembrance as it did in the moment it happened. In it a cloud covered the tabernacle, and a blinding light filled the place of worship. Over a white beam connecting two pillars was written: "In the beginning was the Word, and the Word was God, and the Word became flesh." Then a figure I assumed was Jesus bowed at the altar and cried tears that flowed into a stream to the left of the altar.

A gate facing east opened, and Jesus's spirit rose heavenward and lifted me into the inner court, and from that vantage point I beheld such splendor no mind can imagine. Then Jesus infused within me his spirit which slowly rolled through my insides with the comfort of an internal massage, leaving me feeling as though floating over all space and dimension. Jesus declared to me: "Heaven is my throne, and the earth is my footstool. Where is the house that you will build me? And where is the place of my rest? For all those things my hand has made, and all those things exist, but on this one will I look: on him who is humble and of a contrite spirit and who trembles at my word."

Next, singers praised God from two inner court chambers, and the altar of sacrifice appeared with water flowing south of it. Four horns were at each corner of the altar, and inside a hearth made of two ledges and a single base. Goats, bulls, and rams were led to the altar, as people carried grains, oils, and salt. Then a towering angel appeared and said, "Offer sacrifices of joy in his tabernacle—sing praises to the Lord!" What happened next evoked the profound emotion that awoke me: Jesus strained to carry a cross to the altar. Others surrounding him tried to relieve him of the cross, but he rebuked each one that tried to do so. Jesus's dragged his worn body to the edge of the altar, barely able to stand, and with all his strength pushed the cross over the top the altar.

"The last sight I saw in my vision," I explained to Elian and David, "was a figure draped over the top of the cross that lay upon the altar."

"Was it Jesus?" David asked.

"That would be the obvious choice," I answered. "But, no, I think the figure was someone else. I felt as though I was atop the cross and it was very real."

"If you look at the temple altar, nothing is on it." David replied.

"No, I saw someone on the altar in my vision—I swear it."

"No one can sacrifice themself on the altar," insisted David. "The altar was rebuilt for a sacrifice of food in remembrance of Christ's sacrifice for us."

Elian helped me sit upright. "Perhaps you witnessed the ultimate sacrifice," he said.

I thought for a while—what was the ultimate sacrifice? Then it dawned on me. "The ultimate sacrifice is to give my all to the one who gave me his all," I said.

Elian just smiled.

"Where's the prime minister?" I asked.

"She was ushered back to a holding site after the shooting," Elian answered. "She's fine."

David jumped up like a giddy five-year-old. "We have a surprise for you. You'll be as pleased as a punch. The two prophets—they are in the temple square—you'll want to meet them. They have been declaring the words of God day and night."

This was all too much too quickly. David and Hudson helped me walk. Elian insisted that he stay behind for "just a while" before joining us in the temple square. We walked through the cloisters (of the outermost court) upon varied cold stones of all kinds. My eyes glanced upon the second court, where there was a partition made of marble all around, very elegant, and from the floor rose brilliantly white pillars—"declaring the law of purity," as David explained it.

David stopped us before we entered the "sanctuary," up fourteen steps from the first court in which we stood.

"We cannot enter the innermost court," David said. "Do you see the gold embossed gate with no doors?"

"Yes," I answered.

"These represent the universal visibility of heaven. It is through those gates, into the sanctuary, that our Lord will appear—the most sacred part of the sanctuary where the presence of God resided in Solomon's time."

280

Chapter Thirty-Two

"For the second coming of Jesus Christ," I said.

"Yes—he resides within you now, does he not?" David asked.

Then it came to me. The sacrifice on the altar that I viewed. That person was truly me! I was to be sacrificed so that the spirit of Jesus Christ might be released.

"I am the sacrifice!" I shouted.

David's contorted face looked at me as though I were a lunatic.

"Brother," he said, "let us first meet God's prophets."

As we stepped easterly, seven lamps greeted us on either side of the hallway leading toward a large public courtyard. Declarative voices boomed out from the courtyard.

What first struck me were sweet-smelling spices. "Incense replenished from the sea," as David explained it, "signifying that God is the possessor of all things that are both in the uninhabitable and habitable parts of the earth."

"The same fragrance I smelled on Amanda's body," I said.

Twelve loaves sat upon a table within the courtyard. *The Last Supper*, I thought. None of this made sense to me, yet it all played out in perfect harmony with my soul.

Large candle flames danced throughout the dimly lit courtyard to the rhythm of the gentle winds. By now the mysterious prophets' voices rang out boldly from behind the courtyard pillars.

"Reuben, the Lord is with you!" declared a deep voice. A robed figure walked from around the pillar into the courtyard with arms outstretched, his face hidden beneath the saggy hood. The tall prophet glided across the floor toward me. I must admit that the figure's rather cryptic appearance froze every muscle in my body. David stepped forward.

"Reuben, may I introduce you to Elijah?" he said.

"*The* Elijah? The one who ascended to heaven without dying?" I asked in awe.

"Yes, I am he," Elijah said while pulling back his hood to reveal a tawny-colored face with brown glassy eyes that warmed me. "It was because I did not die on earth that I could visit it again for this most precious time."

I was speechless.

"Did you bring him?" Elijah asked.

"Who . . . you mean the spirit of God—Jesus?"

Elijah nodded.

"I've been told he resides within me, if that's what you mean."

Elijah walked within one foot of me and boldly pressed his hand over my heart, tightly closing his eyes. He stayed there for at least two minutes while breathing deeply.

"No," Elijah said. "Though God's spirit is with you always, his full presence is not in you."

He could just as well have punched me in the gut. After all that had been said and done, to think that I had failed my mission . . .

"Still," Elijah said, "to be sure . . ." He waved his hand. "My brother, it is time to greet your old friend." Elijah turned toward a hidden dark corner.

My so-called old friend emerged from the darkness draped in a flowing white garment with his covered head bowed. The floor received the prophet's gliding feet that seemed to float toward me. The figure walked not ten feet from me and paused, then lifted his head and slowly pulled back the hood.

"Munny Chin!" My Vietnamese mentor who had led me to Christ when I was an agnostic. My dearest friend who disappeared during the plague while sharing the truth of Jesus Christ in Israel.

Munny pulled my body to his so forcefully that he almost knocked the two of us over.

"Reuben, my dear friend!" he said while squeezing me. "I have longed for this moment." Munny kissed me on the cheeks and forehead—a trait he undoubtedly picked up in heaven, given his formerly proper demeanor on earth.

"I can't believe—Munny! And you've grown hair!"

Everyone laughed.

"We have much to catch up on," Munny said, "and we'll have to do most of that in paradise, my friend. Time is running short. I overheard Elijah's word as to whether God's spirit was inhabiting you. I'm afraid, my dear friend, that our Father's Shekinah presence is not within you."

"Shekinah?"

"His glory," Munny explained. "I'm sorry."

"But how—I mean, everyone said as much. The Holy Spirit resides in each believer, doesn't he?"

Munny's exceptionally wide smile revealed teeth I'd never seen before. "He meets with us from without now. But soon, very soon, my dear friend, he will purge the earth of unrighteousness so that he can reside with his children face-to-face."

"A new earth," interjected Elijah.

"A new garden of Eden?" I remembered this from David's earlier words to me.

"Paradise," Munny answered, "a resurrected garden of Eden that will flow out of its hidden place under this earth. And on this earth our Lord Jesus Christ will reign with you and me for a thousand years."

This was all too amazing. I knew God's presence would need to be restored in the temple, and to my profoundest disappointment, I had failed to deliver.

"I'm so sorry," I apologized.

Munny placed his hand under my chin to lift my head, his piercing eyes looking straight into my heart. "You did bring him here, Reuben. He was always with you."

Two tender hands grasped my shoulder from behind as someone gently rested his head against my neck, imparting the most wonderful assurance. He then stepped gracefully to my right.

"Elian," I said. "Thank you—"

"Lord and Master, the great I Am," declared Elijah and Munny as they kneeled down before Elian and kissed his feet.

"Oh my—God." I dropped to my knees.

"Yes," Elian replied to me.

Imagine my sheer stupefaction. All this time . . .

"I was walking and talking with Jesus Christ, and didn't even know you."

"You knew me," Elian responded, "as one closer than a brother."

Elian motioned for Elijah and Munny to rise while giving them hugs and kisses. "One way or another I am always with my children."

"But all this time . . ." I had to take a deep breath hoping my heart would stop flapping around like a loose kite. "I should have known. It was written over my heart—you are always with me."

"Be at peace," Elian, or rather Jesus, said. "Though I am with my beloved always, few trust that it is so."

"Why didn't you just tell me?" More importantly, why didn't I know it was him? What telltale signs had I missed? His carefree demeanor had thrown me off. I expected Jesus to be more . . . somber—yes, because of the world's rejection of him, because of all this ugliness around. Now that I look back, I should have known that his joy came from transcending the evident to the reality of God. He lived in a place separate from me. I was so caught up in the duality of this world and the spirit world that I failed to grasp that my reality should have centered on the person of Jesus Christ, who was always with me. If I had just stilled myself in the presence of Jesus, I could have found the joy that Elian exuded.

"You needed to first believe," Elian said. "Faith activates true relationship."

"You promised that everything would turn around for good, and I doubted you." I could barely speak through my emotional heaves. "In heaven . . . I knew you so intimately."

"That was in heaven, surrounded by my glory, Reuben. Blessed are those who believe yet do not see."

"Sounds familiar," I said. And then an overriding conviction filled me. "This will be the question I will ask myself from this point forward: 'What must I do knowing that Jesus is beside me?'"

Going forward, no space in my existence would be void of Christ's presence. He is always with me, whether I see him, or hear his word, or whether he speaks in the silence or is in fact silent—he is always with me. While strolling I will walk and commune with Jesus. He shall dine with me, and work with me, and we can play together just as we did in the flesh. No more can I think of my Lord as an invisible, imagined companion. He is real beyond sight, smell, sound, or touch. Jesus's reality existed in his promise that he was always with us.

I knew now that Jesus would always sit in the chair next to me; he would hug me in my time of loss, he would always rejoice with me, and pray with me. "I believe now, Jesus, that you were always with me regardless of whether I knew it or not," I said. "Even before you met me after the plane crashed, you were always with me; you had never left. My believing you were with me didn't change the fact that you *were* and *are* with me. You were with me before and after the rapture—always—because you promised as much."

Elian—Jesus—smiled a river of comfort. "Knowing is believing." His face relaxed with the understanding look of a kind teacher patiently waiting for his student's epiphany. "My children know my voice."

"Your word—it was all about your word, your promise, wasn't it?"

Elian firmly grasped my arms while drilling his eyes into mine. "Beware of just *knowing* my word, beloved. Even Satan knows my word. My word can only come to life when translated into *your* word. With one voice we can speak and act in one accordance. Then, and only then, my promises will constitute your reality."

"If only—" and then I caught myself as Elian cupped my head with his hand.

"Have you forgotten my patience and forgiveness? Just ask, and you will receive anything."

"So please tell me what to do," I pleaded.

"Listen with your spirit," he said while pressing his hand into my chest. "Wisdom is my voice. Now be at peace, and let wisdom rule in your spirit. Once I speak a word, whether it be over two thousand years ago or even now, from my lips or the lips of my prophets, or through your thoughts as reflected by my truth, these words must be fresh to you each moment of your life. For I am the living word, and I am always with you in spirit and in truth."

"Thank you, Lord," I said while kneeling down.

"Let's always keep in touch," Elian said with a smile and a touch to my head.

I'd pay everything to see that smile again and again. Come to think of it, I *would* see his smile, always—just like I *would* smell his sweet perfume, and feel his warm embrace, and hear his encouragement, and everything that is good. That is, everything of Jesus Christ *would* stay afresh with the renewal of my mind by my listening to God's wisdom, and worshipping him and expecting his presence to be in my midst. So that Elian and I would never say hello or good-bye; we would always be together.

"Are you ready?" interjected Elijah as he reached for Jesus.

"I am," declared Elian as he gave me one final squeeze.

Munny and Elijah grasped Elian's hands on either side to escort him toward the stairs leading up to the Holy of Holies sanctuary.

Watching the backside of Elian walking toward his destiny filled me with hope. I also dwelled on the tender memories of my fellowship with Jesus that I had so carelessly taken for granted.

The solemnity of this holy time pressed my soul with that one lingering question: What would I have done or thought differently had I known Elian was really Jesus? More importantly, how would I act going forward knowing he was with me even now?

I knew now to substitute his words for my words with the confidence of a kindred soul. His promises would trump my realities. I had an eternity to get to know him.

I followed close behind, understanding that I could not ascend the stairs with my Savior. Only he could enter the chamber as the only one untainted by this world.

Anticipation stilled the midnight air with not a sound anywhere. The silent wind blew crisp with freshness. Moonlight mixed with dimmed lantern lights cast a silhouette of our Lord marching up the steps. Step by step he hesitantly trekked as though about to enter a deeper shade of dusk—through death's door again?

Munny and Elijah gracefully let go of Elian's hands. Christ took the final steps before entering a place none of us could comprehend. Adrenaline pulsed through me. Peopled jammed around me with frozen anticipation. Jesus appeared now a faded figure. And then the wind surged and blew out the flickering candles around him, surrendering him to the darkness.

Munny hurriedly stepped down to stand at the base of the temple. He embraced me with that knowing look. "God only gives us grace for this moment," he said. My mentor was still offering me sage wisdom. "Do not worry about yesterday, because our Lord keeps only that which is good from our yesterdays. And do not worry for tomorrow, because only our Lord is in tomorrow—and if so, we need have no worry of the future. And do not worry for today, because the Lord is our provider."

"Thank you for those living words," I said. "The Lord is with us."

A beam of light cut into the black around Elian. I could faintly see him at the entrance to the inner chamber. His moonlit face looked back in my direction, his eyes gleaming with that ever-present look of confidence and compassion as he waved, turned, and disappeared into the Holiest of Holies.

Everything was about to change.

⟡ Chapter Thirty-Three ⟡

Bakr sat on the tatami floor of an austere room with a straight spine, closing his eyes and opening them just a little bit, then placing his hands on his knees with index finger and thumb touching, palms facing up. A single meditation chime stood atop a small table in the corner alongside a bowl and two candles.

A half-open sliding door made from wood and paper let in the stagnant earthen air. A shadowy figure pressed against the illuminated paper walls appeared to listen—probably some curious guard hoping to learn of an escape from the confines of this tunneled tomb.

"Sa-Ta-Na-Ma," Bakr chanted over and over. "Father Ra, thy will be done." Though the spirit of Ra no longer fully possessed him, Bakr still maintained the core chakra of Ra. That subtle body or force center that comprised whorls of energy that could transmit from one place to another through rotating vortices of ethereal matter. Thus, he could still commune with Ra.

"Yes," Ra responded through a spiritual voice box akin to extrasensory perception. A ghostly, rather ghoulish, broadcast from the underground new Babylon, where Bakr resided, to Jerusalem, Ra's otherworldly haunt for the moment.

"That we might be one again," Bakr continued.

Ra's words lingered in the musky air. "I will ascend with the Christ—to challenge his position."

Too bad about Reuben, Bakr sarcastically lamented, forgetting momentarily that Ra could tap into his every thought.

"Yahweh's presence was not in him, so it did not matter whether we killed him or not," Ra answered. "When the Christ rises from the temple to assume his place of judgment, then I will ascend with him."

"The final battle," Bakr said.

"For the rights to the new earth," Ra said. "My spirit will indwell you again in the new earth—our world, but not until the Christ is defeated."

"You will cause him to sin," Bakr said.

Ra let out a smothered laugh. "Remember in Sodom and Gomorrah, my perfect den of pleasures, how Yahweh said that if only ten were found innocent, he would save it from destruction?"

"Yes."

"So," Ra continued, "there are 144,000 innocents, and yet the Christ still intends to destroy this earth once he assumes the judgment throne. Will this messenger of grace not save this world for the sake of those innocents? He promised as much."

Bakr wrapped his arms around himself while scrunching up in the most childishly delightful pose. "I see now," he said.

Ra eagerly elaborated: "If but the Christ were to forsake the will of Yahweh for the grace he would bestow on these innocents—to save them from destruction—he would deny the will of Yahweh."

"Yes, yes." Bakr rapidly flapped his tongue. "And to deny the will of Yahweh is to sin."

"The Christ will ask for grace, just as Moses did for the people of Israel when Yahweh was about to judge them—against the will of God," Ra said.

"Moses lost favor with Yahweh when he refused to trust in his God's judgment," said a perky Bakr, "never seeing the promised land of Canaan."

"Yes, Moses was punished for denying God's perfect will. And likewise the Christ will never inhabit the promised new earth," said Ra.

The intoxicating thought of Jesus being dethroned had blurred Bakr's wits. He wiggled his head with childish delight. Everything he really knew he had learned from his master's feet. "Christ is always the intercessor," Bakr said, "always trying to save the humans. His grace will be his own downfall—brilliant!" Bakr lay on his back against the cushioned floor, clutching his thoughts like a child embracing its favorite toy.

Ra waited for Bakr to relish in their dastardly scheme. Bakr breathed in Ra's ashes as though smoking the rarest cigar. Ra's spirit fed off of decay. Vulture of the oppressed. Reviver of the dead. Wonderful.

"This plan is so perfect only we can appreciate it." Bakr leaped to his feet. "Christ cannot reign on the throne of God if he defies the Father's will. What good is a redeemer who is corrupted by the very disobedience that stains humankind? It would be like a rescuer trying to save a child from his dishonesty by lying to him."

Bakr drank in his intoxicating scheme while Ra rained down oppression over all of Jerusalem. Bakr envisioned it through a vicarious looking glass. He could see the netherworld thundering down a season of gloom through winter lightening over a spring-starved world without Christ as its covering. Gloom hailed down. Ra's sprinkling of malaise was a thing out of season because now was, according to the Christ's prophets, the spring of hope promised by God's end-times word. But with a boom and thunder Ra spread defeat over moonlit heads in Jerusalem—by planting doubt, fear, and above all, indifference. "And they will call you supreme once the Christ has fallen," Bakr said.

"The Christ will choose compassion over Yahweh's righteousness," Ra answered. "Bleeding heart—the Christ always places the needs of his precious humans over his own suffering. Only, this time it will cause him to disobey Yahweh for the first time. Once the Christ sins, he loses his place on the throne."

Bakr bit into his arm, drawing blood, and sucked it as though drinking in refreshingly cool lemonade—sweetened just so, and tart enough to leave a desirable aftertaste. Just like tasting the blood of the innocents. Fresh, wholesome blood that sweetened the pleasure of corruption—a deadly cocktail of deceit.

Finally, Ra would tempt the Christ with something he could not refuse: saving his children from certain slaughter, with Yahweh left holding the butcher's knife.

"Ra, Master, one more thing. Of course our motivation is to create a new world in our image, but it never made much sense that Yahweh would give us free reign over this earth during this so-called tribulation period."

"He thinks like a gardener," Ra said. "By not fertilizing the earth with his presence, he allowed the weeds of sin to grow out so that he could easily separate those rooted in evil from those who were merely oppressed by wickedness. The souls we possess thrive in decadence; those souls who struggle to find the truth wither under such conditions. His bleeding heart looks upon the heart of a human. He always seeks to save anyone he can, and that's how we will take advantage of his weakness."

The silhouetted figure outside Bakr's paper wall crumbled to its knees. It must have been an angel. Only an angel could still have feelings for the Christ. No matter. It could do nothing.

Hope deferred turned to hope lost.

You'll get over it," Bakr whispered. "Just turn your love inside."

𝕔 Chapter Thirty-Four 𝕕

The vapory fingers of Ra's spirit overlaid the temple in which Elian, the Christ, kneeled—confined within the austere Holy of Holies. Intricately laced drawings of Jesus Christ's first journey on earth were carved into the cedar wood walls. His first and final act of salvation.

All of Jerusalem reeked of the moldy stench of Ra's decaying expressions, making new, old, and fresh, decay. His ashen mist caused multitudes to cough upon inhaling the caustic fumes, much like cigarette carcinogens; only, these were toxic to the soul.

Ra listened outside the sanctuary to Elian's short gasps, his pleas to Yahweh. The Christ was unable to avoid Ra's reach. Ra could see that Elian's arms shook as he gripped the altar and pushed it vigorously, not realizing his enemy lay in wait. Sweat pressed through the Christ's forehead, much like it had when he prayed at the Mount of Olives before his betrayal. It was as greasy as the oil used to anoint his dead body in the tomb. Death was Ra's domain, and he would gladly smear the oil over the Christ's head to welcome his nemesis's final death. The Christ was strong, wrenching Ra with reverent words understood only between the two holies. Ra envied the union of the Son with the Father.

Closer and closer the Christ came to relinquishing his spirit to Yahweh—Ra knew it—sensed it just as when the Christ gave up his spirit at the cross. The moment breathed sweet gold frankincense and the amber resin from myrrh. Even though the Christ's words were foreign to him, he still knew the moment was soon, as the sky turned red with fury.

Anticipation rippled through Ra as he withdrew his grip over Jerusalem only to strengthen himself to grab the Christ's risen spirit. The cold impressed itself against Ra—he could sense everything now, excited with the expectation of causing the final abomination.

The Christ's damp hands slipped from the altar as droplets of wine tears rolled down his tensed face. Ra now extended his vaporous tendrils, ready to catch the airy spirit of Christ. Then it happened—the man called Elian in an instant released the spirit of Christ unto Yahweh with an explosion of greens, reds, purples, whites, and oranges.

An angular geometric form began taking shape through the resulting brume. The Christ's morphing body appeared veiled within a transparent silky covering as it bulged from its fetal cloud. As though catching the wind, Ra reached outward with every vile expression he could muster in order to entrap the Christ spirit within his web of anguish. He succeeded in halting the Christ's ascent with his freezing breath and debilitating odor of decay.

The Christ emerged as an effervescent figure with radiant eyes and a body like flowing pearls mixed with liquid diamonds set over billowy rainbows. Gargantuan, angular, translucent, with hair rippling as if cut from a waterfall. Even Ra could barely contain his reverence for the Christ.

It took every ounce of Ra's vengeance to hold off the Christ's convicting glare, using his last semblance of strength to tempt the Christ:

"You cannot kill the innocent, Jesus," Ra proclaimed.

Heat emanated through the Christ's laser stare into Ra.

"This world has turned against YHVH," the Christ answered. "He can only look upon that which I have redeemed."

"So you intend to kill those whom you redeemed? Even in Sodom and Gomorrah you would not kill the innocents. Now, ask Yahweh to withhold final judgment upon the world for the grace you long to give," Ra said.

"You tempt me once again," replied the Christ, his voice the tenor of a roaring lion. "You know that I am full of grace, and so you think I will deny the Father's word to satisfy my compassion for the innocent?"

"You are Life, are you not? It is right in this case to impart mercy over judgment so that you might save those who are cleansed with your blood."

"You reason as though judgment is not a part of mercy," Jesus answered.

Ra arched his back with the force of a riled horse. "To kill is not mercy!"

"You never knew me, Ra, otherwise you would know that I am merciful to those I judge. If it were not so, I would not have spared those who daily reject me."

Ra cowered at the fearsome sight of Christ's glory that shone brighter than the human eye could behold. "Adam and Eve disobeyed. Did they not warrant judgment? And yet, your mercy prevailed. They lived on—"

"They lived without the communion they enjoyed with me before their rebellion," Jesus said. "Separation from me was their judgment. However, YHVH found a way to bridge that separation through me, did he not?"

"You ransomed yourself in hell—gave me what was left of the world, in return for those who inherited your bloodline." Ra moaned before the Christ. "Now, Jesus, I demand that you give me this world as promised—tell your Father that you will grant mercy—save the innocent, and leave me with the rest. And all will be well."

The Christ fumed with righteous anger that seared Ra with conviction, burning his mildewy odor to a smoky waft, and affecting Ra's *character*—the essence of all spirits—causing Ra to remember his loss again: absolute abandonment. Ra languished in the pit of streaming nightmares remembering the Christ's resolve to always follow Yahweh's script. How could he believe this would be any different? Yahweh and the Christ were not only of one accord, they were truly one, and how could any deity speak a word of conviction while disagreeing with it?

"You never understood YHVH's judgment," said the Christ, "because you never understood his love."

Truth always brought him to himself. Ra, like every spirit, could only exude those qualities fundamental to its core, and so he detested the Christ for reminding him of his own depravity. The truth always shut him down.

293

"Judgment is revenge, plain and simple," he said.

The Christ's countenance turned somber, an expression Ra had seen before in the face of fathers who had lost their prodigal sons and daughters. "If only you had accepted my authority," the Christ said. "If onlys" always followed the loss of hope.

"YHVH's judgment is not revenge," said the Christ, "it is righteousness."

"Doing right?" Ra's rage weakened his resolve, made him like a child throwing a temper tantrum. "So destroying the earth and life is right?"

"Only he who has perfect understanding knows what is truly right," responded the Christ. "Judgment is righteousness, but only when done in perfect love."

"Perfect love does not violate its own law—to kill is to sin, according to you," Ra rebutted. Ra's hot indignation melted the sense of futility he'd felt before. If only to call out the Christ's hypocrisy, it was worth struggling through his defeat with what vitriol was left.

"Sin is the outcome of failing to love with YHVH's love," the Christ said.

"Then all have sinned and been condemned to die." Ra snickered.

"No one merits life, Ra—and those without my lifeblood are dead already. How can anyone have life if I am not in him? Those who reject me have made their choice. To destroy the body is nothing. However, to deny the spirit life means everything."

"And what about me?" lamented Ra. "I did not choose death."

"Then can you choose me now?" Jesus asked.

Ra turned his head downward. Of course he could not, would not, repent, because the hardness baked within him was fundamental to his being. *Enough*, thought a defeated Ra. The Christ could not be tempted. Death would be his and his alone.

"I hate you," Ra said to the Christ—for all he had left was hate. And all he could do now was view the Christ ascending to the throne accompanied by his angels through the crystalline effervescence around heaven's gate—a brilliant homecoming that served to dull his own bluster even more.

The Christ's masterful frame faded into the angelic masses who lavished him with adulation until he disappeared entirely into the blinding light. After which the billowy gates of heaven closed, leaving a shroud of darkness again over all the earth.

Ra for his part would depart, at least for now, through the sludge of hell's emissions into barren hopes. The new earth would not be his this time.

ᛒ Chapter Thirty-Five ᛒ

In the temple courtyard, Munny raised his hands shouting "hallelujah" into the sky as the moonlight spilled through clouds. The crowd of people below looked up but nary a word was spoken. I knelt, pressing my knees against the stone floor. The moon's glow impressed a faint image of winged angels against the temple walls. Cobblestoned streets were kissed with the reflections of praying faces.

The air was crisp, clear, and expectant. No more death on the inside, only the light of hope.

I prayed again and the sky began to move with the accompaniment of rolling thunder. Readiness tugged at my heart like a magnet, waiting for its release.

Standing up and raising my arms, I walked under the direct moonlight with my bare feet, pausing to feel the brush of wind against my tensed face.

I didn't want to stop quite yet, but three more steps and I could hardly stand. The weight of the air thickened and pressed downward, hard, as if to push something out of the heavens.

We were all exiles of the world now. Men and women driven out of useless homes destined for refuse. Our new home awaited. Soon the storm would break and there would be unending days of sunshine that children would dance under. The countryside would turn a brilliant green. Fences would be torn down as formerly divided lots turned to open fields. And we would dance together!

How long had we waited? The full moon slowly gave way to a sliver of sunlight, directing its rays upon the temple's dome reflecting brilliant gold splashes. Memories of heaven instilled a soothing confidence within my heart. I lifted my head with rising hope.

The clouds parted. I closed my eyes, listening to the sound of the thunderous sky, and then opened them again. Light broke the distant sea into shards of watery glass. I shivered in the heat.

A burst of light consumed the darkness. It was suddenly daylight— only brighter, as with a million blinding headlights raining from above.

Drawn to the sweet fragrance that rained from sky, I raised my arms, wanting to bathe myself in the comforting wash of light. White beams stretched over everything, turning dull colors to vibrant hues. People's faces glowed.

Even the buildings became vibrant with bobbing heads from windows, arms waving, rooftops teeming with restless bodies. Light flooded into the streets below where trees had been felled and apartments crumbled. And the shimmering figures dancing on the streets looked like moving dots on a crowded pegboard game, periodically breaking off with hands clasped together. Closer to me the temple square was mobbed and rejoicing. It was Sunday worship without walls. Jerusalem was wonderful when people laughed together. I could hear it for miles. It made me feel free and happy.

I reached out even higher, heat tingling through me, trickling down from head to toe like tickling currents enlivening every sense. Even the air buzzed so much so that I looked for electric lines above only to find none.

A grand scale of celestial voices shouted from above: "Praise the Lord! Glory to the King of Kings! Salvation and glory and power belong to our God. His judgments are true and just. He has punished the great devourer who corrupted the earth with his immorality. He has avenged the murder of his servants." A chorus of angelic voices rang out in perfect unison: "Praise the Lord." Over and over they shouted praises.

The crashing of ocean waves to the west resounded through blue sky in a melodic hymn in sync with the voices of a thousand choirs: "Praise the Lord! For the Lord our God, the Almighty reigns. Let us be glad and rejoice, and let us give honor to him." The masses all around Jerusalem repeated what the angelic multitudes sang.

Trumpets resounded with the boisterous proclamation of several baritone voices: "For the time has come for the wedding feast of the Lamb, and his bride has prepared herself. She has been given the finest of pure white linen to wear." Ribbons of undulating silks interlaced the buttermilk sky.

"It's as the Bible says," spoke a tearful Munny. "In Revelation: 'For the fine linen represents the good deeds of God's holy people.' Our Lord Jesus Christ is preparing the wedding feast for his church."

"Mighty God!" Elijah shouted. "Look up!" Blankets of rippling white linen pulled back across miles of azure to reveal a regal-looking white horse, and atop it the most glorious figure resplendent in flowing pearly garb with long snowy hair and eyes like the stars.

"Behold the Lamb of God—for he is Faithful and True!" declared Elijah. "For he judges fairly and wages a righteous war." The Lord's eyes burned with reassurance at everything over which he viewed, and he scanned all things in one fell swoop of his gargantuan frame.

A jagged crimson stain wrapped around the base of his robe, and then I noticed from his garment dripping pools of . . . "What's that he is issuing from his robe?" I asked the two prophets.

"Blood—the blood of the Lamb," answered Munny. "Do you hear his name being softly spoken through the wind?"

I closed my eyes and prayed that God would open my spiritual ears. "The Word of God," I said.

"Yes," affirmed Elijah. "He is the Word of God."

Tears of crimson blood wafted from Christ's robe, mixing with the mist and turning into silvered raindrops that fell upon us without wetting our clothes. This heavenly rain imparted assurances of God's promises to each soul as all of us dropped to our knees crying joyously with relief.

In the distance on a small hill, those who refused to participate in our worship wailed with haunting cries while on their knees, bobbing up and down. Drenched with Christ's rain, they shouted lamentations of all kinds—agonizing cries of a greater weight than any mourning I had ever heard. Their icy breath puffed out smoke circles as their blank faces darted up, down, and around with the jerkiness of birds.

"They cannot turn back," Munny explained. "God's truth is comforting to us, but condemning to them. Their hearts are completely hard and unable to accept the grace of our Lord."

And then one by one their cries went silent as they fell to the ground. The light from above that warmed us burned their bodies instead, turning the mass of still figures to dust particles that quietly blew through the wind.

Munny wrapped his arms around me. "Their stone hearts broke with the conviction of their hopelessness," he said.

"They died of broken hearts." At first I was surprised that I couldn't grieve with the lost—not these last-day ones. They had long since been dead, living only in possessed or empty shells, and in the end they existed as zombies seeking to devour whom they desired. Creatures without a conscience, feasting on innocence. I knew that some might find this insensitive, even cruel, but if they were to look into their souls, they would see a beast and not a person—and they might even deduce that they chose to be so when all they needed to do was believe in the one who offered them life after they had been given almost endless opportunities to accept.

I looked up to hundreds of thousands of towering angels sitting atop white horses, their white gowns flapping in the wind. Then the Word of God spoke, but not with syllables or any language; his words came forth in sparkling expressions like Christmas glitter. My spiritual ears must have picked up on their meaning, because without hearing anything in the natural, I understood, just as you would from a close loved one who could just look at you and you knew what they were saying. God was speaking the language of love, saying, "I love you" through that tingling sensation that left me entirely comforted.

"See his personhood?" Munny asked me. "His character of righteousness is showering down upon the earth. And through it the wrath of God has purged the earth of all unrighteousness." Munny beamed like a child as he pointed to the Lord's robe. "See," Munny said with a grin. "Listen with your spirit, Reuben. Hear with your heart—what is written on his robe. See the unseen, my brother!"

I could not. So I closed my eyes and it came to me. I sensed God's silent words: "This is love—that I have given my Son for you."

"Yes!" cried Munny. "Your heart can see what your eyes cannot. God has given of himself. Now, keep your eyes open and close your mind with the hearkening of your spirit. Simply believe."

I saw—whether through my spiritual eyes or not, I couldn't tell—a giant surreal figure reflected through what seemed like a waterfall, sculpted in silver like Michelangelo's statue of David and highlighted by the speckled rays of yellow sunshine. "Come," the figure commanded. "Gather together for the great banquet God has prepared. Come and partake of the ruins of kings, generals, and strong warriors; of horses and their riders; and of all humanity, both free and slave, small and great."

Legions of massive figures clothed in shining garments swooped from the sky and vanished into the distance. My fellow believers around the temple lay prostrate on the ground, covering their heads against the raging fires that surged across the lands as far as the eyes could see.

It was all so glorious and devastating at the same time. And I knew—I knew as much as I knew anything—that it was all as it should be, and that the best was yet to come.

☙ Chapter Thirty-Six ☙

"**R**un, Serge, run!"
The long tunnel shook them like raggedy dolls. Bakr and Serge hurried hand in hand toward a waiting room lined with stone walls several feet thick. Trembling guards waited to shut the doors behind them.

Ten-foot-tall doors announced their closure with a hard clunk, followed by Bakr and Amato dropping to the floor and heaving. Bakr reached into his pocket to retrieve a handkerchief soaked with his own blood—from where it had come, he knew not. Still, he wiped his brow, caring little of anything.

"Are you possessed with his spirit? Are you whole?" Amato asked.

"No," Bakr gasped. "I am alone. Ra is somewhere—I don't know. He's abandoned me. I could die, Serge!" Bakr grabbed Amato and pulled him by the collar. "Without Ra's spirit I could die!"

Amato pushed Bakr away as though he were a bothersome dog.

"Good grief," Amato said. "Get a hold of yourself. Where's your dignity? Your people made this underground fortress to protect us from all this."

Bakr spoke through chattering teeth: "Yes, we did, didn't we?"

"So we're safe—aren't we?" Amato asked with a hesitant tilt of his head.

Bakr went limp. "Safe?" He spoke listlessly. "This is our tomb now. The asteroid has fallen. The earth is caving in on us and sealing us in this pit, Serge."

Suddenly a weird, startling cry sounded in Bakr's ears, and everything around him seemed to heave and shake. He clutched Amato's shirt, yet found that he too was quivering, while the cry grew even more and more shrill.

"What is that sound?" Bakr screamed. "I can't stand that sound!"

Amato's dismissive look grazed Bakr with that condescending appearance of one looking at a demented cripple. "It is you," Amato answered. "You hear yourself."

Bakr walked aimlessly in circles while wringing his hands. Finally he fell to the floor and carelessly wiped the baseboard with his head and hair, sobbing as would a baby pricked with a blunt needle.

"We're doomed like burrowed insects, for a thousand years!"

#

As the asteroid swallowed the earth with its devouring flames, layers of rock and soil caved in upon Bakr's iron fortress, imploding with red-hot lava down to the depths of his deepest tunnels. In time its cooling would leave hardened black stone over the top of those tunnels through which no man could exit, regardless of his ingenuity.

The surface had become like an expanding volcano erupting from the core of the earth's foundation—to its origin. Every creature above ground or in the sea was dead, except for the redeemed and a few others not yet fully dead.

☙ Chapter Thirty-Seven ☙

Clumps of earth fell into a cavern that coughed up funeral fires. Smoke arose from what once stood as the Mount of Olives, a lone olive tree jutting from a recently made cliff. Ancient monuments fell helplessly down a newly formed embankment formed from the split hillside.

Less than a mile away flames rose and fell like lava fountains. Pounding turbine sounds spoke deep within a bottomless crater, whose sulfuric breath and open mouth threatened to devour those of us standing at the temple site.

For now the temple mount stood. Operative words: "for now." USA and Jewish believers huddled around the holy site either prostrate or on bent knees. Waves of caked earth crumbled like brittle sand castles. A domino effect of rippling earth and debris moved toward us, threatening to consume us as if we were an afternoon snack.

Occasionally, praying believers would peek at the encroaching implosion of earth that sucked in multitudes of people. Trailing cries could be heard en mass as twisting figures fell into a black hole—sacrifices to a dying Mother Earth—some cursing God.

Thousands of statuesque angels cloaked in purple robes surrounded our majestic Lord above. The wind tousled Christ's hair, sending brilliant white strands through the crevices of the angels' tightly ordered black horses. The Lord's filaments appeared as lightning rods against the cobalt-blue sky.

I looked over at David; his jaw practically scraped the ground while looking upward.

"I'm gobsmacked," I said to him.

Only after a few seconds did David look my way. "I am dumbfounded," he said. "No idea what gobsmack means."

"Now what's going to happen?" Hudson shouted from about six body lengths down. Before answering, I noticed the absence of Hudson's tagalong partner, Lila—or, as some of us referred to her, "The Temptress." I asked him where she was.

Hudson's face waxed somber. "She became hysterical, ran away, and then the earth caved under . . ."

"She made her decision, Hudson," I said. "You couldn't change her heart."

"But when she saw our Lord, she knelt before him as though she accepted him as Lord," Hudson said catatonically.

"That doesn't mean anything," I responded. "Who wouldn't bow down before the spectacle above us?"

"I was beginning to . . . care for her," Hudson said with a slight adolescent-sounding crackle in his voice. The ravages of lost affection had quickly matured our young friend. He showed less swagger, and his face expressed the blended seriousness of a man who knew through life's greatest loss the earnest requirement of true love.

I walked over a few praying bodies to get to my young friend, then placed my hand on his shoulder. "Trust God, Hudson."

"Still . . ." Hudson's eyes welled up. "She was close."

"You might have thought so, but she was hardened to God," I said. "God knows our hearts; he knows when someone's reached the point of no return."

Hudson wiped the tears from his eyes.

"No matter how many miracles happen . . . life is never perfect—never," Hudson murmured.

I reached my hand over his shoulder. "No, it's never perfect through our eyes."

"Ugly in fact," Hudson said.

"That's why we need to see things through God's eyes," I said.

Hudson nodded lethargically and walked away.

A pulsing current broke in the faint distance. Gigantic watery rolls gathered strength through the far-off misty light. Ocean currents welled up hundreds of feet tall before crashing against the craggy bluffs. The battling high surges of fires against the cold waves produced vaporous explosions miles high, and the shifting earth created a tsunami like none other.

People around us stood and began screaming.

"Reuben, over here." I turned to see David shouting at me through the din, arms crisscrossing wildly.

I pushed through awestruck bodies to get to him. He swung his arms around me.

"The ocean waters are coming!" he shouted. "They're pouring through the caved-in earth."

Indeed, a blanket of muddied currents rapidly spread over Israel, carrying with it cars, houses, and large ships. A colossal amoeba of debris spreading toward us.

"So we're about to drown?" a woman next to us asked.

"Regardless—we'll be with our Lord," I replied. I preferred to look at the waters as champagne to toast our Lord's arrival. I imagined the sun's brilliant rays dancing through swift currents, waltzing us toward heaven.

The frightened cries from many spoke otherwise—of doom. How could anyone perceiving the majestic Lord of Lords breaking through the clouds think of anything but awe? How deftly our flesh tied a dastardly knot to separate us from our God-inspired spirit. Our thirst for existence extinguishes the flame that burns for a loftier life with Christ.

"Listen!" Munny startled me.

The faint sound of a horn blared through the sky, followed by drums pounding. The angels retreated atop their horses, revealing the Lord's eminent frame. His white horse fell back on its muscular hind legs and fiercely whinnied. The Lord's white mantle bristled like long soft feathers through a gust of wind that settled cozily upon us.

"What's happening, Munny?"

"The land and waters you see welling up from below are from the garden of Eden," he answered.

"What?"

"Deep below, the first earth and ocean waters are pushing through the outer strata to form a new earth."

"You're saying that the garden of Eden was buried for millenniums until now."

"Yes," said Munny. "What's happening is an inversion of the earth. As the old earth implodes and then explodes, it is pushing up the original layer of God's perfect earth."

"Amazing!" An understatement.

A loud snap rang from the heavens. At first I thought the sound came from thousands of flags flapping in the wind. Then looking up I saw Christ's dangling sleeve fluttering as he waved his hand over all of Jerusalem. He appeared to look directly into my eyes. And in that moment everything turned silent.

Quietly I approached Munny and whispered, "What's he doing now?"

"He's waiting for you, Reuben."

"Me?"

"Give the word for his will to be done on earth as he has decreed it in heaven," Munny said.

"And what would that be?"

"Ask him."

Remembering Elian's word to trust God, I closed my eyes asking the Lord to give me a word. *How shall I pray, Lord?* I waited patiently. *God, still my spirit.* I gave up all matter of time and circumstance. A confident calm impressed me with the words to shout:

"Let the new earth begin!"

The Lord nodded toward me and straightened with the satisfaction of a proud father. He repeated my words in a surprisingly hushed voice.

"Let the new earth begin."

Immediately the earth heaved. Huge flakes of land crumbled around all of Jerusalem. They whistled through the air down the deep canyon before crashing into the ocean depths below. Echoes of clashing rocks bounced against the remaining jagged cliffs. Restless waters surrounded the towering earth miles below its surface crashed against bluffs with deep gushing sounds.

Several emerging rocks dripping with waterfalls peeked out of the deep-blue rolling waves. Jerusalem, now an island city, stood as a shining city on a hill above the ocean's crested waves.

The sea broke into pounding shards of watery glass while crashing against the jagged coastline. As if setting off a chemical reaction, the mixing of hot waterfalls with the swirling sea erupted into a mass of boiling foam. And then a towering column of molten lava erupted miles high from the ocean's depth.

I looked to see the searing lava burning many skyscraper-sized holes into the cliff's side. The red-hot sludge tunneled its way deep into the rock, leaving a porous contour that reminded me of coral with deep and wide crevices stretching as far as the eye could see. Passages hundreds of feet wide and long dotted the seaboard. It looked like a giant—and I mean *giant*—ant farm as far as the eye could behold.

A jet stream of hot liquid earth spilled over onto our surface, rapidly oozing its way toward us like an expanding glob about to swallow us up. As the snaking sludge streamed toward us, tens of thousands around the temple screamed.

"We're going to heaven!" David shouted through the loud burbling noise.

"It looks like boiling-hot tomato sauce," said Hudson.

"I'm speechless," David said—a first.

Strange how we viewed our encroaching death as just another doorway to the eternal. "Lord—have your way with us!"

People began shouting praises to the Lord: "Almighty God" and "Lord of Lords." The Lord's countenance shone more brilliantly with each praise as he pleasantly breathed them in.

"Praise you, Jesus!" I shouted, wishing my lungs strong enough to declare his glory. A chorus of angels bellowed out praises to God through a billowy vortex behind the Lord. In the distance I witnessed their figures bathed in golden light, grouped together in seraphic beauty and with melodic voices beyond any earthly description.

Trumpets resounded—at least a thousand, I presumed. All of us were now shouting praises, despite our impending doom by the molten earth now less than a mile away. We welcomed the end of our world and the beginning of a new one. It entreated us to the ultimate communion with our Lord and Savior.

David danced, as did others. "We're going home, Reuben, we're going home!" He hugged me while twisting my body in the air as though it were a feather. I felt like a kid again, waiting for the amusement park gate to open so that I could rush to all the rides. I was giddy. Simply giddy with anticipation!

Our Lord's voice boisterously rang out: "It is finished."

What happened next took the air out of us all. Our Lord's translucent figure began gradually fading into the hearty wind until resting simply as an afterglow. Gone. Our Lord was gone from the firmament. All we had left was the light of heaven pouring out from the whirling mass of clouds above. His remnant, I supposed.

We could only wait, not my strong suit, but by now I knew to wait on the Lord meant a future better than the present. Which in this case would mean seeing Jesus again—and this time I wouldn't miss him.

༐ Chapter Thirty-Eight ༐

I turned my view to the hot earth. Moments until the end. And then through the vortex above, an arctic rush of wind rained twinkling icicles upon the lava. Steam began rising from the cooled land as it hardened. All the while our mass of believers basked in the warm bath of the light.

My feet tickled from the ground upon which I stood. I looked down to see sparkles as though millions of soft diamonds had been imbedded in place of the dirt. I could barely look upon the ground because of the light's reflection.

"What's going on?" Hudson asked.

"Look," said a giddy woman to my left. "The earth is sprouting flowers, and the ocean—beautiful—"

I gazed out toward the distant sea beyond pristine fields. It was like the paintings that master artists used to do on blank canvases with perfectly blended colors, and it used to be such a pity that one could not walk into the scene. But, now I could walk into the artist's rendering, replete with the emotion of the scene, smelling the perfume of innocence that wafted from heaven's throne, hearing the rhythmic waves as music, and feeling the evocation of God's artistry. It was all so real now, the imagination's dreams coming to life.

"Watch out!" A man started pushing people in an attempt to run. "A lion!"

Indeed, a lion lumbered toward us. The beast stopped not three feet from me, lay down, and started licking its paws. I walked over, placed my hand over the lion's mane, and began petting the gentle creature as it yowled.

"The air—the air smells wonderful!" said a man whose nostrils flared to the point I thought they might tear. Refreshing rain swept breezes that enhanced every sensation. My body felt as though I were lounging in a warm bath.

People began frolicking all about in childlike abandonment. They ran onto fertile ground that had once burned with red-hot sludge and now sprouted new growth before our eyes. Fields of deep-blue hues mixed with tight, small buds of pink roses, purple blooms, silk petals of fragrant gardenias, sun-drenched daffodils, and lavender spreads.

The deserts and mountaintops bloomed with life. Trees danced with gentle breezes, vibrantly colored butterflies twitted from limb to limb, turquoise-colored streams splashed onto cushiony petaled fields, and virgin air enveloped everything with freshness. Even the temple softened after being set aglow by the tender sun.

A little girl with rosy cheeks frolicked through the rainbow-colored mix of tulips, her long black hair flipping through the accommodating breeze, robustly singing "Mary Had a Little Lamb." Her mother skipped along with her, arms raised high.

"Isn't it amazing?" the little girl asked.

The mother peered all around as if wanting to drink in the entire splendor. Birds whistled cheery tunes and grown men rolled in the fresh, soft grass. "It is amazing," the mother answered. "It is more than amazing, dear." She cried tears of joy while dipping her hand into a sparkling stream and sprinkling the water over her giggling daughter.

"Look!" A young man tapped me on the shoulder, pointing toward the vortex above.

A flight of gemstones formed step by step from the gold-hued arena in which the angels stood above us. The cascading stairway extended from the sky down to the ground where we stood, and then branched down into the naturally lit tunnels below, forming transparent arteries connecting the heart of Jerusalem to heaven.

After these translucent extensions touched the earth, figures in long flowing white garments began walking down the stairs. At least twenty could rest on just one step as the mass of serenely faced bodies gracefully walked downward to earth. They glided with rhythmic artistry, descending in free flow as human spectrums of light.

In short time, the first to touch down waved toward those of us standing in awe. Their vibrant human forms were perfect in every way, just like us, only without any blemishes. A young man lapping up water from a pond stopped, his mouth agape. "Jacob's Ladder," he said.

"Reuben's Ladder," joked David.

"God's Ladder," I returned.

The people coming off the ladder or stairs began intermingling with those of us already on the new earth. They hugged, kissed, and held hands—sharing their praises to our Lord. Talking as familiar friends who'd know each other forever.

I walked toward one athletic and beaming man who ran from the stairs toward our group. He was at least six feet tall, maybe twenty-something. "Hello," he said to me while turning. "I was told you're Reuben."

"Yes," I responded.

"Pleased to meet you," he said while extending his hand.

"Likewise, brother," I said while returning his gentle grasp. "Who are the people coming down from heaven?"

The man grinned wide. "We've yet to be glorified, brother. We were the ones martyred during the time of judgment."

"So you haven't been to heaven as yet?" I asked. I was itching to ask him the question that burned inside me, but for now, I let him answer out of courtesy.

"We've been to paradise, brother," he replied. "But, believe me, from the glimpse of the third heaven we saw, if we had gone there, we wouldn't have come back."

I was confused. "I thought once to die and then to heaven," I asked.

The man ruffled my hair. "Reuben, you've been to heaven, right?"

"Yes."

"Then you know. There are heavens, just like there are different cities and countries. Places filled with all kinds of wonderful activities. It's all good—don't worry about it. Our Lord will reveal these things to you soon. Besides, I have someone wanting to see you."

"Amanda! Tell me my Amanda is with you! Did you see her? She . . . tell me she's with you!" I shook the poor wiry gent as he sort of wiggled in my arms. Perhaps he was too shocked, because he failed to answer me.

By now the robed figures had descended the stairs and were comingling with their earthly brothers and sisters in a grand celebration of life. Several brought musical instruments with them and played inspiring melodies I couldn't begin to describe. Even the freshly grown trees swayed in merriment. Yet I couldn't get Amanda out of my mind. Our separation was not the conclusion; our brief reunion had not been our final time together. God never left a picture undone, no story untold, for those who stilled themselves in his presence. Oh God, let me see Amanda . . . please!

Anything was possible at this point, yet the mere thought of whom the young man mentioned tensed me like a child on Christmas morning. A group of white-robed persons stood around the young man, and then everyone parted while peering at one angelic-appearing woman who slowly glided down the sky-born stairs.

She walked like a ballerina on two strong legs, gracefully touching each step with the tip of her toes. Her white skirt floated as light as the wings of a butterfly. As she gently descended, the woman sang with the most soothing voice. Her anointing inspired everyone to still themselves as the angels hummed a beautiful song along with the woman's poetic mastery:

"There was a time when men were hard
When their actions were mean
And their deeds destructive
There was a time when life was marred
And the world was a cry
And the cry was seductive
There was a time
Then God said good-bye

I prayed a prayer in love gone by
When hope was gone

314

And all appeared lost
I prayed that God would lift love high
I prayed knowing Christ had paid the cost
But then I was naïve and scared
And prayer was wasted in my despair
There was my comfort that God cared
No more cries, God would his love declare

My Lord Jesus came at night
Speaking words that rang as thunder
As they sealed my heart with light
As they swallowed all my shame

He touched me with his arms stretched wide
He filled my void with speechless wonder
He took my weakness in his stride
And stayed close by when darkness came

I prayed a prayer my life would be
So apart from the eclipse in me
So different from the hell I made
Now God has birthed the prayer I prayed."

As she touched the ground, the most striking woman I had every laid eyes on elegantly reached out her arms toward me. Her beauty matched her song. She looked intently through me with familiar green-marbled eyes. And then this rapturous woman embraced my frozen body, melting everything hardened within me.

As she stood back, her hands wrapped firmly around my arms, and with a steady and confident voice she said, "I've been cheering for you all this time," then planted a kiss on my cheek so familiar.

"Amanda!" My heart swelled ten times its normal size. She was more striking than I ever imagined—willowy with long, chocolate-colored lustrous hair. Almond-shaped eyes topped with arched eyebrows.

"I almost didn't recognize you," I said as we wrapped our arms around each other, and I breathed in heaven's fragrance that anointed her skin.

"Everything in heaven grows more beautiful," Amanda said. "Our bodies are completely satisfied in the presence of our Lord with no more wants or desires."

As we pulled apart I closed my eyes to savor the moment. With my head cupped in my hands, everything went silent. Even the angels were silent. And then almost in unison the masses of people all around shouted, "Praise Jesus!" They chanted the name of Jesus Christ over and over. Even the mountains declared his name through their faint echoes.

Amanda and I embraced again and then released as I gazed into her smiling eyes. She stood straighter than ever before—tall in the confidence of her newfound strength, shoulders wide. Our love seemed purer than before, full of understanding. *Oh, God, thank you! Let my thanks ring a thousand times stronger in your ears!*

"Your suffering helped save many souls on the former earth," I said to her.

"I don't even remember the suffering, Reuben, just the pleasantries that meant so much to me—and us."

My soul danced. "Isn't it wonderful how God takes away our cares and makes them his?"

"Yes," Amanda said while grasping my hand in hers. "And how he makes his words ours?"

Trumpets resounded from above, barely audible now through my euphoria. I turned upward to see seven angels blowing their curved horns beside the beginning steps toward earth. A golden-hued light emanated from rolls of satiny linens in the sky. Suddenly the trumpets turned silent, and the linen coverings over the firmament drew back to reveal the mist through which a lone figure walked.

My body shook feverishly with anticipation, as did others. Amanda almost swooned as I braced her in my arms. I wanted to cry out but could not; I was paralyzed by an overriding and inexplicable joy. The figure's body glowed brilliantly as he seemed to almost glide down the stairs in a matter of but a few minutes.

Soon his face began to take form. His forehead was relaxed and serene and very delicate. His oval face, with his olive complexion without spot or wrinkle, was tinged with a soft red against a delicate ruddiness. His nose and mouth were perfectly formed, and his beard was thick, not very long. Under brows that grew together, his eyes soft blue shaded into brown—clear, and quick above his prominent nose His countenance was reverent, innocent and mature, inspiring both love and fear, and his hair was the color of chestnuts down to his ears, wavy at his shoulders.

As he touched the earth, a barrage of bleeps and creaks began to sound, underpinned by something like the tone of a *Star Wars* laser battle at first until fading into the impression of song. And then the ground began to fracture with the staticky crackle that followed the earth's cracking like ice as waters began to flow from Jesus's feet. The fissure widened into a river as it stretched toward the western ocean. Its cobalt-blue deluge that started as a trickle at Jesus's feet now appeared as raging rolls of waves that eventually cascaded over the cliff, creating a thunderous roar down to the ocean's surface.

It all calmed with an appearance of a slight breeze, along with the sound of birds in the distance and the expanding greenery and sprouts from the river's edges. Jesus touched the dribble at his feet, which caused a fountain of water to pour from heaven down the stairs and into the river as Jesus stepped away to face his crowd of believers, who watched in awe. As for me, having seen a glimpse of heaven, I understood that the river of life emanated from Jesus wherever he traveled, providing life to whomever or whatever drank from it. It was absolutely spectacular to see it in the physical.

Munny and Elijah walked to the base of the stairs and greeted Jesus with a kiss, and he returned their greeting with a smile of friendship. The multitudes bowed down toward the man I knew as a friend, and now as Lord. I was not twenty feet from Jesus; however, I couldn't possibly move. Jesus spoke pleasantly and with more gravity than I remembered him when he'd been Elian. He conversed in a temperate way, modest and supremely wise.

His person bespoke love with understated elegance. He was truly love incarnate. His hands softly touched peoples' heads, whispering words to teary-eyed faces. With tenderness Jesus spoke to each person words of encouragement and thanks. Then my Lord walked directly in front of me as my knees remained bent. His eyes glistened with compassion.

"Have you found the answer to your question?" Jesus asked.

I waited hoping to please him with an answer, stupefied with reverence. "What question?"

"What's it all about?" Jesus replied. "You had asked me that when you were left alone."

I didn't need to think on that one, not now. It was so clear to me. "It's about relationship—closeness with you and with each other. It involves making our way your way, and trusting you along the journey with no need to question why. Giving everything into your hands. Just being in your presence is enough—knowing that you're always with me, listening to you, trusting you, and doing what you say. It's all about being with you, being in you."

"And so it is," Jesus said with his all-so-familiar smile. "For he who is in me is blessed to be and to do as I am." Then he ushered a word I'd never heard before—it sounded like *sayla*, only more beautiful coming from his mouth. He understood my confusion at the unfamiliar word.

"It was the first word I spoke to Adam," Jesus said.

"What does it mean?" I asked.

"You can only understand it in your heart, beloved," he said. "The closest meaning in words is no separation, no divide—complete intimacy."

All the ups and downs of life were about achieving *sayla*, or whatever that word conveyed. This I now knew. Creating a pathway toward intimacy, communion with God and with each other. All the busyness of life and the selfishness had interfered, when all this time God had simply wanted to be close to his children. He would settle for nothing less than *sayla*.

I think I grasped why no language on earth could express that oneness; it had been abandoned the first time humankind trusted in someone besides God. Every other word substituted for it was empty, a cliché.

Jesus turned to the crowd while holding my hand.

"Blessed is he who mourned . . ." he began.

"For I was comforted," I said, my voice fully returned.

"Blessed is he who hungered and thirsted for righteousness," Jesus continued.

"For I am satisfied," I responded.

"Blessed are you who were persecuted for the sake of righteousness, for yours is the kingdom of heaven." And Jesus spread out his arms as he declared it to everyone through a voice that echoed throughout the new earth's expanse.

"Now I am with you, beloved," Jesus spoke—his hearty voice heard by everyone through nature's sound system. "You who are humble in spirit, now inherit the earth. As you were merciful, so I give you mercy.

"Because you denied the ways of the world, now I can have fellowship with you, face-to-face. For you did not rely upon your way, but mine. And for this, my beloved, I give you my kingdom." And Jesus spread his arms wide as though offering the world for everyone to partake of. A feast of the eyes for all, because the earth had never appeared so grandiose and beautiful.

With those words, people above and below shouted thanksgiving to Jesus. I joined in the chorus of praises. Imagine a thousand stadiums with cheering fans—that would sound like a whisper in comparison.

Jesus knelt down within a nose hair of my face, kissing me and engulfing me with his sweet embrace. He then pulled me up and cupped my face with his soft hands.

"Now you believe," he whispered with playful eyes.

"Yes, I believe your word," I said. "I believe you."

"Good," he said. "Because I believe in you, my beloved Reuben—I have always believed in you." With that I crumbled to my knees and wept more unabashedly than ever before. The perfumed scent of Amanda drew my attention.

Amanda came alongside Jesus and rested her head upon his shoulder. Jesus returned her touch with gentle kisses and hugged her, then released her and glanced at both of us before placing his hand on each of our shoulders.

"Now you know love, my children," Jesus said.

"Yes, Lord," she said confidently. "Because we know you."

"And so it is for all who abide in me," Jesus said. And then he spoke loudly for all to hear:

"And you have known and believed the love that I have toward you. God is love, and he that dwells in me dwells in the Father, and the Father in you."

So it is. So it will forever be. I was home.

It had been a long time since I wrote; I was a journalist at one time, you know. I took out a notebook from my pocket and with childish excitement began to scribe my first journal entry on the new earth. It felt good to write again.

Today Jesus descended the stairs of heaven to begin the first chapter on this new earth. He welcomed us to Eden as our new residence, evoking thoughts of home, and how it is a sanctuary for our souls.

Everything seems to lead back to a place called home. A safe haven in a place of warmth and security. A place of belonging to something greater than oneself. The earth that served as home to generations from the ancient civilizations to the modern age exploded into eruptions of a new earth for those of us who would begin a fresh chapter in human history.

Would this new earth last forever? Someone once said that change is the only constant. Though true in nature, I think not for the spirit. Even though the solar systems last for eons of time, their planets and stars never stay the same. All seems to disintegrate through the course of existence. I'd rather believe that everything that dies brings forth a new design from an old friend. Even this garden of Eden upon which I stand was restored as God's perfect homestead for humankind, though it's not really our home.

I think of heaven, our final abode, and how it will last forever. Now that's a place in which any one of us would enjoy living. And I suppose that I should be giddy with the promise of life eternal in a paradise that will never end. However, even heaven is not home to me—not anymore. It's been said that home is where the heart is, and if so, then my home is where my spirit resides, and that would be with my Lord Jesus Christ.

My home is where my spirit can soar with its creator, in the sublime inner sanctum of his presence, which comforts and cements the relationship between an unfathomable God and a simple-minded man. My search is over. I will no longer strive for a place to call home. Wherever I may find myself, on whatever ground, I will always be at home with the one who is always with me and within me, closer than a brother.

For me, the last earth upon which I placed my foundation was the place of my physical birth. Even after I was born again into a new life with Christ, I still considered home a place where my body lived. No more. My foundation lies with Jesus Christ, in a place where I need never worry.

I had the former world to make it painfully obvious that it was not home. I have Amanda to thank for showing me how our bodies are not home, and I thank my good friend Elian for teaching me about the joy of coming home, and I have Jesus to thank for providing me with a home in which to live. As Jesus recently said to all of us, "Those who dwell in him also dwell in the Father." Praise God for bringing me home.

"The Lord reigns!" David shouted. "Let the earth rejoice!"

I put down my notebook and breathed in the soothing wind. Amanda reached her hand to mine, and I returned her grasp while pulling my body close to hers. I had never felt so close to her before this moment, truly united as one in spirit and in trust. No words were adequate to describe.

Those of us who knew one another in the former earth looked upon each other with *sayla*. No more words needed to be spoken, not even "I love you," for love spoken from the heart was all that mattered, and we were very much in love because Jesus gave us his all.

All is well with my soul. Amen.

THE END

"I will never leave you or forsake you." Hebrews 13:5

"But they that wait upon the Lord shall renew their strength; they shall mount up with wings as eagles; they shall run and not be weary; and they shall walk, and not faint" (Isa. 40:31)